BATTLE FOR FOREVER: VOLUME I

I0690882

ALEXANDER

EDWARD SAVIO

BABELFISH
PRESS

SAN FRANCISCO

BABELFISH PRESS
237 Kearny Street, Suite 9179, San Francisco, CA 94108

ISBN-13: 978-1-63124-016-4

This is a work of fiction. Names, characters, corporations, places and incidents in this novel are either the product of the author's imagination or used fictitiously. Any resemblance to actual events, locales, organizations, or persons, living or dead, is entirely coincidental and beyond the intent of either the author or the publisher.

For reprint permission: permission@babelfishpress.com
All other information: info@babelfishpress.com

*This volume contains material previously published as
The Eternals Book 1: Prelude, and Book 2: Revelation.
It has been restored to a single volume, revised
and reedited to reflect the original vision of the author.*

FOR SPENCER & JESSE

PRELUDE

"I WOULD HATE TO BE IMMORTAL FOREVER."

—ALEX MERAZ

ONE

This Year, Like Last Year, My Birthday Gift Is A Punch To The Side Of The Head

Okay, first off, if you're reading this, *είμαι πατήσαμε!* I'd rather not translate that. Let's just say, I'm breaking about a dozen rules here. Easy. I'll probably get grounded for it. And by grounded, I don't mean I'll have to stay in my room unable to go out the next twenty-five Saturday nights, I mean, *grounded*. Into dust. And buried under a thousand pounds of rock.

That kind of grounded.

But that's the least of my worries.

The fact that you're reading this means that wherever you are people can still print things or electronically disseminate information. You're alive. You might even have electricity. I hate to tell you, I'm not sure how long that's going to last.

You see, they have a plan. And believe me when I say this, time is on *their* side.

I have no idea who you are or how you got a hold of this, but for my sake, I hope you're under a hundred.

Someone once told me my name means "the defender of mankind." Unfortunately, it may actually come to that.

They call me *Alexander the Pretty Good*.

Which is probably about right.

I'm a junior at Middleton—

No, wait...that was the last one.

—*Monument* High School in a small town with a big name, nestled in the Berkshires, which are these really beautiful low mountains in the Middle of Nowhere, Massachusetts. The biggest thing that ever happens here is people come from all over the world to see the leaves turning colors in the fall.

Dead leaves. That's the highlight.

And in less than an hour, I've got a mammoth end of semester U.S. history test given by a teacher who rambles on like she knew our founding fathers *personally*—especially Thomas Jefferson, 'He was a cad,' she'd say with a grin—and looks old enough to actually have known them.

But this isn't about the misery of my second period history class or some wry, witty, angsty journal about my high school experience. Believe me, I wouldn't be putting one word of this *faex* down if it wasn't a lot bigger than that. Maybe you've got your own issues and think you don't have time to hear this. Maybe things seem pretty good where you are. Or maybe you're dealing with the kind of shit that comes down in buckets, and maybe you want to know why the hell that is. Maybe this will help explain. More importantly, maybe it'll give us a way out of this mess.

Maybe.

"You study?" My friend, Daniel, looked worried. The kind of worried you are when you get a bloody nose in shark-infested waters.

"I'm ready."

"That didn't answer my question," he wheezed.

We were jogging along the shortcut through the woods that led to school.

"Trust me, I'm ready for the test."

"Great," he said, getting very excited. "So, when you write, put your hand this way." Daniel motioned awkwardly with his arm, wrist, and fingers in a way that was supposed to mean something, I figured, but just made him look like an idiot. "That way I can see your answers."

"My answers?"

"Yeah, so, you know, you're not covering them."

"You're not copying off me."

His face turned white as if I had just run over his favorite childhood stuffed animal with a dump truck.

"Wha-why not?" His voice went up an octave. "C'mon, you gotta help me out. I'm not as smart as you."

I stopped on the dirt path and waited for him to catch up.

He did his best to look pathetic and helpless. Which wasn't that difficult for him. Like a dog watching you eat a turkey sandwich.

Hungry. Pitiful. And lazy.

"Daniel, if I just tell you the answers, I'm not gonna be helping you."

"Yes, you will," he said, nodding like a bobble-head on a bumpy road. He was still catching his breath.

"It might seem that way, but trust me, long term, I won't be doing anything more than setting you up to always doubt yourself. And by the way, you *are* as smart as me."

He didn't seem to believe me. On either count.

"I am soooo not prepared for failure right now."

"Daniel, this isn't that hard. I've endured so many years of U.S. History to know—" I caught myself.

"What are you talking about, 'so many years?'"

"I've taken the class before. Another school." I pulled my history book out from my backpack and gently slapped it into his chest. "Here."

He didn't take the book. Like it was radioactive or diseased or covered in pink hearts.

So I opened it for him.

"I've highlighted the portions I think are relevant." I'm actually a lot cooler than I was sounding at the moment. Being smart is cool. Although you wouldn't know it from high school. It can even save your life sometimes.

Daniel groaned as I pointed out my color scheme of pink, green, and yellow, denoting important information from lowest to highest probability of being on the test.

Much, much cooler.

"I just wanna know how you do so well in every one of your classes *and* play sports *and* hang out with me *and* go to every party *and* have a billion excused absences *and* never sweat about it, ever. SparkNotes? You hacking the computers and stealing answers? What is it?"

"Time. You gotta put in the time." I looked at my watch, "You've got fifty-five minutes. Just study the highlights, especially the yellow, and you'll be Ace, okay?"

He winced at the word 'Ace,' and I cursed myself. I try to avoid using slang. I don't always get it right. But then I realized he was simply questioning his entire year plus friendship with me. His eyes said it all. A real friend would just give him the answers.

"Actually, a real friend would do what I'm doing," I said.

That snapped him out of his brooding. "How do you do that?"

"Do what?"

"Read my mind."

There's a *huge* difference between knowing what people are going to say and reading their thoughts.

I ignored his comment. "Hard work beats brains."

"Yeah, *beats* 'em to a pulp," he said as he finally, reluctantly, took the book from my hands and started down the path again. "I hate school."

I followed after him. "You have no idea," I said under my breath.

We were about a quarter mile from campus. I could see it below, the grounds and the building carved out of a stand of trees. A convergence of oaks and sugar maples.

The leaves were turning late this year. The yellows popped like they were superimposed on the forest, and the reds and oranges and lime greens and red-browns were stunning. There is perhaps nowhere in the world besides this area of New England where the change of season is so visually spectacular.

I told you, dying leaves are a big deal here.

Caught up in my admiration of the foliage, I wasn't paying attention. I'm usually more alert in these situations. I would've been dead a couple of hundred times over if I wasn't normally a lot more diligent. But they came out of the woods right at the start of a clearing, where the underbrush got the most sun and was the thickest.

Three of them.

We were maybe fifty feet from the school grounds, but Daniel and I were completely hidden from view by the dense growth.

The perfect ambush.

"If it isn't Alexander The Grating and his sidekick, *Ohhhhh Danny Boy.*" He sang the last part like an Irish tenor.

Craig Coulter was the most popular kid in school. He was also the meanest. He was somewhat of an anomaly in that he was the class president, the star football player, *and* the biggest asshole. Most mere mortals could only pull off two out of three.

It was quite an accomplishment, actually. I'm sure his father was very proud. And his mother was reaching for another vodka and Vicodin tonic.

Craig had a couple of his football buddies with him. I had never actually seen the guy travel alone. Two was the minimum contingent. One on either side.

Most of the time, he walked around with his entire offensive line surrounding him. I guess we were just lucky today.

One of the bookends was built like a Sub-Zero. The other had arms the size of my legs. The Fridge grabbed Daniel and pushed him to the ground while Thigh Arms made sure he stayed there.

Craig strolled up to me. Alone.

Pretty brave of him, actually.

The guy stood about a foot taller than me and outweighed me by at least fifty pounds.

Alexander the Still Growing.

"So, what's up with you?" he said, casually, as if we were sitting around eating pizza and watching the Patriots play on the big screen.

"Not much. Got a History test. Thanks for asking."

He let out a fake laugh. That was his standard response to sarcasm or anything he didn't really understand. "Where's your big stick?" he said, knocking my backpack with his fist, which held my books and binders, but none of my lacrosse gear. "Too afraid to play football?" Craig glanced toward the bookends. "How's that dirt taste, Dinga Lang?"

So clever.

My friend, Daniel Lang, couldn't really answer. But I figured he was thinking maybe school lunch *wasn't* the worst thing on the planet.

"I play football," I said, drawing Craig's attention back to me.

"Yeah, I saw you at tryouts. You made a couple of lucky catches."

Lucky, because I didn't get my head knocked off.

Craig here, star quarterback, was lobbing up passes at tryouts so that the "rookies" would get clobbered by his upperclassman pals playing defense.

"Just want you to get the feel of a real game," he said at the time.

I've dealt with guys like Craig before. And played on the gridiron enough to know how to pull down a ball without getting creamed. Even when my quarterback was being an asshole.

"Then why'd you chicken out and go for lacrosse?" His finger stabbed my chest with each word. "That's a pantywaist sport for—" He lowered his voice to a church whisper. "—*pussies.*"

I barely heard the word as if a mosquito had hissed it into the wind a mile away.

His eyes darted about, worried the single word could bring more punishment than his ambush of Daniel and me. Given the mentality of my current school's administrators, he might've been right.

"If you're going to call me a pussy...you might want to avoid, you know, *sounding like one,*" I said, mimicking his whisper.

Probably not the smartest thing to say.

But I couldn't let Daniel take all the punishment.

Craig knocked me to the ground, repeating the word loud enough so that I figured every feline in town would be heading our way. He pushed my face into the rocky path. I had no choice but to breathe in the dust he was kicking up. I started coughing as it got into my lungs.

"See? You're not even '*The Pretty Good*,'" he said. "So, how does the dirt taste to *you*?"

"I prefer a bit more grass with my soil," I managed to hack out. "Although the clusters of rocks offer a crunchy satisfaction."

Craig kicked me in the stomach, knocking the wind out of me. His heart wasn't in it, though. I could tell he wasn't punting me as hard as he could. Didn't matter much—it still hurt like crazy.

I caught a glimpse of Daniel out of the corner of my eye. My vision was blurry, my tear ducts flooding in response to the pulverized Precambrian particles getting stirred up.

I could see the two bookends were starting to mess with Daniel a bit more than was necessary. They didn't seem to have Craig's restraint. If they weren't careful, they were going to actually hurt him.

Daniel's one of those kids who's nice, easy going. He's able to make friends with almost anyone. He's not competitive. He doesn't screw up the curve. He doesn't play sports. He makes you laugh. And most kids like him. At least, no one *dislikes* him. In high school, that's saying something.

He may not be much of an athlete, but in a straight line, Daniel Lang was by far the fastest kid in our class. He attributed his quickness to the fact that he was constantly being chased around his old neighborhood by the bigger kids. He wasn't so much born fast as he was forced to develop speed.

I told him there were tribes who trained boys to be warriors by having men with clubs chase them and beat them if they got caught.

He said growing up in his old neighborhood was pretty much like that.

I had to do something to help Daniel.

This wasn't about him at all. Craig Coulter's problem was with me. Plain and simple. And I couldn't let Daniel get hurt because of that.

Craig had a pretty good hold, keeping my face planted firmly in the ground. He had made me swallow enough of the path that I figured I'd need to use a Dirt Devil to vacuum out my lungs.

I could've surprised Craig with a spear hand strike to the throat. He wasn't defending against it because 1) in this position, it would be a behind-the-back move for me, and 2) why the hell would anyone suspect I was trained in something as dangerous as Ninjutsu?

But you can't be halfway about using something like a throat jab. Either you do it full tilt or don't do it at all. I considered it, but I'd easily crush his windpipe. Craig was a prick and an asshole, but he didn't deserve choking to death. At least, not yet, anyway.

I had to be careful what reaction I chose. You know, sleepy little town. You don't want to bring too much attention to yourself. I didn't feel like having to move again so soon.

I figured a less straightforward approach was probably the best idea.

"Craig," I said, so smoothly, so evenly, that he didn't even bother to answer. "I want you to reeeally focus on pushing my head into the ground." My voice was calm, confident. "Can you see my cheek going into the dirt? Do you feel the power rushing through your hand as you press my skull into the path?" My body was relaxed. "Focus. Can you feel it? Just picture it in your mind the way it's happening in real life."

"Will you shut the *hell* up! You're taking the fun out of this," he said.

I waited a moment.

"You're breathing. Feel it? In and out. Cool going in, warm going out. Then there's that itch at the end of your nose." He wriggled his nose. "The blood running past your eardrum. Hear it?"

He twitched.

I was so calm, my voice so fearless, that I knew it was unsettling. I could feel the pressure lessen. His grip relaxed slightly.

He was focused.

Exactly as I needed him to be.

In one quick movement, I rolled my head, looked straight into his eyes, snapped my fingers, and said sharply, "Sleep."

I had to put my arms up to keep his full weight from landing on me. Not that it wouldn't have been satisfying to let him drop face first into the dirt. But I needed him to be pliant. Crashing to the rocky path would wake him.

He was heavy, and I struggled even though most of his body weight was on the ground. But I couldn't risk asking him to move on his own just yet.

"I want you to tell your friends to leave Daniel alone. You have no quarrel with him. As for me, your feelings haven't changed, but your anger is gone. For the rest of the day, you may feel like you've forgotten something. But you haven't. You've remembered everything about what has happened here except that I'm speaking to you now. Okay?"

He nodded.

"I *could* make you cluck like a chicken whenever I say the word pickles."

Craig dutifully, although very quietly, complied. "*Buck-buckaaah,*" he whispered.

I *could* have made him flap his arms, too, or pirouette, or suck his thumb like a baby. But that stuff just comes back to haunt you.

"This is over with. We're our normal selves, quietly loathing each other."

He nodded again.

And then, I snapped my fingers. "Awake."

I turned my head and pretended to be sucking dirt under his weight. Craig seemed put out by the situation. Like it was too much trouble to be hassling me. He pushed himself up using my head as leverage. Which really hurt. I should have suggested something a little more graceful for him.

He turned to his buddies. "What the hell are you two doing? You're going to hurt the poor kid. I've got no quarrel with him."

By the look on his face, I don't know whether Craig even knew what the word *quarrel* meant.

His buddies were dumbfounded. Certainly a common feeling for them.

Craig pulled me to my feet. Not gently. Not like a guy lending a hand to a teammate. He was making the face you'd make when picking up a pumpkin that had rotted on your front steps six weeks after Halloween.

He looked me in the eye. A hollow gaze.

"Later."

"Later," I said.

As Craig and the bookends headed toward school, Daniel and I dusted ourselves off as best we could.

That's when I saw him at the other end of the path. Where the trail disappeared into the woods. With dark hair and even darker eyes, Braeden Ellis was a senior, but new to the school, a transfer student who had shown up a few weeks ago, causing a significant stir with the female students and a few of the female teachers as well.

He seemed to be walking out of the forest, just as we had done a few moments earlier. But it was like a movie where the director yells, "Action!" and then the actors start walking.

It didn't feel right.

Braeden caught me gazing at him, and he smiled as he passed by me. "We're gonna be late," he said as if he and I talked all the time. Only I can't remember saying one word to him. Ever.

The encounter left me far more uneasy than Craig or his goons ever could.

We ducked through a hole in the fence and all of us—Craig, his thugs, Braeden, Daniel and me—emerged onto the far corner of the track that surrounds the practice field.

There was a gathering of girls with their phones out, chatting furiously. Not into the phones, these were used almost exclusively for anything but talking. Most were texting at the moment...probably each other.

Craig's girlfriend, Phoebe, was right in the middle, *her* phone in her pocket. She was speaking with one of the other girls, Emily, whose downturned, tearful gaze was in contrast to the mood around them. Emily had recently lost her mom to an illness. Phoebe gently placed her hand on Emily's upper arm. The gesture was touching. Emily nodded and looked up, something like a smile or hope in the creases of her eyes.

Phoebe sensed our approach before we said a word. She had dark hair and light eyes, and she flashed them in our direction.

She glanced at Braeden in that way a person does when they're trying very hard not to appear to be glancing at them.

Phoebe detached herself from the group and strolled smoothly up to Craig and kissed him. On the mouth. A nibble of his lower lip briefly coming away in her teeth.

Daniel winced.

It wasn't the idea of making out that bothered him. Just the idea of anyone making out with Craig.

When Phoebe saw me, she gave me this disinterested, almost annoyed look. Like I was bothering her. "Alexander! You're a year older. That why you decided to show up today?"

"Yeah."

Both of us were talking louder than normal.

"Where've you been? Sick aunt, toothache, food poisoning, trapped in an elevator?"

I narrowed my eyes. That wasn't some random list. I had successfully deployed each of these excuses over the past year and a half.

"Yeah."

"See you in history, Old Man," she said, her eyebrow arched. "That is if you don't cut class again."

"Yeah."

I smiled. I couldn't have stopped myself even if I wanted to.

And that's when the suggested calm I had planted in Craig Coulter drained away. Hypnosis works only so long as the subject is suggestible.

Everyone was all smiles. Craig especially.

The bell rang.

"See you later, Cs," Phoebe said to Craig as she kissed him again.

"Later," he said, grinning.

Once her back was turned and she and the rest of the girls were hurrying to homeroom, Craig wheeled around and punched me right in the side of the head.

For the second time in ten minutes, I found myself on the ground. Only this time, I dropped like a cartoon character. Board straight. Landing flat on my back. Little stars floating around my head.

It seemed like a long time before Daniel's face appeared over me. "Dude," he said. "I'm so sorry." He stared down at me, a puzzled expression hinting at the baffled thinking going on behind it. "I totally forgot."

"Yeah," I said. The sky was very busy. And lying there on the grass, I could see a lot of it.

"It's your birthday."

"Yeah." My head was still buzzing, still fuzzy, making it hard to think, hard to say anything coherent. Hard to remember where I was or even who I was.

I took a slow, deep breath.

I'm a junior. At Monument High.

Great Barrington, Massachusetts. The United States.

Today is my birthday.

My name is Alexander...*Grant.*

And at precisely 3:16 this afternoon, I turn fifteen—

—hundred years old.

- TWO -
90% Of What You Read In History Books Is Half Wrong

I know what you're thinking.

A moment ago, I was bragging about my Ninjutsu skills. If I'm so extraordinary at deadly Japanese hand-to-hand combat, why didn't I get on my feet and stand up for myself, right?

I mean, better than lay there like a candy-ass. Or as Craig would mutter in a fearless whisper: a *pussy*.

Well...

First, there was the not wanting to draw too much attention to myself. I liked this town. I wanted to stay awhile. And second, there was the not knowing whether I could stand up at all, let alone for myself.

It's not like I haven't—

—you know—

—hurt people...before. It's something I try to avoid as much as possible because the people you harm, the unfortunate incidents...they pile up until it feels like a mountain of rock is on your chest, crushing you. It probably doesn't surprise you that I have reoccurring dreams about being buried under tons of rocks.

Right now, everything was just foggy. Kind of swirly.

Craig Coulter had come about as close to knocking me out as you can without actually doing it.

I had this sense of *déjà vu*. You know the feeling that what's happening right now is something you've experienced before. I'm kind of used to it. Having fifteen hundred years jostling around my brain to compare with the present, it isn't a big surprise when something matches up.

Usually, you can't remember the previous event in detail. But lying there on the twenty-yard line, my head throbbing, I had a good idea what was causing me to feel like I'd been here before.

Because I had.

Only I think I made it to the forty-yard line last time.

It was my 1,499th birthday. A senior thinking I was a wiseass and a bit too popular. A punch to the head. Me on the ground. The details aren't important.

I've been going to high school pretty much since there *have* been high schools. So I know how to play the game.

Be halfway decent at sports. Halfway decent in school. Halfway decent at the social scene. Cut only so many classes that they don't try to put your parents in jail—good luck finding mine. Pick your friends wisely. Pick your nose in private. Don't pick your ass at all.

And most importantly: have a sense of humor. If you can make them laugh, it goes a long way to easing the tensions of being the new kid, believe me.

Just don't *look* like you're trying to be funny. You never want to be the class clown.

That loses you points. And can get you punched even more often.

It's a tightrope. Most people fall a few times. The only reason I'm any good at it is I've been doing it for so long.

Daniel was looking at me so that his head was upside down from my point of view.

"You okay?"

"Yeah."

"You sure?"

"Yeah."

My brain was still foggy.

I could tell Daniel was trying to come up with any reason, any reason at all, not to study, not to take the test. Maybe if I had a concussion, a cracked skull, even a case of whiplash, he wouldn't have to. I guess he figured he'd accompany me to the hospital like he was my legal guardian or something.

"You're not moving," he said.

"Yeah."

"You're saying 'yeah' a lot."

"Yeah."

"You're not paralyzed or anything, are you?"

The fog was lifting.

My words were slow and stilted. "I'm not going to the hospital, Daniel, and you're not getting out of taking the Am-Hi exam. My head's just a little fuzzy."

He thought about that for a moment.

"So, you're saying I probably shouldn't trust your answers on the test?"

That snapped me out of it. I jumped up and started chasing him as the rain began. But like I said, in a straight line, Daniel was the fastest kid in our class. Even in a downpour.

∞

I can hear some of you right now: *Craaaaaaazy!*

Fifteen hundred years old. Right! Get out the straight jacket and book him a padded room.

Listen, I understand. It's difficult to accept. Believe me, it took me years, literally *hundreds* of years, to come to grips with the surreality of my situation. It's not easy for a kid to understand why everyone around him is changing, growing, dying while he just stays the same.

I *look* pretty much like any other fifteen-year-old. (Actually, I can pull off looking from fourteen to seventeen, depending on how I dress and act.)

I've got some facial hair that's been coming in slowly since the late 1960s. I've been battling acne for the past three hundred years. I've tried every potion, cream, and treatment there is, from ones made by medicine men to the ones sold by snake oil salesmen to the ones formulated by the biggest pharmaceutical companies on the planet. Including one concoction that involved having a frog urinate on my face. They all work about the same, which is to say they hardly work at all. It's getting tiresome. Throw in the fact that the same blemish-causing hormones are battling it out early in the second quarter of puberty—the body hair, the *smell*, the mood swings, the curious things you feel whenever a pretty girl walks by showing any skin whatsoever—and I'm basically a moody, constantly hungry, libido-driven mess.

Just like every other kid at school.

But I'm *not* like every other kid at school.

Like I said at the beginning, I'm breaking some pretty serious rules writing any of this down. Bad things happen when people like me talk. Like what went down at Halifax in 1917. A dozen of us. Two thousand others. Killed. It's kind of a boogeyman story told to Eternals everywhere. So if you're reading this, my situation has deteriorated. Putting this out there might not help me. Might make matters worse. But I'm gambling that the risk will be worth it, that this will provoke you to take action, to inspire others to take action by giving you an understanding of what we are up against.

And when I say 'we,' I mean everybody.

You may be safe now. But don't count on it for long.

I can't tell you everything. I can only tell you what I know, which is this: there are perhaps a thousand people like me in the world. No one's exactly sure why, but a genetic defect in our DNA short circuits the natural clock inside our bodies. Of course, we didn't know about DNA until recently, and a lot of crazy things were attributed as the cause of our unusualness. Like some other genetic defects, this doesn't show up right away. The first year and a half or so we develop like any other baby. We learn to walk, talk, all the normal things. But as we approach our second year, physical growth slows down dramatically, until it settles into a constant, diminished rate.

I age roughly one day for every one hundred days I'm alive.

Some age a bit faster than that, some a bit slower, but generally, that's the way it works.

One day for every one hundred.

This genetic trait is passed on from mother or father to child. But not every time. My father has had hundreds of children, but none of them—other than me—have been this way.

I'm the tenth in my family to be called Alexander. Which makes me Alexander X—the *Tenth*, same as Richard III is the *Third*, but I prefer to pronounce it like Malcolm X and for the same reason. I may be known at the moment as Alexander Grant, but…I have no last name. At least, not one that means anything to me.

I was born in a house on a hill overlooking the Sea of Marmara in Constantinople, just after the fall of Rome, when Constantinople became the sole seat of power in the Roman Empire. You've probably heard of it as the Byzantine Empire, but that's purely a modern convention, a name historians began using only a couple of hundred years ago. To me, to everyone who lived and died from the time of Augustus Caesar to the day the Ottomans took control of Constantinople—sixteen centuries—it was known, first in Latin: *Imperium Romanum*, and then in Greek: Βασιλεία Ῥωμαίων, simply as the Roman Empire.

I can remember flashes of my mother, Delicia, even though I was basically a two-year-old for the rest of her life.

She was beautiful and kind and had a quiet strength about her. She handled the life-long task of raising a baby that didn't age with elegance and dignity. She died in my fifty-sixth year. It's hard to know what you don't have when you've never had it, but I've been around enough families with loving mothers to understand exactly what I lost.

I cling to the fragments of my memories of her.

My father…well, he looks a bit like a gladiator when he takes his shirt off. Or an MMA fighter. Chiseled features. Lean. Perpetually tan. The kind of muscles I wish I had. Not the bulked up, juiced up, better-living-through-chemistry freaks. Real muscles. But along with that power and brawn, there is a regalness about him. Not an air of privilege—well, maybe a little—more a sense of breeding.

He is, by the way, something north of four thousand years old.

At times, he still speaks to me as if I'm a child.

Let me get one thing straight: This isn't a fairy tale. This isn't some myth. I am not a descendant of the gods. I am not a wizard. I have no superpowers. I don't feed off other people's blood. I'm not immortal. If I step in front of a train, I die. I am simply a human being whose body—because of a genetic defect—ages at an incredibly slow rate.

My father calls us *Eternals*.

I usually say, *people like me*. Makes me feel less odd for some reason.

This is real.

There is no magic here, although there are many "magicians" among us. I'm pretty decent at magic myself. But what I do has nothing to do with sorcery. In fifteen hundred years, I've never seen *anything* that would make me believe *real* magic exists.

We've all seen an illusionist do something that seems unbeliev-able. Pull a dozen boxes out of an empty bag. Make playing cards appear to change in our hands. Cause the Statue of Liberty to vanish.

I'm awed whenever I see these things.

It's amazing.

It's exciting.

It's always a trick.

That doesn't take away from the beauty, the elegance, or the boldness and sheer confidence it takes to pull off something that spectacular.

In fact, I find it even more amazing when you know positively something is a trick and you still can't figure it out.

The truth is, what we call magic—what people only a few hundred years ago feared—takes a lot of planning and a lot of practice. The greatest magicians and illusionists have worked at their craft for years before wowing the world.

Today, the best of them make millions doing shows on stage and on television. A thousand years ago, the best influenced armies, rulers, and even empires.

Just imagine how supernaturally masterful some of my kind would appear when they've been practicing every day for a thousand, two thousand, even three thousand years.

Actually, it doesn't matter what it is: magic, music, mind games, martial arts...war.

Given enough time, put in enough effort, *anyone* can become great.

And that's the problem.

Because although everyone has the ability to be great, not everyone has the ability to be good.

Not everyone wields power responsibly.

This is true of people everywhere. There are those who are good and those who are not.

But most people, whether good or bad, don't have the time to amass enough knowledge, wealth, and power to affect the course of history.

There are about a thousand of us who very much have the time.

And unfortunately, there are some who work only for their own benefit without *any* regard for the effect on others.

Some are corrupt. Some are malicious. Some are just lazy.

A few are diabolical.

You see, there is nothing special about us. We simply have more time to be whatever we already are.

Good or bad.

But here, in the quiet, sweet, somewhat boring little town of Great Barrington, Mass., Craig Coulter was about as bad as things got.

Nothing I couldn't handle.

What I *couldn't* deal with was that I was about to take my 2,198th history test.

I know for some of you, it may seem like you've been in school for a thousand years.

I really have been.

I walked into history.

Most of the class was already there. Heads turned and eyes darted toward the door as I entered. Everyone relaxed when they realized it was me and not Mrs. Avery. You could smell the fear in the room. A couple of kids were cursing themselves for thinking it was a perfectly sound idea to bail on studying last night and do a few hours of gaming instead.

Daniel was in his seat, pouring over my history book, trying to glean as much information as possible in the time remaining before class started. He was cramming, stuffing every piece of data, every fact he could fit into his head. I don't think two hours from now he'd have any recollection of what he'd read, but I had to give him credit for trying. Daniel would remember long enough to pass, I was pretty sure.

He glanced up and growled at me. I pointed at the book.

He glared in my direction another few seconds, then put his face back in the Civil War.

I hated the Civil War.

Phoebe walked into the room and avoided my eyes as she sat in her seat, which was just in front of mine. She kept her back to me.

I could hear her breathing. It was heavy. Through her nose. As if she were angry, annoyed, something. After a moment:

"You okay?" she said without turning.

"I'm…fine."

When she finally glanced at me, she seemed surprised.

"Looks like you're trying to give birth to a golf ball." Her fingers touched her head in a mirror image of where mine hurt.

I ran my hand over the area where the pain was coming from.

"I think it's going to be a…Titlest," I said.

The smallest hint of a smile flashed in her eyes. But it was gone before it ever made it to her mouth.

The bump was throbbing.

I've been hit harder before. One time, after I was captured in France and mistaken for an English spy when, in fact, I was working for the Americans who were allied with the French, Napoleon himself took the handle of his sword and clobbered me. I ended up becoming a valet and trusted ally of the man. The history books say he was short—five foot two or so, but back then I was five foot two, and he was at least four or five inches taller than me.

That's the problem with history. The people who are actually there are too busy trying to stay alive to write it.

"He's got a lot of pressure on him. Homecoming Game this week," Phoebe said without mentioning Craig's name. "Sometimes he can be a bit—"

"—of an asshole?"

She glanced down at the floor. "He's really very nice." After a pause, she added, "To me."

My head hurt. I wanted to say, *Hey, I get it. You're beautiful. You run around in a cheerleader uniform. Of course, the King of the Cool Kids likes you. And why wouldn't he? On top of everything else, you're funny. You're charming. You run up and kiss him whenever you see him.*

I don't even think his mother ever did that. Even when he was a baby.

But Phoebe was a good person. I decided to cut her some slack.

"What do you see in that idiot anyway?"

Not that much slack, I guess.

"He's captain of the football team, senior class president, annoyingly good looking," Daniel said without looking up. "That's what history really teaches. That the biggest pricks get the hottest chicks—"

"Daniel!"

He looked up, startled.

"Was I saying that out loud?"

I nodded and gave him an irritated scowl before returning to Phoebe.

"Listen," I said. "I've known a lot of guys like Craig Coulter in my life. Some of them turn out halfway decent. But most of them become horrible husbands and terrible fathers. And the worst of them, turn into bullying assholes."

She looked at me, quizzically. "Your *extensive* life experience tells you that?" she said, sarcastically.

"Trust me, I'm an expert on the subject of assholes."

She turned quickly, her hair gently twirling to catch up with the movement. I caught a glimpse of a displeased frown and a hint of jasmine. The scent reminded me of something, but I pushed it out of my mind. It was too painful.

Mrs. Avery walked into the room, and I heard a couple of audible gasps. She was carrying...a stack of paper at least ten inches high. "Good morning. Seats, please." Her eyes found me. "So nice of you to join us, Mr. Grant." She began handing out tests, dropping one face down on each student's desk. It had to be twenty pages, at least.

Mrs. Avery looked about a hundred years old, spoke like she was three hundred, and moved like she was twenty. She could hear a snide comment from across the room and be dragging you out the door by your ear in three seconds flat. I secretly wondered if she was like me. She had a huge schoolgirl crush on Thomas Jefferson and spoke about him in the present tense.

Last time my father was home, it was Parent/Teacher conferences, and I asked him about it. I thought he might tell me I was being silly or laugh at the question in that hearty, unrestrained way that he does. The way I've seen kings and generals and others of great power laugh.

But he didn't.

He sat across from Mrs. Avery and watched her as she told him that my class work was satisfactory, but that I needed to take history a little more seriously.

I nearly choked on that.

By the way, seeing my father sitting in one of those classroom chairs, listening to know-it-all teachers and helicopter parents is almost worth going to school every day.

Afterward, in the car, my father told me he was certain she wasn't like us, but I still had my doubts.

"Take history more seriously?" I asked rhetorically. "What is that supposed to mean? I know everything there is to know about the past thousand years. I've either lived it, learned it from those who lived it, or studied it till I was sick of it because *you* made me." I looked out the window into the darkness. "Take history more seriously."

My father smiled. "You still have a great deal to learn, Alexander. Believe me."

"I know!" I sighed heavily. "And I'd like to learn by *doing* something. Living this quiet, laid-back life is killing me."

"I understand how difficult this is for you."

"Do you? I bet you weren't sitting in a classroom at my age."

He was quiet, his eyes searching far down the road. "I was doing what people at that time were expected to do. You're doing what people are expected to do now. It is very important you keep yourself and your talents in check."

"Yeah, I know that, too."

It's not easy being inconspicuous when you've lived a hundred lifetimes.

I wanted to be more. I could be great—*monumentally* great—if only he would let me.

There've been periods when my father forced us to remain anonymous, to live quietly. But there were other times when he allowed me to show off my skills.

But that was in the past.

Lately, it had become increasingly difficult to be who I am—who I can be—and not be discovered. It used to be easy. I could hide in plain sight. Be a child prodigy, a protégé, a boy wonder, and then move on. But the modern world made that nearly impossible.

Cameras on everything from stoplights to cell phones. The ever-present media. The ability to communicate instantly across the globe. It all meant that anyone doing something extraordinary would gather attention, be recorded and, more importantly, be *remembered*.

Indefinitely.

The fact that there is a picture of me, looking pretty much the same as I do now, in every major newspaper in the world on May 18, 1948, after I came in third at the World Chess Championship held in The Hague and Moscow...still causes my father to get furious at me.

And so, for the past five-plus decades, we have moved from city to town, small town to even smaller town every few years. I've enrolled in more than a dozen schools, taken the same tests over and over, had the same three teachers time and time again.

The good. The bad. And the horrible.

Sure, every once in a while, a teacher stood out. But I found even the good ones not so great. It wasn't their fault. It's just difficult to hear someone droning on about Napoleon or Thomas Jefferson or Joan of Arc or Catherine The Great or Shakespeare, listen to them blather on about what these great men and women were really like, what their motivations were, what they were thinking about, when you've actually met these people yourself.

By the way, Shakespeare is one of us. He's a writer in Hollywood now. Television, mostly. And you know what? He still makes the actors say every one of his words. As written. He's kind of a prick that way. He only gets away with it because his dialogue is still the best.

As for Mrs. Avery, I'd rate her somewhere between bad and horrible.

"Now, class," she barked, "I want you to put your books away, keep the test turned over and only begin after I tell you. You will have the full period to complete the examination. If you happen to finish early, you may walk up to my desk, hand it to me, then sit quietly in your chair until the end of class. There will be no talking. And everyone, eyes on our own papers."

She looked directly at Daniel as she put the last exam in front of him and not-so-gently closed the book in his hand.

"Begin!" she ordered sharply, startling half the class as if a gun had been fired in the room.

I turned over the stapled stack and began the test.

Like the thing with Napoleon's height. Most of history, at least the history that gets written down, is just plain wrong.

Take, for instance, question number twenty-six.

> *In what year was the island of Manhattan acquired?*
> *By whom, from whom, and for how much?*

The answer Mrs. Avery was looking for was: The island of Manhattan was purchased in 1626 by Peter Minuit from a local Wappinger tribe for beads and trinkets worth sixty guilders (often said to equal $24).

This makes the Indians look pretty stupid. I mean, a whole island, some of the priciest real estate in the world, for twenty-four bucks worth of junk? Dumb.

Problem is, the only thing correct about that answer is the year.

After Shakespeare "died"— I'd been a scribe for him—I moved around Europe for a few years and found myself on a Dutch ship, heading to America for the first time, landing in New Amsterdam, which sat on the southern tip of Manhattan Island.

I had money, troves of it, stashed throughout Europe. But it isn't like today where a small rectangle of plastic or a chip in a cell phone can give you access to thousands, even millions of dollars. Wealth until recently was unwieldy. And not very portable. It would've taken a small armada of ships to bring my fortune to the New World. So much for blending in.

Instead, I came with almost nothing.

And so, because I could pick up languages easily, I earned my keep by translating between the settlers and the local tribes.

What really went down in 1626 is that *Pieter* Minuit gave 60 guilders (a couple of thousand dollars in today's money) worth of technology including ax heads to the Canarsee tribe who didn't even live on Manhattan but inhabited an area that is now Brooklyn. Minuit never acknowledged this mistake. Over the next few months, the Canarsee wiped out the local tribe on Manhattan, clearing the way for the Dutch to settle there.

Not as cute a story.

It's like instead of buying a house from the owners, you hire a hit man, then move in once the former occupants have been taken out.

This wasn't the only question I had a problem with.

The first President of the United States was *not* George Washington. We did *not* declare our independence on July 4, 1776. Maine is *not* the easternmost state in the U.S.

Of course, if you answered these questions accurately, you'd almost certainly fail your history test.

George Washington was actually the ninth "President" of the United States. John Hanson was the first, followed by seven others between 1781 and 1788 under our original constitution, each serving a one-year term. Washington was the first President elected after our second and current constitution was ratified in 1788. The first one was so bad we realized we had to scrap it and start over after only seven years.

As for the Declaration of Independence, we declared our independence on July 2nd. In fact, John Adams, who would become the *tenth* president—the one after Washington—wrote his wife saying, "The second day of July 1776, will be celebrated by succeeding generations from one end of this continent to the other, from this time forward forevermore."

Not…really. The 2nd of July I'm usually packing to go somewhere for the 4th.

The final *text* of the Declaration of Independence written in Jefferson's hand was *approved* by Congress on the 4th, but that was just a formality over some minor text changes. I held the beautifully lettered parchment for the five seconds it took to ferry it between Jefferson and John Hancock who, as President of the Congress, was the only man to sign it. That original document was lost almost immediately. The copy sitting in the National Archives didn't get signed until August 2nd. It's Jefferson's words, but not his handwriting.

As for Maine being the furthest east? Seems like a no-brainer, right? Except several islands in the Aleutian chain are so far "west" of mainland Alaska, they're in the Eastern Hemisphere. Making Alaska the westernmost *and* the easternmost state.

I answered question number twenty-six "correctly." Minuit, $24, 1626, blah, blah, blah.

This was what passed for knowledge in the present world of Alexander the Pretty Good. Alexander *the Great*, his teacher was Aristotle. Mine was Mrs. Avery.

Out of the corner of my eye, I could see Daniel straining to get a peek at my paper. You had to admire determination like that.

But it was something past Daniel that caught my attention and made my chest tighten.

Braeden Ellis.

The recently arrived senior was watching me through the windows that ran between the courtyard and our classroom. Unlike his slyness in the woods, Braeden made no attempt at pretense, no effort to hide his gaze.

His stare was fixed, black eyes unmoving.

Like a shark.

I've lived through so many events, had so many experiences, from the horribly frightening to the embarrassingly funny, that I'm not easily rattled. But something in the way that Braeden's eyes drilled into me stirred up trouble in the pit of my stomach.

Which I realized is how much of the rest of the class felt *before* the test.

Ready to puke.

- THREE -
A Pussy Sport Played With
500 Warriors On A Side

Even with Braeden eyeing me like a lion eyes a gazelle, I finished the test early. Seventeen minutes early. Not a record. Not even close. But still a little intimidating for the other students.

I heard Paul Polanski say, "You're kidding me!" a lot louder than he meant to when I put my pencil down at 8:28, got out of my chair and strolled up to Mrs. Avery with my test outstretched.

The ancient-faced teacher glared at Paul.

Then she looked at me.

And I looked at her.

It was a standoff.

I heard bad Spaghetti Western music in my head. Don't worry if you've never heard of gunslinging pasta. Spaghetti Westerns are a sub-genre of Westerns shot in Italy and Spain in the '60s and '70s, instead of the American West. Motion pictures have been around for more than a century. They're still kind of new for me. I've barely gotten over photographs.

Anyway, the theme from "The Good, The Bad and the Ugly" was whistling in my ears.

Mrs. Avery seemed like she was expecting me to ask a question—hoping, I think—especially since she had scribbled the words NO QUESTIONS DURING TEST in huge letters on the blackboard behind her, which she would casually point to after you asked her something.

She's not the only teacher I've had that enjoyed making her students feel like complete morons. But she took more pleasure in it than most.

Only I had no questions. Other than: how come your test was so flawed and inaccurate, Mrs. Avery? If that even *is* your name.

But I knew I wouldn't get a constructive response to that. I'd have been instantly ear-pulled down to the office to see Mr. Gulivin, which was more torture than I could take.

And it wasn't the ear-pulling I objected to.

I'd rather be burned at the stake—and believe me, I very nearly have been on several occasions, including the time I stupidly performed a magic trick in public while passing through Barcelona during the Spanish Inquisition—than be forced to endure five minutes with Mr. Gulivin.

If there are only three types of teachers—the good, the bad and the horrible—there are only two types of principals: The mean. And the meek.

The mean are militaristic ultra strict ex-drill sergeants (or frustrated wannabes) who believe that children should be seen and not heard and that any creative spark should be snuffed out of them immediately.

Kids need to understand their place in the world, which is a millimeter above pond scum and be grateful that it isn't a hundred years ago where they'd be working fourteen hours a day in a factory or out in the fields under the scorching sun. These I-hate-you-cuz-I-really-love-you types claim they want "to prepare children for the real world" where we're just gonna become another cog in the wheel.

Uplifting, isn't it? Who wouldn't be inspired by that?

"Lower your expectations in life, young man," a principal once said to me. "That way you won't be so disappointed."

And adults wonder why kids hate school.

The meek, on the other hand, are overly comforting, too kind and want you to talk about your "feelings." They fawn over you and say things like, "I know you can do better Mr. Grant. All you have to do is believe it, too," and "I'm going to let you get away with it this time, Alexander, because I know you're not a bad kid at heart."

Only some kids *are* bad. And pampering them isn't going to make them suddenly good.

You never heard me say this, but kids need boundaries, even though we'll never, ever admit it.

Without rules, things get out of control. And quick.

Mr. Gulivin was neither one of these types.

No, Mr. Gulivin was that rare specimen of undiluted mediocrity. He was both meek *and* mean, and worse, he was profoundly bad at both.

He wanted you to "understand" his thinking, but his vocal cords produced the sound of a mouse with a heavy Boston accent sneaking by a sleeping cat. What you could make out from his garbled, squeaking whisper always ended with, "en yah be spindin yah ahfta noons ahrrr-ite he-ah beside may."

With my somewhat excessive number of absences, tardies, and early dismissals—all of them excused by scrupulously forged notes—I tried to avoid Mr. Gulivin as much as possible.

I let go of the exam. It dropped with a thud on Mrs. Avery's desk.

She gave me a suspicious look that screamed, *are you sure you wanna hand it in so soon?*

"I'm sure," I said out loud.

Mind reading snot, she was thinking.

My answers were all *correct,* even if many of them weren't *right.* So, unless Mrs. Avery was looking to me for enlightenment, for something other than the "facts" in her flawed *The American Experience* textbook, I expected she'd be compelled to give my answers a reluctant "A."

I would've finished even sooner if I hadn't gotten bogged down by the aforementioned questions.

Some days it was harder than others to get my pencil to scribble out what the writers of history wanted me to believe instead of what I had witnessed.

I don't mean to imply that everything in these books is wrong. It's just that the simpler and easier-to-understand the authors try to make an event, the farther away it is from what really happened.

They say that those who don't learn from history are destined to repeat it.

I think that's true.

Which is why it's even more important to know what the hell actually occurred.

∞

"I think I did okay," Daniel said in the hallway after class. "How dumb was that tribe for selling Manhattan for beads? Seriously."

I doubted Daniel's life would ever depend on knowing what really happened, so I decided not to correct him.

"You finished in like three minutes," he said.

"Thirty."

"Whatever. It was annoying. I did enjoy the fact that you had to park it for the rest of class, no book, no phone, no games, no texting. Nothing to do but sit '*quietly,*'" he said, making quotation marks in the air. "Torture."

"Yeah," I said. But I really didn't mean it. Unlike most kids my "age," I don't have the need to be entertained every second. I enjoy moments of contemplation, where I can think, meditate, or just clear my head. I don't find it painful or boring. I find it peaceful.

Besides, I spent most of the time watching Phoebe. Her hair. Her breathing. The movement of her arm as she filled out the test. Stupid, I know. It's not like there aren't a lot of other attractive girls in this school. But there is something about her.

"You wanna get some pizza after school?"

"Practice," I said. Daniel knew this. But every day he would ask me anyway.

"Right. It's the big game Saturday," he said. "Oh, and your game, too."

I gave him a fake laugh that sounded like a goat getting kicked in the stomach.

"After practice?"

"Sure, if your social calendar isn't too filled up." I swiped my history book out of his hands and started walking away.

"Your highlights helped," he said. "Although the actual answers would have been much more efficient."

"You'll thank me someday, Daniel."

"I highly doubt that."

Even though he tried to act cool, I could tell he was relieved and more than a little happy about how he had done.

The rest of the day crept by.

Third period, fourth period, fifth, sixth, seventh. *This* was torture. I know some of you know what I mean.

I don't want you to get the wrong idea. I crave learning. I seek out knowledge. And I genuinely love school.

That is, the first hundred times I went through it.

When the day's final bell rang, I sprinted out of class and hurried down to the locker room.

This was the one part of the day I really enjoyed.

I changed into my gear and got ready to play *tewaaraton*.

Almost a thousand years ago, not far from here in what is now upper New York and southern Ottawa, the Huron and Iroquois created a game that was part sport, part boot camp, part religious ritual.

Played to honor The Creator, it was known by many names on both sides of the St. Lawrence River: *dehuntshigwa'es* ("men hit a rounded object"), *baaga`adowe* ("bump hips"), *kabocha-toli* ("stick-ball").

When I played it in the late 1620s and early 30s, I knew it as *tewaaraton*.

I was eleven hundred and something years old—still about a century from hitting puberty.

I only spent a brief time in New Amsterdam, which back then encompassed only the land on Manhattan Island below what is now Wall Street.

I found the New Amsterdam settlement a little boring after being in Europe. To me, all the action was with the tribes.

They were getting pushed inland, either by force, by trickery, or by shady land deals—none of them as famous as Pieter Minuit's, but with outcomes pretty much the same.

I used my language skills to get friendly with various tribes. Over time, I traveled up the Muhheakantuck River—what is now called the Hudson—and finally settled in with a tribe that called themselves *Kanien'kehá:ka*. People of the Place of Flint. But you know them by the name their enemies gave them: Mohawk. *"Man-eaters."*

Tewaaraton was their favorite sport.

I've taken part in games with as many as five hundred to a thousand combatants on a side, played on the plains that ran between villages. Some contests spanned an entire valley.

We would spend days, sometimes many days, sunup to sundown, fighting our way through the mass of men to get a single chance at glory—shooting the deerskin ball at the goals.

We would eat and sleep in the field of play.

It may be difficult to imagine a *game* of such great magnitude, a thousand men, miles of terrain and only one ball, but these contests were a mix of beauty and brutality, of elegant strategy and brute force.

Across the Heron and Iroquois Nations, the Creator's Game was played to resolve conflicts among tribes, to heal the sick, but most importantly, it was played to develop, to hone, to chisel boys into men, and men into warriors.

Despite the fact I was a paleface, the leaders of the Mohawk trusted me, adopted me as their own, and so I was given the chance to learn the ways of the warrior and complete the transition into manhood.

I became friends with the eldest son of the Chief, a boy on the edge of turning twelve.

Actually, Deganawa and I were best friends. He was the same size as me, and our speed and strength surpassed all the others of our age. We were highly competitive one-on-one, but on the playing field, we fiercely protected each other.

I closed my locker, making sure it was secure by absently

spinning the combination lock longer than I needed to. I laced up my cleats and secured the Velcro straps for support. Much better traction-wise than the leather moccasins I wore on the plains. I put on my helmet, snapped the chin guard, pulled gloves over my fingers, stretching open my hands to loosen the leather. I closed my eyes and breathed in slowly, held it for a moment, then I grabbed my stick and headed out to join the rest of my team on the rain-soaked practice field.

I owe my life to Deganawa.

My lighter skin made me an easy target for the opposing tribes. Although not as pink as most whites, I was clearly not "of the people."

On the eastern end of the sprawling Mohawk Valley, I stared at the Oneida across the valley floor. Even at that distance, I could see the men and boys of this tribe were not to be taken lightly. There was much riding on this game. Money, gold, even wives and children had been wagered on the outcome. But for Deganawa and me, the stakes were even higher. It was our first chance to play the game against *men*.

In the middle of the field, the deerskin sphere was tossed into the air as the leaders of the two teams dove for it.

It was impossible to see the ball. It was nearly a mile away. But the swarming movements of the men made its location clear enough.

All day, the action around us was fierce and territorial.

After more than three hours, fatigue setting in, I was caught off-guard and blocked in the head with the end of a stick.

Deganawa, as he had many times before, came to my rescue.

"Are you injured badly?"

I felt warmth running down the side of my forehead and over my cheek as blood dripped out of the wound.

I didn't answer.

One of the things you notice when you live a long time is that history repeats itself.

Often.

I have found myself knocked silly more times than I'd like to admit. I could take up your entire life listing them off for you.

I'll spare us both.

Now, killing an opponent on purpose had become less common, but it was still part of the game. And as a white man, the Oneida might not think the Mohawk would take any offense at my death.

They were mistaken.

Deganawa fended off three members of the Oneida. Then without much effort, he dragged me by the back of the neck and pulled me at least a hundred yards, knocking more attackers out of the way, until he dropped me into a small depression carved in the field by the annual rains.

I was hidden, which meant, I was safe.

There was still a slow trickle of water running through the long grass, home to about a million mosquitoes. Half of them started feasting on my exposed flesh, the other half waiting for the leftovers. As soon as Deganawa let go of me, I felt the coolness of the still water and the warmth of my own blood.

"Do you think you can stand?" he asked me.

Without thinking, my body started to get up.

"Stay. Do not move."

A second later he took out another attacker with the end of his stick. An Oneida brave landed next to me with a squishy thud.

He was looking at me. Or maybe it was through me.

I could tell he was only marginally conscious. There we were, both of us, staring at each other, half out of it.

Deganawa patted me with his stick to keep me awake, to let me know I would be all right. "We will be men soon."

Saturday finally came.

Homecoming. The final home game. Sunny. Fifty-two degrees. Winds from the south.

The football game was at 2:00 PM. Our contest would start at

10:30 AM on the same field. They'd have about two thousand people in the stands. We'd have less than a hundred.

Didn't matter.

We'd play like there were ten thousand watching us.

Coach gave us his traditional Homecoming pep talk, which was pretty much the same pep talk he gave us before every other game of the year except he added a bit at the end—with an even bigger scowl on his face than he normally had—that during halftime of the football game, the Homecoming Queen and her court in their long, pretty dresses would be paraded across the field in classic cars, while during *our* halftime, Ken Swiner, the school's three hundred and fifty-pound groundskeeper, would spend the entire fifteen-minute break picking at his enormous ass as he rechalked the lines.

Pretty much the whole team winced at the image that popped into our heads. I'm not sure how coach thought this helped us, but the team was 10-0 on Homecoming Day in the decade he's been coaching.

We charged out onto the field to face our arch-rivals, Housatonic Regional. When adults weren't around, we called them Who'sMoronic.

The weather was crisp. The sky was clear. My stick felt good in my hands. A perfect day for The Creator's Game.

An hour later, the game against Who'sMoronic was going along fine. The score was 24-23 in our favor.

As I expected, the stands weren't very crowded, certainly not as full as they would be when the football teams took the field, but there were more spectators than normal. Ironically, Who'sMoronic had a larger number of fans than we did. Partly because they had twice as many students, but mostly because a dozen chartered buses packed with Who'sMoronic football fans not wanting to make the trip from Pittsfield by car arrived early to tailgate and barbecue.

Both goalkeepers were doing an incredible job. It had been more than ten minutes since the last goal. Lacrosse is a high-scoring sport. And to go that long without either team getting a goal was unusual.

One of Who'sMoronic's middies stick-checked Richie Z., popping the ball loose from my teammate. The middie scooped it up and carried it across the midline, then fired it down the sideline to an attackman behind the goal, who took three giant steps, leaped from the back of the crease into the air and shot the ball over the top of the net.

It bounced off the shoulder blade of our keeper and went in.

I cursed under my breath, then jogged up to our keeper and knocked him on the pads for encouragement.

Richie Zedman was our captain and one of the best players I've ever seen. *And* one of the most competitive. He hated to lose even more than I did. He ran up to me. I figured he was going to chew me out for not getting downfield fast enough to help him. Instead, he seemed mildly impressed. "These guys are good," he said, quietly.

I nodded. "It was a pretty shot."

"Circus shot." He meant it as a compliment. "They're pressing down low. We might catch them out." Richie Z. hit me on the back with his stick.

"*Nia:wen,*" I said when I realized I had survived.

"You're welcome." Deganawa was watching something in the distance, his pupils fixed. "Can you stand up?"

"I think so."

"Good." He looked around. At what, I couldn't see. "Do you think you can run very, very fast?"

"I'm not sure."

"If you could be sure, I think that would be something we should do," he said matter-of-factly.

I stuck my head over the ridge of the depression and saw at least fifty attackers heading our way with an equal number of Mohawks in pursuit.

And something else—the ball.

Flying straight at us.

It bounced once at the top of the ridge and landed right in front of me, rolling to a dead stop at my ankles.

Normally, any brave would consider themselves blessed by the Creator to have such good fortune fall at their feet. Some men went their entire lives without being this close to the ball. Me, I cursed in at least six different languages.

But eventually seeing the ball inches away jolted me like a lightning strike to the groin. Injured or not, I could have lifted a boulder at that moment.

There is a fever that one gets when playing this game, the need to take the ball and defeat the enemy. The native word for it is not important. It's extremely long and hard to pronounce. What it describes is a powerful feeling. One that takes over your entire body.

It's more than the adrenaline surging through you when seeing a hundred warriors aiming for you. It's more than the need for competition. Or even survival.

It is all of those and something else. Something basic.

It is the need to prove one's existence. To matter.

Lunging with his hands far apart on his stick, Deganawa took out the first of the Oneida to reach us. The dumbstruck brave wheezed as the wind was knocked out of him and he landed right on top of his brethren.

"Run!" Deganawa screamed at me.

Without any thought, I snatched the ball from the ground with my stick and raced off, fighting through a thicket of Oneida.

The fact that Deganawa and I came out of nowhere surprised everyone, including our own tribe.

I was running for my life.

Literally.

And I did not look back.

I sprinted nonstop for over a thousand yards—about three-quarters of a mile flat out. I blew by the last defenders and left Deganawa behind.

I shot the ball at the narrow space between the two twenty-foot high posts. The deerskin sailed through the hot, heavy air and past the keeper.

I didn't stop running.

There were a hundred screaming braves chasing me across the amber fields.

Deganawa later told me that I sprinted another mile before I collapsed. I was so far out of play no one bothered me. They had all turned around after a few hundred yards to celebrate or mourn.

It was one of the young women of the tribe who found me. She had been gathering roots for the dinner when she stumbled upon my unconscious body sometime later.

I remember a warm hand on my skin.

Her name was Alanu.

The only daughter of the tribe's medicine man. A pretty girl with large, brown eyes who not long after that day would marry Deganawa in a ceremony that filled me with great joy…and a little jealousy.

I understand jealousy. It's why I didn't fight back against Craig Coulter. It can make a person irrational. Hitting him would've been easy. Holding back, that's much, much harder.

Phoebe's voice cut through the grunts and groans and clashing equipment. "Goooooo, Grant!" Whenever I had the ball or made a play, I could hear her voice cheering above the rest.

The cheerleaders had arrived midway through the second half and were doing impromptu cheers as a warm-up before the football game. Phoebe was the only one on the varsity squad who knew any of our names.

"Zedmaaaaannnnn!" she hollered.

I always want to win. I'm…fairly competitive. But having her watching from the sidelines added an extra urgency. A little caveman, I know.

We were tied with three minutes left. A lot of goals can be scored in a hundred and eighty seconds, and they had gotten the last two. It felt like we were playing on our heels, reacting instead of attacking.

And it cost us.

A minute later, they scored again. This time with a shot from ten yards out that blew by our keeper.

He didn't have a chance.

Richie Z. came toward me again.

This time he was not as cordial. "Hit that guy, A.G.! He never should've gotten a clean shot like that!"

I nodded, dipping my head. Richie was right.

I went for the ball instead of the man. I was trying to get cute instead of just checking him to the ground.

I walked to the center of the midline to take the face-off. I am one of the three midfielders and can go the entire length of the field. The three attackmen have to stay on the offensive side, just as the three defensemen must remain in the defensive end—unless one of the middies swaps out.

Two minutes to go. We had gone from being up by two to being down by one.

∞

I laid my crosse down on the grass, horizontal to my opponent's crosse along the midfield line. The heads of the sticks were inches from the ball.

Since at any given moment the vast majority of the players spread across the valley were nowhere near the ball, the primary object of *tewaaraton* was to defend against and disable as many of your opponents as possible.

I found it funny that Craig Coulter called lacrosse a game for pussies.

Tewaaraton literally means, "the little brother of war."

And like war, the game was deadly for some.

Craig would've lasted about thirty seconds on the grassy plains before he'd be knocked out cold—or worse—by a stick to the head.

One way or another, by the end of a game of *tewaaraton*, there were no pussies left.

When I began preparatory school in the early 1800s, I played rugby, golf, and tennis, by the middle of the century in what would become *high* school, baseball became my favorite sport. And in the early 1900s, I added football and basketball.

I avoided lacrosse.

I had played in some of the most epic, adrenaline-inducing games in history. Modern lacrosse, confined to an area about the size of a football field including end zones, didn't inspire me.

For sixty years, I played football in the fall. I broke my arm twenty-seven times.

Bet Craig Coulter can't say that.

Then one day I saw Rutgers defeat Syracuse for the NCAA championship. The announcer called lacrosse the "fastest game on two feet."

Watching that game and the celebration afterwards brought back memories of glory.

I looked at lacrosse differently now—ten men on a side versus a hundred or a thousand—but cradling the ball, smashing through defenders, the acrobatic shots at the goal, the quiet tension before the ball is put in play, it now brought me the same joy as it did three centuries ago.

I've played it almost every year since.

I went out for football this year, just to change things up, but after dealing with Craig Coulter and his friends at tryouts, I decided I'd rather play a game I loved with people I liked.

We waited for the whistle from the ref.

I could hear my opponent breathing.

He was mumbling something, either to me or to himself. It sounded like, "Ball is mine."

The whistle.

I grabbed my stick off the turf and scrambled for the ball. I tried to clamp it under my crosse, but the kid was pushing down on my stick, and I couldn't flick it out. Finally, I was able to roll it behind me. I slid my crosse under my legs and poked the ball back to Richie Z. who scooped it up and carried it into the attack zone. He got slammed to the ground by a defenseman, and the ball came free. Another of our players picked up the ball but was checked off it.

I came rushing in and shouldered the defender just as he was about to pass. The ball blooped into the air, and I pulled it down into the netting of my stick, stealing it from the sticks of several other players.

"Go, Alexander," I heard Phoebe shout.

I could see Craig Coulter watching me from the sideline. The football team was beginning to show up. They were forced to dress in suits and ties before games, which always seemed like putting a tuxedo on a gorilla. The gorilla didn't like it. The tux didn't either. Craig glanced over at Phoebe as she cheered me down the field. His face turned red. I had the distinct feeling that at some point in the near future, I was going to get another visit from his fist.

Craig had anger issues.

I don't care how nice he was to her, he was an asshole.

Like I said, I understand him being jealous—Phoebe was one of the prettiest girls in our school—but he had no reason to be upset with me. A dozen *other* guys, sure, but not me.

I don't mean to sound arrogant, but if I really wanted to steal Phoebe Amara away from Craig Coulter, I think centuries of experience, the years I spent with Shakespeare listening to him compose love sonnets or learning from Leonardo da Vinci how to draw out the inner beauty of a subject, transcribing poetry for Shelley, Wordsworth, and Keats, delivering proposals for the matchmakers of Dublin, if I applied all of this knowledge—any of it!—I'd have a pretty good chance of winning her heart.

And maybe the real reason I didn't fight back, didn't give him the beating he deserved is because he was right in a way. I hadn't tried to hit on her. But that didn't mean I didn't want to. Phoebe Amara made me notice her. No matter where she was or what she was doing, some part of me was paying attention.

Nobody understands chemistry, of course, why one person likes another person. I'm not guaranteeing one hundred percent I'd be able to win her over, but I could certainly make it a lot more difficult for Craig if I wanted to.

It would be so easy to say and do all the things that could make her fall for me. Not because I felt them, but because I had seen them work a thousand times before.

And that's one of the most difficult things about being fifteen hundred years old.

Not showing off.

I almost got clobbered because I wasn't paying attention.

At the last second, I hit the ground and rolled, avoiding the hit. The middie aiming for me tumbled awkwardly as he grabbed at an armful of air.

I almost forgot I still had the ball. I flicked it to Richie Z. who passed it behind the net to Tommy who sent it back to me after I got to my feet and rushed the net.

I jumped into the air to get some height over my defender and fired a bullet at the upper left corner of the net.

The keeper reacted late and clumsily stuck out his stick and—somehow—caught the ball.

We all were frozen for a moment.

I think everyone expected my shot to go in.

The keeper lobbed the ball downfield, catching us off guard.

All of us were down low, just our three defensemen were back.

Thirty seconds left.

A Who'sMoronic attacker caught the ball and ran behind our net. He was ragging it. Taking his time, trying to run down the clock. He should have pitched it to his teammate along the crease. They had us outnumbered.

His hesitation gave me and the other middies time to get back.

As I was closing in on him, the attacker finally passed the ball out front. But Ben Lasker reached up with his long defenseman's stick and stole the ball. Ben charged back the other way, looking for a fast break.

Anticipating his steal, I had already turned and sprinted toward the midline. I got out in front of Ben, off to his right. I called for the ball, but he flicked it to Richie up the middle who raced straight toward the goal.

Two defenders closed on Richie from either side.

Ten seconds left.

He pulled back his stick. I thought he was going to shoot, but he no-look passed the ball back to me over his shoulder just as the defenders sandwiched him.

It was beautiful. With Richie double-teamed, I was wide open. I cradled the ball, rocking my stick back and forth to maintain control.

I could've shot, but I was pretty far out. The keeper would have time to react. He'd proved he was lightning fast. I wouldn't make the same mistake.

I ignored the defender charging at me.

Five seconds.

Richie Z. was still under the two defensemen. The rest of my teammates were covered or behind me. Not enough time left to wait for them to get open. I had the only shot. If I timed it, if I was patient, I thought I could beat the keeper and tie the game.

But I was about to get a defender in my face.

I leaped. I was soaring. Before I could wrist it toward the upper right corner, the defender, who was at least fifty pounds heavier than me, smashed his stick across my arm. I felt a searing pain that spread through my whole body.

He not only slashed me but then brought his stick up under my chin.

A graphite fiber uppercut.

I heard the horn sound—game over—and almost immediately, things started to go black.

I don't remember anything after that.

- FOUR -
I Don't Particularly Like
Having A Nuclear Weapon
Aimed At My Crotch

I came to as the paramedics were locking me into a head strap. I could see Phoebe looking down at me.

I was disoriented. The crowd in the stands seemed huge, like I was on the field in the middle of a Patriots game.

As I woozily glanced around, I saw Braeden. Him again. What was it with this guy?

And then I began to remember.

Braeden watching me from the sidelines. His stare more intense than even Craig Coulter's. Craig was no longer satisfied with simply pushing my face in the dirt. The new Craig Coulter wanted to kill me—I can only imagine what Braeden was thinking.

After the vicious hit—as I was losing consciousness—out of the corner of my eye, I saw Braeden sprint onto the field. Was it before the horn? I couldn't remember. He shouldn't have been on the field either way.

He was running directly at me. I was expecting another blow. I was defenseless. I was half unconscious and still in the air, heading to the ground. But he didn't hit me. As best as I could remember, and it's a little fuzzy, Braeden slammed himself into the defender that had taken me down.

"What's your name, son?" one of the paramedics asked me.

On a good day, if you catch me off guard, I might not be able to answer this question correctly. I've had so many names over the years.

"Alexander...ummm...." I've almost always been Alexander, so that's easy enough to remember, but the rest of my name has changed. Right now, my father and I are running through the surnames of famous generals. "...ummmm, Grant."

The guy didn't look too pleased.

"Alexander Grant," I tried to say more convincingly.

"Where are you?"

Another trick question.

"Lying on a gurney."

He didn't smile. "What town?"

I could see Phoebe's face. She was worried.

For almost a hundred years, I knew this place as *Mahaiwe*.

"Great Barrington."

"What day of the week is it?"

"Saturday. Homecoming."

The paramedic nodded.

"Okay, we're going to take you to the hospital just to be safe."

"It's just a bruise on my foreARRRMMMM!" my voice raised as I touched my limb and was hit with shooting pain. I tried to recover quickly. I wanted to avoid the hospital. I told them I didn't want to go. But the coaches said *blah blah blah* liability *blah blah* insurance claims *blah blah blah* to make sure I was okay.

The crowd cheered as they slid me into the back of the ambulance. Once the doors were slammed shut, we drove across the field, the ambulance followed by a cop car. My parade beat the Homecoming Queen's by a good hour and a half.

I don't really know how any of us have survived, and by us, I mean all of us, when you consider what goes on at the local emergency room.

It seems like if I were actually in need of medical attention, I'd be entirely dead by the time they got around to helping me.

For a place whose very name supposedly advertises that this is where you come during an urgent situation, no one seems to move with any great speed, enthusiasm, or urgency.

I had to be very careful dealing with the doctors here. The multiple injuries I've had, the pathogens I've come in contact with that no one alive could have been exposed to could bring unwanted attention.

For people like me, the most dangerous time is from birth until sometime in our "toddler" years. For *any* child born before the twentieth century, this early period was perilous. But we are young for so much longer, it brings added risk. It's not surprising that I rarely catch a cold, that my immune system is better than most of yours. It's simply that those of us who didn't have a superior resistance to disease…died.

Most before they could speak complete sentences.

The second most dangerous time for us is during puberty. Hormones are coursing through our bodies causing drastic changes as we transform from adolescents into adults. It's slightly less of a problem with normal teenagers because these hormonal changes happen over a few years. For me, it's been a few centuries. And the effects on my mind and body are profound, pronounced, and irritating.

We're more vulnerable to injury. And more likely to do stupid things to get injured.

Luckily, like a small portion of the general population, most of us have a variation of the gene involved in building proteins that help repair neurons, making me less susceptible to concussions. We didn't know this, of course, until very recently. We just thought we had harder heads.

"You check out fine in the cognitive tests," the doctor said. He had asked me some of the same questions—what's my name, where am I, how old I was—but I was feeling much better and answered them quickly.

"I'm a little concerned that you passed out," the doctor said.

"Did I? I don't think I did."

"That's the thing about passing out, you don't remember doing it."

"Probably as much from dehydration," I tried to offer.

"Maybe. Any headache at all?"

I paused as I took stock of my brain. Concussions were nothing to mess with. I didn't feel any symptoms.

"None."

"Hmmm. Okay, I'm not going to order a CAT Scan at the moment." He looked at my arm. "But I do want to X-ray that arm in case there's a fracture."

Yeah, that makes sense. Worry more about my arm than my head. There was nothing wrong with me, I knew that. I certainly didn't want either test, but of the two, I would think he'd err on the side of my brain. But no.

"Listen, doc, I've broken my arm before, and this doesn't feel like that. It feels bruised."

He jutted his lips out and pursed them. "Probably, but I wanna look at it anyway."

I tried a few more times to get him to change his mind, but I got the impression I was earning myself a CAT Scan as well if I didn't shut up.

I shut up.

I was wheeled up to the Radiology Department even though my legs were perfectly capable of taking me there on my own. To be honest, I was in a lot better shape than the person pushing me. The nurse behind me had to weigh at least three hundred pounds and had an asthmatic, here-comes-a-piece-of-my-lung cough that could only be cured by her next cigarette. Her ancestors probably had a leg up in surviving long stretches without food. But here in the calorically overabundant present, her genetic superiority was killing her.

Of course, I didn't get *directly* to the X-ray room because my nurse had to stop for fuel along the way—two pit stops, actually, a light-on-the-dressing green salad at the cafeteria and then, only ten yards from Radiology, three candy bars out of a vending machine.

I figured this would somehow all end up on my hospital bill.

The nurse wheeled me into the X-ray room.

The space was much bigger than it needed to be. It was probably built when X-ray machines were three times the size they are now. I found it more comfortable this way than years ago when it was cramped and stuffed with ominous equipment.

The technician asked me if I needed help getting out of the chair—*again*, as if it were my legs that were the problem. I said, no, and I crawled onto the table and under the crosshairs of the X-ray machine.

I always find it discomforting when someone is aiming a nuclear weapon at my body. I don't care how much lead they give me to shield my testicles, I'm still a little annoyed by the fact that no one has come up with a better way to see inside my body than to shoot radioactive material in my direction and send it careening through me.

"You guys put these things in the freezer?" I asked the skinny radiologic technologist as my bare skin touched the table. (Yep, that's what they prefer to be called, radiologic technologist. Not to be rude or anything, but he's an X-ray technician. It's like calling the guy behind the counter at the gas station a fuelologist.)

He was standing next to the nurse, and they were talking to each other like they had a secret between them. It seemed like they liked each other. When they were together like that, they looked like a giant "10."

"No, that's just the way it is," he said after a moment. "The metal dissipates the heat of your body. It's a function of the fact that our bodies are at ninety-eight point six degrees and the temperature of the room is somewhere around seventy-four." He paused. "Even if I were to pump the heat up to eighty-five or ninety, which wouldn't be comfortable, the metal would still seem cold to your skin."

I stopped listening halfway through. I thoroughly understood the thermal dynamics of the situation. I was just annoyed my ass was freezing in addition to the humiliation of having it hanging out of this stupid gown.

With all the advances I've seen over the years, I've gotta believe someone out there is capable of making a gown that doesn't expose your ass so that everyone in the hospital snickers at you as you walk down the hall.

So far, no one's come forward.

That's another tricky thing about being fifteen hundred years old: Embarrassment. Unlike any other emotion, embarrassment simply doesn't fade with time. I am still as mortified by the stupid and cringe-worthy things I did in Rome in the 1400s as the idiotic things I did last week.

I sat there as the X-ray tech lined up my arm.

Tweaked the machine. Moved my arm. Tweaked. Moved. Tweaked. Moved. Okay, just right.

He and the nurse walked behind the protective lead wall.

I knew what was coming. The windup of the machine. Heard the little zap. Could almost feel the radiation percolating through me in that instant. Then the wind-down. And the final clunk. Whatever hazardous thing that is.

The tech stuck his head out from behind the barrier.

"Turn your arm to the right."

I did what he said. He shot me with more radiation.

A few minutes and it was over.

And then I heard him make a sound. The one they always make.

Something between a question and punch in the gut.

People like me are able, in essence, to replace and regenerate damaged material in our bodies. Everyone does this to an extent, but our bodies continue to produce a steady trickle of stem cells, basically blanks, which give us the building blocks to counteract the wear and tear of everyday life. This is a side effect of our "defective" genes. But there's a downside. Blank cells can become anything. And some of those anythings are malignant. Which can mean painful and heart-wrenching ends for the young of my kind. If we make it through our toddler centuries, it means we not only have a powerful immune system, but we're less susceptible to cancer.

But like the rest of you, the rebuild isn't perfect.

If you look closely, you can see traces of a few of the scars I've received over the years. Accidents. Battles. Lacrosse games.

My forty-seven broken arms (twenty-seven of them, as I mentioned, from football alone) have all healed well, but the aftermath of some are still faintly visible. Maybe a dozen.

When the tech came out from the protective booth, he had a look of grave concern on his face.

"Son, is there anything that you'd like to tell me?"

He was maybe twenty-six. The paramedic—in his forties—I'll let *him* call me "son," but this guy...

I took a breath. *Let it go,* I told myself.

"I play sports all year round," I said, nonchalantly. "I've also done a lot of rock climbing. Had a number of falls."

He looked at me suspiciously. I knew I had blown it. I had a perfect answer ready for him, delivered a little too quickly. Like I was waiting for the question.

"I think I have to call someone about this. It's very unusual."

"Listen, I know what you're thinking. I would tell you if something was going on. If anyone was hurting me."

"I'm sorry, but I need to inform the doctor. And we'll have to report this to the Department of Social Services. More than ten breaks on a single arm. What else would I find if I X-rayed the rest of your body?"

I didn't answer. He wouldn't believe me if I told him.

I understand that in order to protect kids who really are being abused, it's important to have people looking out for these things. But most times, a broken arm—even forty-seven of them—is just a broken arm.

"Social Services will need to speak to your parents."

Well, that's a bit of a problem.

My mother's been dead for one thousand four hundred and thirty-five years.

And my father...well, my father was somewhere halfway around the world fighting evil. And I don't mean just any evil. I mean the kind of evil that takes thousands of years to develop.

Like I said, there are good people in the world and bad people in the world.

But when you've been alive for three, four, even six thousand years, have had all that time to amass great knowledge and even greater wealth...let's just say: When one of us turns bad, it's extremely dangerous.

So, wherever my father was, whatever he was doing, was way more important than having to deal with Social Services red tape.

Of course, I couldn't say that to the X-ray tech. I don't often talk to people about my father. When I do, the conversations generate questions not easily answered. *What* does your father do again? What's his phone number? Where exactly *is* your father? Who takes care of you? Are you living alone? Should I be calling Child Protective Services?

It never ends very well.

The less said, the better.

I had to think quickly in order to get the X-ray technician off my back.

I came up with the only thing I could think of.

"If I showed you how I got most of these injuries, would you drop it?"

"How are you going to do that?" he said, as he reached to pick up the phone.

Without answering him, I slowly slid off the table and got to my feet, took in a deep breath through my nose. Focused. Then...

I ran straight for the wall.

The X-ray tech dropped the phone and instinctively tried to stop me, but I was already out of his reach. The nurse tottered into action too late as well.

Just as I was about to smash into the four-foot-thick concrete barrier meant to keep in stray X-ray particles, I jumped and walked two steps up the wall, did a flip-twist-360 and came down facing the opposite direction in a full sprint away from the wall and back across the room.

I propelled myself off the edge of the X-ray table, launching toward the other wall, kicked off the wall, then the elbow of the robotic arm of the X-ray machine, then the wall again, then side-flipped onto the top of the machine.

I was twenty-five feet in the air in less than ten seconds, looking down at the X-ray tech and the nurse, who were both staring up at me completely dumbfounded.

The nurse's leg was wet. I thought maybe she spilled her drink, the one she had gotten on the way up here, but it was still in her hand. She had pissed herself.

"Spider-Man," she whispered.

"More like Jackie Chan," the tech said.

I took two steps on the X-ray arm like a gymnast on a balance beam, jumped down to the elbow, did a front straight-leg walkover, landing gently with my right foot, then left foot on the X-ray table and immediately side-flipped to the floor.

My bruised arm never touched anything.

I was now standing in front of the X-ray tech and the nurse.

"You don't get that good without failing a bunch of times," I said. "Can I go now?"

The tech nodded.

"I'll walk myself downstairs."

The nurse nodded.

It wasn't until I was strolling away from them toward the door and past the wheelchair that I realized I had done all that flipping and twisting wearing nothing but a backless hospital gown with my ass and probably my balls hanging out for all to see.

As I passed the chairs in the hallway, I grabbed my clothes and confidently headed toward the stairwell, my hospital gown continuing to flap open and closed in the turbulence created by my movement.

FIVE

I'm Not Paranoid.
I'm just Well Informed.

I prefer the stairs over elevators.

It's not like elevators have ever done anything wrong to me. I've never gotten stuck in one. Never had one fall while I was in it. Well, except that one time in the Tower of Galata—not the new one, but the old one—when, so I'm told, the peasants working the pulleys decided to stop holding the ropes after their repeated requests for more food and water rations were denied.

I was young, only about a hundred, so I don't remember the details. No one was seriously hurt, if you don't count the peasants after they were caught, but whenever I get that sensation in my stomach like being on a roller coaster, my heart starts racing.

I just feel more comfortable walking on something solid, rather than being raised and lowered in a box that dangles hundreds of feet above a concrete slab.

People think elevators are a modern invention. They aren't. Variations have been around for over two thousand years. The elevator may be the safest mode of travel in the world *now*, but until Elisha Otis created his fail-safe braking system in 1852, I never used them after that incident in the tower.

Instead, I'd climb stairs. Scale scaffolding. Leap from rooftop to rooftop.

It just seemed safer to me. Besides, taking the stairs is great exercise for your legs, your heart, your lungs, and your mind.

I think about taking care of myself more when I'm at a hospital. You have to understand, until recently, hospitals were places you actively tried to avoid. The doctor came to you. The home was the medical center of the past. Hospitals were gateways to death. They were incubators of infection and disease visited only by the destitute and the desperate. Even doctors wouldn't go near them in the early days. The fact that patients had to pay a deposit on admission to cover their burial didn't engender much confidence.

Even with all the advances, you look around a hospital today and realize, the longer you can stay away from a place like this, the better.

It's not like I haven't faced death in my fifteen hundred years on this planet. I've come close to it more than a few times. And in both brutal and quiet ways, I've seen a great deal of it. From the simple passing of time to the savagery of war.

When I was assumed to be a boy of only eight or nine—in those dark years before the creative explosion of the Renaissance—I was forced along with many others of my age to be a soldier. Mere children ordered into the army to protect England from its foes.

It was vicious. It was unforgiving.

Because I had centuries of training and experience, I fared better than most.

When you read about war or see it on a movie screen or immerse yourself in a video game, it might seem exciting, dramatic, heart-pumping.

But war...

Real live war is terrifying. It's panic-inducing fear, mixed with unbelievable stretches of boredom, hunger, and deprivation, followed by terror, shock and pain, and many times death.

It's the waiting that's the most stressful part, I think. If war were *always* intense, you would, at least, not worry about what's going to happen because...well, it *is* happening. You can prepare for battle. You can't as easily prepare for boredom. Waiting for something to happen while having to be constantly on guard, always looking out for a danger that only comes when you finally stop expecting it. It's taxing on the mind and the body.

War isn't like a video game where you choose when and where to play. War plays *you* whenever the hell it feels like it.

War for me has always been about the smell more than anything else. You could always turn away or close your eyes. But you couldn't stop breathing.

The choke of smoke. The sulfuric bitterness of gunpowder. The fetid reek of garbage. The stench of human waste. Of blood. Of decay.

Within the sterile walls of modern healthcare facilities, places like Fairview Medical Center, death smelled pleasant in comparison. But still, I tried to avoid them.

I stepped out of the quiet stairwell and into the busy lobby.

I don't consider myself completely paranoid or anything, but I instinctively scan a room when I enter it.

I mark the exits, calculate the fastest way to each. I instantly target obstacles. Humans or objects that might slow my escape. Judge the best course to neutralize each. And while all this is taking place in my brain, I try to get a feel for the attitude of the room. The vibe the people are giving off.

Friendly.

Agitated.

Festive.

A powder keg about to explode.

Finally, I look for anyone out of place, people trying not to be noticed, anyone dangerous looking or strange.

Now, there are some of you who might mistakenly call this obsessive-compulsive behavior a disorder. I call it proper planning.

Sprinkled around the room were a lot of odd people—it *was* a hospital waiting area after all—but I didn't sense any obvious threat.

In the center of all the strangeness was Daniel, sitting in a blocky sofa that appeared to be made out of giant Legos covered with industrial strength fabric. This was furniture specifically designed to make waiting excruciatingly painful. The message was clear: we don't want you here. Even less than you want to be here.

Daniel's face was a mask of anxiety and unease as he glanced around at the injured and/or disease-laden people surrounding him.

Every time someone coughed, Daniel stopped breathing, the color of his face moving far past red, toward purple, until he couldn't go another second without oxygen.

When he wasn't fighting off some feared pandemic, he was staring at the television hung uncomfortably high on the wall, delivering news, entertainment, and neck strain.

Suddenly, the doors from the outside blew open, startling the waiting room occupants. Paramedics wheeled a man hurriedly through the entrance. He was maybe sixty or so, and they were working on him as if every organ in his body was failing. It was hard to watch.

As the paramedics rushed the man past me, with doctors and nurses joining in, pumping his heart, giving him oxygen, sticking tubes everywhere, the man, to the surprise of everyone, lifted his head off the gurney.

"You. Are. Doomed," he said, staring straight into my eyes. After the words had left his mouth, he seemed relieved to have said them. He let his head fall back. He was going to accept his fate.

And then he was gone, disappearing into the treatment area.

The doors whooshed closed, and an eerie silence descended over the room.

Once again, my guard was down. I let myself get distracted by the mechanics of the doors to avoid having to think about what just happened, and I didn't notice Braeden approaching from my four o'clock until it was too late.

I reflexively made a quick defensive move, twisting my body, tensing my forearm, and hardening my hand into a formidable weapon.

Braeden was not at all as big as Craig Coulter, but he carried himself like someone who walked down dark alleys without fear. My first Wushu Master said over and over and over again that victory is never about size. He was four foot ten. I once saw him take down a three hundred pound sumo wrestler with a single, elegant, one-handed move. Another time, I watched him fight off sixteen heavily armored swordsmen with nothing but his fists and a handful of sand.

When it comes to fighting, size doesn't matter as much as leverage and ingenuity.

Despite Braeden's slender build, I sensed...something. Power. Strength. Danger.

I was already setting my feet, getting ready. It's surprising how often my body tenses up in anticipation of an attack. I've always thought of myself as a calm, easygoing individual, but I don't notice anyone else ratcheting up their personal defenses as often as I do.

Great Barrington was a place where I usually felt at ease. But I'd been hit too many times in the last few days, and I hadn't heard from my dad in months.

I get on edge when I'm alone.

Braeden noticed my stance. "I'm a friend," he said.

I studied him, my body still prepared for battle.

He was scanning the room in the same way I had earlier.

I realized he wasn't concerned with me, so much as he was worried about something or someone else.

"Every time I look up, you seem to be there, staring at me. It's a little creepy."

"I don't mean to be."

"Well, you are. And my *friends* just say, 'Hey' or 'What's up?' They don't formally announce, '*Sum amicus.*'" I watched his face for the slightest hint of recognition or confusion.

There was neither.

He took a step back, giving me space.

"Hey, what's up? You're not dead!" Daniel was running over. He had apparently just seen me.

Without thinking, Braeden knocked Daniel to the floor with a shot to the solar plexus. Daniel lay on the ground, gasping for air like a goldfish that had made an ill-advised escape from his bowl.

I glared at Braeden as I rushed over to Daniel.

"Sorry," Braeden said to me. "Reflex."

"Tell *him*."

His hand outstretched in friendship, Braeden gazed down at Daniel. "I am sorry."

Daniel put up one finger, indicating he needed a moment. "I'll just—" is all he managed in a pained whisper.

While Daniel caught his breath, Braeden pulled me into the far corner of the lobby.

It was quieter. Less crowded. More defensible. With an easy escape. Exactly the spot I would have picked.

"Φιλαλέξανδρος," he said, which came out *Philalexandros*. Friend of Alexander. "Vidi patrem tuum."

It wasn't that I was surprised to hear Braeden speaking Ancient Greek and then quickly switching to Latin. I had already assumed he was like me, just a few hundred years older.

It was what he said.

"You spoke to my father?"

Braeden nodded. "He asked me to look out for you."

My face flushed red.

"What are you, my babysitter?"

"Call it what you like. He sent me."

"When?"

"Three weeks ago."

Now, my twinge of embarrassment turned to jealousy. Like I said, I hadn't heard from my father in months. Not that long ago, not hearing from him wouldn't seem strange. There were times I wouldn't see my dad for decades or hear from him for years, but now, with instant worldwide communication, it was more than odd. It meant something was wrong.

"Where did you see him?"

"I can't say."

I pushed him aside. "Then leave me alone. I don't know you." I started to walk away.

"Remane filiolum."

I stopped. *Stay here, my little son.* Now, I was really angry. I wanted to lash out, but I quickly got control of myself. "Only he gets to call me that."

"It's what he told me to say. So you would know it was him. His message was very clear. *Festina lente.*"

"Make haste slowly."

He nodded. "Don't leave Great Barrington. Don't pack up and move. No matter what. He asked me to look after you. Contact you only if something changed."

"So, you *are* my babysitter."

Braeden said nothing.

"What changed?"

"I've not heard from him in a couple of weeks."

Now I was more pissed. "*Where* did you see him?" I asked again.

"I can't tell you because I don't know myself. I was picked up. Taken to a plane. I wasn't able to open the window shades. When we landed, wherever it was, he came on board. We talked. He left. The plane took off and brought me to Boston. I had no idea where I was until I walked off the plane and into the terminal."

"How long did it take?"

"Seven hours. Maybe eight. My watch, phone, they were all taken."

My head hurt, and I was reminded why I was standing in a hospital. "What were you doing running on the field?"

"The other player...I thought he was coming for you, I thought he was trying to hurt you."

"That's *exactly* what he was trying to do. It's lacrosse. He was trying to kill me."

I said these words as a figure of speech, but from the look on Braeden's face, I could tell he was serious.

"You really thought he was trying to kill me?"

"Things are very precarious."

"What things, Braeden? Could you be a *little* more specific?"

He was silent.

After a moment, I turned and started for the exit.

He said, "You are in a great deal of danger—"

I glanced around. No threats. Just the sick and the injured. "Yeah, terrifying. C'mon, Daniel." I headed toward the glass doors that led out of the emergency room and into freedom.

Daniel was being tended to by a pretty nurse, but he got to his feet and followed me.

"Where are you going?" Braeden asked, not moving.

"It's Homecoming. I'm going to watch a football game and then go to the dance with a pretty girl."

Braeden looked confused. Being a few hundred years older than me, I'd bet a million dollars that except for his brief time at Monument, he'd never gone to high school. Let alone a Homecoming Dance.

I waved my hand in front of the sliding glass doors, whispered, "Open Sesame," and instantly, they opened. A hundred years ago, that would have been called magic.

Now, it's just a motion detector.

~ SIX ~
Revenge Is A Dish Best
Served With A Little Chicken

Before we could see the field, I could hear the fans cheering loudly.

Walking through the narrow path carved into the hill that hid the stadium, Daniel and I arrived at the gate. The stands were full now, not mostly empty like they were for my game. I wasn't jealous. Not really. It's just more fun playing in front of a packed stadium. At my last school, in upstate New York at the very edge of Canada, lacrosse was the major fall sport, and the games were almost always sold out. I loved hearing the rumbling that builds as you race down the sideline, the roar that reaches a sustained fever pitch until you miss the shot and it dies, or you score, and it erupts.

Okay, maybe it annoyed me a little that Craig Coulter got to play in front of at least a thousand people every Saturday. A thousand fans make a lot more noise than a few dozen.

Even though the game was well into the fourth quarter, we had to pay to get in.

As we approached the field, I could see Craig talking to Phoebe at the foot of the stands. You could tell he was upset. His face was red and the veins in his neck were bulging more than they normally did.

I started to say something to Daniel, but he beat me to it.

"He's tweaked because she immediately ran out onto the field and tried talking to you when you were unconscious. Jealous much?"

I let out an exasperated sigh. "What's his problem?"

Daniel looked at me. "Really?"

I didn't answer.

"You stare at the back of her head every day in class for the entire period. I have no idea how you pass, never mind get straight A's."

That was one of my weaknesses. Not Phoebe, but grades. I had trouble acting stupid. For someone like me, someone trying to stay under the radar, it was a lot smarter to play dumb. I had trouble doing that.

"I get it," he said. "She's cute. She's smart. She's pretty. She's hot. She's got sass. She's sooooo hot. And I think you—" He wanted to finish the thought, but he let what he had already said hang in the air.

I pretended to be interested in the game.

Our defense had stopped Who'sMoronic on their own forty-yard line, forcing them to punt. Craig would have to go out onto the field in a moment. One of the coaches was calling to him—yelling at him, actually—to grab his helmet and get his ass over to the sideline.

Craig had more to say, but he couldn't ignore his coaches any longer. Phoebe looked well past wanting to discuss the subject, whatever it was. The punt return team was running off the field and the offense—his offense—was huddling up waiting for their leader.

His eyes flashed with rage.

Showing a bit of control, he didn't unleash his anger on Phoebe. Instead, as he stomped toward the field, pulling on his helmet, he roughly pushed one of his teammates, who stumbled into a cheer-leader, knocking her to the ground.

"He really is an absolute, total tool," Daniel said as we reached the crowded stands.

I nodded.

It was when I saw the cheerleader laying on the grass, struggling to her feet that I decided I would expose Craig Coulter for who he really was. I laughed to myself as it hit me that I had already seeded the way to do it. All I needed was a little help from the public address system.

But as soon as I climbed into the stands, heading toward the press box, people started grabbing me, shaking me, screaming at me in long, guttural battle cries. I had a flashback to the Battle of Agincourt in 1415 when I was "enlisted"—more like kidnapped—into service as a longbowman for Henry V. There was a lot of that kind of shouting back then.

When one guy in the crowd slapped me on the shoulder, I yelped, wincing in pain. Another fan yelled, "He hurt his arm, idiot!" before turning to me and saying just as loudly, "That was amazing!"

I glanced stupidly at Daniel who hit his forehead with the palm of his hand.

"Dude, I'm an idiot." He put up his hand to high five me. "That was the most unbelievable shot I've ever seen."

"What are you talking about?" I said, leaving his hand hanging without returning the high five.

Daniel stared at me, then at the surrounding fans cheering me, then back at me.

"I'm talking about your shot that tied the game. The crowd went absolutely berserk." His face lit up like he had swallowed the sun.

My mind was clear. Any residual effects of being knocked unconscious had been wiped away.

"My shot?"

"Yes. The one you took after getting bulldozed. Somehow, I don't know how, it went in the far upper corner before time ran out."

I tried to process this. I had begrudgingly accepted the fact that we had blown the lead *and* the match, which wasn't easy. I hate to lose. I don't much like winning in a rout either, but losing ignites a fire in my belly that isn't easily put out. Maybe it's part of the makeup of who I am, of what makes me more of a throwback to an earlier time. A time when survival was more uncertain. I am in many ways not as advanced as people born today. When I was a child, winning meant life. Defeat more often than not spelled death.

You didn't get ribbons just for participating. Usually, you just got killed.

I replayed the last few seconds of the lacrosse game in my mind. Anything is possible, of course, but it seemed improbable that I could've gotten enough speed on the ball after being hit so hard.

"I— I—"

Daniel stepped into the uncomfortable silence. "Who'sMoronic was so completely demoralized, we beat them in overtime almost immediately. Richie Z. banked in a shot off the goalie less than three minutes in."

"We won?" I said without much emotion. The victory felt empty. I guess because I couldn't remember it, but now, the crowd's reaction to me made sense. "I'm sorry I missed it."

Daniel smiled. "Don't worry. About a million people got it on video. I'm sure it's already on the web."

I cringed.

So much for laying low. That's just the kind of video that goes viral. A hundred thousand hits later and my father would be in my face saying, "This is exactly the kind of thing I told you to avoid."

I just wanted to live, play, make mistakes.

"You are going to get sooooo much attention from this," Daniel said. "I bet you get scouted."

"You understand people fought and died for the right to the freedom and privacy that people now give up for nothing more than free access to a website?"

"What are you talking about?"

"Never mind."

It was a lost cause trying to explain to Daniel that someday not that far in the future, he would be going out into the world and getting a job, meeting a woman, getting married and maybe running for public office, and out there preserved forever will be the time he made milk come out his nose. It's up on the web right now. You can see it for yourself.

For obvious reasons, I've tried to limit my public exposure as much as possible. But long ago I accepted that if I was going to do anything—and be remotely good at any of it—there was going to be some record, an oral history by a Mohawk chief, a painting in oil, a photographic plate, a gramophone recording, a YouTube video, something.

Besides that chess championship photo of me in every major paper in the Western world in 1948, there are probably dozens of films of me playing sports in the '50s, '60s, and '70s, hundreds of videos in the 80s and beyond. But it wasn't until the last few years that everything exploded.

High definition cameras in phones can upload video to the Internet within seconds. In another year and a half, I'd move and start high school all over again—recently I've skipped being a freshman and gone straight into tenth grade. I don't need the hassle—somewhere far away, Montana, Canada, Alaska. Even taking these precautions, it wouldn't be long before the images of me would catch up to the reality of me.

Someone, somewhere was going to notice the striking resemblance between me and that kid who once made a one-handed touchdown catch in Cedar Rapids to win the Iowa state championship in 1976.

∞

The crowd was restless. It was late in the fourth quarter, and we were up by ten points. The Housatonic fans were getting ready to leave. The students on our side were thinking about the Homecoming Dance later tonight, what they would wear, who they would ask to dance.

It didn't help matters that Craig had run two conservative running plays up the middle. It was third down and nine on our own 25-yard line. There was less than three minutes on the clock.

Who'sMoronic's defense was pretty good, second in the conference. They had a fair chance of stopping us and getting the ball back with decent field position. At least, make a game of it. Now, a professional quarterback could do a lot with two-plus minutes, but Who'sMoronic's quarterback was no Joe Montana or Tom Brady.

The game was over, and everyone knew it.

Still, Housatonic called time out. It ain't over till it's over. You had to give them credit.

I was making my final assault on the press box but was being slowed down by people high-fiving me as I scaled the steps of the bleachers.

Maybe it was the commotion around me that drew his attention, but the announcer spotted me, frantically waving his arms and motioning for me to come over, even though that's exactly where I was headed.

He was losing the crowd. I was running out of time.

Our needs converged.

The announcer was a Monument student, part of the A/V contingent at our school. The press box was enclosed on three sides with an angled roof. The side facing the field was open with a short half-wall at the back of the stands.

"And here is Alexander Grant," he said in his deepest sports announcer voice, "whose last-second, jaw-dropping shot with no time on the clock snatched victory from the jaws of defeat, sending today's varsity lacrosse game into overtime, where Captain Richie Zedman put it away with a goal at two minutes and fifty seconds of OT."

The kid motioned to one of the other students in the booth who pushed a button on his computer. Suddenly, an audio replay of the kid announcing the lacrosse game blared out of the P.A. speakers.

"Housatonic is making another run for it, holding on to the ball, hoping to protect their lead until time expires. They're passing it around the edges of the box. Wait! Lasker picks off a pass, scooping it out of the air. Monument gets the ball back! The Wolves are hungry. Thirty seconds to go. They're down by one. Grant is wide open up ahead, but Lasker tosses to Zedman, who is making straight for the goal. Housatonic scrambles to defend. Two defensemen close on Zedman. Fifteen seconds to go. He's going to get sandwiched.

No way he can—Oh! He passes back to Grant who's all alone but still a long shot away. Ten seconds left. One defender is making a desperate sprint as Grant charges up the far sideline. It's a race to the finish. Can Grant get close enough to the goal in time?" You could hear the crowd in the background counting down, six, five, four. Even I was getting anxious and excited as I listened. "Grant cocks back his stick, he's going to shoot, he's…oh no! A crushing hit. A stick to the chin. Grant is knocked off his feet. But—he's gotten off a shot. It's in. It's in! It's in! It's in! I don't know how he did it, but it's in!"

The crowd roared. Both the one on the recording and the one listening.

As the replay stopped, I could see Craig looking up at me from the field. His eyes burning into me.

I was stealing his moment.

Just you wait, I thought.

The announcer kid suddenly turned Pulitzer Prize-winning reporter. "You were knocked unconscious and had to be taken to the hospital. But you seem like you're okay."

Before I could answer that I was fine, the kid snatched the microphone away from my mouth.

"Anything to say to our boys in blue?"

Just as quickly, he shoved the mic back in my face.

"Uh," I stumbled for a second, my brain still wanting to respond to his previous remark. But then I remembered why I was standing there. Operation Sack The Quarterback. "It's Homecoming, let's make it a clean sweep with two wins today." Another cheer from our side, boos from Who'sMoronic. "And to everyone out there, let's all just be thankful for pickles."

Some of the people in the stands laughed, some of them clapped, some of them had quizzical looks on their faces. But I had said the magic word. The one I had offhandedly embedded in Craig's mind when my face was in the dirt.

The timeout was over.

Craig Coulter was about to go up under center when he began—without warning—to cluck like a chicken.

Buck Buck-ah.

He was juking his head around, like a rooster while strutting back and forth behind the line of scrimmage. His teammates were trying to figure out what formation they were supposed to be in.

Then suddenly, Craig began to flap his arms.

Wildly.

A pass? Is that what he's calling?

Now, his coaches and his teammates were yelling to him.

Craig ignored them and, instead, pecked at his running back, who tried to get away.

Buck Buck-ah.

Craig Coulter had become a full-on Chicken Man. Had he been wearing feathers and a rooster suit, I don't see how it could have gone any better, been more satisfying. The Housatonic fans started laughing and cheering him on with chicken calls of their own.

And to be honest, a lot of our fans did the same.

It was one of the most embarrassing displays I've ever witnessed. And I've witnessed some pretty embarrassing moments.

Part of me wasn't all that proud of what I had done. It wasn't the most enlightened act. But Craig was a tool. If I'd been the only one Craig had bullied, I would've let it go. But it was the way he treated Daniel. The way he pushed his teammate in frustration and by doing so knocked over that cheerleader. How he took Phoebe for granted, and how he looked down on everyone else with his smug, superior attitude and open disdain.

He had it coming.

Scattered people in the stands started doing the "Chicken Dance." Craig would be seeing more of that later tonight as he was crowned Homecoming King, and again in the hallways and classrooms of school on Monday and beyond. People were taking video, which would go viral on the web and never disappear.

Ever.

Payback is unforgiving.

The coaches had to lead Craig off the field. He kept getting away from them in that infuriating way that chickens do. Slow and meandering until you reach out and grab for them, and they speed up just long enough for you to miss. Once out of range, they go back to their unhurried zigzagging.

Craig was still clucking. *Buck Buck-ah.* This forced the team to call a timeout to avoid getting penalized for delay of game. At this point, pretty much everybody was laughing, and those that weren't, were frankly, mortified.

Here was our star football player roostering up in front of a couple of thousand people.

The ref's whistle seemed to scare Craig, and he finally scurried off the field.

They sent in the junior varsity quarterback to fill-in. You could tell, he was nervous. Partly from coming into a big game cold and partly because watching your starting QB suddenly go cuckoo was unnerving. He made a good play to get the first down, which pretty much ended the game. Our fans counted down the last ten seconds and after time expired, everybody rushed onto the field, including the Homecoming Queen in her long dress, her high heels sinking into the grass until a couple of linemen lifted her by her underarms. She looked like she was floating across the field.

Craig was clucking around on the sidelines. I figured I should put Craig out of his misery, snap him out of it, and let him regain whatever dignity he had left.

The announcer was in the middle of telling everyone to drive home safely when suddenly, his voice cut off and I heard a deep creaking, like the sound you hear on the docks at night as the ropes moan and the ships grind against the piers.

Only...

It was more metallic than that.

The sun disappeared, the world becoming darker as if an unexpected solar eclipse had occurred.

"Alexander! Look out!"

I glanced up, realizing seconds before it was too late that the sun's disappearance was caused by a bank of stadium lights that had somehow become detached from its tower.

A bus-sized rectangle plummeted directly toward me.

I had just enough time to dive out of the way before three tons of steel and glass crashed edge first into the bleachers, barely six feet from me.

I covered my face, protecting my eyes and exposed skin from the glass shrapnel that hit me a second later.

I stood there, along with the rest of the crowd, frozen in awe, staring at the structure balanced on its side.

Had that really just happened?

I didn't have time to fully ponder the question because the monolith moaned, the bleachers becoming unstable underneath my feet. The bank of lights was pitching ever-so-slowly in the direction of the press box.

"Get out!" I yelled. No movement. "Now!"

People flew out of the press box in every direction as if it had exploded.

With a deep, drawn-out wail, the light structure tipped over and smashed into the press box, flattening it.

Luckily, everyone had escaped the path of destruction.

All except for the student announcer who sat, dumbstruck, still gripping the mic, his headphones at an odd angle.

I was able to reach in and pull him over the lip of the half wall seconds before debris from the roof fell right where he had been.

We didn't have time to celebrate.

The impact of the lights and the weight of the twisted steel caused the bleachers to groan under the massive burden. There was a stampede as hundreds of people rushed to get off the stands, pouring onto the field like a wave crashing the beach.

The kid announcer was clinging to the floor of the bleachers.

"We've gotta get off this thing!" I said.

He shook his head. He wasn't moving from that spot.

"It's going to collapse!"

Then I realized, he couldn't move. He was scared. In shock.

I tried to get him to his feet. But when someone doesn't want to be picked up, it's like trying to lift a hundred pounds of Jello.

The stands were swaying. I had no other choice.

I grabbed the kid's feet and pulled, dragging him down the center stairs toward the field, his head smacking hard on each landing until finally, he'd had enough and used his hands to help. We reverse wheel barreled toward the bottom, then jumped to the grass an instant before the entire main section of the stands imploded.

He yelped, holding the back of his head. "That hurt!"

There was a final, earth-shaking crash as the stadium was reduced to dust.

"Not as much as that would have," I said, looking at the devastation.

Gazing at the rubble, he nodded. "You saved my life." He turned to others in the crowd. "He saved my life!"

From out of the sea of stunned onlookers, Braeden appeared, his jaw set and his look determined. He gripped me tightly by the arm. "This way, now!"

Braeden calmly, but briskly pulled me through the panicked, confused crowd in the direction of the woods as the kid yelled again, "He saved my life!"

This time, I didn't fight Braeden.

SEVEN

A Journey Of A Thousand Miles Begins With A Single Step-Brother

At the far end of the field, opposite the entry gates, was the start of a path that led to a ridge. Part of the hill had been cleared of trees and carved out to make way for a baseball diamond, leaving a crescent-shaped scar that sloped sharply down toward the home run fence at the edge of the outfield.

The path was used by the cross-country team as part of their 5K course. It was steep and narrow and left no room for error. One misstep and you'd tumble down the embankment. But if you alternated between the far right and the far left of the path, you could find a foothold in notches in the dirt that had been etched by a decade of pounding feet.

"What's going on?"

"No time," Braeden said, charging up the near-vertical trail.

I like to think of myself as in shape, but I was breathing heavily as I got to the top of the ridge. If Braeden was fatigued, he didn't show it. About halfway around the crescent, the path took a hard left into the woods and descended along a rocky path that appeared to be a dry creek bed. As we dipped deeper into the woods…

Quiet.

The sounds of the cars and buses and voices, the commotion, the shifting debris of the stands, all of it was silenced.

After another moment, I could hear the rush of water somewhere nearby. A few steps further and the meandering Housatonic River appeared through breaks in the trees. But the wide, slow waterway was not the source of the sound.

We came to an outcropping of rocks, and Braeden quickly ducked behind the formation which concealed a low waterfall from an underground spring that poured into a stream that led to the river. Only then did he settle down. I wouldn't call him relaxed. Just slightly less ready at the slightest provocation to rip someone's head off.

"Start talking," I said, my voice having more edge than I intended.

Either Braeden didn't notice or he was ignoring me. Instead, he rapidly scanned the area. "We have a good vantage point of all directions. This will do for the moment." Satisfied, he turned his gaze back to me with those eyes that had been watching me for the past two days. "Do you think it was a coincidence that a light tower happened to fall out of the sky and land two meters from you?"

"I—I don't know." It hadn't hit me until that moment of exactly how close I'd come to being crushed.

"I do," he said. "That was deliberate."

I shuddered. And then, perhaps in reaction to my fear, I got angry. "Since you seem to have all the answers, why don't you start telling me what's going on."

"Your father is in danger."

"My father is always in danger!" I said in a loud whisper.

For as long as I can remember, my father had vowed to disrupt the plans of those of us who abused power. To keep them from doing too much harm. And keep our secret safe.

As a young boy, I would lie in bed and picture my father battling demons and monsters and giants, images from stories that had been taught to me as a child, mostly in secret because talk of them had been outlawed.

It was centuries before I understood that these superhumans, the Roman and Greek Gods and the fantastical creatures of mythology, were stories that had been told for thousands of years in an attempt to answer questions about life that did not have easy answers.

It seems silly *now* that anyone ever believed the god Apollo dragged the sun across the sky each day in a fiery chariot pulled by flying horses. But they did.

When I came to realize who my father was really fighting—our own kind—it was, for some reason, more terrifying than any monster could ever be.

"I know all about my father and what he does."

"I'm sure he's told you many things," Braeden said without much emotion. "But he hasn't told you everything."

I could feel my face flush red. I wanted to strike out at Braeden, but I didn't. Not because I was afraid of him, although I probably should've been, but because he had found my weakness. If I reacted, it would only make my vulnerability more apparent.

The cunning warrior waits for his foe to act rashly.

"Why don't you enlighten me. What do you know that I don't?"

Braeden gazed at me. His eyes not as hard. "I am your brother."

I'm not sure what my face looked like, but my body felt like someone had put dry ice down my pants.

I have known scores of siblings over the years, whether through birth or marriage. I have watched them grow up, become old, and wither away. None of them were like me.

My father has had many, many wives. But a few hundred years ago, he stopped getting married, stopped having any more children.

He once told me his truest loves had lasted far longer than their lives. It was simply impossible for him to add any more weight to the tremendous burden of loss he carried.

I already felt the heaviness of time and the pain of loss, and I hadn't experienced watching my wife or my children fade and perish before my eyes.

I may not know everything, but of one thing I was certain: my father had no other children like me. There had been one, many years before I was born, but he did not make it past six hundred years old. The boy died in an attack that left my father severely wounded and the boy's mother dead.

I was the only one.

"My father doesn't have any other Eternal children," I said to Braeden.

"Your father is not my *biological* father."

My mother was not an Eternal. She did not have the genetic defect that slows my body's clock to a crawl, the defect that would have allowed her to see me grow up.

Braeden could see my expression.

"My mother is like us," he said. "She and our father were married when I was very small, a little over a hundred and fifty years old."

I looked at him. He was definitely not as young as he was pretending to be. "How old are you?" I asked.

"Two thousand one hundred and eighty-six."

I tried to picture what the world was like six hundred years before my birth.

Just then, we heard voices from the top of the ridge.

"Alexander! Alexander!"

It was Daniel.

"Alexander!"

Phoebe as well.

"How well do you know them?" Braeden asked.

"Better than I know you."

They were getting closer.

"Alexander!"

"Alexander!"

Braeden let out a heavy sigh. "I'll take the boy. You grab the girl. We need them to shut up immediately." I could tell from his look this wasn't him being irritated by the interruption, there was danger in it. He nodded to me, his raised brow silently asking, *Do you understand?*

I nodded back.

It happened in the blink of an eye.

Braeden appeared out of nowhere, grabbed Daniel by the

shoulder and put a hand over his mouth, muffling a scream. You should have seen Daniel's expression. It was priceless. I wished I had taken a picture.

I couldn't see Phoebe's face, but I assumed she was just as surprised when I covered her mouth and dragged her behind the rocks.

They were both breathing heavily. They were scared, confused, embarrassed and extremely pissed off.

Daniel hurled a string of obscenities our way the second Braeden pulled his hand away.

Braeden clapped his hand over Daniel's mouth once again, this time pushing my friend's head into one of the rocks.

"Oww! That hurt!"

Braeden pointed his index finger right between Daniel's eyes. "I need you to keep quiet."

Braeden pressed his hand harder into Daniel's face as he looked over at Phoebe, studying her. Braeden had given Daniel only a cursory glance, having sized him up at the hospital. I didn't particularly like the way Braeden was eyeing Phoebe. He was judging whether Phoebe was a threat or not, but, still, something about it bothered me. There was more to his gaze.

He finally let go of Daniel. And I released Phoebe.

"You shouldn't have come here!" growled Braeden. A fire raged in him.

Phoebe glared at me. "We were looking for our *friend*," the last word dripping with contempt after what I had done.

"Well, you've found him," said Braeden. "And a whole lot of trouble as well."

Daniel perked up. "Trouble? Nobody wants trouble. I know I don't."

Phoebe's demeanor changed as her eyes flitted between Braeden and me. "That wasn't an accident, was it?"

"She's smarter than you are," Braeden said to me. He turned to Daniel and Phoebe. "Stay here. If you see anything, signal." He handed them each a stone. "Do *not* call out." Then he dragged me from the protection of the rocks.

"What exactly are we looking for?" asked Daniel.

"You'll know it the moment you see it," said Braeden, ominously.

I could tell Daniel had a lot more questions, but he wisely kept quiet. I don't think he really wanted to know the answers.

Braeden led me to a second outcropping, a little higher up. From our vantage point, we could watch the ridge and the river and still keep an eye on Phoebe and Daniel.

"What *are* we looking for?" I asked.

He didn't answer me for a moment. "I was hoping to lose them. But I fear your friends have given us away."

"Who is *'them'*?"

"An old threat returning," he said. I had the sense he wasn't trying to be cryptic. I don't think he knew much more than that. "You are coming of age. And with that, you are becoming a concern for those we fight against. Father believes you are a target."

I knew this day would come. My father and I often talked about preparing for it. It was why I spent decades as a young boy in China, and then more recently, in Korea and Japan, studying various martial arts. Why I attended military academies—Sandhurst in England, École Royale Militaire in Paris, Kriegs Akademie in Berlin, Whampoa in Guangdong. Why I learned stick fighting in Africa and trained in hand-to-hand combat in the Philippines.

So I would be ready to fight.

"The best course of action from a tactical perspective would be to leave. But I assume you don't want to abandon them," said Braeden, nodding in the direction of Phoebe and Daniel.

I watched as Daniel nervously chewed on his nails. It looked like he might eat down to his knuckles if we stayed here too long.

"No."

Braeden glanced up at the cliff behind us. "That complicates matters," he said. "Then we wait."

We stood, both of us, listening to the sounds of the forest, listening to the water and the wind, listening for any disturbances.

After a moment, I broke the silence. "What happened?"

"What do you mean?"

"What happened between your mother and my father?"

Braeden's head whipped around as a twig snapped in the distance. He breathed again only after it was clear it was an animal in the underbrush.

"They were together for nearly five hundred years," he said, glancing at the ground, a bittersweet expression on his face. "He left to marry your mother. To become *your* father."

I find it ironic that today's society makes a huge issue of the problems associated with coming from a broken home. Because I can tell you that the modern family has nothing on the intrigue, betrayal, and treachery of the ancient family. What people today consider a "traditional" family didn't even exist four hundred years ago.

Part of me wondered if Braeden's claims were true. Perhaps it would be more honest to say: I wanted it all to be a lie.

I had the sense, though, that he was telling the truth.

I pictured him as a young boy. The pain of losing the only father he had ever known. He and his mother would've felt intense resentment about being left behind. About my father's new wife. About his *new* son. No wonder he glared at me the way he did at school.

"I'm sorry," I said, thinking how much I missed my father.

Braeden nodded. "He has made it up to me over the years."

I didn't respond. I couldn't. I felt like I had been punched again. Not only had I been unaware of Braeden's existence, but my father—*our* father—had kept an important and ongoing part of his life a secret from me. A boy he treated like a son.

Why? Why would he do that?

All these years, I would've appreciated having a sibling that aged as I did, that didn't grow old before my eyes.

A brother. There was nothing I wouldn't have given for that. Nothing.

Maybe Braeden was right. Maybe I didn't know very much at all.

I felt sick.

I tried to catch my breath.

That's when I heard the snap of a twig, heard it over the sound of the water. Then I heard another crack. And another. Not animals this time.

We caught a glimpse of two hulking men, making their way from the direction of the fields.

"It's been decades since I've been in a battle. I'm not ready for this."

"Well...ready or not...here they come."

There were six men, actually. The two coming down the ridge. Two coming across the river. And two that were approaching out of the forest to our left.

Braeden's eyes tracked the three sets of attackers. "You should encourage your friends to leave. They won't survive."

I knew he was right.

Staying low, I quickly made my way down to Phoebe and Daniel. "You need to start moving up that hill," I said.

Daniel looked at me. "Are you crazy? That's not a hill!"

Made almost entirely of white quartz, the cliff behind us rose three hundred feet into the air and glimmered in the sunlight. The scree—the rocks at the base—looked like salt and pepper, angling away from the face at forty degrees. Difficult but not impossible to climb. However, the cliff itself was nearly vertical with some outcroppings and crags along the way.

"There's a trail at the peak that leads back down toward the school." I tried to recall the time when Deganawa and I came to *Mahaiwe* to play *tewaaraton* against the Mahicans. We had to escape into these hills after Deganawa kissed the daughter of the local Chief. "If you stay to the right, you'll find a crevasse and a series of footholds and ledges that lead to the top." I pointed toward the area, hoping it hadn't changed in the nearly four hundred years since Deganawa almost got me killed.

"And why would I want to do that?" Daniel asked.

I motioned in the direction of the men headed our way.

Daniel saw them and was about to scream out when Braeden appeared and pressed his hand over Daniel's mouth, squelching the sound and banging his head into the rock again.

"Mmmmmmmmouuuuwwww."

"Next time, I'm going to cover your mouth *and* your nose and hold it until you pass out. Now, those men want to take Alexander, and they will kill us without hesitation to get him," Braeden said. "Do you understand?" He only let go after Daniel nodded.

Phoebe had been quiet the entire time. "Take Alexander? What are you talking about?"

"We don't have time to explain." Braeden turned to me. "They're betting we can't make it up that cliff."

Daniel stared up at the wall of rock behind us. "And *they* would be correct."

"I agree. It's unlikely you two will make it. But the alternative is certain death."

Phoebe glared at Braeden. "Listen, I love the upbeat we're-all-gonna-die attitude. The whole sullen, brooding thing sort of works for you...you know, for me. But you don't know me. Don't tell me what I can't do. I bet I get to the top before you."

"Then perhaps you'll survive today."

"That's the cheery outlook I was looking for."

"Hey, I've seen enough movies to know, we go out in the open, and they'll pick us off one by one," said Daniel, his voice cracking. "We'll be like ducks in a shooting gallery. Pow. Pow. Pow. Pow."

"They won't use guns," said Braeden.

"Why not?"

"Because it would be dishonorable," I said.

"*Dishonorable?*" Daniel asked as if he had never heard the word before.

"They will only kill us with their hands," said Braeden.

"Oh, well, if it's only with their hands," Daniel said. "Much more honorable." He started mumbling to himself. "Now, I feel so much better."

"Unless you're prepared to fight to the death, kill or be killed, we need to leave immediately."

Daniel's eyes widened.

Phoebe was about to say something when four men dropped out of the trees, catching us off guard.

We had been focused on the six men heading toward us over land. We were thinking two-dimensionally. A tactical error.

We were surrounded.

"Run!" I screamed. This seemed to startle Phoebe, who had up to that moment been extremely calm. I thought she was going to make her escape. Instead, she aimed a high leg kick toward my head. Her foot went over my shoulder and collided with the face of one of the attackers. The kick hadn't done enough damage to put the man down, but it stunned him. Before he had a chance to lift his hand to his stinging cheek, I whirled around and jabbed him in the throat. He gasped, trying to get oxygen into his lungs, and after failing to get enough, fell to his knees.

Another attacker from the trees grabbed Phoebe. I pulled him off her and spun him away, then roundhouse kicked him across the face, knocking him into Braeden who turned the man on his head, pile-driving him into the ground.

In that instant, the blade of a sword, of a metal and design I had never seen before, a sword so polished I could see the leaves on the trees above in its reflection, came swinging through the air and sank deep into Braeden's side.

Immediately, he screamed in pain.

Everyone froze for a moment.

All I could focus on was the blood.

So much blood.

The sword was coated in it.

Braeden grabbed the back of the blade, along the dull edge, gripping it with his fingers against the bottom of his palm. He pulled the blade from his flesh, letting out another gut-wrenching scream.

In that distracted moment, I struck out against Braeden's attacker and dropkicked him in the chest, sending him hard into a tree.

Phoebe turned and sprinted toward the base of the cliff. One of the men chased after her. I instinctively stuck out my arm and clotheslined him.

He landed hard on his back.

A fist rushed at my face. I moved too late, but it wasn't meant for me. I felt a breeze as it passed. It was Braeden's clenched hand, aiming for a guy about to club me in the skull with a wooden fighting stick. His fist connected. The guy didn't move. He just stood there as surprised as I was that Braeden was up and walking around. Then the guy just dropped.

I turned toward Braeden in disbelief.

"Are you okay?"

"It doesn't matter."

I could see the bright white of his hipbone. That was the good news. It meant there was a chance the blade hadn't sliced through his internal organs.

There were too many attackers for me to take on alone. Even if Daniel and Phoebe had been trained to fight…

Braeden was my only hope.

Movement to my right. A swoosh as a blade aiming to sever Daniel's head rushed toward its target. The same man, the same strange blade that had gravely wounded Braeden.

I swept my leg in a wide arc in a desperate attempt to save Daniel, connecting with his ankles, knocking Daniel off balance. He crashed to the ground. The sword sliced through the air where Daniel had just been and lodged deep into the trunk of a tall maple. The man wielding the sword could not pry it free. Landing hard, Daniel had the wind knocked out of him and was sucking in deep breaths. Somehow he gathered enough strength to roll away from a kick to the ribs.

The blade was stuck. The man seemed glued to his weapon, unwilling to leave it. I took that instant to strike at him with a thick, fallen branch. The blow would have killed most men. It barely stunned him. But it did, just long enough for me to hit him again. Then again. Then again. Then again.

He slumped to the forest floor, his fingers finally, reluctantly releasing the hilt.

He had brownish red hair that was cut short. Hair made redder still by blood oozing from a cut in his scalp.

Phoebe was making progress up the rock face. It was slow going. But no one seemed interested in her.

"Daniel, if Phoebe can make it up there, so can you."

Daniel was in shock, staring at the sword that had nearly sliced him in two.

The other six men converged on us.

What happened next, I can only give you fragmented details. These are events driven by adrenaline, the need to survive and consist of moments you can't remember until they come back to you in nightmares to poison your slumber.

Braeden and I fought back-to-back. We moved in fluid motions. There were no hesitations or wasted effort. A ballet of violence.

We waited until the last second, until they were close and bunched together. They attacked. Two at each of us. Two staying back.

I saw the flash of a knife. Reacted. Blocked. Defended. Disarmed.

Two of the men were holding wooden sticks about four feet long. I caught the handles in my hand, pulled myself up and kicked the two other men that had been laying back, stunning them. I kicked up my right foot, catching the man on my left off guard. A long breath in, and then I seized the wrist of the man to my right, bending it down, then twisting it counterclockwise in one movement. He countered by somersaulting into the air and unwinding his arm. His feet tapped the ground just long enough to spring-board into a spinning hook kick. The sole of his foot came around and nearly took off my head. I ducked at the last second, and his foot glanced off the top of my head instead of hitting flush with my right cheek. Still, the force was hard enough to snap my neck to the left.

The way Braeden was fighting, you'd assume his wounds weren't as bad as they looked. But this was life or death. He was running purely on adrenaline.

I spun out of the way of another kick, then launched into the air, grabbing a tree branch above. I released and landed with my full weight on the attacker I was fighting.

Then I got hit in the head with a rock. I was stunned. I turned around and saw Daniel. His face, bright red.

"Seriously?" I had a lump on the back of my skull the size of a walnut.

"I'm sorry! I was trying to help."

"Don't. Any more help like that and I'll end up dead."

"But they're getting—"

I jumped up, grabbing the branches again. Two of the attackers had gotten up and were rushing at me. I swung my legs behind me to get some momentum, then shot forward, my knees hitting the closest man under the chin, knocking him out and slamming him into the other attacker.

I saw a look of disbelief on Daniel's face.

I turned my head to check on Braeden. He had two men down and was battling the third. That split second cost me. The first attacker I had jumped down on had gotten up. He grabbed my throat. I stumbled back into Braeden, which made him miss a punch. Braeden got kicked in the head a second later. He fell to the ground. He was losing a lot of blood. His attacker paused, his eyes flitting from the open wound, the white bone and a medallion hanging from Braeden's neck. Something like fear flashed on the attacker's face.

I used that instant to kick up—using the man choking me as leverage—and wrapped my legs around the neck of Braeden's attacker.

Braeden could no longer defend himself. I kept my legs wrapped around the other man's throat to keep him from getting to Braeden.

I was starting to lose consciousness as the man crushed my windpipe. I tore at the hand around my throat, gaining a few sips of air, and focused on squeezing my thighs together. It was a contest to see who would pass out first. Finally, the man locked between my knees fainted from a lack of oxygen. And as he fell, my legs were pulled downward. Building on that momentum, I leaned my weight forward into the man at my throat, tipping him back, his feet shuffling in reverse to keep his balance until he smashed into the trunk of the large maple, the uneven bark ripping into his flesh with a force that caused him to cry out. I jerked my body, swinging my weight from side to side. His right shoulder slammed into the blade edge of the sword stuck in the tree, spilling blood. Immediately, he released his grip. I grabbed at the thick chain around his neck which held a heavy medallion similar to Braeden's. Struggling to find my breath, I hesitated, and he was able to recover enough to catch me in the cheek with his closed hand. Reflexively, I yanked on the chain while whipping my head back around and rammed my skull into his chest, bringing it up under his chin, snapping his neck back and knocking him out cold.

I stood there, panting like a dog, trying to catch my breath. I checked my body. Everything still attached.

Hyper-vigilant, I slowly backed toward Braeden.

Daniel looked at me. "What, what, what was that?" He had no ability to articulate anything else. He asked me the same question half a dozen times.

I shook him. "We have to get out of here."

"Why…why aren't you dead?" He checked my body for lacerations at the same time I did.

There was hardly any evidence of having done battle. I remember blades and fists and parts of trees coming at me, but a thousand years of people trying to hurt you hones your reflexes.

I reached Braeden and bent to check his wound when I heard one of the men at the edge of the fighting writhing on the ground. The sound made me turn my head, and I realized the redheaded attacker had crawled away and was weakly raising a crossbow and aiming it. His hand shook, but once he found his mark, his grip steadied. The arrow tip was not fixed on me, but on Phoebe who was struggling up the face, the tinkling of falling shards of basalt echoed from the cliff.

She was not too far away to be hit, and I judged this man capable of marking her.

I rushed him, jumping directly in the path of the arrow. I was confident he wouldn't release his dart, at least not to kill me, he could have done that already. He seemed resigned to my stopping him.

When I was two lengths from him, he surprised me. His taking aim at Phoebe had been a ruse to draw me to him. He nimbly got to his feet, lifting a long branch and thrusting the blunt end into my stomach. My vision blurred, and bright spots swirled around the edges of my sight. I could hardly see. Or breathe. I tried to control the panic. But the most effective way to do that is to breathe in and out slowly and deeply. But I couldn't get my body to inhale. If you've ever had the wind knocked out of you, you understand. The blow not only takes away your precious oxygen, it paralyzes the diaphragm momentarily, which seems like minutes.

The man let out a guttural roar and swung the detached tree limb. I used the last of my strength to move just enough to make him miss.

He was expecting the branch to hit, preparing himself for the sudden stop, but when the branch found nothing, his body weight was thrown forward. He lost his balance, stumbled over, and tumbled down the hill toward the water's edge. But he wasn't done. This man was a warrior. Whoever he was, wherever he came from it was clear that he had done nothing his entire life but fight.

He rose up, slowly at first, then finding his footing, he charged at me, this time with the jagged edge of the branch aimed directly at my skull. The frenzy of battle, the rage of adrenaline was overriding the desire to take me alive. I hadn't yet regained my breath. I tried to make myself move. I could feel my limbs moving in my mind, reacting, but in reality, I remained immobile, defenseless.

I would be dead in seconds.

Daniel screamed, "Alexander!"

I don't know how, but Braeden pulled himself up and got to his feet. He quickly limped forward. As the cutting end of the makeshift weapon neared its target, Braeden grabbed at a branch that hung low, and used it like a high bar in gymnastics to launch himself at the man, feet first. He struck the attacker in the chest, driving him to the rocky ground. And both of them rolled further down the embankment.

Finally, my diaphragm reflexively contracted and pulled air into my lungs. Braeden had expended all his energy, all his strength. He had nothing left to defend himself against the man who was once again rising to his feet. This man who refused to give up.

What the hell was driving him?

I struggled to my feet and stumbled toward Braeden. He had saved me. It was my turn to save him.

To stop this redheaded menace.

As I lurched down the hill, I saw the man pick up a rock two feet in diameter and lift it over his head with ease. He was about to drop it on Braeden's skull. I sensed an attacker coming at me from behind, but I had no time to fend him off first.

I let out a guttural scream as I crashed into the side of the redheaded man, the rock he was holding over his head coming down hard, knocking him unconscious. The other attacker rammed me in the back and sent me to the ground. He scrambled over to the fallen redheaded man and picked up the stone, struggling with the weight where the other man hadn't. Didn't matter. He could lift it high enough to finish Braeden with it.

My friends would not understand what I had to do, but there was no other way.

I got to my feet, closed the distance in a second and thrust the ragged edge of the branch into the side of his chest.

He dropped to the ground.

I heard Phoebe scream.

It was an awful, awful sound.

Exhausted, Braeden pushed the man's lifeless body into the river.

Daniel ran down to us. "What the fuck!" he was panting as he watched the man's body float away. "Is he dead? You killed him?" He was hyperventilating as he grabbed me by the shoulders.

He wouldn't let go. I had to push him away. I had to tend to Braeden's wounds.

As I bent down, Braeden was already shaking his head, no.

What I couldn't see until I got closer and changed my angle of view was that when Braeden landed, he had come down on branches. They wouldn't have done much damage, if any, they were mostly rotted, except that one had slipped through the gash already opened in his side.

"Braeden," I whispered.

He continued to shake his head.

"You must leave this place immediately," he said. "Leave Great Barrington," he added, making his meaning clear.

Phoebe, her face smudged with dirt and dust from the cliff, appeared a moment later, her white cheerleading shoes now gray.

Through the pain, Braeden said, "You are no longer safe here. You do not have much time." He was looking around. Almost sensing the air. Feeling something. "There will be more. They will be here soon."

"We can't just leave you here," Phoebe said.

"That is exactly what you have to do. They do not want me. They want you," he said, looking at me. "I am of little value to them."

"Why *me*?" I asked.

"Because of who you are, Alexander. Because of our father. *Your* father." He paused. "He's been a great man, Alexander. A great many men."

Phoebe and Daniel looked confused.

Braeden turned to Daniel. He reached up and grabbed him with a bloody hand and said, "Are you brave?"

I was pretty sure Daniel was about to take a dump in his pants.

"Yeah, sure. Brave," he said, quivering.

"Hold your right arm out in front of you. With your finger pointed, rotate as far as you can."

Daniel did so and got two-thirds of the way around so that if he had started at twelve, like the hands of a clock, he had ended up around eight.

"Now, take this." Braeden removed the shorter of the two necklaces he wore, a small stone amulet hanging from a thin cord of what looked like leather. He gave it to Daniel. "This will give you power." Braeden's breathing was labored. Once the necklace was around Daniel's neck, Braeden said, "Now, try it again."

Daniel rotated his upper body. Only this time, he got all the way around to almost eleven o'clock.

"That's amazing!" Daniel said as he stared at the amulet.

Like I've told you, this isn't a story about magic. It's a story about people. Braeden could've had Daniel do the same thing with a crumpled up piece of paper instead of the talisman. And he still would have gone further the second time. It's simply a matter of mechanics. The first twist, the body is tight. The second twist, the muscles have already loosened, allowing you to go farther.

It's not that items don't have power. A ring on the left hand of a woman is very powerful indeed.

A lucky charm, a sacred stone, a rabbit's foot. It's not the item itself, but the meaning we pour into an item that gives it its power. A talisman draws attention to itself, becoming a powerful focal point, allowing the wearer to do more, to be more because they aren't focused on the thing they fear, the thing that distracts—the pain, the surroundings, the danger, whatever it is.

If there is any magic, it is that we can, with our minds, turn a stone, a hunk of metal, a piece of wood into a receptacle and amplifier of our most powerful selves.

I don't know if Braeden truly believed the carved stone pendant would help Daniel access his inner strength, or if he was counting on the simple placebo effect. But it worked.

Daniel looked down at the amulet hanging from his neck. "I, I don't know—"

"It is yours now. Help him escape. I can no longer."

Braeden was losing too much blood. He wouldn't survive very long at this rate. I reached down and scooped up a handful of mud from around his feet and plastered the wound as best I could before Braeden, finally, calmly, told me I had to leave immediately.

There was something in the serene way he said it that I knew it was time for me to listen to him.

Then he said something else, a message from my father. It was faint, barely a whisper. The words a mix of parlances. Parthian and Greek and Vulgar Latin. It took a moment for me to comprehend. *The key is at the beginning of time.*

One of the men was beginning to stir. Braeden noticed.

"Go straight to the safe house in New York. Do not go to your home," he said forcefully. "They will know where you live."

"The house is probably compromised," I said.

Daniel was squinting at us, quizzically. Because we were conversing in some foreign way. Perhaps, we were speaking Ancient Greek, or Latin, or maybe even English. I have spoken so many languages over the years it's easy to slip between them without realizing.

"Do *not* go home," Braeden said, repeating the warning.

"I won't."

I didn't want to leave him. He was in terrible pain. I wanted to help him and treat him. I wanted to *know* him.

Braeden's eyes fixed on mine. "Tell our father, I'm sorry I could not take you all the way." He peeked at his wound, almost laughing when he saw blood seeping from the edges of my improvised dressing. Then as his smirk disappeared, he gripped my upper arm, squeezing it so firmly I winced. "*Everything* depends..." a stab of pain caused him to swallow hard, "...on you getting away. Millions will die if they ever catch you."

I was momentarily stunned. I could tell by his grave expression he meant the warning literally. That millions would die.

"Now, go!" he barked, pushing me away. "Go!"

With the strength that comes to you when there is nothing else you can do but face the truth, I nodded. "Be safe, my brother."

I wouldn't say Braeden smiled, but he looked comforted. "And you as well."

∞

As we ran out of the woods, I called 9-1-1 on my phone. Told the operator several people had been injured, at least one of them severely. I gave the emergency personnel the location in longitude and latitude from memory. I wiped down the screen and every surface with my shirt, making sure not to hang up the call, then dropped the phone, leaving the line open.

By the time we got to the main road, I could hear the sirens.

- EIGHT -
You Never Forget Your Six Hundred and Fifty-First House

The first thing we did was go straight back to my house.

Daniel wasn't pleased about this as we navigated a shadowed walkway that led from The Red Lion Inn deeper into the middle of the block where my house was hidden. "I thought he specifically said, 'Don't go back to your house!'"

"Yes."

"That going there would be dangerous."

"Yes."

"Am I missing something?"

"Nope."

"Then why are we here?"

Phoebe questioned my decision to come back as well. "I can't believe I'm saying this...but don't you think Daniel might be right?"

Someone leaving one of the adjacent guest cottages caused a door to slam shut.

"Hit the deck!" Daniel screamed as he dove to the ground.

Phoebe and I gazed down at him.

"What are you doing?" I asked.

"Gun sh—" his voice trailed off when he realized neither Phoebe or I had flinched.

"Get off the ground," I said, stepping over him. I continued onto the front porch, pulled out my keys, my fingers instinctively finding the set of professional picks I usually used. I fumbled for the real key. Now was not the time to practice my lock skills. I was just about to slide the brass key into the door when Daniel grabbed my hand.

"But..." he said, and then whispered, "...someone could be in there."

"Someone *could*. An elephant, a monkey or even an expendable solid-fuel rocket booster *could* be in there."

"Really?"

Phoebe rolled her eyes. "Noooo."

I glanced at Daniel's hand on mine, then up at him. "Braeden told me not to come here loud enough so the men lying half-unconscious on the ground would hear it. This is the last place they're going to be looking."

Daniel tightened his grip, keeping me from turning the key. "Did we kill people back there?"

My eyes were fixed on him. "I have to get inside."

He finally loosened his grip, and I unlocked the front door, which was painted bright red. In colonial times, a red door let weary travelers know this was a place they could come for rest. There were many times as I wandered the colonies from Charleston to Boston that I found comfort and a hot meal behind a scarlet door. And it reminded me of my time in China, as well, where a red door symbolized the mouth of a home. But mostly I liked it because crimson added a pop of color to the gray wood siding, white trim and black shutters of the house.

The darker palette stood out from the other buildings along the street, most of which were ivory or white.

It's hard to call this house a home. I've been here just over a year. I try to set up certain parts of my homes the same for consistency. Kitchens, bathrooms, and bedrooms, if possible. And I try to appreciate and enjoy the parts of each that are different. But my home is Constantinople. Although even that doesn't feel much like home anymore. It's not at all the city I knew as a boy.

This is my six hundred and fifty-first house. I'm not counting the places I've stayed in while earning room and board or homes where I was a guest. Or the tents, teepees, and caves I've sheltered in over the centuries. Six hundred and fifty-one represents the houses I've owned, or when I was younger, my father owned.

Buying real estate when you're pretending to be a high school student isn't easy. Realtors and banks want to deal with an adult. Even if it were, how many teenagers have the money to purchase a house?

Of course, I've had to devise methods to get around bankers since my father's often unavailable for months or years at a time, usually in another country, on another continent.

I've been pretty much on my own since I was nine hundred or so.

Years ago, I'd pay a surrogate to handle the details. Some were unscrupulous, and I learned my lessons the hard way: by losing money. It's easier now. Much of my dealings are done through corporations. For the past several years, I've used a lawyer who lives in a small town in Connecticut. I hired him, offering him a top salary, despite the fact that the big New York firms had rescinded their job offers when he got in some trouble at the end of law school. We both have a healthy suspicion of each other, which seems to work for us.

My father has taught me to plan well. Not just to earn a good return on my investments, but to have as many options as possible for myself when it's time to move on. I have the ability to own hundreds of homes, although I usually don't have more than a few dozen at any one time.

There is a farmhouse nearby that I bought when I first came to town. It has a working farm that sells vegetables in the summer, Christmas trees in the winter, and fresh, free-range eggs all year round. There are horses and pigs and chickens and thousands of acres where I spend at least one weekend every other month deep in the woods. I walk in carrying nothing but a knife and a flint. I hunt my food, build shelters out of whatever's available. I survive only on what I can find or kill.

Mostly, I do it to stay sharp. But sometimes I do it to get away.

My father and I saddle a pair of horses and take them into the hills whenever he comes into town. It reminds me of when we would ride in the valleys of the Pyrenees in Spain or the rolling hills of Tuscany.

I miss those times with him. I miss having him around. Our relationship is complicated.

Anyway, I like the farmhouse. But the place is too big for me. I hired a married couple in their fifties to act as caretakers. Both are skilled with horses, good cooks. The husband runs the fields, and the wife runs everything else.

Over the last eighteen months, I've grown to care about them, and I know they feel a need to be surrogate parents.

They think my father neglects me.

As much as I enjoy them and the farm, after the first few months, I decided I wanted to live somewhere else. The farmhouse is my official residence as far as school is concerned, and I sleep there a few times a month and do my treks into the wilderness, but I wanted to live closer to people. I prefer living in town or in the city versus out in the country. So, I rented this gray house with the red door that sits nestled behind the Red Lion Inn. The Inn is made up of a large main guest house and several guest cottages which surround my house. There are other cottages down a little lane across the street. The lighting at night is warm, and I like to go into the dining room and eat with the guests. There are several regulars that come in. They know me now. So do the people who run the place.

I like the mix of new people and familiar faces.

There are sitting areas inside and out on the porch where you can chat with guests or play a board game.

It feels comfortable. There is a painting of the Inn under a blanket of snow done by Norman Rockwell, which captures the warmth the place radiates even in the dead of winter.

∞

As soon as I walked in, I knew no one had been in the house.

There were several things I wanted to get. Personal items. Some IDs. Maybe a weapon.

I ran upstairs and scanned the bedrooms. I've gotten so used to moving, so conditioned to leaving places that there wasn't much I wanted to take. I opened up a drawer and pulled out two rings from the sixteenth century. A hardcover thesaurus. A few other items. I grabbed a pair of my sweats for Phoebe to change into.

If there was one major difference between me and every other teenage boy, it was that my room was neater.

I'm not a clean-freak or anything, not at all. I'm just not in any one place long enough to accumulate crap.

I'm...uncluttered.

I didn't see anything else. I thought I would want more.

Daniel was pacing the living room when I came down. He saw me carrying barely a fistful of items.

"You're not packed," he said. "I thought you were packing. Do you need help? Cause I think we need to, you know, fffffffft, leave." He accompanied the fffffffft with a gesture that ended with his index finger aimed at the front door.

"I think you two should get out of here."

"I'm not leaving," Phoebe said.

I looked at her. "This isn't your problem."

"We left a classmate dying back there!"

"I called for help."

"But we left him!" I could see Phoebe was upset. "We should have—we should go to the police."

"And tell them what?"

"That there are dangerous men running around hurting people."

"They're *very* dangerous. But they want me. They won't hurt anyone. Unless someone tries to get in their way. We get the police involved, and people will start getting hurt."

"People are already hurt!" Tears rolled down Phoebe's cheeks. "We shouldn't have left him there. We should've stayed with him." She had suppressed her feelings until now.

Her emotion crashed against the wall I'd put up since leaving the woods, since leaving Braeden, but didn't penetrate it. I had the urge to comfort her. I resisted. The sooner we got out of here, the better.

The back wall of the living room was filled with books. I stepped up to the middle shelf and tipped the spines on several hardcovers in a specific pattern.

I couldn't bring myself to look at Phoebe as I said what must have sounded to her like the lamest excuse ever given. "It would have offended his honor if I didn't leave."

I found my copy of The Riverside Shakespeare and pushed on it until it hit the back of the shelf.

Phoebe was about to respond to my cowardly-callous explanation when part of the wall opened, revealing a large metal door. I swung the heavy bookcase outward.

I know it's cliche, bookshelf, secret door, but it's not my fault, really, the house came with it.

Daniel's eyes widened. "What the—*what* is that?"

Inside was another door that looked more like a giant wall safe, this one with a modern keypad. Okay, I upgraded a few things.

"It's a secret."

I punched in the code: 1-0-6-6, then pulled open the thick metal door.

Disbelief flashed on their faces. Inside the safe was a wheeled cabinet with flip-up doors hiding its contents. I ignored what was inside and rolled it out of the way, pushing the storage tower into the middle of the living room. Then I reached up and grabbed the edge of the ceiling panel, getting my fingernails in a tiny gap. I gently tugged downward, and part of the molding came away, unveiling another keypad. This one was horizontal with numbers running from zero through nine and the letters from A through F. I punched in a series of numbers and letters much more complicated than the first.

With a loud click, three bolts retracted. As I pushed on the back of the safe, the metal wall swung away. I stepped through the safe into a room which was used to hide weapons and people from the British during the Revolutionary War.

Daniel let slip a few choice curse words as he got his first glimpse of the room's contents. The safe had surprised him. This room made him giddy.

An array of guns from rifles and shotguns to handguns and assault weapons were lined up neatly. Some were mounted on the wall, others rested under plexiglass in a display case. Revolvers on the right, pistols on the left. Bullets for the guns were housed under the case in drawers labeled by caliber size and gauge, smallest to largest. The weight of the bullets made the drawers difficult to open. A rack of swords from around the world and across the millennia hung on another wall. I won't bother with the details. Let's just say they were kept sharp and very deadly.

There were various types of explosives in unlocked cabinets. And another wall that held an assortment of medieval and martial arts weapons.

The most dangerous items in the room, however, were kept behind glass. They were the half dozen or so photos hanging on the walls of me in various poses, the earliest from the mid-1800s. To the modern eye, they might look like some Photoshopped image you'd buy on a trip to Frontier World or some other tourist trap. A digitally aged sepia-toned shot of you dressed in rawhide in an Old West ghost town. Or your face dropped into a shot of passengers waving excitedly from the deck of the *Titanic*.

Only these were real.

I was on the *Titanic*. And the photograph to prove it was hanging right behind Phoebe's head.

Phoebe briefly glanced over her shoulder at the photo, but I was one of a hundred faces looking down from the top deck at the photographer on the dock. She didn't seem to notice me. No, the picture that caught her eye was on the opposite wall. It was the oldest in the room, but the people in it were clear. The faces close up.

The image was faded. Surrounded by several men in uniform, I wore a grim expression. The soldiers posed with me as if I were their pet. The harsh lighting and the dirt on my skin made it hard to see that it was me. It could easily be mistaken for a relative of mine.

The photograph was taken at the Battle of Gettysburg, though you wouldn't know it from the image. Just outside of the frame, nearly one hundred thousand men choked the camp all around us. Yet, they were invisible. It looked more like a picture from a camping trip. Except no one was smiling. Part of that, of course, was the wretched circumstances after two days of fighting, but mostly no one smiled because in those days you had to hold perfectly still for an excruciatingly long time so as not to ruin the picture. It was harder to smile without moving than it was to maintain a blank expression.

The image was taken on the evening of July 2nd, 1863. Two days into the longest three days of my life.

The Battle of Gettysburg, like most battles, wasn't *a* battle at all. It was made up of several acts broken into innumerable scenes. Like some horrible, lethal version of a playoff series in baseball. You might win an inning, even a game or two, but that doesn't mean you win it all.

I said I hated the Civil War. But the truth is, I've hated every war I've been involved with. I've especially despised the wars that I was forced to fight, and even more, the ones where I was not allowed to. That may sound strange. But think of war as a game of chess. I'd much prefer to be a knight or a bishop or a rook than a pawn.

The day after that photograph was taken in the Union camp, I was a lowly pawn caught in the middle of what is now known as Pickett's Charge. We called it what it was: a suicide attack by Johnny Rebel meant to slice into the center line of the Union troops in an attempt to capture Cemetery Hill and the roads into Gettysburg that our high ground positions defended. Across from us was an imposing line of 12,500 Confederate soldiers nearly a mile across ready to attack. It was one of the most frightening, awe-inspiring, terrible things I've ever seen.

Against this onslaught of men, I was armed with nothing but a large serving spoon.

But even a pawn, if it can get to the back of the board, if it can get all the way to the heart of the enemy's defenses, can become whatever it wants to be.

Throughout the third and final day of the Battle of Gettysburg, artillery from the Confederate side pounded us. I was an army cook, having been pulled into service by the local militia as all the able-bodied adult men were needed to fight. Hardly anyone had an appetite that day. The constant explosions rattled the nerves and squeezed the hell out of everyone's guts.

Despite the clamor, the shelling did very little damage to the Union's position.

There was one shot that blew up one of the "sinks," which were nothing more than open latrines.

As bad as that sink reeked before, it smelled a whole lot worse after it was blown sky high. Luckily, no one was going to the bathroom at the time, but an officer everyone hated, Lieutenant T.K. Butler, got the worst of it. He was passing behind the sink and had to be dug out from under a half ton of excrement. Fitting, actually, since he was full of it most of the time.

To this day, I think the Southern generals saw the explosion, saw us scrambling for cover, and thought they'd hit one of our munitions stores.

It wasn't the only mistake they made that day.

These proud, but ill-fated men charged across the open field. A dozen thousand men running straight toward us.

The Union cannons blasted away. They tore into the attack, exposing the weakness of that outdated way of war, of men charging shoulder to shoulder in lockstep. It worked when wars were fought with swords. Less so when archers were added. Once the rifle came, it seemed immoral to stand up a line of men as human targets, hoping a few of the ones behind them would get through.

The few Confederate soldiers able to reach the low wall that protected the Union ranks couldn't hold their position, and almost all were forced to scramble back to their line in full retreat.

They made for easy targets.

There was one man who made it past our defenses. I think the Union soldiers were so shocked to see this lone man refuse to retreat, they just let him through. He screamed the entire way, the bayonet on the end of his rifle outstretched in front of him.

I was standing there just as dumbfounded to see a Rebel in the midst of our camp as everyone else.

By the time he got to where I was, there was no one else around. I was the only victim in sight. He headed straight for me. He had spent his shot on the charge, but he was determined to kill a Yankee, any Yankee. Never mind that I had lived in the South almost as much as I had lived in the North. Actually, that probably would have made him more angry.

When I realized he was aiming the tip of his bayonet at my chest, I stood *en guard*, holding the spoon. I felt ridiculous, but the serving spoon was all I had.

I thought about turning and running, but not far behind me were a group of women—nurses and cooks. They would be his target if I retreated.

I readied myself. In my mind, the spoon was a sword. A short one, like a Scottish dirk.

I stood sideways, giving him less of my body to hit.

I balanced my weight. And prepared to perform perhaps the most important parry of my life. I had one shot to strike my opponent's blade and deflect it. I had no guard on my weapon to protect my hand if I didn't do it quickly or powerfully enough. Properly executed, I would be in a good position to strike back.

With my spoon.

His howling did not stop or grow louder. It remained constant, even as he tried to run me through with his bayonet.

With the tip only a few inches away from my ribs, I parried, twisting my right wrist as if I was looking at my watch.

Any sooner and I would have mistimed it. I drove his blade to the side and down. I grabbed the stock of his Enfield with my free hand. The force of my blow knocked him off balance, and his momentum carried him into me, but turned as I was, he slipped past. I struck him once in the head with the spoon, sending his hat flying.

He staggered around, his battle cry just a whimper, then he turned to run at me again. He was exhausted and no match for me now. I would easily take the rifle out of his hands on this pass.

I never got the chance.

I heard a single shot a second before the man's chest exploded. He fell to the ground.

Thirty paces to the right, a soldier nodded to me, somberly, then he glanced down, opened the gun and cleared the priming from his rifle.

Pickett's Charge, like the charge of this unknown Confederate, failed.

Casualties ran over fifty percent.

It was a terrible, terrible day.

One that changed the fate of the United States. After Gettysburg, the Confederate Army would never regain its momentum.

A few months later, I watched President Lincoln give his elegant Gettysburg Address from the top of Cemetery Hill, not far from where I had defended myself with a spoon.

I had the barest sense, a tiny but powerful niggling in the back of my brain that I had just witnessed something important.

Lincoln's final line still fills me with emotion.

> *"We here highly resolve that these dead shall not have died in vain—that this nation, under God, shall have a new birth of freedom—and that government of the people, by the people, for the people, shall not perish from the earth."*

Seeing Lincoln speak on the same ground that had been littered with the bodies of forty thousand dead and wounded, reminded me of the lone soldier who came so close to me, I could smell the foul salted pork on his breath.

That one man, and the Union sharpshooter who killed him, brought home the cost of that war more clearly, more personally than the half a million others that died.

Phoebe moved in closer to the picture. Then she looked at me. More like *through* me.

"That's you in the photo."

I nodded.

I always had an answer ready for these type of situations, but Phoebe had a way of clouding my thoughts.

"I—" I stumbled. "I took part in a Civil War reenactment a couple of years ago when I lived in Pennsylvania."

"You don't look very happy."

"It's exciting at first, but once you see your friends lying on the ground and realize what those soldiers went through, see their graves, it hits you."

"I don't know much about the Civil War. Seems pretty depressing. History's not really my thing."

I knew that wasn't true. Her lying made me smile. Craig was probably threatened by dating someone smarter than him. "I took a peek at your test."

"You cheat!"

"*After* I handed mine in. You're smarter than you give yourself credit for."

"Maybe, but it's not like a guy ever said, 'Hey, look at her. Nice brain.'" She motioned a big, busty head with her hands.

"A guy can't like both?"

"Can they?" She eyed me, holding the stare for a moment before returning to the photograph. "They did a great job on this. It looks so real."

People's inability, even in the face of truth, to fathom that someone could be a hundred times as old as they are has probably been the biggest reason we haven't been outed before.

Daniel saved me, thankfully, when he punched me in the arm and yelled, "You are a horrible friend, do you know that? The worst!"

"And why's that?"

"I've been to your house how many times?"

"I don't know. How many?" I said, feeling like I was in the middle of a comedy act.

"Like a thousand."

"More like fifty."

"A lot, okay? And you never showed me this?"

"There's a reason for that," I said, as he started to pick up a kama, which looked like a small sickle or a slender ax with a knife blade coming out the top at a right angle. "Don't touch those!"

"A good friend," he eyed me, "would let me touch whatever I wanted."

"Apparently your definition of a good friend is someone who let's you maim yourself. I don't want you slicing off your hand. Or worse my hand or Phoebe's."

Phoebe nodded emphatically in agreement.

Daniel slowly, reluctantly, pulled his fingers away from the kama. He continued examining the array of weapons with his hands behind his back as if he were in a museum—just to highlight his displeasure.

Phoebe glanced around the room, trying to take it all in. She didn't have the same kid-in-a-candy-store gaze Daniel had. Her expression was cautiously curious. If she hadn't witnessed the attack against me in the woods, the fact that I had a room like this would have completely freaked her out.

Smart girls don't date boys with weapons caches in their homes.

Which, come to think of it, is a rule everyone should follow.

Got more than a hunting rifle or two. Red flag.

I guarantee if I walked into someone's home and saw this arsenal, I'd be quickly leaving through the closest exit I had scoped out upon entering.

I understand people are fascinated by guns and knives and

swords. But I have witnessed these weapons in action. How easily and indiscriminately they can kill. How a momentary impulse can have a permanent consequence.

I don't pick them up lightly.

I respect their power.

To respect something, you have to fear it without being afraid.

Most of these weapons took years for me to master.

If I'd had any one of them, the fight in the woods would have gone very differently.

I would not be weaponless again.

I wished I could arm Daniel and Phoebe. I didn't stand much of a chance without help. Even with Braeden beside me, it had been barely enough.

I picked up a shinai, a rounded bamboo stick with a carved handle. I hefted it in my hands. It wasn't sharp, but I've been hit with one more than a few times and, to be honest, I much preferred being stabbed than getting whacked with one of these.

I handed it to Daniel.

"Start with this."

As he began swooshing it through the air, I grabbed one of my bokken, the wooden swords I used for training during my studies under the Samurai. Bokken allowed us to practice realistically without killing each other.

I offered the bokken to Phoebe. "You handled yourself well out there."

"Fear, mostly. Mixed with six years of gymnastics, three years of cheerleading camp, and a year of taking the bus with the football team."

"I would have been down in the first minute if you hadn't stunned that guy with a kick to the face."

She nodded and absently played with the bokken. Her movements were natural, fluid.

"You should take that," I said.

She held the bokken up to her face and studied it. "I'm still trying to make sense of everything. Those people. Why did they want to take you?"

"I'm not sure. Probably something we shouldn't try to figure out here."

We had been in the house less than ten minutes. I didn't want to stay much longer. I needed a weapon. But which one?

"So...you know how to use all these?" Phoebe asked, gently poking me in the chest with the wooden tip.

I didn't mean to answer her so directly, but I had already picked up the qiang and was in the process of throwing the Chinese spear when she asked.

"I don't practice as often as I should," I said, truthfully.

The spear pierced the heart of a training dummy.

"Yeah, you seem rusty."

I grabbed a kunai and sent the throwing knife into the wall, killing a fly that had been buzzing around the room. I grabbed the other two in the set and slid them in my back pocket.

I swung a mace. Too bulky.

Flicked at the air with a set of nunchaku. Maybe.

I wasn't satisfied with any of the weapons, except the kunai, but they had limited use.

I wanted to take the katana, but I couldn't just walk around with a sword.

Despite my warning, Daniel put down the shinai, and before I could say anything, picked up the katana. Maybe he thought the samurai sword was similar to the shinai since the deadly blade was concealed within a lacquered wooden scabbard. It looked harmless. As soon as he swung the sheathed sword, however, the scabbard slid off the blade and hit me in the crotch. The weight of the blade almost knocked him over and he began waving it indiscriminately as he tried to regain his balance. I was bent over in pain and was spared a beheading. Phoebe barely had enough time to raise the bokken, deflecting the tip of the katana away from her face. The blade continued slicing through the air until it finally connected with something. The razor-sharp katana effortlessly lopped off the head of my practice dummy. The decapitated head caromed off the spear I had just put in the dummy's chest, then the head landed on the floor with a loud thud, rolled into a floor lamp, knocking it over, causing it to graze Daniel's back. He reacted by whirling around too quickly, sending the katana flying out of his hands where it buried itself, BOING!, in the middle of the forehead of a portrait on the wall right next to me.

"And that is why we don't touch the swords," I said as I gently pulled the blade from between the eyes of the unknown female figure in the one of a kind, never-before-seen sketch given to me in Florence by one of my mentors. It was signed simply, LDV.

Getting Leonardo's sketch remounted in a new airtight frame without drawing attention would be difficult. But it would have to wait.

It was time to leave. No more delaying.

I charged out of the secret room. I would take the katana. I placed it on a side table near the door that held several days worth of mail I hadn't opened. I picked up a cordless phone from the table and started to call a cleanup crew I trusted. There was one about thirty miles from here, across the state line in Connecticut. I put the phone back in its charger, deciding to wait to make the call until we had gotten safely away.

The damage to Leonardo's drawing wasn't the only thing tightening my guts. I suddenly had a bad feeling about coming here.

Phoebe and Daniel followed me out of the hidden room.

"I'm starting to think I don't know you very well," said Daniel.

"Don't talk to me right now!"

Daniel started to speak again when my stare caused him to close his mouth quickly. He nervously began picking things up and playing with them.

His silence lasted all of ten seconds.

"Is your family in the mob or something? I mean, who has a secret room full of deadly weapons and a safe house in New York?

Which, by the way, Braeden specifically told us to go to instead of coming here."

Daniel had a knack for choosing the most dangerous items in my house.

"Don't play with that bat!"

"Listen, I'm sorry about the sword, okay? It's just a bat! I know how to handle a bat."

I pulled on the knob at the bottom, withdrawing a slender sword.

"Okay. Remind me never to hit you with a pitch." He ran his hands tensely through his hair. "When I get stressed I need something to occupy myself. And I'm very stressed right now. Is this okay?" He flicked an umbrella that was resting by the door into his hands.

"That! has a needle in the tip that can inject you with deadly poison."

Daniel gingerly put the umbrella down. He picked up the most innocuous item in the room, a baseball.

"And don't touch the baseball!"

Daniel froze. "Are you kidding me? What's in the baseball? Explosives? Some sort of nerve gas?"

"Babe Ruth signed it."

His body instantly relaxed and Daniel took a closer look at the ball, studying the signature.

"I thought you were a Red Sox fan."

In Great Barrington, being anything but a Sox fan got you painted as a heretic, a traitor, and several other things I can't mention. I started to tell him the truth, which is that The Babe signed that ball when he was with the Red Sox, but Daniel turned the ball with his fingertip until we both could see the words "To Alexander" written in faded ink.

He glanced up, and I sensed his dawning comprehension. "You make money counterfeiting sports memorabilia! That's brilliant."

Or maybe not.

"No, that's stupid and would land me in jail."

I grabbed the baseball, and with a sleight of hand, made it disappear into thin air.

"How did you—?" Daniel was looking around the room, trying to figure out where the ball had gone.

I'd pulled off the trick cleanly, even though my hand movements were a bit sluggish. I like magic. I find it relaxing. But ever since that misunderstanding where I nearly got burned at the stake, I rarely did it in front of people.

My prestidigitation had its desired effect. I had distracted Daniel.

The ball was safely in my backpack atop the sweats for Phoebe. The pack held several other items I thought we might need and the handful of items that were dear to me.

I went to zip it up, then stopped, staring at the sweats for a moment.

"You know what? I need to leave. You need to go home. Both of you."

Phoebe glared at me. Daniel was still looking for the ball, and it took a moment for him to realize what I had said.

"Just go home," she said. "Like nothing happened?"

They deserved some sort of explanation, but anything I told them would only put them in more danger.

This wasn't the goodbye I wanted. I wanted to do it properly, but I needed much more time than we had.

Not that I don't know how to say goodbye. Believe me, I've gotten very good at leaving places, leaving people.

Of all the things you have to master to successfully live as long as I have, learning how to leave may be the most important.

In the time it takes me to look one year older, I've left behind twenty to thirty sets of friends. It makes it difficult to open up to people. To get close. Because you always know...you're going to leave. Maybe not today or next week, but soon. Three or four years. At the most.

Usually, I had time to prepare myself, but this felt like cutting and running to me. It didn't feel right.

"I'm probably..." I gathered my thoughts. "I'm *not* coming back. I've enjoyed living here." I turned to Daniel. "You've been a good friend."

I gave Daniel an awkward hug, made worse by his refusal to let go of me. I finally pried myself away from his sobbing grip, then turned to Phoebe. I wanted to tell her the truth. Not about me being fifteen hundred years old, but about the crush I've had on her since right after our first conversation.

But it seemed stupid to say it. If she didn't feel the same, I'd feel like an idiot. And if she did, it would just make it so much harder.

I don't have much experience when it comes to normal dating relationships, but the experiences I have had, haven't worked out well.

I've rehearsed this moment, saying goodbye to her, probably a hundred times, at least. Gone over the words in my head and out loud, practicing the timing, the phrasing. Trying to explain how I feel and why I have to go without revealing too much.

"Phoebe, I hope you realize..." I said, my heart pounding in my chest. "I want you to know...you deserve someone much better than Craig. He may be nice to you, but he's an arrogant prick to everyone else. And sooner or later, he's going to be a prick to you."

Wow. I hadn't seen that coming. Not the way I'd rehearsed it.

Don't get me wrong, I've wanted to tell her Craig Coulter was a world-class jackass less than five minutes after I'd met him.

Her eyes showed hurt. She was still holding the bokken. I thought she might hit me with it.

I let out a deep sigh. "Listen, I'm sorry. I'm sure you bring out the best in him."

She watched me as I began locking things down. "Where are you going?"

I pulled the rear door of the safe closed, punched a locking code into the keypad. There was a low clunk as massive bolt cylinders extended into the surrounding frame, sealing off the secret room.

"Somewhere else."

I pressed the molding until I heard it click. Once in place, it was impossible to tell a keypad lay hidden behind it. Then I returned the rollout cabinet into the safe.

"So, that's it?" said Phoebe. "See ya later. Nice knowing ya."

"Unfortunately." I started to close the heavy metal door.

"What about the stuff in the safe?" Daniel said.

I stopped. Glanced at the contents, realized some of it might be useful. I grabbed one of several cell phones off a shelf in the back. I handed it to Phoebe.

"You have your phone?" I asked. She nodded. "Call it from this so I have your number and you have mine. If there's any trouble. You call me. I'll get you help."

With the bokken tucked under her arm, she moved toward the front door to get a better signal.

I opened several of the flip-up doors on the rollout, revealing racks with gold bars and wrapped bundles of cash stacked inside.

Daniel couldn't believe what he was seeing. "Who *are* you?"

I stuffed two stacks of hundred dollar bills into my bag. There were some smaller denominations, fifties and twenties, and I took two stacks of twenties and a stack of fifties as well.

"You're just going to leave all that behind?" asked Daniel as he stared at the four gold bars and two dozen half-inch stacks of bills I was abandoning.

A quarter million in cash. Something north of two million in gold.

"Take it," I said. "But leave the gold." The bars were heavy and cumbersome, and two teenagers trying to peddle gold ingots without knowing what they were doing would attract the kind of attention that could put them in jail or get them killed.

Daniel stared at me. He didn't move toward the money. Like maybe it was marked or would explode if he touched it. "Seriously, who *are* you?"

A man appeared in my living room doorway. "Alexander Grant," he said.

Rugged looking, with an air of power and authority, the man was in his mid-forties. He had a slight scar on his face and his skin was that deep olive color that people from around the Mediterranean have, especially if they spend time in the sun.

His body looked strong. His arms, powerful. But he wasn't bulky.

He was holding the katana sword I had left on the entryway table.

Adrenaline shot through me. My stomach twisted. Escape routes. He was blocking the front door. The bookshelf that was swung open prevented me from getting out the back exit cleanly. The couch was in the way of my reaching the window quickly.

He waved his index finger as if to say, *no, no, no.*

I had the strangest feeling, an immediate need to show him respect. The only way I can describe it is, he commanded it.

NINE

Both My Adversary And My Deliverance Come Right Through My Front Door

Like any kid in the middle of their teens, I have all of the classic symptoms of the untreatable disease known as *puberty*. The more than occasional adolescent angst, the hormones, the feeling of invincibility, the need to rebel against our elders. But on this last point, how I treat—and even defy—my elders, this is where I am different from those who are biologically the same age as me. Part of this difference is that centuries of experience have tempered and enlightened my mind. Time makes you humble. Truly. Even as it makes you more confident. Given enough of it, you will run up against someone who is better and stronger and faster. As much as I know, as much as I've learned, as many skills as I've mastered, there is always that place in the back of my mind where a healthy dose of doubt and skepticism lives. A place that reminds me that I have seen far too many others filled with pride and puffed up by overconfidence who have failed. Often tragically.

Over the last hundred years, there has been a seismic shift in the way people raise their children, and how they think about the world and privilege, class, social order, and rank. Kids are treated better, are listened to by their parents more, all of which is good, but it has led to the people of my age—at least, the age I appear to be—to have a cockiness and a confidence that isn't always warranted or deserved. In today's world, presidents and even kings are spoken of irreverently and made fun of.

I grew up in a time where I feared my elders. I don't want you to think I was afraid of my father, but I was afraid of disrespecting him. The years apart gave me the confidence to handle my own affairs even at a young age, and with that came a strong will and strong opinions. But I would never dare to cross my father.

And not just because he was my father.

There have been over the many years a number of people who deserved a kind of respect and reverence far beyond what is expected of children toward their elders. These men and women commanded and received deference not just from the young, but from powerful adults and the most hardened soldiers.

It may be difficult for people facing the harshness of urban life to believe, but the world has become a kinder, more forgiving place. I did not grow up in this gentler time. And except for the fact that I feel constrained by the need to keep my identity and my talents and my longevity a secret, I enjoy the advances of technology and the blossoming of a more accepting society. But as I stood there, gazing at this stranger, I was sent back to a time where one should be very careful about even looking directly in the eye of a man like this.

"You know my name."

The man smiled. "I know who you *are*."

My eyes narrowed. "You sent those men."

"I have to admit, that was quite impressive. I didn't anticipate the other boy being there. Still, you did far better than I expected. I figured you would be like your father. If I had known you were so talented, I would have sent three times as many."

I ignored the comment about my father even as I felt it burn in my gut. "And yet, here you are, alone."

"I am. Seems strange, doesn't it?"

When he moved, it was fluid, relaxed. Nothing rushed about it. Always in balance.

"What happened to the other boy?" I didn't dare say Braeden's name. I wasn't going to reveal his identity.

"Your friend didn't make it."

I heard Phoebe gasp. She was about four feet to his right. He hadn't seen her because a short section of wall jutted out into the living room, obscuring her. He swung the blade in the direction of the sound so that the tip was only inches from her face.

"What have we here?" The man moved closer to her.

"He wasn't my friend," I said, harshly, drawing only a glance from him.

I tried to look disinterested, tried to cover my sorrow and my concern even as all the air left my lungs. Phoebe was sobbing. I tried to keep my composure. Seeing the danger she was in made my heart race. I could tell she was trying to keep it in, but it was too hard. Sometimes fear keeps people quiet. Sometimes it makes them bold.

"You mean your people murdered him?" she said, defiantly.

"An unfortunate loss." The man looked at her. "He wasn't your boyfriend, was he?"

This made her swallow her tears. Her face blushed red, and she shook as she held it together. "No," she said, the first consonant straining on her tongue.

He leaned in, keeping the point of the blade to her throat and sniffed her. "You smell..." He sniffed again, breathing in the pleasing scent I often enjoyed in History class. The hint of a grin spread across his face. "Hmm...older. What is your name?"

She was about to answer when I put up my hand for her to keep quiet.

"Who are *you*?" I asked.

"I'll let Marcus explain that when he comes to save you."

Marcus is my father's name.

The man made a motion with his hand that said, let's get this moving along. "Now, as brave as that performance in the woods was, I want you to come with me. Peacefully." He said it in a casual, almost friendly tone. "I would hate for anyone else to die."

Maybe his words were calculated to get a response. Maybe they were unintentional. Either way, the words cut me. My friend's deaths would be my fault. Just like Braeden's had been.

Braeden. Dead.

This wasn't the way things were supposed to happen. We could die. I knew that. Accidents. War. Disease. There was the explosion in Halifax, but I'd never met any of those people. In my entire life, I had personally known only one like me who died before Braeden. It had given me a false sense that we were immortal.

I stood there nodding for a moment, putting my hands up in an okay-give-me-a-second sort of way. I was stalling. Trying to come up with something. I couldn't just go with him. What would that say? That Braeden's death was for nothing. If I was going to give up, I could've surrendered to the men in the woods and saved his life.

No.

They would've murdered Daniel and Phoebe. Maybe Braeden as well. Even if I went.

Daniel and Phoebe. That's why he died.

I relaxed my arms. "Fine."

The man with the scar lowered the tip of the katana slowly.

Without warning, while his attention was on me, Phoebe slashed with the bokken, knocking the tip of the katana down and away, then she did a handspring tuck off the coffee table—feet coming down on the sofa cushions—into a twisting double back somersault that vaulted her over the couch. She stuck the landing. She was as much surprised by her actions as the rest of us. I shoved Daniel into Phoebe and both of them into the hallway.

"Go!"

If they did the smart thing and left through the back, they'd get away with their lives.

I could hear Daniel say, "C'mon!" to Phoebe. There was a shuffling of feet.

Now, it was just me and the man with the scar.

"Well done. I can see why you are enchanted by her."

"I'm not."

"Hmm, of course you aren't."

I couldn't let him get to me. I bit the inside of my mouth and drew blood to keep myself from thinking about her. Or Braeden. I savored the metallic taste and focused solely on the man.

He was bigger. Definitely stronger.

My only advantage was that this was my home. My turf. He might have cased the place, but I doubted it. It didn't matter. The edge it gave me was small. There was a common four-over-four room floor plan to these colonial homes. This one was slightly different to make the hidden room possible, but other than that, it was a standard layout.

This man, whoever he was, was over four thousand years old. He would know his way around these homes.

He slashed at me with the sword. It missed my chin. Not by much. I could feel the wind as the blade rushed passed.

I had to be careful. I needed to keep myself between the man and the hallway. What were they doing? I hadn't heard the back door. I didn't want Phoebe or Daniel getting hurt. I also didn't want the man using them against me.

I glanced around the room for something, anything I could use to defend myself. If I could just get to the bat, I would have a proper weapon.

He swung at me again. The blade came even closer this time. He was playing with me, letting me know he could hurt me at any time. As he gave a halfhearted third swing, I picked up the floor lamp next to me, ripped the plug from the wall, tore off the shade and held the brushed nickel pipe out in from of me. I swung it around, guarding against the katana. He seemed pleased that I had decided to put up a fight. He charged at me. I flipped the lamp, and using the round, flat base, rammed it into his chest. The force of the blow halted him for a beat. I may have knocked the wind out of him slightly. But not for long.

He was stronger than he looked. And he looked powerful.

He knew how to use the katana. He came at me and I deflected the attack as best I could with the lamp.

It was obvious he didn't want to kill me. He wanted me alive.

"I know what you're thinking," he said. "And you are right, I do not want to kill you. But alive does not necessarily mean *unharmed*." As he said the last word, he thrust the sword at me and this time he was more serious about it.

When I say serious, I mean his efforts were more earnest, more determined. Because the look on his face was anything but solemn. It was clear he was enjoying this.

He rounded on me and with a good, strong swing of the blade, he sliced the floor lamp in half. The impact caused the plug and cord to whip me in the face, catching the corner of my eye. It stung.

The pain drove me to lash out. I wrapped the cord around the katana, pulling the blade to the side. For an instant, I was able to get close enough to drive my knee into his groin. I might not have caught him directly in the balls, but I hit something with a great deal of force. He stepped back but didn't give me the satisfaction of seeing him wince. Then he circled around the couch, spending a moment to untangle the sword from the wiring. He lashed at me with the cord.

It may not seem warrior-like or worthy of my ten centuries of training at deadly combat skills, but I snatched several pillows off the couch and threw them at him.

He was startled. Then he laughed.

This gave me just enough time to make a move for the bat. I kicked the sofa and knocked the coffee table into his shins. He didn't let out a sound, not a peep, but I could tell from the creases at the corner of his eyes that I hurt him.

I reached out with my leg and flicked the bat into the air with my toe.

I grabbed it.

I didn't pull the sword out right away. Keep it a mystery a little longer. I didn't want him to know just yet what I really had in my hands.

Instead, I swung the bat at him, wildly.

I hit mostly air. But the bat glanced off his shoulder twice.

This was a man who could take a heavy pounding. He had already endured several powerful shots from me. Okay, maybe not the pillows. But the lamp. My knee to his balls.

It was going to take a brutal direct hit.

There is a way to block a blow from a bat. The trick is keeping your arm parallel to the barrel of the weapon. If you've ever watched a relay race at a track meet, seen how a runner waits with his arm back for his teammate to pass the baton by slapping it into their open palm, you have some idea of how to defend against a bat.

A club, a bat, or a stick is most deadly when it strikes at a ninety-degree angle. When it hits its target perpendicularly.

No matter how good this man was, if I could get one shot at him, just one good slug, this bat would do some damage.

I only had to make sure that I did not swing the Louisville Slugger too wildly. If I did that and whiffed, if I didn't connect with anything, I'd throw myself off balance.

Do that, and you're out of position, defenseless, usually with your back to your opponent.

We did not speak. We didn't engage in clever banter.

There was no need for discussion.

He wanted to take me. I didn't want to go.

Every once in a while there was a tiny "yes" or a barely audible "very nice" that escaped from his lips.

I took another swing at him. As I figured he would, he used his forearms to deflect the attack. I was careful to make sure he couldn't grab the bat. I altered the speed and angle of my swings. If he seized the bat, he might disarm me or, at least, reveal too soon what was inside.

Showing superior ambidextrous ability, he fought with his left and right hands independently. This wasn't merely him using both arms at once. He was aggressively defending against the bat and attacking with the sword in a complicated, discrete way.

The blade of the katana sliced at me. He meant to end this fight. I caught the blade with the bat and knocked it aside. Force against force. I was going to lose a battle of sheer power. He was using one arm while I had both hands on the bat handle to keep his sword down. It wasn't enough. I took one hand and grabbed the ricasso—the dull section of the blade just above the hilt—to sustain the hold. He came face-to-face with me, pressing in on me. And then, with his free hand, he slapped me across the face.

Not punched. Slapped.

Like I was a disobedient child.

He glared at me. "I said, I want you to come...*peacefully.*"

We held that pose for five seconds. I could feel his breath on my face. It was hot and smelled vaguely of garlic and olives. He did not sneer at me. He never took his eyes off my eyes. I blinked a dozen times before he blinked once.

After pushing me away, he increased the speed of his attack. The sword disappeared in a blur.

I am a fair swordsman. I don't fence with partners often because the weight of the weapons used in the sport—even the heaviest, the épée—were delicate and less taxing than the burden and unwieldiness of an actual battle sword.

Okay, I'll admit, I'm better than fair. But this man was obviously more skilled. And not just with the blade, but in hand-to-hand combat and strategy.

I knew then it would be impossible for me to defeat him.

Once I accepted that, I understood what I had to do.

I swung the bat at him again, only this time I telegraphed my actions. He twisted his arm and grabbed the entire barrel just like the runner's baton. Exactly as I wanted him to. Using a burst of strength more powerful than anything I had gone up against before, he ripped the bat out of my hands. The barrel went flying and smashed through the front window, sending shards of glass everywhere.

He smiled.

Until he looked down and saw the slender blade left in my hand.

He had overextended himself, left himself open. Not completely.

He knew I would try to defend myself by some other means, but he assumed he had disarmed me, that he had taken away my most lethal available weapon. Before he could blink, I shoved the blade at his throat, sending the tip straight toward the hollow under his Adam's apple. His shirt opened a bit and I saw the edge of a scar just below his clavicle in a shape I'd seen before. In the woods. Hanging from the neck of Braeden and the redheaded menace.

Despite being caught with his defenses down, he responded more quickly than my attack. He deftly raised the hilt of his sword just enough that the edge struck the cross-guard. Instead of piercing his esophagus, the sword point slipped across his cheek.

There wasn't much blood. It was more of a scratch than anything. It mirrored the deeper scar on his right cheek.

That's when he hit me again with his fist. This time it was a close-fisted punch.

I saw stars.

I don't know what it's like to get hit by a heavyweight boxer in their prime without gloves, but I'm pretty sure it felt kind of like this.

I had made him angry, and this distracted him more than the surprise appearance of my sword.

In that instant, Phoebe appeared in the front hall and ran at him. She flung a decorative pewter plate she must have grabbed from the eighteenth-century breakfront in the dining room. The heavy metal disk nearly took my head off. It struck him right above the ear. As he flinched, I drove him back, using my legs.

Daniel appeared from around the corner and opened the door to the cellar. With a final shove, the man tumbled backwards down the stairs. He grabbed at the railings and kept himself from smashing his head against the sharp edges of the steps and the concrete at the bottom.

We only had a few seconds.

I slammed the door to the cellar, then turned to Daniel and Phoebe. "Get out of here now!"

Daniel sprinted out first. If there had been a line of pregnant women pushing infants in baby carriages in front of him, he would've bowled them all over without hesitation or remorse.

Phoebe looked at me. "What about you?"

I glanced around, catching sight of the umbrella. I could use that if I had to.

I turned to her. "Get out of here. Now!" I grabbed the umbrella. "Now!"

She wanted to say something. I don't know what. Perhaps it's the nature of all teenagers, their need to defy orders, any orders, even those commands that will save their lives. Finally, she turned and ran outside.

The house was suddenly quiet.

I could hear the man getting to his feet. I backed away from the cellar door. I didn't want to be in its path when he forced it open. And he would. He wasn't going to remain down there for long. Was there anything in the cellar he could use? I tried to picture the basement. I'm sure there was something down there.

It didn't matter. I would be ready for him. As ready as I could be anyway.

I positioned myself slightly to the left of the door, the side it opened from. I had to keep him pinned on the stairs. He would have less room to fight. Behind me, the front door was open. I could have turned and run, but he had found me. He had cut through the layered veil of my secrecy as if it was tissue paper.

I wanted, I needed to know why he had expended so much effort to come for me. He had a plan. A plan that included my father rescuing me.

"Alexander!" the man with the scar called out.

He was angry, but I could still hear the smile. As if he was wiping blood from his lips and enjoying the taste of it.

I heard a disturbance outside. Screeching tires. Someone yelling.

"Who are you?" I asked.

From behind the door, I heard that incredible laugh again.

Followed by the meaty part of his fist pounding against the wall, not with rage, but with pleasure. "You really don't know, do you?" he said.

For some reason, his words annoyed me. I guess it tapped into that same feeling I had when Braeden started telling me things about my father I didn't know.

Like I've said, there is no emotion more powerful and lasting than embarrassment. And there is nothing more embarrassing than not being let in on a joke.

I had been kept in the dark. My pride was hurt.

The door flew open, kicked with a heavy boot. It smashed into the wall after coming off its hinges.

He stood on the top step and stared at me standing there with nothing to defend myself but an umbrella. It wasn't even open.

"Really?" he said, mockingly.

"It's deadly enough. You underestimated me once. I wouldn't do it again."

I was ready to jab him with the tip if I needed to. There was a small button that released the poison. If I tapped it briefly, it might only incapacitate him. But even if I was careful, there was a good chance the man would die.

I didn't want that. For a lot of reasons. He was like me for one. Killing one of our kind brought repercussions. And a dead man in my home would bring too many questions.

But I would kill him if I had to.

He smiled again, his head turned noticeably to the left so that his right eye bore into me more than his left.

He held out his hand. I thought he was offering it for me to shake. Honor or no, I wasn't going to take it. But as he opened his palm, my heart skipped. In it was the poison tip of the umbrella. I hadn't noticed it was missing.

Now, I really *was* just holding an umbrella as a weapon.

Talk about embarrassing.

I should've run when I had the chance.

He charged at me, and I did the only thing I could. I opened the umbrella. Believe it or not, the awkwardness of it caused him to grope for me, blindly.

There was a crash. Louder than his kicking the door off its hinges. This time everything became hazy. Noise and dust and dirt filled the air. There was commotion all around me. Debris was everywhere. Dazed, I glanced around. The front porch had been destroyed, and I was staring at a pair of brake lights.

Phoebe had backed a car into the front porch, smashing through the wooden steps and into my home.

"Alexander?" she said, her voice steady.

I didn't stop to think. I jumped onto the trunk and slid down the passenger side. I clawed at the door handle and pulled it open, then leaped into the front seat. I wasn't all the way in when Phoebe hit the gas, and the car lurched forward, sending a blast of colonial-era debris into my living room. The flying splinters of wood kept the man from coming after us. But the car was stuck. We had gone only ten feet.

"Put it in reverse," I screamed.

"What?"

"Put it in reverse. And floor it!"

Phoebe jammed the transmission in reverse and slammed her foot on the gas pedal. The car jerked backwards. I could hear the high-pitched whine of the spinning wheels, smell the acrid odor of burning rubber as the friction caused the tires to smoke.

"Now, throw it in drive."

She popped it in gear and stepped on the gas. The rear wheels spun, spitting out more fragments of the two hundred and fifty-year-old house. The car rocked forward and jumped over the remnants of my front porch, sending grass flying. The tires squealed as they hit the pavement.

I was not going to get my cleaning deposit back.

It was at least a minute or two before any of us could speak. Daniel looked like he'd seen a ghost: his own.

After carefully rubbing away the dust and slivers of wood from around my eyes, I blinked and looked around.

"Whose car is this?"

"I don't know."

I stared at her.

Daniel blurted out, "She stole it! The guy was running into the little store across the street, probably for some milk for his kids so they could eat cereal in the morning, and she just stole it. We're living Grand Theft Auto!"

I nodded. "Huh." I was impressed.

She let out a sigh, all the tension leaving her, and she suddenly looked as if we were out for a leisurely drive. "Where are we going?"

"NewYorksafehousegottagettothesafehouseinNewYork," Daniel said this as if the entire sentence were one word.

"We're not going to New York," I told him.

"But that's where the safe house is. I'm not feeling very safe at the moment. I could really use a safe house. Even a safe condo. A safe apartment. I'd even take a nice, safe prison cell right now."

"The place in Manhattan isn't the only option."

"You have more than *one* safe house?"

I turned to Phoebe. "Boston."

TEN

If He'd Only Seen The Sawdust, He'd Be Alive Today

The drive up to Boston was not pleasant. Oh, the foliage was beautiful. The little towns we passed through were charming and picturesque. The cute little cafe we ate in served up delicious food. To Phoebe's relief, we found some UMASS sweat pants in her size at a gas station. She changed out of her cheerleading outfit. The ones she picked out fit much better than the pants I brought. They didn't have tops in her size, so she had to wear the baggy sweatshirt I packed.

We mostly avoided the constant highway roadwork that usually accompanies a trip across Massachusetts. And as evening came, the sunset was simply stunning.

The reason the trip was unpleasant was because Daniel peppered me with questions the entire way. Even if I wanted to tell them, which I didn't, I wouldn't know how to begin or explain it so they wouldn't think I was straightjacket, padded-cell crazy.

At least it was easy to ignore Daniel. It's not that the questions weren't annoying. They were. It's not that his interrogation wasn't constant. It was. I could disregard his queries because the questions were pointless and absurd.

They weren't even questions. They were statements. Each one sounding more ridiculous than the last.

"Okay, so you're in the mob..."

"Maybe you're a gunrunner..."

"You're like a merchant of death or something..."

"You're a smuggler who ran off with whatever you were smuggling..."

"You're a criminal mastermind who kidnapped a mythical creature for ransom..."

"You're an international spy only pretending to be a high school student..."

There were a hundred others of these.

I stopped denying them after a dozen or so. I was starting to cut my tongue on my teeth from saying, "No. No. No. No."

Phoebe's scrutiny, on the other hand, was not as easy to dismiss.

About an hour into the drive, after having been quiet since we stopped to eat, she said, "The baseball." Then nothing else for a full minute. You could tell she was thinking. Her mind tossing the thoughts around. "It said, 'To Alexander.'"

I didn't respond.

"Babe Ruth," she added with emphasis. She kept her focus on the road, but I could feel her watching me out of the corner of her eye.

"That's why I like it," I said.

She couldn't grasp the truth, I knew that. But she sensed something wasn't right. While Daniel was going off the deep end trying to figure out what alien planet I came from, Phoebe was slowly constructing a framework of understanding, building a fence around the tidbits of information and facts she had gathered. And with each passing mile, each new thought that came to her, she was getting closer to completing that enclosure and corralling the truth.

"You're really amazing at so many different things. A little too amazing, actually. I can understand being great at lacrosse *or*... playing the piano. *Or* mastering karate or whatever you did in the woods." She waited. I said nothing. "But you don't even have a piano."

"Cause he doesn't play the piano," Daniel said, groggily from the back seat. His constant questions had slowed as the food hit his system and made him sleepy.

"He plays."

"No, he doesn't."

"Yes, he does," she said, glancing at Daniel in the rearview mirror. She turned for the first time to look at me. "I heard you. One time after school. There was this beautiful music coming from down the hall. I peeked in the window. You were playing with your eyes closed. I stood there listening for at least twenty minutes. You didn't have any music in front of you. What was it, Beethoven?"

"Chopin."

"It was mesmerizing. You were sitting there in your grass-stained lacrosse uniform, playing this incredibly intricate, passionate music. You still had your muddy cleats on."

She looked at me, her eyes begging to understand. She wanted to know. She needed to know. She wanted… Was it me? Or just my secret?

"My father forced me to take years of lessons when I was younger."

Which was true. Hundreds of years of lessons.

Phoebe tilted her head. "But...like I said, you don't have a piano at your house. How could you play something that complicated that well—without sheet music—and not practice every day?"

She was quiet. The only noises were the engine, the wind, and the tires on the road.

"There's something you don't want people to know about. And it's not just what's in that hidden room."

"And what about all that money and gold in the safe?" Daniel said.

Phoebe shook her head. "The gold. The money. The ability to play like a classical musician. Those aren't what he's hiding. They're symptoms of whatever it is."

The fence was about to be finished.

Daniel started up again with his theories.

"You're the last of your race and your enemies are trying to kill you..."

"You're a vampire and you're in love with a mortal girl..."

"You're in witness protection..."

"Daniel, will you shut up!" screamed Phoebe. "You're making me want to crash this car into a tree!" She composed herself, then turned to me. "Whatever it is you're hiding, I did things I'm going to get in a lot of trouble for. I think I deserve to know the truth."

"So do I," Daniel chimed in from the back.

I put my finger to my temple. My head was throbbing. More from the conversation of the last few minutes than the slug to the head the scar-faced man had given me.

I know it's just an arbitrary line on a map, but I let out a sigh of relief when we reached the city limits and I saw the sign: Entering Boston, Est. 1630.

I know Boston better than I know any place else in America. There were people we could turn to and secure places we could hide, including a brownstone my father kept in Back Bay, a tightly packed neighborhood of row houses that edged the river. It took me a while to warm up to the place because the land underneath it had once been tidal flats that flooded twice a day. The shallow shore was part of a Boston I used to know. A Boston surrounded entirely by water. A Boston that no longer existed. Beginning in the 1860s, the land was slowly filled in. Houses were constructed as lots gradually became available so that traveling west, house by house, block by block, you could clearly see the evolution of architectural tastes and styles from the 1860s through the early 1900s.

The house in Back Bay was our goal. It was less than a mile away and my father had been there recently. Maybe there would be a clue to his whereabouts.

"Telling you would put you in too much danger," I said.

"We already seem to be in danger!"

"*Nothing* compared to the danger you'd be in if I told you."

As if on cue, as we approached the intersection, the lights in every direction turned green all at once. My eyes saw it, but it took an instant for my mind to catch up.

By then, it was too late.

Our car was T-boned by a vehicle speeding through the cross street.

It happened so fast.

The vehicle impacted our car along the center pillar separating the front window from the rear. This may have been what saved our lives. Glass shattered against the curtains of inflating airbags, protecting us from the flying shards.

I was disoriented by the loud pop that preceded the deploying airbags.

Then...

Everything went silent.

Just a ringing in my ears.

And...and the clicking of something electrical in the car. Perhaps it was the ignition trying to engage. I heard a hiss coming from my right and saw steam rising out of the radiator of the other car.

My heart pounded in my chest. I pulled myself together.

"Are you all right," I asked Phoebe.

"Yes," she said. "But I can't start the car."

She was in shock. I put my hand on hers and pulled it away from the key.

"It's okay." I nodded calmly. "Daniel?"

I heard cursing come from the back seat, and I knew he was alive and well enough to complain.

"We have to get out of the car." I grabbed my backpack.

Phoebe was gripping the steering wheel. An airbag had blasted from the middle and was hanging like a shower cap. Two shower curtains hung from the dashboard.

"Right. We have to get out of the car," Phoebe repeated. "We should wait for the police." She thought about it. "No, we can't wait for the police. I stole this car. I stole this car, Alexander!"

"Yes, you did."

"Why did I steal a car!?"

"I can't get out." Daniel was trying to open the back door. The passenger side doors were useless, but the impact had twisted the frame, jamming the driver side doors as well.

The radiator steam was making it hard to see.

No, it wasn't steam. It was smoke coming from somewhere. I couldn't see any flames inside the car, at least, not yet.

Daniel started to panic. He was kicking at the door, trying to get it opened. We had to exit immediately. I wasn't worried the vehicle was going to explode, although, I guess I should have been, seeing as that's exactly what happened. I was concerned about the smoke. It could kill us quickly. Simple asphyxiation.

Even worse, the interior contained plastic and other materials that created toxic particles when burned. Once in our lungs, they would irritate the delicate lining, causing swelling and airway collapse. Some molecules could disable the cell's ability to absorb oxygen. These effects could develop hours and days later.

We could survive the flames and still not survive the fire.

"Cover your mouth. Breathe through your clothes," I said, coughing through the last few words.

I used my backpack to clear away the glass fragments on my window, then ripped out the deflated airbag and laid it across the opening as a barrier against any sharp edges. I saw a flicker of orange coming through the floor. I pushed myself out, sliding onto the hood of the other vehicle. I helped Phoebe out of the car next. Then she and I grabbed Daniel by the shirt and pulled him through the window just as the car was engulfed in flames. He continued kicking his feet. I thought maybe he was in shock, still trying to kick at the door, but it was because the soles of his shoes were smoking.

I told them, "Get to the middle. I'll meet you there." I pointed toward the wide, tree-lined mall between the two directions of Commonwealth Avenue.

"Aren't you coming?"

I motioned with my head. "The driver of the other car."

Daniel started off toward the trees, but Phoebe didn't move.

"I'm not leaving you."

Roaring in frustration as I turned back to the scene, I yelled, "Then get some help!"

The fire had spread to the other car. I tugged on the driver side door. It was stuck, but I could feel it budge. When it finally broke free, I was sent crashing to the ground.

I got up and did a visual check of the driver.

"Are you injured?" I asked.

She was staring at the flames like they were a television show. She turned slowly toward me. When she saw who I was, she started yelling. "You ran the red light! I had the green."

I glanced up at the signal lights. They were all green. Every direction.

There was a riddle that a jester in the court of Queen Elizabeth once told me. The only clue was this: *If he had only seen the sawdust, he'd be alive today.*

I could ask yes or no questions. If I asked anything that demanded an answer other than yes or no, or if I guessed incorrectly, the jester would repeat, "If he had only seen the sawdust, he'd be *alive* today." It was frustrating how many times I heard that sentence. The phrasing was always the same, but the word he emphasized would change. *Alive. Seen. Sawdust.*

I thought about giving up. At one point, I even begged him to tell me the answer. The jester just looked at me and said, "If he had only *seen* the sawdust, he'd be alive today." I wanted to strangle him. It took me days to figure out. Hundreds and hundreds of questions to narrow it down. And then...as if a bolt of lightning had struck, it hit me. A nugget of an idea so ridiculous, I had to be on the right path. When I finally solved the riddle, I screamed, I was so elated and proud, like I had cured polio or invented fire.

"Everybody had the green," I said to the woman.

"Everybody can't have the green!" she shouted. "If everybody had the green there would be chaos. People would be getting into accidents all the time."

Sawdust, I thought. She couldn't see the sawdust.

I looked around. People were approaching, a few from every direction.

"You need to get out of the car now, ma'am."

I pulled a penlight from one of the zippered pockets of the backpack and shined it into her eyes. Her pupils reacted slowly.

As people arrived at the scene, I grew tense. I wanted to run. My survival instinct kicking in. Some were just watching. A few were taking pictures and video. These images were getting posted to the Internet in real time. Thankfully, others were asking if we needed help. I furtively gazed at every face, looking for an enemy in the eyes of each stranger.

Phoebe found one man who looked like he was in charge of people, maybe a foreman at a construction site.

"What can I do?" he asked.

"We have to get her out of the car. She's stuck and in shock and we don't have much time before the fire's going to reach her."

I pointed inside the car. The man saw it, too. She was wedged between the seat and the steering wheel.

He immediately enlisted several people to help, shouting commands.

I went back to the woman.

I heard Phoebe's voice. "Alexander...the fire..."

I looked up. She was staring at the flames moving across the hood.

You're not supposed to move people after an accident, but we didn't have any choice. The fire was about to engulf the car and anyone inside it. For a moment, I forgot about my own concerns and focused on freeing the woman.

I couldn't get the seatbelt to release. I had to reach around her belly on each attempt.

"What are you doing? Don't touch me."

"I have to get you out of the vehicle, okay?"

"It is not okay!"

She was fighting me. I pulled out a butterfly knife from the backpack and flicked it open.

She screamed. "Help! He's trying to kill me!"

"He's trying to help you," Phoebe yelled.

I cut through the tightly woven nylon of the restraint.

The woman could see the flames getting closer, burning hotter. She fainted.

Once the seatbelt was gone, the foreman instructed two men to push up on the steering wheel, while he and I and another man struggled to extricate her. We finally slid her free and dragged her away from the car.

We were not ten feet away when both cars erupted into a massive fireball. A second later, the stolen vehicle exploded. Everyone hit the deck.

I pushed Phoebe to the ground behind a truck as the mushroom of fire rose into the air. The woman was face up, and I covered her body as best I could to protect her. I felt small pieces of hot debris hit my back. I shook them off before they burned through my clothes.

When I thought it was safe, I peered through the smoke and dust. There was nothing of the car we had been riding in but fragments of red-hot twisted metal.

I glanced the other way and saw Phoebe staring at me from under the truck. My ears were ringing. I mouthed, *Are you okay?*

She nodded.

The woman came to and immediately started screaming. "Get off me! Help!" She pulled out a rape whistle from around her neck and started blowing.

"Seriously, lady! What the hell is your problem?" shouted Phoebe. "He just saved your life! If he was going to cop a feel off anyone, I think it would be me!"

"It would be her," I said to the woman as I got off her.

She didn't respond or yell or blow the whistle. She had lost consciousness again. I noticed blood seeping onto her pants and her ankles were at right angles. The force of the collision had crushed her legs, fracturing them just above the bony humps of the medial malleolus.

More people were getting out of their cars, peeking through apartment windows, or joining the growing crowd. A couple of men at the edge of the throng caught my eye. The sight of them triggered warning signs in me.

"Phoebe," I whispered as I pulled her to me. "Stay close."

I bent down as the foreman came over.

"She's losing a lot of blood," I said.

I noticed several traffic cameras. I did my best to keep my face turned away. I wiped my forehead, my cheeks. Rubbed my eyes. It was perfectly normal to be doing these things, I had just been in an accident.

"Now I feel horrible for being rude to her," Phoebe said.

"People react differently to intense stress. She reacted badly."

I tore some fabric off the bottom of my shirt and turned the strip into a tourniquet that barely had any effect. A woman saw what I was doing and handed me her Hermes scarf.

"Here, this'll work much better."

I slipped the butterfly knife from my pocket and cut the scarf in two and slid the strips under the woman's leg and tied each one with a double overhand knot. The spread of blood slowed.

I used the knife to trim away the excess fabric of her pant leg. I wanted to have it out and available to use without seeming threatening.

"The tourniquets should slow the bleeding. Can you stay with her and make sure she's okay?" I asked the foreman. "I have to go check on our friend. He's disoriented and dazed and babbling nonsense."

"Isn't he always like that?" Phoebe whispered under her breath.

I shot her a hard look.

"Sure," the foreman said. "I called it in. Paramedics should be here soon." He looked at me strangely. Like he was concerned for me. Was I cut? Bleeding? "You okay?" he asked.

"Going on adrenaline. I don't feel a thing."

I could hear the sirens. I wanted to get as far away from here as possible before the police arrived.

"Make sure they know that her legs are broken before they move her," I said to him.

He nodded.

I went back to Phoebe. Staring at the remnants of the two cars. The enormity of what had happened was sinking in.

"I was such a bitch to that woman," she said, tears flowing.

"You were protecting me."

She nodded. "I was." She was trembling. "We were inside that car, Alexander."

"Yes," I said. "But we got out."

I instinctively wrapped my arms around Phoebe, and she relaxed her shoulder into my chest. I felt her breath, warm against my neck, and I closed my eyes. It's not like I've never brushed up against a girl in the last century. There have been hundreds of dances. Proms, sock hops, fancy balls. Thousands of notes passed back and forth. But it never felt like this. Never felt like time just stopped. The warmth of her body against mine. The scent of her hair. How could it still smell so good after all we've been through?

I was lost in the embrace, breathing her in. I had started out comforting her. But it ended up comforting me.

I've said it before, *nobody* understands chemistry. Not even someone with centuries to ponder it. That spark of attraction, that feeling that runs through your body, it *is* a chemical reaction. And true chemistry is when the thousandth touch feels the same—or better—than the first.

I would never get to that thousandth touch with Phoebe. Maybe not with anyone.

I wanted to tell her how I felt. The words were forming on my lips when she spoke into my chest.

"My parents are probably freaking out right now. And I can only imagine how angry Craig is going to be."

I tensed up. And she noticed.

"I didn't mean—"

"It's okay," I said.

I didn't flinch because of what she said about Craig, not

completely, at least. It was that her words made me open my eyes, and I realized I hadn't been paying attention. We were vulnerable. I couldn't relax until we were someplace secure, and even then, I couldn't let my guard down. Not until I understood what was going on. If my house hadn't been safe, I wasn't sure any place would be.

"Let's get Daniel and get moving."

I grabbed Phoebe's hand. Pushing through a line of onlookers, I stumbled over something. It was one of the two men I had been worried about. He was lying on the ground, unconscious.

I had a good grip on Phoebe's arm, which saved me from falling flat on my face.

We made our way across the eastbound lanes of Comm Ave. and found Daniel pacing the grassy mall that divided the avenue. He was not pleased to see us.

"I'm feeling very angry right now! You and you! Both of you! You leave me here! All by myself. I don't know *where* you are. I'm totally having a breakdown and what are you two doing—"

"Saving someone's life," Phoebe said.

"Oh, you…you always have the perfect excuse, don't you?" He instantly lowered his voice to a whisper. "People…are trying to kill us."

"They're not trying to kill us," I said.

"No, no, not you. Us." Daniel motioned between himself and Phoebe.

Her mouth curled in irritation. "Which is it? Are you pissed we left you? Or are you pissed being with us is dangerous? You can't have it both ways." Phoebe turned to me and saw something in my eyes. "Are you okay?"

"Is *he* okay?"

Why was everyone asking me that? Did I have a piece of sheet metal sticking out of my forehead? I put my hand to my cheek, ran it through my hair. It came back dirty and smudged, but there was no blood. No pain.

I guess it was the look in my eyes that worried everyone.

Maybe it was anger. Maybe it was fear. Maybe it was the steeliness that arises when fear and anger meet. I've been trained to fight, to survive, to play an orchestra full of instruments, but I've never had one of my own kind after me.

I wasn't okay, but I nodded, halfheartedly. "We need to get off the street as soon as we can."

Daniel kept glancing back at the smoldering wreckage and the pillar of smoke, saying, "Oh, man," over and over.

I took a peek only once. The signal lights on every corner were still green. Just that one intersection. I had that feeling in my chest and in my gut, the one you get when you know this wasn't some random act, some error in the system. Streetlights flash red when they fail, or they go dark. They don't simultaneously turn green.

I put my head down and tried not to look like we were in a hurry.

"You don't think that was a coincidence," Phoebe said.

I didn't say anything.

"Like the lights at the stadium," she added.

"You think somebody hacked into the traffic light controls and did that on purpose?" Daniel asked. "C'mon! Glitches happen all the time. It's not like they've got state-of-the-art laptops running these things. They're like decades-old technology. It's lucky they work at all."

This coming from the guy who had been spouting conspiracy theories the last hundred and fifty miles. "You're a cyborg coming back from the future..." Now he was the sane one?

"You have to admit it's a little strange we just happened to be driving through that intersection the moment the glitch happened," said Phoebe, raising an eyebrow. "A second later, we'd have been through without a scratch. A few seconds earlier, and other cars would have crashed or started honking, and we'd have stopped to avoid the danger."

Daniel scrunched up his face while he shook his head. "That would mean coordination on a massive scale."

"Yes, it would," I said.

That made him swallow hard.

"It's the sawdust."

"What?" Phoebe said.

Daniel turned around and started walking backwards. "Again with that stupid ass riddle!"

I had tormented Daniel for one very, very, very long evening where I told him the riddle and forced him to ask me questions until neither one of us could keep our eyes open. Daniel tried to give up after ten minutes. I finally told him after several hours, but not before he'd heard me repeat, "If he had only seen the sawdust, he'd be alive today," at least three hundred times.

The "he" was a dwarf. And not just any dwarf, but the smallest man in the kingdom. As such, he was given a title, money, and servants by the King. The dwarf was only nineteen, but his legs were not well-formed, and he needed a cane to walk.

There was another man in the kingdom—less than an inch taller—who because of that minute difference lived a wretched life. Poor. Hungry. Persecuted. It was this man who began to secretly whittle away at the shorter man's cane, sanding fractions of an inch off the bottom each week.

The shorter man became alarmed, thinking he was getting taller. If he grew any more, he would lose his title and his life of ease. The other man would gain the favor of the King and all the comforts he had enjoyed.

The King, you see, had no use for the second smallest man in the land.

So the dwarf went to an apothecary, asking for help. The apothecary gave him an array of potions. Poisons, really. Things to make him stop growing. He drank the foul liquids every night. They made him sick. They made him vomit. But they didn't prevent his increase in height. Of course, he wasn't growing. The second shortest man was paring down his cane week after week. The dwarf went back to the apothecary and asked him to make new potions that were even more powerful. The apothecary warned the dwarf of the danger, but the diminutive man would not back down. The apothecary gave in and prepared stronger potions.

The shortest man in the kingdom took the poison that would take his own life. Willingly. Knowingly. But...

If he had only seen the sawdust, he'd be alive today.

I told Daniel how amazing it was to finally figure it out, the satisfaction I felt, leaving out the fact that it had been hundreds of years ago, in a kingdom that didn't exist anymore. He just looked at me. "You spent several days, asked hundreds of questions—"

"Thousands."

"Thousands of questions, just to figure out that one midget was trying to off another midget?"

"You know, before television, before people had computers, game consoles, and smartphones, people used to actually use their brains."

"Sounds like a nightmare."

The way the jester told me the details made me wonder if it was more than just a riddle, that perhaps there had been some truth to the story.

It also made me realize that the smallest details can have serious consequences.

If I had only seen the lights turn green and acted immediately, we could have avoided the accident. If I had only noticed the missing poison tip on the umbrella, I would have chosen another weapon against the man in my house. If I had been more observant, watching the trees, not just the forest floor, we wouldn't have gotten outflanked in the woods, and Braeden might still be alive. Hyper-vigilance is taxing on the body, but I would need to be much more attentive if we were going to make it out of this alive.

"What riddle?" Phoebe asked.

"This stupid riddle about a midget."

"Dwarf."

"Aren't they called 'little people?'" Phoebe asked.

"He's tiny!" Daniel and I said at the same time.

"All I'm saying is, if he'd only seen the sawdust, he'd be alive today."

Daniel cupped his hands over his ears. "I can't hear that one more time!"

Phoebe stopped. "What the hell are you two talking about?"

Daniel was right. Strange things happen. People are too quick to tie them up in a neat bow and say, "I'm cursed," or "I didn't forward that chain letter email to eight friends and look what happened," or "we're the target of a giant conspiracy."

Maybe I was letting the struggles of the last few hours get to me. I was drained.

The constant dumping of adrenaline into my system was taking its toll. Just playing lacrosse got me pumped up, then add in how close the game was and getting knocked on my ass at the end. My encounter with Braeden at the hospital, the stadium lights crashing into the stands at the football game, the attack in the woods, fighting off ten men, the scar-faced man walking into my house, having to fight my way out of my own home to get away, and then being slammed by a speeding car, pulling my friends and the other driver out of the cars seconds before the vehicles exploded. My body had burned itself out. I was still running on adrenaline. But there's a point where you physically shut down. Could this be paranoia brought on by fatigue? Perhaps. But sometimes, like William S. Burroughs said, "Paranoia's just having all the facts."

"All right, so, there's this dwarf and—" I stopped. "It doesn't matter. We should assume anything is possible and that seemingly unrelated details could matter very, very much."

"What's the 'sawdust' in this scenario," asked Daniel.

"Being wary and watchful of Braeden and completely missing the real threat. Thinking that because I've got a house even my father doesn't know I have, I don't need to take better precautions. Having signal lights turning green in all directions simultaneously."

Daniel thought about it for a moment.

"Braeden show's up, you don't know who he is. It's his fault for not telling you sooner to expect trouble. And someone showing up at your secret lair, okay, not good, but, again, that's on Braeden. He led them to you. It's not a stretch to imagining them following you home from school. But controlling signal lights? That's a whole different level of upsetting. If you have people after you that can do *that*..." Daniel stopped. "We might as well just lay down right now." To prove his point, he laid down on the path. "We're dead."

"Get up!"

"What for? This isn't a little sawdust from sandpaper. If they can hack a signal light at the exact moment we're passing under it, this is a woodchipper. What kind of chance do we have against a woodchipper?"

"Not much with you lying on the ground."

"How far is this house of yours?" Phoebe asked. She was exhausted and needed to get off her feet.

I was spent as well, but I couldn't let her or Daniel know that. I had to be strong. For them. I breathed in, filling my chest. The cold air pierced my lungs, the pain doing what I had hoped it would do. Stimulate me.

There've been many instances in the past when I had to draw on my reserves. My monthly sojourns into the woods were part of keeping that skill honed. Hunger. Cold. Fatigue. They can sap your strength. Dull your senses. Slow your mind. Fear is a great motivator. On the battlefield, it can keep you awake, and keep you alive. The problems begin when the body stops. Rest is for the weary. It's also for the dead. Rest in *peace*. You don't rest in war. Because once a drained, worn out body relaxes, all too often, it shuts down.

Another shot of adrenaline jolted me, a hot rush flooded my core as I caught a glimpse of the man with the scar. I realized immediately, it was someone else. Just a man heading home. Still, my muscles tensed up as he passed. The man with the scar had rattled me. It wasn't just because he had held a sword to my throat, it was his magnetism, his confidence, his force of being that demanded respect and fealty. I've met kings, and I've met presidents, and even among them, very few had a presence equal to the man with the scar.

Rare is the person—my father being one—that commanded such a sense of power.

I have fought for myself, protected myself, taken care of myself for over five hundred years, but I knew I needed my father's help if a man like this was after me.

I spun around, trying to get my bearings. We were on Commonwealth Avenue close to the restaurants and shops on Newbury Street. About three short blocks from my father's house. Eight long blocks away from Boston Common.

The brownstone was close. Two minutes away at most. Warmth. Rest. Safety. I pushed the thought of rest out of my mind. It was a dangerous thought at the moment.

"C'mon, it's this way."

Phoebe followed immediately. We didn't bother to wait for Daniel who was still on the ground. Either he would come or he wouldn't.

He caught up with us about half a block later.

"You were just going to leave me there?"

Both Phoebe and I answered. "Yes!"

We got off Commonwealth. It was less conspicuous to make our way along the side streets. We were close to the brownstone now.

The man in my house had found me. I had to assume he knew where we were. Maybe he knew everything.

I could evade the police. Slip from one identity to another easily. Keep myself hidden from the government. Stay off the grid. Remain anonymous. But *this* was beyond my abilities. I was in no way prepared for eluding someone who had all my skills and an additional three thousand years of practice, training, and resources.

It was a block later that I realized someone was following us. I couldn't make out who the figure was, but I knew that it wasn't the man with the scar or any of the attackers from the woods. No, the person tailing us was much smaller. The pursuer wore a black hoodie that obscured their face.

"C'mon," I said, quickening the pace.

"What is it?"

"Probably nothing."

Daniel looked around. "When has it been nothing so far today?"

The figure passed under a street lamp, but the hood cast a shadow so that there was nothing but blackness where the face should be. It reminded me of the Angel of Death, and even though my rational mind didn't believe in any of that, I still found it unnerving.

The safe house was just around the corner.

The person's gait was unsteady. Awkward. Was it a chronic state, an injury, or was there something else affecting the stranger's walk? A weapon?

We reached the next intersection. My father's house was thirty seconds away if we sprinted. I could see it, half a block on the left. I had one foot in the crosswalk when I saw someone on the steps of a house across the street from my father's. They couldn't know about this place, could they? I didn't think it was possible, but I watched the man suck on his cigarette, the tip glowing orange as he leaned against the iron railing, his foot on the stone half-wall. Nobody smoked like that here. They'd take a walk, or smoke on the roof or the back porch. Not on the steps. Not in *this* neighborhood.

Okay, maybe I was overthinking things. It was probably nothing, but given everything else that had gone on, I couldn't risk it. I quickly changed directions. "This way."

I hurried Daniel and Phoebe around the corner.

I knew this street, the houses, the places to hide. I glanced to the right and saw a darkened alcove beside the steps of one of the row houses. Before they could protest, I pushed Daniel and Phoebe into the cramped, shadowy space.

"What are you doing?"

I put my fingers to my lips. "Shhhhh."

We waited in silence. I heard the footsteps as the person turned the corner. The steps quickened for a moment and then stopped. Whoever it was realized we couldn't have made it to the end of the block that quickly. We had to be somewhere close.

The footsteps started and stopped several times, but the person didn't seem to be approaching.

Then…

Nothing.

The night air was cold. Daniel was against a door that led under the house. Phoebe was against him, and I was pressed against Phoebe. I could feel her body, her chest rising and falling with her breath. We were packed tightly together. Even more than the warmth, the closeness of Phoebe comforted me. I fought hard to keep my attention focused on the street.

The door in the alcove creaked on its hinges at the weight of us against it, and I felt movement behind me.

"Oh, God. Daniel, what the hell—"

"Shhhhhh!"

"I'm sorry. I'm sorry. It's—just the adrenaline."

"Seriously?"

"It's not my fault."

"Be quiet and keep still," I whispered.

I couldn't see it in the darkness, but I knew Daniel was turning red with embarrassment and sporting a hard-on. Phoebe exhaled an annoyed sigh in my direction.

"Disgusting," she said under her breath.

"Not my fault."

"Both of you…shut up." I whisper-shouted. I tried to calm my breathing and listen.

After a moment, the footsteps started up again. Slowly, then more confidently. At the sharp sound, a cold shiver ran through me. The clack-clack, clack-clack was uneven. It could be a shotgun causing the asymmetrical pattern. Or maybe a sword. Although, I doubted that. No one wanted their blade at the unnatural angle hiding it in a pant leg would require. Besides looking ridiculous, it made unsheathing the weapon difficult and awkward. With a sword, quick reaction and easy access were paramount.

Not likely a sword then.

I ran through disarming a person with a long barrel gun in my mind, picturing different scenarios depending on the hand the stranger shot with. My advantage was surprise. The stranger knew we were somewhere on the street, but they didn't know exactly where. I knew by the sound precisely their location.

They were approaching from our left.

The footsteps began to speed up and grow louder, echoing through the quiet street. Closer. Louder. Closer. Louder. Just a few feet away now. As the small figure passed by the alcove, I launched out of the darkness and grabbed them.

Wrapped in my hands was nothingness. A ghost. Fabric without substance. I continued to hear the footsteps, but there was no one making them. No legs. No shoes. No body.

Suddenly, I was struck by a stick or a pole or something.

Phoebe and Daniel screamed.

Then someone jumped off the front steps of the row house and landed on me. I grasped at anything I could get a hold of, which wasn't much more substantial than the nothingness I had snatched at the moment before. A fist flew by me, a flash of spotted gray-white flesh that missed my cheek by a few inches. And that's when I saw it. They were holding a gun. Not a shotgun, or a pistol, but a stun gun. The armed hand reached for me, and I quickly ducked out of the way. Phoebe jerked instinctively to the side. There was no one left but Daniel. The stun gun connected with his chest and sparks flew, illuminating the darkness like lightning in a bad horror flick. He shook violently. I knocked the person's hand away, lessening the jolt Daniel received. In an instant, my friend was laid out on the sidewalk. A twitching rag doll.

I thrust my forearm into the stranger's throat and forced them against the brick wall. The arms and shoulders were bony and frail. The skin on the hand holding the weapon was pale and wrinkled.

I whipped off the black wool scarf covering the face, and I heard Phoebe gasp behind me. I have to admit, I was shocked as well.

"Mrs. Avery?"

"Mrs…" Phoebe trailed off. "…Avery?"

What the hell was my U.S. History teacher doing here, a hundred and forty miles from home?

I figured the best tactic was to ask her. "What the hell are you doing here a hundred and forty miles from home?"

"Get your hands off of me, Grant. Striking a teacher. That's a suspendable offense," she said in her rough, untold-decades-of-being-a-smoker voice.

Even though we weren't in her classroom or the halls of Monument High, I had the feeling I was about to get sent down to the principal's office. It might seem strange that with as many teachers as I've dealt with—the great and the grating—I would be hesitant to face down someone as frail as Mrs. Avery. But she had taken years to perfect her intimidating craggy and cantankerous persona.

I had never seen anyone as old as Mrs. Avery, at least, not anyone that was still upright and walking around. That she could follow us at our hurried pace and then jump off a staircase onto my back, it boggled the mind.

But we weren't in school. And she wasn't a teacher here in the shadows.

"I'm sorry, Mrs. Avery, but right now, I'm the one asking the questions. And you're the one that needs to answer them correctly."

She stared at me as if she was considering whether or not I had the guts to stand up to her.

I pressed my forearm a little harder into her throat. "Don't test me tonight, Mrs. Avery. You won't like my answers."

"Alexander," Phoebe said, her voice calm and velvety.

I think she was hoping her tone would defuse the situation, but my mood was a cool kind of dangerous.

"It's okay, Phoebe."

I glanced down at Mrs. Avery's feet. She was barefoot. Her toes were gnarled and the nails were thick and yellow. She had a marking on her ankle. Tattoos had become commonplace. There were kids at school who were inked. Not me. I wouldn't go as far as to say it was forbidden, but I needed my body to be clean and clear of any markings, piercings, anything that could give me away. My face and DNA were enough. Still, it was a little strange for a woman as old as Mrs. Avery to have a tattoo. It was a simple design. Two triangles facing point to point, somewhat reminiscent of a Roman numeral X with the traditional bars on the top and bottom.

The hoodie and the cloak were spread out on the sidewalk. I rifled through the jacket. In the pocket, I felt something hard, rectangular. I hunted for the opening, found it, reached inside, and pulled out a smartphone. This was the source of the footsteps. A memo app's date and time stamp showed the recording was made only moments ago. The cloak was wrapped around a cross made from two metal rods like the ones from the alarm company yard signs that peppered the neighborhood. Hooked to the jacket was a long strand of translucent monofilament. Fishing line was almost as useful as duct tape. You could do a lot with fishing line. You could catch fish with it, but there were myriad other uses that might mean the difference between living and dying. It was an effective weapon around someone's throat. You could set traps with it. You could use it to hang food in the woods or pictures in the house. You could cut a cake with it. Nice, even slices. You could even create a life-sized marionette that might trick someone into thinking you were walking down a darkened street.

"Clever."

"You aren't the only one that's capable, Mr. Grant."

I was fairly sure Mrs. Avery wasn't like me. My father had assured me of that after my Parent-Teacher conference. Unless…

"Did my father send you?"

"You aren't that smart, are you, Grant?"

Honestly, I wasn't feeling very smart at the moment.

I looked into her eyes that were slightly cloudy from cataracts. Old yearbooks testified that she had been at the school for decades. My father preached planning, multiple exit strategies, contingency plans, stockpiling. I had chosen Great Barrington myself. Of course, I selected it from a number of options my father and I had discussed over the last half-century. It was possible Mrs. Avery was working for him. My father paraded in and out of my life. He was a caring father, but not a doting one. I've always known there were people in his employ whose only task was keeping an eye on me. More now than when I was younger. I was easier to control then. It was a game he and I played. I'd try to figure out who his minions were so I could keep some of my teenage life private, and he would devise new ways to thwart my efforts. Technology was good for certain kinds of intelligence, but any spymaster will tell you, it's boots on the ground that give you the greatest advantage.

Then again, Mrs. Avery could be working for someone else. Unless she could give me some verifiable information, something like Braeden had, I couldn't trust her.

I pulled my arm away, and she breathed fully for the first time in over a minute. I grabbed her makeshift puppet and used the fishing line to bind her hands.

"I've been following you since the football game." She turned to Phoebe. "Nice job stealing the car, young lady. I always knew you were a juvenile delinquent."

Phoebe was taken aback.

"And that one," she nodded toward Daniel. "Was he dropped on his head as a child?"

"What did I do?" Daniel asked, still mostly unconscious.

"Absolutely nothing," she sneered.

"And what have you been doing?" I said.

"Trying to save you idiots. There were two of them following you." She kicked at the stun gun. "I took both of them out for you. You're welcome. I bought you some time to get away. But more are coming."

I thought back to the man I tripped over. My instincts told me to be wary of him when I noticed him at the scene. And then... there he was, lying unconscious on the pavement. Mrs. Avery had apparently safeguarded me at a vulnerable moment.

"Come with me, Grant. A safe place is very close."

It all fit together. Maybe too well. Which is why I couldn't trust her. The two men might be her accomplices. She may have knocked them out or had them pretend to be unconscious to gain my confidence.

"I'm not leaving them. And we're not leaving with you."

I finished tying the knots. Not too tight. Just enough to hold her for a while.

She glared at me, her milky blue eyes boring into my soul. "How do you do it? Tell me. "

"Do what?"

"The tests. Do you break into my office and steal the questions?"

No, she was not like me.

"I know my history." I picked the hoodie off the sidewalk and put it over Mrs. Avery's shoulders. "You should be able to get out of that in about fifteen minutes."

"You'll never get away with them weighing you down," she said.

I watched her for a long moment. She was being sincere. At least, she believed what she was saying.

"Excuse me, can somebody tell me why I'm lying on the ground?"

"And he's back with us," snapped Phoebe.

"I can't move," Daniel said as he looked up from the ground. He actually was moving. Well, twitching at least. He would feel like he ran a marathon when he stood up.

Mrs. Avery sneered in Daniel's direction, then turned back toward me. "Darkness is approaching," she said. "Autarky." The word came out of her as if it were a death curse. But I knew she meant it as a warning. The word and her delivery sent a chill through my body. "Only *those* prepared will survive."

I stepped back from the old woman. Phoebe became visible in my peripheral vision. She was watching me. Concerned. In a moment, I was going to lose her respect, and probably destroy whatever feelings—if there were any—she felt for me.

I glanced at the fishing line wrapped around Mrs. Avery's wrist. I couldn't risk her getting free no matter how unlikely. "I'm sorry I have to do this," I said as much to Phoebe as to Mrs. Avery.

I snatched the stun gun off the ground, pressed the electrodes into Mrs. Avery's right pectoral muscle, pulled the trigger, and shocked her. It was a quick burst, no more than an instant. Mrs. Avery slumped to the ground.

Phoebe let out a horrified cry that she muffled instantly.

Daniel and Mrs. Avery were less than a foot away from each other on the cement, lying face to face. He gazed into the old woman's blank stare. "I have wanted to do that all year," he said.

Phoebe went to her. "You could have stopped her heart."

Putting two fingers to her neck, I checked Mrs. Avery's carotid artery. Her pulse was steady and surprisingly strong.

After spending a semester in her classroom, I had the feeling it would take a lot more than fifty thousand volts to kill this woman. "She's fine. We have to keep moving. C'mon, get up." I tried to help Daniel to his feet only his legs weren't working. In fact, his entire body didn't seem to be functioning. "Daniel, I need you to get up!"

I bent down and stared into his face from above. Like he'd done to me when Craig Coulter laid me out near the twenty-yard line on my birthday.

"I'm moving my legs," Daniel explained.

"No, you're not."

"Well, they're moving in my head."

"I need them moving on your body."

I motioned to Phoebe, and she stepped to the other side of Daniel. We lifted him, our arms locked under his armpits. It was like trying to make water stand up.

We dragged Daniel along the sidewalk, the front of his sneakers making a popping noise as they caught the cracks in the cement.

"Keep your legs moving. That will clear the lactic acid. And increasing your circulation will also get more blood sugar to your muscles."

"I want a candy bar," he moaned.

"We need to get you something to eat."

My father's house was only a block away. There'd be food and maybe answers to my father's whereabouts.

Phoebe glanced back in the direction of Mrs. Avery. The old woman wasn't visible from the street, she was hidden behind the steps of the row house.

"Do you really think she'll be okay?"

I nodded.

She was quiet for a moment. "You were protecting us back there," she said. "Being overly cautious. I understand."

A wave of relief rushed through my body. It lasted only a moment. A beautiful, wonderful moment.

Then I saw the man smoking on the steps across from my father's house. That would mean four cigarettes, maybe five. He was waiting for someone. Waiting for us.

I made a sharp right at the intersection, slipping past my father's block. I tried to keep the pace as fast as I could without drawing attention to ourselves.

"We're not going to the safe house?" gargled Daniel.

"I don't think it's very safe."

Phoebe let out a frustrated sigh as she stopped and grabbed my arm. "I want to go home." Her voice wavered, but her resolve didn't.

"I know." I didn't want her to go home. "We'll get you home."

"I want to stop walking like I'm made of Jell-O. I'm really tingly. What happened?"

Phoebe shot him an acid grin. "Mrs. Avery zapped you with fifty thousand volts of electricity."

"She never liked me." Daniel stared down at his feet, which I was kicking forward with each step. When my blows began to elicit yelps, meaning the feeling was returning, he dared to put more weight on his legs. After a few steps, we were able to let go of him.

With the burden of Daniel's dead weight lifted, Phoebe and I moaned in ecstasy. You never understand how painful something is until it stops.

"Why was Avery talking about anarchy?" he asked.

"Not anarchy. Autarky."

"What the hell is that?"

"It means to be self-sufficient. A country, a city, a group that can survive without outside help."

"Is she saying only preppers will survive? Survive what?" Phoebe asked.

"I don't know."

Darkness is approaching, she said.

It felt like it was already here.

We cut back up to Commonwealth and took the path in the center of the street.

"Where are we going now?" Phoebe asked. I could hear the weariness in her voice.

"We need more than a safe place. We need help." And I knew where to find it. Beacon Hill was just north of the Common. "Another ten minutes at most."

Commonwealth Avenue dead-ended at the Public Gardens. We cut through the park, past the statue of George Washington, drawing his sword, which was missing its blade this evening. It had been stolen so often, it was now replaced with a plastic sword when it was replaced at all.

We took the bridge over the lagoon, then across the street to the Common.

Phoebe took my hand. I wasn't sure if she did it to make us look like one of the other couples walking in the park under the evening sky, or if she wanted to hold my hand. Either way, it felt nice.

"I've only been to Boston a couple of times," Daniel said, looking around.

I wondered if he'd hit his head in the crash, or maybe it was the stun gun had something to do with him acting stranger than normal.

"We go to the aquarium every single time." He paused. "I hate fish."

When we reached the far edge of the Common along Beacon Street, I stopped.

"What is it?" Phoebe asked.

"Shhh. I'm trying to figure out which way it is. The street's only a block long, and if you're off, you miss it. I haven't been here in twenty years." As soon as the words left my mouth, I knew, I had screwed up. I tried not to react.

There was a second of nothing, and I thought maybe I had gotten away with my colossal boneheadedness. We waited for the traffic to pass, then we crossed Beacon.

We weren't halfway to the other side before Phoebe said, "Twenty years?"

"It's a figure of speech."

She nodded. Then a second later: "No. A figure of speech is 'I haven't been here in a million years' or 'This suitcase weighs a ton.' 'I haven't been here in twenty years' is pretty specific."

I could tell she was having trouble getting over that last hurdle, the one that led straight to the truth. It was an enormous mental obstacle. Too high for most people to climb.

"It's not much farther. It's this way."

We turned left on Chestnut.

Phoebe was processing everything. The events of the day. My flimsy explanations. All the various trails of sawdust I'd been leaving behind the past year and a half. I could see the truth starting to bubble up inside her. And then, the final realization exploded in her head.

Her feet kept moving, but they were just mindlessly following mine.

"There's something wrong with you."

I felt a stab in my stomach.

She let go of my hand.

A few steps later, forehead wrinkled, she looked at me. "Why would you fake an autographed baseball signed by Babe Ruth… to you?"

I kept walking. This was definitely the way. The modern street lights were gone, replaced by gas lights.

"And those pictures…" She stepped away from me. As if I was contagious.

I couldn't have picked a worse time to lead us up a narrow, dark, mist-covered, gaslit alley, but this was where we needed to go.

Acorn Street was one of the oldest in Boston and one of the last with its original cobblestone.

"It's up ahead at the top of the hill," I said.

She hesitated, gazing into the dark passage that was so beautiful in the daylight and so foreboding at night.

"We just need to get to the last house on the right, and we're going to be okay."

"No, we're not going to be okay. Nothing is going to be okay." She started to shake like there was an earthquake within her. "Is this where you take your victims?"

Still a little out of it, Daniel had been blissfully ignorant of the scene playing out until now. "Victims? Whoa! Hold on. What are you talking about?"

I stepped onto Acorn followed tentatively by Daniel a few paces behind with Phoebe lagging at the back.

"I'm still on this 'victims' thing. Why are we walking up this horror-creepy—"

"—historically enchanting—"

"—disturbingly spooky ass street."

"You both have to trust me. I don't want you to get hurt. On this street, we'll find shelter and protection."

"Yeah," Daniel said. "That doesn't sound creepy or weird at all."

Acorn was eerily quiet. The tiny cobblestone street rose up from

West Cedar, lit dimly by gas lamps along the curbs. More illumination escaped the white-paned, black-shuttered windows and brightly lit doorways of the brick row houses. The slope to the top was gentle. This wasn't San Francisco, although Boston reminds me of that Bay Area City. The hills in Boston were no longer as steep, having been leveled over the years to fill in the surrounding water. A few yards up Acorn and any semblance of modern Boston disappeared. The houses surrounding us stood as they did before cars and electricity. The street was cleaner now and didn't smell of horse shit and hay, but a fire burning in one of the living rooms dropped smoke into the street, and the scent and the haze brought me back.

I could almost hear the carriages in the distance.

Our footsteps echoed off the brick walls. Daniel's shoes were the loudest, the heat from the burning car had melted the bottoms of his soles, causing the spongy material to harden. The sound of our steps was irregular as we tried to navigate the uneven cobblestone. I found the hiss of the gas flowing to the lamps comforting. A light dew had fallen as night washed over the city and there was a sheen of moisture on the stones.

I didn't hear Phoebe's approach or feel her reaching into the backpack and pulling out the baseball until she blocked my path. She stood staring at the ball, rolling it over and over in her hand.

"People are chasing you, ramming cars into us and you take a baseball?"

"It's important to me."

"Why? It's a fake."

She cocked her arm, about to pitch the ball down the hill, and I jerked toward her, clawing at her hand, at the baseball.

"Noooo!" I seized the ball. Held it. I don't know why this damn thing meant so much to me. Me and my father at Fenway, I guess.

Phoebe stared at me. But I didn't meet her eyes.

"It's not a fake," I said. I stepped around her.

As we got to the top of the rise, everything began to look familiar.

I headed up to a black door with a "2" on it, the house flush against the street.

I gently ran a fingertip over The Babe's signature. They had won that day. He'd pitched a good game. Struck out three times. Hit a home run.

"What does that mean?" she asked, gesturing her chin toward the baseball.

I shrugged. This was not the time or place for explanations. I'd have to reveal the truth to Phoebe and Daniel. Taking them here made that inevitable. Sooner or later, they'd figure everything out whether I told them or not.

"What does what mean?" Daniel said.

I knocked on the solid oak door. Number 2 Acorn Street. And waited. The gaslights hissed. A breeze meandered through Beacon Hill and up over the cobblestone street. I breathed out and let my breath mix with the drifting smoke from the chimneys. On the other side of this door was safety. On the other side of this door was help. On the other side of this door was the one person who would know what to do. After a moment, a man who appeared to be in his late eighties answered.

When I saw him, the stress drained from my body like water after stepping out of a pool.

I smiled and felt the grin spreading across my face. His amber eyes lit up.

"How are you?" My words were muffled as I hugged him.

"I was expecting you," he said.

I raised an eyebrow. "Really? That's not good."

"Perhaps not. But it *is* good to see you."

I turned to my new friends and introduced them to my very, very, *very* old friend.

"Phoebe, Daniel, I would like you to meet Stephen Engel. He's my oldest friend in the world." I heard Engel chuckle at my words.

Phoebe's head snapped toward me. Daniel didn't understand. And I relaxed.

We were safe. For the moment.

If he'd only seen the sawdust, he'd be alive today.

And if I'd only known these historic homes and this quaint old street would be obliterated in less than three hours, I might have taken a longer look before I stepped inside.

REVELATION

"REVELATION CAN BE MORE PERILOUS THAN
REVOLUTION."

—VLADIMIR NABOKOV

- ELEVEN -
The Oldest Man I Have
Ever Known

It didn't go as smoothly as I expected, and believe me, I had expected it to go not smoothly at all. Yet, to fail even my lowest expectations was a stunning achievement in its own way. Trying to explain to my friends that, although I look about fifteen or so, I'm actually a hundred times that old was the least of it.

Engel was genuinely glad to see me, but I could tell he wasn't as pleased to meet Phoebe and Daniel. I've known Engel since I was a child, and he's been ancient for as long as I can remember. I don't mean that figuratively, I mean, really, truly, *ancient*. Still, this slender, nearly nine thousand-year-old man's intense gaze filled me with apprehension. A look that revealed his displeasure at my bringing outsiders into his home.

Even though I've been alive for fifteen hundred years, seen just about everything the world can throw at me: war, famine, disease, it's amazing how in times of stress we run to those who have comforted us as children. And that, more than any other reason, was why I had come to Acorn Street.

I needed help. I needed comfort. And I knew Engel would offer me both.

We stood in the foyer. Phoebe was trembling. Daniel was trying to get someone to tell him what was going on and why everyone was so uptight.

I managed to get Phoebe and Daniel settled in the living room.

I asked Engel's housekeeper, Mrs. Dunn, if she could offer them water and aspirin and something sugary to help Daniel recover from getting zapped with the stun gun.

"Maybe they would like some rum. I have some excellent rum," Engel offered. "Or scotch. Scotch is good for the nerves."

"Yes," said Daniel at the same moment I said, "No."

Mrs. Dunn gave her employer a hard look, then started for the kitchen. "I'll get something appropriate for them."

"I'll have you know, Mrs. Dunn, I was drinking beer from the time I was a baby," he said. "It was that or wine."

"Yes, because it was safer than drinking fresh water back then."

"I still think it is."

Engel pulled me into the small library off the main hall. The rooms were miniature in comparison to more modern homes, but there was a warm charm to the place. Everything was handcrafted. The house was worth millions now, but even when it was built, it cost Engel a great deal of money.

"Have you lost your mind?" he said, calmly. "What are you doing bringing them here?"

I filled him in on the situation. He already knew most of the details. There were news reports about the tower collapse at the football stadium. The stolen car. The damage at my house. There was nothing on the news about Braeden or the others in the woods.

"Braeden is dead," I said.

Engel's reaction was limited to a slightly stronger than normal exhale through his nostrils. "I am sorry to hear that. I've heard his praises."

"I know it was stupid, but I called emergency services. There should be something on the news about it."

Mrs. Dunn brought Engel a glass of rum.

"Leave the bottle," he said.

"Do you want anything for yourself?" she asked me.

"No, thank you, Mrs. Dunn. How are you?"

"Much older, Master Grant."

It had been almost twenty years since I was last here. Mrs. Dunn had been with Engel for five years at the time. She was somewhere in her forties then. She looked different. Time had etched its effect on her face. And I'm sure working for Engel had a part in that as well. But she still had the same mischievous glint in her eyes. I've never met or heard her talk about the elusive *Mr.* Dunn. Taking care of Engel seemed to be her life.

"You look the same. Handsome as ever," she said.

I blushed.

Mrs. Dunn gave us some privacy, leaving the room and closing the door.

"It's unlikely those men in the woods would have left his body behind. There would be too many questions," he said.

"I know, I'm sorry. I wasn't thinking. I just wanted to help him."

"It's understandable." He took a sip. "It doesn't look like any harm was done."

"Except to Braeden."

"Yes, except that."

Engel's glossing over my stepbrother's death wasn't callousness on his part, at least, not intentionally. As much as my stomach twisted at the thought of Braeden's face as he lay there, urging me to go, to leave him, I had to forgive the old man if he paid little attention to the life of one person he didn't know.

Engel had been alive for every moment of recorded history. He had literally seen *everything*. Seen us rise from a disorganized band of nomads to the society of today. Seen generation upon generation of men and women live and die.

The enormity of what he had witnessed was staggering.

I wasn't able to let Braeden's death go so easily. I wondered if I would become as desensitized after a few thousand more years. I hoped not.

Despite having known him for almost a thousand years, Engel was a mystery. My only knowledge of his life is what he told me. These morsels of information usually came out late at night after he'd consumed a good measure of rum or wine or beer. And not beer you picked up at the corner liquor store, but a concoction he brewed in the basement from barley and farro, ancient yeast and uncooked malt.

He'd been told, when he was old enough to understand, that the tribal leader, long since dead, had named him Enhegal at his birth. Exactly when and where he was born, even he wasn't sure. It was somewhere along the banks of the Tigris River, so long ago the sporadic settlements had no names.

He spent his childhood and early adult years living between the Tigris and Euphrates Rivers in what is now Iran and Iraq, and what two thousand years after his birth would become the cradle of civilization, Mesopotamia.

To understand just how old Engel is, let me tell you about a science class I was in some time in the mid-1970s. Science is one of the few areas of study that holds any interest for me. Not because I'm particularly good at it, but because it isn't always the same thing, decade after decade. Languages change, but it might take a hundred years to notice any real difference. Math could go centuries without a major development. How long has it been since Algebra or Geometry were invented? Now, I know there are people—mathematicians, mostly—who will argue that math is a constantly evolving study of blah, blah, blah, blah, blah. Whatever. Let me just say: $2 + 2 = 4$, and it's been that way for three thousand years. But in science, there were new discoveries all the time. Which, for a kid who's taken more than a century of these classes, gives me something to look forward to. So, I was sitting in class, and the teacher started talking about new geological modeling helping us understand the past and how Great Britain used to be connected to Europe until around 6500BC by land that was now underwater (cue computerized 3D graphic) and it hit me right then: Engel was alive when the English Channel was still *forming*.

Even for me, that's hard to grasp.

Historians separate *history* from *prehistory* at around 3000 BC with the development of coherent writing systems. When humans stopped living only in the present and became interested in their past and in their future as well.

I once asked Engel what had changed. Writing is what scholars used as the demarcation, but writing things down was a symptom of some change in humans, not the cause. We were sitting in the library room. It was Summer then, the light filtered in and played on his face. Engel thought about it for a moment. "I think when we started to plant our food, stay in one place. When we could know that the next day there would be enough to eat, I think that is when we started to think about tomorrow. No one can contemplate the meaning of the world or even the meaning of their own life when their belly is empty. Actually," he said, putting his hand to the side of his mouth to get more amplification, "Mrs. Dunn, I'm a little hungry." Mrs. Dunn was much younger. As she made him something to eat, he glanced over at the three walls of books that ran from floor to ceiling. "I wish I could remember more. But there's so much I've forgotten." On his shelves were books by Plato. Socrates. The complete works of Shakespeare, of course. A dozen or so modern classics. And a surprising number of mystery novels that took up two whole rows. But the vast majority of Engel's library was made up of history books. "I like reading history," he said. "They're like fiction for me. I find myself yelling at the authors a lot. They're always so damned sure of themselves, like they actually know what the hell they're talking about."

"You know, I still can't get over the fact that you're *prehistoric*," I said.

Engel smiled and sipped his liquor. "I don't think of myself as prehistoric. I tend to look at the world as pre-rum and post-rum. And really, anything before rum doesn't really matter in my opinion. You really should try it. I make it myself."

"No, thank you." I've had Engel's rum before. What happened post-rum was never pretty. Besides, I wanted to steer the conversation back to our current dilemma. "They already know."

"How much?"

"Enough."

"So, not much."

"I think they deserve to be told the rest. They helped me escape."

"If I told everyone who ever helped me or saved my life, half the world would know about us by now."

I stayed silent. I wasn't going to argue with him. There was little chance I could change his craggy, old mind, and he wasn't going to change mine. Mrs. Dunn clanged a pot in the kitchen. I raised my eyebrow at Engel.

He studied me for a long moment. Then made a noise, almost a snort, when I think he finally realized I was determined to do this.

"I trust her. Do you trust them?"

I thought about it for a moment. I wanted to make sure I was thinking clearly, that this wasn't some rash decision. Trust is not an easy thing to give. Especially when you're entrusting your very existence to someone.

"I do."

"Really?"

"Yes."

"Because we could correct your misguided decision to bring them here by sending them home right now. Which is what you *should* have done in the first place. Send them home. It's safer for everyone."

"I don't know if it is. Phoebe probably already knows enough to be a problem."

"Who's going to believe her? She's how old? Sixteen, maybe? What actual proof does she have?"

I shook my head almost imperceptibly. She had none, of course.

"Exactly." He knocked back the rest of his rum and poured another inch in his glass.

Engel was right. Who would believe her?

Part of what has allowed us to keep our secret across the millennia is that it's such a laughably ridiculous tale. Anyone who's ever tried to reveal our existence has been looked upon as crazy, a lunatic, out of their minds. The story has been out there for a long time. But it's been misunderstood and distorted over the millennia, twisted until it's become the basis of mythology, the gods, sorcery, even vampires.

"If we send them back now without a good explanation, I know her, she'll try to figure the rest of it out on her own. She'd never do anything to expose us on purpose, but just digging around, asking questions, is going to bring unwanted attention. I think her curiosity might be more dangerous than us telling them the truth. We have to trust them."

"Your record on who to tell the truth to is not very good," he said.

"That was a foolish mistake. I let my feelings cloud my judgment."

"And what are your feelings now?" He glanced across the hall toward the living room where Phoebe was sitting on the couch.

My face turned red, but only for an instant. "Do you trust me?"

"I trust you. I don't always trust your judgment." He poured himself another glass of rum. "But that is what growing up is all about. Developing good judgment after using bad judgment."

I know this seems strange considering my age, but as much as I've lived and learned, my brain is still developing. Just as we physically age more slowly, we progress mentally at the same decelerated rate. The prefrontal cortex—the part of the brain that weighs consequences of behavior, considers the future, balances short-term rewards with long-term goals, and manages impulse control—is one of the last regions of the brain to reach maturity. I *look* fifteen, and although I hate to admit it—and would never acknowledge it to anyone but myself—in terms of my emotional development, I *am* fifteen.

Engel swirled the rum in his glass. "I know what you're doing."

"What are you talking about?"

"You don't think I've seen this a thousand times before? Felt it myself? You want to make the pain go away. You want companions who understand you. Who can peel you away from that dark chasm you find yourself standing at the edge of whenever there's a quiet moment. People who just might keep you from going under and sinking when the memories flood in."

I felt my heartbeat speed up, my ears grow warm.

"But it never ends well. For us. Or them."

I took in a breath and tried to slow my pulse. "What about you?" I nodded toward the door. "Mrs. Dunn. What about that?"

"I'm so old, Alexander, I might actually die before she does. She's been a good friend."

I was quiet. "Why don't we all live together? Wouldn't that solve a lot of this?"

"It's not the way we are. A hundred years is far too long to be in the company of anybody. Especially people like us. Never mind three hundred or thousand. It takes a certain kind of drive, determination…ambition to survive as we do." He swirled his drink. "We would have all killed each other long before you were born." He put the glass to his lips and savored a swig. "You need a better reason than you *think* it's a good idea."

There were a thousand reasons to send them back to Great Barrington, back to their lives, their families, change my name, change cities. I had done it uncountable times before. It was easier. It was safer for me. It was less complicated.

There was only one reason not to.

"They've been part of three incidents," I said. "The woods. My house. The car crash. Beyond the police and any legal consequences—"

"Those can be smoothed out," he said.

"*Beyond* those, they've been seen. They fought with me. By my side against the people trying to kidnap me. They helped me escape. That makes them targets. The men in the woods would have killed them if they could have. They wanted me. No one else mattered. And the man at my home, he scared me more than all ten of the attackers in the woods." I knew I was rambling, but I had to convince Engel that I sincerely believed they were at risk. "I didn't leave them. He knows they're important to me. He's willing to use me to get to my father. He'll be willing to use anyone in order to get to me. If they go home now, not only will they be in danger, but their families will as well. I won't let that happen."

Engel studied me with perhaps a hint of disappointment. After a long moment, he finished the rest of his rum and got to his feet. "I think we are being rude. Let's join our guests." He went to the door and gazed through the window panes. "By the way, where's Mrs. Avery?"

TWELVE

I Spill The Beans And The Molasses

There was a pit in my stomach. I wanted to throw up. I hoped the anticipation was worse than the event because I didn't know if I could take any more.

The problem is, where do you begin? How do you tell someone you're a hundred times older than they are? And in Engel's case, that you're older than recorded history. Short of locking us all in a room for the next ten years, there was no way to demonstrate the phenomenon to Phoebe and Daniel.

I opened my mouth. At first, nothing came out.

Nothing.

Eventually, the words came, but they were halting, baffling, and unclear.

I won't go into the details because you know them already. When and where I was born. How we think it works. All that.

They listened.

There was confusion, then shock, which surprised me since I thought Phoebe had figured some of it out. I guess *speculating* I was the one in those old photographs is one thing, *knowing* it's true is another. And I really think she thought I was a vampire, which is ironic because we are—well, one of us is, at least—the reason for that crazy myth.

Daniel skipped over shock, wizards, aliens and the undead, and went straight to denial.

"That's stupid. What are you talking about? You're younger than I am. You can't even drive," he said before turning to Phoebe. "Why aren't you calling bullshit on this bullshit?"

"It's not bullshit," I said.

I reached into the backpack, pulled out a hardcover book, and handed it to Daniel.

He glanced at the cover. "A thesaurus? You think I need help coming up with synonyms for 'prick?'"

"Open it."

Daniel turned a handful of pages, revealing a lockbox set into the book. I rolled the numbers into sequence and the cover released. Daniel removed the lid. Inside were photos. Some of them were old and fragile. He lifted them gently from the container. There were images of me and John F. Kennedy, Franklin Delano Roosevelt, Amelia Earhart, Albert Einstein, Marie Curie, Rosa Parks, The Beatles, Martin Luther King, Edison, Tesla, Wild Bill, Buffalo Bill, Annie Oakley, and a number of other famous and infamous faces. As he shuffled through each, he handed the photos to Phoebe. I looked pretty much the same in every one. Same stupid grin. Same slight tilt of the head. The hair got longer or shorter or poofier or flatter with the style of the day, the clothes ranged from classic to embarrassing. The image of me, of anyone really, in a leisure suit sporting a '70s perm should have elicited a sarcastic comment, a chuckle, a shake of the head, something, but Phoebe stared at the pictures as if they were autopsy photos.

Daniel sneered "Oh, c'mon, people forge things all the time." He pointed at the baseball. "How hard is it to fake a signature? And the Photoshopping? It's not even good. These are all fuzzy and out of focus. What you're saying is ridiculous. It's impossible. It's *bullshit*. If anybody had ever lived that long, we'd have heard about it."

"But you have." Engel tilted his head toward several large, colorful books spread out on the coffee table. There were titles about ancient gods and books on mythology, reincarnation, and medieval magicians. "It's just that you don't believe."

"Those are just *stories*," Daniel said.

"Just because they aren't true, doesn't mean there isn't truth in them."

Daniel stared at the books, uneasily.

"Listen, we're not gods," I said, flatly.

"Although, at one time, I truly believed I *was* a god," said Engel, ruefully.

"But we're not. And we're not superhuman. Or immortal. Or any different than you," I explained. "Except that we live...a lot longer."

Phoebe slumped back on the sofa. "That's definitely different."

Daniel waved his hand over the photos. "I don't believe it."

Engel sighed. "Whether or not you believe something doesn't change whether it's true or not."

Daniel scooped up a handful of pictures and flipped through them. "Photoshop. Photoshop. Your biceps are *not* that big, by the way. Photoshop, Photoshop, Photoshop," he said as he tossed each one roughly.

I grabbed his wrist. "They...are...real!" I gathered the photos gently. "Just like the baseball is real."

My father would kill me if he knew I had this collection of photographic evidence. It was one of my small rebellions. I wish I had photos from earlier times, but the technology didn't exist. I don't know why, but they gave me some comfort as I moved on from one life to another. And I realized in that moment, that I felt lonely. Very lonely. I've been isolated for much of my life. Abandoned by my father for years at a time. Unable to maintain relationships for more than a few years at most.

I have felt this weight in my chest before, but perhaps never more than watching Phoebe grimly—and Daniel dismissively—leaf through my recent past.

"I don't get why we're even having this stupid conversation," said Daniel.

Engel glared at me. "I'm wondering why we're having it myself."

Daniel held up his hand. "Excuse me, I'm still trying to get the image of my stun gun-wielding history teacher being your girl-friend out of my head."

"I don't know if I'd call her my *girl*friend. We're a little old for that, don't you think?"

The thought of Engel and Mrs. Avery together was noisily rattling around in my skull as well. "She's not one of us, is she?"

He shook his head. "I've barely known her a decade. She thinks I'm an arms dealer slash doomsday prophet who's preparing for the end of the world. Mrs. Avery likes her bad boys with an edge." There was a glint in his golden eyes. "I told her you were the son of my ammunition supplier and to keep an eye on you."

"Great," I said.

"So, you believe this?" Daniel asked Phoebe. She didn't answer. He shook his head. "I get it, we're teenagers. We're totally oblivious to our own mortality. We feel invincible. We think we're immortal. But we're not supposed to *actually* think we're immortal. I mean, it's not like I don't know I'm going to die. But it's something I can't grasp right now. And I'm not supposed to. And then you come along and tell me this bullshit that not only am I going to die, but I'm going to die thousands and thousands of years before you are! It's…it's not—" His breathing became rapid, and he couldn't finish.

I put my hand on his back and tried to comfort him.

Mrs. Dunn brought in four glasses of water. She handed one to Daniel.

"I had trouble believing it at first," she said as she watched Daniel gulp down the cold liquid until the glass was empty. He took another.

"So, what? You're not…one of *them*?"

"No," she laughed. "And *he* never told me." She glared at Engel. "I started to realize after a few years he wasn't getting older. It's hard to tell, he's so damn old already." Her gaze softened. "There were other odd things I noticed before that, but…" She paused, shaking her head. "But you dismiss them. Put them out of your mind. He tried to let me go so he could find someone else and pretend he was ten years younger again. That's when I told him I wasn't going anywhere. That he was going to sit down, shut up, and tell me a story. And make it believable."

"Actually," said Engel. "You told me you weren't leaving until one of us croaked."

Phoebe sat on the couch, silent and despondent. Was she frightened that Engel and I and the very nice Mrs. Dunn were raving lunatics? Or did she believe me? And the realization that she would grow old and die before I'd appear to age a single year was what caused her to sink into this dark gloom.

She sat like a statue, her chest motionless as if she were holding her breath. Only her eyes shifted as she examined her body, the UMASS sweatpants, my sweatshirt. When she finally moved again, she ran her delicate hands along the letters on the front, then gasped and sucked in all the air she had been depriving herself of. Without a word, she stood suddenly, trying to rip my sweatshirt off her body, but she was unable to think, unable to do the most basic tasks, and she gave up after a few seconds.

Instead, she ran to the door. She wanted to escape. Her hands fumbled with the locks and handle as she tried to decipher how to open them.

Just as she unlatched the lock, I pressed my hand against the door, keeping her from opening it.

"Let me out of here. I want to leave." There was fire in her eyes. I had seen a glimpse of this in the forest, but it had been directed at others, not me.

My free hand got close to her hair. I didn't touch it. I wanted to. I wanted to soothe her, comfort her, stroke her soft, brunette locks.

I knew enough about women to know she needed space.

I thankfully resisted the urge to pat her on the back, which would have come off as clumsy or condescending or both.

"Come back and sit down."

She remained with her hand on the door.

"You haven't answered why you are telling us," she said loudly, directing her question towards Engel in the living room.

"Yeah, why?" Daniel asked. "Is there something we can do to live longer? Eat more kale? Vitamins? Something?"

Engel shook his head. "There have been many who have sought an answer to that question over the centuries. Who've searched in vain for the Fountain of Youth or the Waters of Life. There isn't any elixir you can drink."

"No offense, but number one, I don't even believe in you, and number two, if I were to believe in you, who knows what scientists might learn from you."

"Perhaps if they dissected us to see how our bodies work," Engel offered.

"Exactly—" Daniel stopped as he realized what he was suggesting.

I quickly glanced at Engel. He didn't look up. He stared down at the rug, gravely.

This is what my father and Engel and every other adult Eternal had warned me about. Telling people is dangerous.

"That's not what I was saying," Daniel said, trying to backtrack.

Engel gazed at Daniel. His amber eyes, almost golden, peered intensely at him. Then he turned to Phoebe.

"Your friend," he said to her, "has chosen to tell you because he believes it may save your life. He's taking a tremendous risk in trusting you, risking his own life and mine. I wonder if you are worthy of that risk."

Engel stood, then turned to leave.

Phoebe's body shook. "Yes!" she said. Engel stopped. "We are."

He studied her, chewing on the inside of his lip. There was a look on his face, something harder than I've ever seen before. The silence dragged on for a long time. He inhaled deeply and exhaled loudly through his nose. "I assume you came for chalk?"

"It would help," I said. "A few pieces for each of us."

He nodded absently.

Phoebe's face scrunched up on one side as if she'd just been subjected to the high-pitched wail of an eighteen-wheeler's squealing brakes.

Daniel's reaction was more...Danielish.

"What are we going to do, draw chalk outlines around ourselves to save the police the trouble?"

One of the reasons I liked hanging out with Daniel so much was his pure entertainment value. I never knew what was going to come out of his mouth, not even close. I could usually tell *when* something was coming, but as for what he was about to say, I never knew.

"That's funny," Engel said. And he meant it.

I didn't want to get too deep into explaining things, so I just said: "A chalked ID is one that's been altered or fake."

"You mean, like, we'll be able to buy beer?"

"No. I mean, if we're lucky, we might be able to fly somewhere safer and live long enough so you can legally buy beer."

"Hold on. Fly? I thought you wanted us to go home. Actually, I need to go home." He flipped open his phone and saw the time. "My mom is going to kill me."

Phoebe nodded. "I took my dress over to Jenny's before the game. We were all going to change clothes there. My parents think I'm at Homecoming. Unless Jenny or Craig called my house looking for me." She was searching in vain for something. "I left my phone in the car."

"You mean the car you stole? The one that exploded?" said Daniel.

Reminding Phoebe that she had nearly been blown to bits caused her to shudder.

Daniel reached into his back pocket and produced her phone. "I grabbed it before you two pulled me out. I figured we shouldn't leave any evidence behind. Not that it mattered."

I got a rush, you know, the one you get when it hits you your best friend's birthday was yesterday or you left your wallet at home and only realize it after unloading your entire cart of groceries onto the conveyor belt at the checkout stand.

Homecoming Dance.

I had completely forgotten about it. Had it really been less than five hours since the stadium lights had come crashing down on me?

It seemed like days ago.

I cursed under my breath. "I was supposed to pick up Faith at seven o'clock!"

Phoebe raised her eyebrows. "You were taking Faith Siniscalco?"

"Yeah, I asked her a couple of weeks ago."

Faith Siniscalco was probably the prettiest girl at Monument High—not to take anything away from Phoebe. She was tall and slender. Her features were symmetrical and soft.

Phoebe had a slight smirk on her face. I couldn't tell if she was jealous or simply entertained by the thought.

"Huh," she said. The eyebrows raised again.

Faith may seem a little aloof to some, but that often happens to very pretty girls. They get so much attention that the only way to handle it is to shut it out. It comes off as stuck up sometimes. In my experience, it's usually a defense mechanism. Don't get me wrong, there are plenty of beautiful girls who are complete snobs.

Faith wasn't one of them.

She was smart. Always made Honor Roll. She dressed nicer than anyone else at Monument. The few times we talked, our conversations were surprisingly interesting and engrossing.

We didn't interact much in school. This was definitely one of those go-out-on-a-limb situations where you ask a girl you don't know all that well, hoping she'll say yes to go to the dance or the prom or out with you on a Saturday night, fully prepared for that ninety-eight percent chance you'll get shot down.

I asked her because I knew I'd have a pleasant, engaging time.

I think she only said yes because she was dating a college freshman who was *no way* going to make the trip home for a stupid high school dance. Which made her the perfect date for me. No pressure. No expectations.

The person I really wanted to ask, the one I wanted to attend the dance with was—in a strange twist of fate—the person I was currently spending the evening with.

She was two feet away from me. Still eyeing me.

"Faith's a little delicate for you, isn't she?"

"Delicate?"

"You know, kind of pretty-pretty. The hair, the shoes. Looks like she's walking on a red carpet all the time."

I didn't mean to laugh, but I did.

Daniel grunted. I knew he was jealous I was going with Faith. I told him there were at least half a dozen girls that would go to the dance with him.

He had to ask though.

Easy for me to say, right? I pretty much got over my shyness sometime in the late 1800s. There still were times I'd get anxious asking a girl out. But as hockey legend Wayne Gretzky once said, "You miss one hundred percent of the shots you don't take."

Let's just say, I'm not afraid to shoot the puck.

Now, Daniel's a good looking kid. He's got great hair. And he's going to have it until he's ninety. He's tall, and maybe a little thin for his height, but he has those scrubbed, boyish 1950s good looks that age well.

He just didn't ask anyone.

I think he was worried about money. You have to rent a tux, buy a wrist corsage, take the girl out to dinner. It adds up.

I told him I'd help him. He refused.

I don't know if his refusal revealed some as-yet-still-hidden do-it-yourself work ethic or just how scared he was.

Daniel was staring at me, giving me a look I'd never seen before. The truth does that. His gaze was making me uncomfortable. My friend didn't see me the same way. He opened his mouth to speak, stopped, frozen like a bass caught in a hook, pressed his lips together, then finally just blurted it out. "Why the fuck do you still go to high school?"

I was so surprised by the question that I laughed.

"No, I'm serious."

I took a moment to answer, thoughtfully. There were a lot of reasons I still went to school—most days. Like my father said, this is what teenagers are expected to do. And it's not like there are legions of interesting, cool people my age just hanging out all day. Unless they're dropouts or drug addicts. I had friends. I played sports. I could do the work in my sleep. Sure, high school sucked, but it was better than being alone. But the truth is, there was really only one reason that mattered. "It's where the women are," I said.

Phoebe arched her left eyebrow sharply. I shrugged.

Daniel nodded slowly. This seemed to be a rationale he could understand. "I see your point."

"Women?" Phoebe said.

"Would you prefer tomato, doll, honey, peach, chicks, *girls*?" I offered as she brushed past me.

"Not helping your case."

Tenth hardest thing about my life: keeping up with what's appropriate to say.

Engel watched the scene, somewhat amused. "Come. Let's get started." He motioned for us to follow.

I can only imagine what one of those young women was thinking right now. Faith was probably, at this moment, shouting obscenities at me on the voicemail of the phone I dumped in the woods.

I should call her. Except her number was in the discarded phone.

While Engel led Phoebe and Daniel down a narrow set of stairs, I looked up the limo service I had hired for the night. They knew Faith's address already.

When I got a woman from the company on the phone, I gave her a message to deliver.

Faith would have, by now, likely heard about today's events, about me being taken away in an ambulance. I made an excuse that I wasn't feeling well and was back in the emergency room being checked for a concussion. I reconsidered that strategy. She would say something to one of my teammates at the dance, and I'd have visitors to a place I wasn't at. I changed the message to say that the doctor had ordered me to rest. No loud noises, no music, no television or socializing, so I wouldn't be able to make it. I urged her to go to the dance. And use the limo to take several of her friends that were going solo.

I ended the note simply:

> *I'm sorry, Faith. I was very much looking forward to spending the evening with you, enjoying your company.*
> *—Regretfully, Alexander.*

"Is that it?" the woman asked.

"No," I said, surprising myself. "Add a postscript that reads: 'I'm sure you look gorgeous in your dress. Be sure to dance.'" The woman repeated the entire note back to me. "Perfect," I said. "Let her know that if she needs anything, anything at all, the driver can take care of it and you can put it on my bill. I want the driver to remain available to her the entire time, as late as she wants."

After hanging up, I went to rejoin the others in the basement.

I couldn't find them at first.

I called out.

Daniel answered. His voice was tiny and far away. I followed the sound, having to trek much farther than I expected given the footprint of the upstairs.

Engel's home was not this large.

It wasn't until I finally located them—after traversing at least two hundred feet of twists and turns—that the extent of his complex became clear.

"You've built this out since the last time I was here."

"Nosy neighbors," he said.

Engel explained that he owned the adjoining real estate. The path we had taken led us under his small yard and through three properties on Chestnut, one street over from Acorn.

I noticed bundles of cable running along the ceiling, like the kind you see used for cable or satellite television, except...the multiple strands were orange.

The basement we were in and the one to the right were filled with printing, laminating, and bookbinding machines. There were digital presses and more traditional offset presses. And everywhere, more of the orange cable. In another room to the left, drafting desks were set around a large, bottom-lit compositing table. Benches covered with tools, some hundreds of years old lined one wall. A collection of metal, wooden and rubber stamps sat in shelves. Large, lighted magnifying glasses were fixed to the tables. I could make out washing machines, heat lamps, ultraviolet lights, and a photo studio through another door.

Daniel glanced around. "What are all these for?"

"Counterfeiting," Engel said matter-of-factly, without a hint of remorse.

"As in printing up fake money?"

"We do some of that, but very little. Only countries where paper money is difficult to come by on short notice. There's no reason to print up banknotes of the major currencies."

"Why not?"

"Because I have plenty of *real* money," Engel said, flatly.

Daniel started to say something else, but nothing came out for a long moment.

"These are used mostly to create documents. Passports. Birth certificates. Driver's licenses. Government, military, corporate IDs, and the occasional forgery."

Engel explained that birth certificates, which used to be easy to fake, were now much tougher because you had to insert the information into the records of the time.

You could create a forged birth certificate that might be good enough to open a bank account or get a driver's license, but if you tried passing it off as genuine with most governments, the military or anything sensitive, it could land you in prison. Or worse.

"That's where the ancestry databases come into play." Engel directed us into the photo studio. He went over to a fixed white backdrop that started on the floor and curved up to the ceiling. He adjusted some knobs, and the backdrop changed color. "Upstairs, we run one of the most successful ancestry websites in the world.

We have more records than any government, including the United States. Even more than the Mormon church. They're our biggest competitors. We use our own algorithms to check information against various sources. When the computers find a gap or discrepancy between different systems, we check into it. If a birth or a death has been misreported, we put it on a list. If it remains uncorrected, we can exploit the error to create identities that have full histories. The anomalies are rare, but with so large a data set, there are more than enough for our needs." He had Phoebe stand in the middle of the backdrop which was now a bluish green. He ignored a large format camera and a high-end digital SLR that were set up on tripods and, instead, stood behind a small plastic box that looked like an old Samsonite luggage case. "Look like you're bored." He snapped a picture. "The website turns a fair profit, even though we don't need it to." He motioned for Daniel to replace Phoebe. "You've just waited three hours for this picture to be taken." He snapped a picture of Daniel. "Now you," he said to me.

The last time I was here, a little over two decades ago, Engel had a few laminating machines and a small printing press. Most of what he did was done manually, chalking and photo retouching. Twenty or thirty years ago no one looked at identifications very hard. Fifty years ago most states didn't have pictures on their licenses.

Back then, if I needed him to make me something, it took a day or two of him hunched over his desk. Most of the time, I was doing nothing more than enrolling as a student, occasionally getting a driver's license. Proof of age, proof of residency, proof of immunizations, that was the extent of the paperwork I needed for school. Aside from the driving test, which I'm not very good at, getting a license was easy. For a long time, all I had to do was present a birth certificate they barely glanced at, get a photo taken that made me look like a criminal, and sit for an interminably long time until the speakers in the ceiling broadcast an unintelligible garble that had the same number of syllables as my name.

Traveling between countries, however, demanded a higher level of skill. Engel sent me a new set of passports every three or four years to keep me in the right age bracket. I didn't even have to show up, he'd been using the same photo the last quarter-century. I'd get a U.S. passport along with ones for Brazil, Germany, Russia, and France. He'd usually throw in one or two others to mix things up. He had his favorites, Hong Kong, Monaco, Yugoslavia (when there was such a place), and the Republic of Nauru, the smallest island nation in the world, whose entire population could be evacuated on a cruise ship. Once—he'd either gotten bored or wanted to mess with me—Engel made me Canadian. It was the only ID he sent. Don't get me wrong, I'm not trying to be rude to those of you joining the fight from the Great White North. I have nothing against Canada. Sure, I've never lived in Canada, and the only time I visited there was when a merchant ship I was taking from England to Boston ran aground in Nova Scotia during a terrible storm— everyone was *very* nice, by the way. And you know, other than the Halifax incident, I hear it's great. Being "Canadian" annoyed me because I had to use the ID to register for school, and on a daily basis at least one idiot at East Buffalo High would come up to me and in a stupefyingly bad impression of a Canadian accent say, "Aboot wot time ahhr ya bringing oowver that bag of homo milk, eh?"

Seriously, Canadians, I feel for you.

Although calling your homogenized milk *homo* milk, you might want to rethink that one.

But everything changed after the terrorist attacks in 2001. It became much more difficult to produce IDs that could stand up to careful scrutiny and enhanced security, but I never imagined the scale and complexity of the process had grown so dramatically.

Our situation demanded incontestable identification for me and Phoebe and Daniel. But more than that, we required IDs that could be sacrificed without compromising our true identities or biometrics.

I was blinded by the flash as Engel took my picture. It was a moment before my eyes recovered and I could see again.

∞

Mrs. Dunn made us something to eat while we waited in the main house for the IDs. I wasn't hungry, so I went back downstairs. I wanted to have some time alone with Engel.

I liked watching him work. As old as he was, as much wear and tear time and living had inflicted on his body, he moved between the machines with little effort. The dexterity in his fingers rivaled a concert pianist.

In less than an hour, he had fabricated four passports and one driver's license for each of us. I told him not to bother with the licenses, but he made them anyway.

Five different identities.

"The man who came to my house," I began as if we were already in the middle of this discussion. "When I asked him who he was, he said I should ask my father."

"He said that, ask your father?"

"Actually, he said I should ask Marcus."

"You've never seen him before?"

"No. He was about forty-five." I didn't need to say *hundred*. "He had a scar on his face. It wasn't deep. It almost went along the natural crease in his cheek. Dark olive complexion."

Engel seemed to purposely ignore my statement. He handed me my four passports.

Two U.S. passports with different names. The third from Ghana. The fourth from Pakistan.

Very clever.

They were all countries that used English as their primary or official language. Both Ghana and Pakistan were inspired choices that gave us instant street cred in various parts of the world. Ghana brought warmer welcomes in Africa, China, and Francophone nations. Pakistan offered easier—if not always friendly—access to the Muslim world. Pakistan had one of the most difficult passports to forge. While a Pakistani passport might be one of the most scrutinized in the world, it was also one of the most trusted.

Engel had been somewhat disingenuous when he said he was counterfeiting. He was using the exact machines, and the same finished materials the governments used. These weren't fakes. These were real passports containing real data. The only thing fake were the biometrics. The pictures and the fingerprints.

And that was the reason for the orange cable. It was primer cord. These machines, these supplies, these houses were rigged to self-destruct if Engel felt his operation had been compromised.

"You never worry about that?" I said, glancing up at the strands of detonation cord.

"Do you worry about living right above millions of miles of decaying gas lines?" Engel rarely conceded a point without challenging it. His way was softer than my father's, yet it hinted at the type of man he might have been long ago. To me, Engel had always been a teacher, a mentor, but looking into his golden eyes, I could imagine him stronger and much more aggressive before the testosterone that had recently begun to course furiously through my body left his. "Dozens and dozens of explosions every year," he added without looking at me. "Every year."

Sure, more than half of the two point five million miles of pipeline in the United States was over fifty years old. And some horrific pipe failures had occurred recently. One blast in Philadelphia destroyed fifty-five buildings. Another in California leveled thirty-eight homes and sent flames a thousand feet into the air. Still, these events were random and rare.

Lining your basement with explosives, on the other hand, was inviting trouble into your home and letting it live there.

"I wouldn't worry about the cord," he said. "It's the ammonium nitrate and fuel oil the cord sets off you should worry about."

I found myself unconsciously rechecking my exit paths. Not that it would matter. The pentaerythritol tetranitrate stuffed inside the orange tubing detonated at a rate of four miles *per second*. You don't light a fuse like this and get to run away. Engel's complex of connected properties would explode instantaneously.

"Braeden said…" I hesitated, trying to wrap my mind around the implication of it. "He said millions would die if they caught me."

Engel grabbed a strip of paper off the desk. "I don't know about millions. But people always die when we clash amongst ourselves."

The room blinked out. I saw Braeden left to die alone in the woods. Then I saw a thousand Braedens dying, then a thousand thousand covering every inch of the forest. Engel handed me the paper, and it took me a moment to make sense of the symbols written on it: a ten digit phone number.

"Put that burn number in your phones," Engel said. "It'll connect you to the automated system set up offshore. Just say the name on the ID or punch in the last four digits, and it'll run a subroutine, deleting the fake record in the relevant databases, and replacing it with whatever had been there before."

I ran my fingers over the raised lettering on the covers of the passports. The feel was exquisite. The interiors, flawless.

"These look perfect."

"It's not good enough to look perfect anymore," he said, annoyed. "Waste of my talent. The artwork doesn't matter."

I understood. Passports were no longer stand-alone instruments.

With advances in technology, it was relatively easy to create believable-looking documents. On the surface. The hard part was duplicating the intricate features: the special reactive ink, the holograms, the seals. The even harder part was inserting the reference data into the respective country's computers. Newer passports contained a vicinity-read radio frequency identification chip. The RFID transmitted passport information to Customs Agents at checkpoints, instantly displaying your name, nationality, gender, date of birth, place of birth, and photo on their screens. A Unique Identifier checked to make sure the data was in agreement. It didn't matter how official the passport looked. If the information didn't match the database, you were in trouble. That's what the "burn number" was for. We would have our real photos and biometrics tied to multiple identities. Deleting that information if we were compromised or once it was no longer needed was critical.

Looking around at Engel's operation, the tens of millions in equipment, the staff of programmers running the genealogy website, the huge chunk of prime real estate in one of the most expensive cities in America, it hit me: the staggering amount of effort and resources it took to allow me to fake a life that was airtight.

"How are you going to plant the data? It's gotta be impossible to hack into the State Department servers."

"*Nearly* impossible. But it's riskier and more difficult than other means."

Engel tapped into a secure network. A map of Boston came up. He zoomed in. I recognized the location.

"That's the passport office here in the city."

"Ah huh. About ten blocks away."

He was navigating through firewalls like a twenty-something hacker.

"By dropping the information into the computer scanning the data, it's as if you handed in your applications in person. The regional offices, although very secure, are easier to hack."

"It's going to take time to populate. The passports still have to be issued, right?"

He spent another ten seconds typing away.

"According to this. They already have been."

I narrowed my eyes, studying Engel for a moment. "You just happened to be dating a teacher at the high school in the town I chose?"

"No. I've been suggesting the Berkshires to you for years. And," he glanced up from his work, "I happen to be dating women in a lot of towns."

It was slightly easier for the Ghanian passports. Security wasn't as difficult to bypass, but the digital infrastructure in Ghana wasn't as good, which slowed the process.

The toughest part was setting up the Pakistani IDs. Their security was just as hard to crack as the American system. Which is why their passports were some of the most trusted in the world.

While Engel seeded the data into the DGIP servers in Islamabad, I found a marker and a piece of paper.

"The man had a symbol," I said. "It was partially hidden, but Braeden and at least one of the attackers in the woods were wearing medallions that looked similar." I put the marker to the paper and drew the symbol. A circle with a box inside with an X inside the box.

I slid the piece of paper in front of Engel, making sure not to knock his hands while he was entering a series of commands. He didn't look directly at it. He continued furiously tapping away at the keyboard, but I could tell he could see the symbol in his peripheral vision. That was born out after he slid the paper back in front of me a moment later.

"He was wearing it?"

"It was branded. In his skin."

"Hmmm." Engel paused his typing for an almost imperceptibly brief instant, and I thought I saw the skin under his eye twitch. He began working more quickly.

"You've seen this before, haven't you?" I said.

He didn't look up from the screen. "Haven't *you*?"

The question caught me off guard.

Suddenly, I heard noises upstairs. It sounded like a half dozen pairs of feet charging through the house above us. The ceiling rumbled. The lights overhead swayed. My pulse quickened.

Engel saw my eyes widen.

"It's just the programmers from the ancestry website. Late dinner."

I took in a deep breath and blew it out slowly. I tensed and relaxed my hands several times, and I squeezed my glutes to burn off the epinephrine that had been pushed into my bloodstream. With my survival instinct heightened, my body was betraying me, overreacting.

"It's Saturday night," I said.

He looked at me, blankly, as if he was trying to discern whether or not I was actually as stupid as I was acting. "It's the Internet, Alexander. It doesn't care what day it is or what time it is."

It was embarrassing to be schooled in tech-savviness by a nine-thousand-year-old man. Seriously, you never want to go up against him in a video game. It's a humbling experience to be beaten at *Nuclear Ninja* or *Golf Bandits* by someone older than the wheel.

He went back to his work.

The question loomed in the air. *Had I seen this symbol?*

I stared deeper into the drawing, letting my eyes go out of focus until the lines were soft.

The symbol was simple and yet had a geometric complexity to it. An X inside of a box inside of a circle. I deconstructed the symbol.

A circle.

A square.

An X.

The first two were geometric. But the X was algebraic.

I turned my head slightly. Without the square, it was the symbol for Earth. A globe with the equator and meridian. Or a compass with the four directions. Or to be narcissistic, the center of every-thing. How old was the Earth symbol? It couldn't be more than a thousand years. Maybe two.

Then my perception switched, and I saw the circle as the letter O.

X and O. Like tic-tac-toe. I used to play a form of the game as a kid. Except each player had three physical pieces you moved around the grid until someone got three in a row.

An X, an O, and a square.

Looking at the paper, my vision blurred again. Coming back into focus, it looked like an hourglass or an angular infinity symbol.

It reminded me of the two triangles Mrs. Avery had tattooed on her ankle. Mrs. Avery and Engel. I got sidetracked for a moment thinking about that.

Focus. Triangles.

The X in the box could be four triangles. Looking at it that way, the symbol depicted the three most basic shapes in geometry.

Circle Square Triangle.

I drew an equilateral triangle with a circle inside with a box inside the circle.

Still only paying attention out of the corner of his eye, Engel chuckled softly to himself and shook his head.

"You could waste your very long life doing this."

He pointed to my newly created symbol.

"The Eye of Providence," he said, solemnly. Then chuckled again. "Well, with a square pupil." He paused. "Or maybe a derivation of the Eye of Reyjou." He rolled the R and contracted his throat over the end of the word.

"Ra?"

"If you insist on butchering the name."

My sketch looked more like the symbol on the back of the dollar bill than it did the icon of the ancient god.

"You don't believe in that nonsense, do you?" I said.

"Bird and dog-headed gods, sun worship, magical spells?" he asked.

I nodded.

"Not anymore."

"Not *anymore*?"

"The consequences of outliving everyone. You start thinking you mayyyybe might be a god or something." He had a slightly sheepish expression on his face. "But I still believe shapes have power. And that symbols have meaning." With a flourish of his fingers, he hit one last key, striking it harder and more loudly. "Done," he said, rolling himself toward my desk. He examined my new drawing. "But that's not the symbol you saw. This one is." He pointed to my original sketch.

Using the padded arms, he pushed himself out of the drafting chair, hovering about halfway to standing as if that was all he could manage. At that point, I offered my hand, silently inquiring if he needed any help. He shook his head, gave it one more push and got to his feet without my assistance.

"A body in motion stays in motion," he said. "A body at rest... tends to fall apart."

Engel gestured for me to remain where I was. "I'll be back."

He left the room, shuffling at first, as if his legs were asleep, then after a few steps, he took his normal, stronger strides. He headed back in the direction of the Acorn Street property, disappearing around a corner at the end of the hall.

I heard his footsteps for another few seconds. Then it was silent. Just the buzz of the fluorescent lights overhead.

I was alone with nothing but my own thoughts for the first time in several hours. I focused on the low hum coming through the ceiling. Maybe it was a refrigerator or the website's servers. I focused on the sound and used this moment of peace to clear my head.

After several minutes, Engel returned with Daniel and Phoebe following close behind. Daniel was rubbing his belly in the way one does when they've eaten too much, thoroughly enjoyed having done so, and are about to hate themselves for it.

Phoebe came up to me. "Alexander, you need to eat. Energy. Fuel. C'mon, there's still plenty of food left. You want me to make Daniel go up and get you some?"

Daniel made a face like *why me?*

"Because you're a gentleman and you wouldn't want to make a girl have to walk all the way back up there to get it," she said.

Apparently, I'm not the only one who can read minds.

"Oh, right."

"I'm not really hungry." The truth was, I hadn't thought about food at all. Of course, as soon as I said I wasn't hungry, I felt my stomach fiercely disagreeing with me.

Engel walked over and placed a metal piece down on the lighted table. Being illuminated from below, it glowed as if it were on fire. I wanted to touch it, but removing it from the light would diminish its stunning beauty, and I was mesmerized by its golden radiance.

But it wasn't gold. It was bronze, an alloy of mostly copper and varying degrees of tin.

The amulet looked similar to my drawing. And similar but not identical to the amulets worn by the men in the woods and the scar on the man.

Giving in to its allure, I picked up the bronze piece and studied it. My stomach was kicking me for not accepting the offer of food, but it ached for other reasons as well. I had a powerful sense of déjà vu. As I've said, living as long as I have, feeling pangs of familiarity is not uncommon.

I *had* seen this symbol before and not just earlier today. But somewhere long ago.

Rolling the piece over in my hands, I felt the weight of it. "I think my father had one of these."

Engel nodded. "He would definitely have one."

"What is it?" Phoebe asked.

Engel sighed and sat down as if preparing to tell a long story. "I don't know when or where or how it came to be. It was some time before I was born. Which is to say a very long time ago. There are symbols like it. Stone formations. Glyphs. Most of them have been destroyed. Some remain. Parts of them, at least. Somewhere along the line, we..." He motioned between himself and me. "We appropriated it as a way to identify ourselves to each other. We generally don't wear them anymore. They're big. Cumbersome. From another time. Unless we believe we will come in contact with another Eternal. And usually only if we're facing that person in battle."

Daniel took the medallion. "Why would you wear something this big and awkward in battle?"

"So we know who not to kill. Professional courtesy. Doesn't happen very often. We don't usually fight each other directly. We use armies and surrogates. If you saw this symbol, they are our people. But it doesn't mean they are our friends."

"What *does* it mean?" Phoebe ran her fingers over the surface.

Engel smiled. "I wish I knew. Over the millennia, many have tried to decipher its meaning. Everyone has their own ideas. I've found that how someone defines it, what significance they put on it, says more about the person than it does about the symbol. I only know what it means to me."

"And what is that?" she said.

Engel put his hands together, outlining a circle. "Being whole." Then he made an X with his index fingers. "Being centered." Finally, he clasped his hands at his chest, so that the fingers of his left hand curled inside the fingers of his right, his intertwined fists forming a box. "Being interdependent."

Phoebe, Daniel and I were silent for a moment as we contemplated Engel's demonstration. As if we'd witnessed something profound, something we couldn't fully comprehend.

"But that's just what I think."

He gathered up all the passports and driver's licenses.

"What about the scar-faced man?" I asked.

"I don't have any idea what he thinks about the symbol."

I glared at Engel. "You know what I mean. You know him."

I could see that Engel was considering whether to tell me or not. My old friend was very deliberate about what he revealed, but I had never seen him so cautious with me. I usually never knew when he *wasn't* telling me something.

He blew out a long, audible breath. "He is a great military mind. That he's come for you...is not a good sign."

This I already knew.

"Who is he?"

Again, Engel hesitated. "He had a weapon with him, and he didn't introduce himself?"

I started to answer that, yes, of course, he had a weapon, and the only introduction I got was to his sword, which I was barely able to defend myself against. But then I realized something.

"Actually, he picked up one of my weapons *after* entering the house."

The man had walked into my home unarmed.

Engel chewed on this information for a while, his expression betraying nothing. Without a word, he handed the stack of IDs to Daniel, then headed back through the maze toward his house.

Daniel watched Engel go. "I've seen this in sci-fi movies," he whispered. "Where you ask the computer a question it can't answer and it just fries its memory chip. It like, completely seizes up."

I hurried after Engel, catching up with him on the stairs. He was surprisingly quick for someone older than paper. Or bronze.

"What is it?"

"You and your friends should leave immediately."

"You're not going to tell me anything? I understand I'm supposed to work things out for myself. It's our way. Nothing handed to us. But someone killed a stepbrother I didn't even know existed, then came into my home and threatened me. I think I deserve to know what the hell is going on."

We reached the top of the stairs. He caught his breath and looked around. "Mrs. Dunn?" She didn't answer, but he heard her putting something down in the kitchen and heading our way. He turned to me. "His name is Elam Khai."

The name meant nothing to me.

I tried to search for anything in my memory that might give me a clue.

My father spoke in vague generalities about other Eternals unless I had met them personally. Most of the time, he railed against those like us who abused their longevity, their money and power. They weren't necessarily evil. In too many people's eyes, if you're not all good, you're not good at all. But the world's not black and white. Then again, it isn't different shades of gray, either.

The ancient Chinese understood.

In the *T'ai Chi*—the *yin-yang* symbol—there is no gray.

There is a black half and a white half, and deep within each half is a tiny kernel of the opposite color. The dividing line separating the two halves isn't straight. It elegantly curves like a raindrop in the wind. The darkness intrudes into the light and light pushes back the darkness.

Still, humans have a habit—a need, really—to classify things. Good or bad, right or wrong, liberal or conservative, traditional or modern. The process of arranging colors, sizes, objects, ideas, even people makes it easier for us to judge them quickly. But putting things in order, painting them in simple, broad strokes doesn't mean we understand them any better.

Opposites are bound together, like yin and yang. They are not opposing forces, but complementary. One cannot exist without the other. At least not for long. Up cannot exist without down. Man cannot exist without woman. We would vanish in a generation. Yet together we've survived for millions of years. Like the waves on the sea. Every rise becomes a fall, which causes a rise that falls again, which in its retreat forms another rise.

On and on.

The old myths I learned as a child weren't simply good guys versus bad guys. These legends told much more complicated tales.

Many of the heroes would be considered immoral and dishonorable in today's world. It may be difficult for you, who—at least until now—have enjoyed the kind of opulence only the richest, most powerful people of centuries past could afford, have luxuries kings and queens and emperors never had, to understand the violent, seemingly amoral myths of ancient cultures struggling to make sense of their hostile and unforgiving worlds. At their core, these stories showed me that what we value most, fear the most, and hope for the most are shared by all people. They also taught me that each person's life is a series of choices. And though these decisions define who we are, the lesson is clear: at any moment, we can redeem ourselves by *choosing* differently.

My father isn't some white knight, but for as long as I can remember, he has fought to keep our influence and dominance in check. Elam Khai didn't strike me as particularly evil, but if he was willing to use me to lure my father, then my father must be an obstacle to something he wanted or wanted to do.

Mrs. Dunn entered the living room, and immediately her demeanor changed when she saw Engel's face.

"Oh," she said. That simple sound escaping Mrs. Dunn betrayed that things were worse than I thought.

Daniel and Phoebe emerged from the basement as I questioned Engel. "Why is my father important to Elam Khai? What does he want with him?"

"Who is Elam Khai?" asked Phoebe.

Engel said nothing. Instead, he nodded to Mrs. Dunn, then marched down the hall to his bedroom.

"He needs his rest," Mrs. Dunn offered. Which seemed plausible until we heard a series of noises that had nothing to do with climbing into bed and sounded a lot more like someone gathering up their things to leave. "I'll show you out. Can I get you anything?" she said, ignoring the clamor. "Some snacks for the road?" She looked at Phoebe. "I wish I had some nicer clothes for you to change into, dear."

"That's all right," said Phoebe, suddenly self-conscious about what she was wearing.

Daniel asked me, "Is this Alan guy the one at the house?"

"*Elam* Khai."

"*Elam* guy…whatever. So who is he?"

"I'm not exactly sure."

"What are you *somewhat* sure about?"

"Nothing. Except that I need to find my father. And have no idea where to start looking."

"Just ask the old guy. I'm telling you, he *knows* something." We could hear the banging and scraping going on down the hall. "I mean, he's been making IDs for all of you. He probably knows everything."

I shook my head. "His entire operation supports a dozen of us. Including him. And me."

Daniel froze. "What? All that equipment down there? Twelve people. You've got to be joking?"

I shook my head again.

"I don't believe it. Maybe that's what he told you, but I'm not buying it. Ask him what he knows."

"It's not that easy."

"Yes, it is! Ask him!" When I didn't move, Daniel started down the hall. "I'll ask him."

"You must go," Mrs. Dunn said. "Gather your things. If you see anything you need, take it."

Daniel knocked incessantly on the last door on the right until Engel emerged empty-handed. What had he been doing in there?

"Listen, sir," said Daniel, following him down the hall. "We've had a very crazy day, as you know. Light towers crashing on our heads, people trying to hack us to pieces with swords, exploding cars, poisonous umbrellas, insane teachers looking to electrocute us—who, I'm sure, make very nice girlfriends—and people as old as the pyramids coming for us. Can you, *please*, tell us who this Elam guy is?"

"No."

Daniel was surprised by Engel's refusal. As if he had been slapped in the face. I have to give it to Daniel, he recovered and pressed on. "All right. Can you at least tell us where Alexander's father is?"

"I'm sorry. I cannot give you the information you're seeking. Only his father or Elam Khai can offer that to Alexander."

"Why not?"

"Because it's not my place to say anything."

"People say things behind other people's backs all the time. I mean, that's what people do. If we didn't, we'd mostly sit around in silence."

Engel was annoyed, but the better part of him wanted to offer some explanation. Actually, he seemed more frustrated than anything else. "Our lives span a great many centuries. We have been many people. And it is part of our belief that who we have been should remain private. And in the past. It is our choice, each of us, whether or not to reveal who we are and who we have been."

"That makes no sense."

"Perhaps to you. But imagine being judged for things you did thousands of years ago under very different circumstances. That's why it is part of our code of honor."

"You mean like not killing each other?" Daniel's words dripped with sarcasm.

"Yes," Engel said. "If Braeden is dead, those responsible will pay with their lives. But if his life was taken in a fair battle, and he refused to capitulate, that is the only exception. An enemy is given the chance to surrender. If he does, his life is spared. He may be turned into an ally, or the victor may exact some price. Such as the promise he remain neutral or disappear or pretend to die. Anyone who does not follow this code, no matter who they are, no matter how noble their cause may be, will be hunted down and offered no such protections in the future. It is the only way we have survived."

"Mutual assured destruction," said Phoebe.

"All of us—" Engel broke off. "—with the exception of Elam

Khai...have at one time or another been defeated. If our way was any other than this, we would all be gone."

"You're trying to tell me this Elam guy's never been defeated?"

Engel ignored Daniel and turned to me. "I can't tell you where your father is."

"Right, I have to figure this out on my own."

"No, I just don't know where he is," Engel scanned my eyes, searching for something. He took a breath and held it. "And as for the rest of it," he said, "if your father would not tell you, I cannot."

Daniel gave up being polite. "You know what? I don't buy any of this 'forever' crap. But you broke your own rule five minutes ago when you told my friend who was chasing him. What's the difference if you give him a few details that might help us?"

"I gave you a name. An ancient name. One that can mean nothing to you. It was perhaps foolish to give you that much. But I am old, and I don't care as much anymore about my safety." He paused, thinking. "Which confuses me..."

"What does?" I asked.

"That he did not tell you who he is. Even stranger that he entered your home unarmed."

"That's what confuses you about all this?" said Daniel.

"You're sure he had no weapon?"

I thought about it. "He picked up a katana I had left by the door. But he entered without one."

"Seeing the sword, he may have felt he had no choice but to defend himself. But he didn't enter as an adversary." Engel paused again, his bright golden eyes looking far off toward some distant place the rest of us couldn't see. "I believe it is within my rights to tell you who confronted you. That, I've done. As for anything else, I can offer you only a way out of here." Engel peered into my eyes. "Do not look too deeply into things. There are times when ignorance is the better path than enlightenment."

"Normally, I couldn't agree with you more," Daniel said.

We were startled by a hard knock-knock-knock on the front door, quickly followed by pounding and banging. Words in an ancient tongue were called out.

"Go," Engel said. "I will delay them. Mrs. Dunn, show them the way." He added, "*Aleximvrotros*," to her under his breath.

He didn't wait for us to go. Didn't say goodbye or good luck or anything at all. He simply turned and made his way down the short set of stairs toward the entryway.

I caught a glimpse of several dark figures in the windows and immediately grabbed my backpack.

"This way," said Mrs. Dunn, leading us past a series of doors and into the last bedroom. Boxes, a shoe rack, luggage, and other items had been dragged out of a walk-in closet and tossed on the floor and the bed. She took us into the closet. Slicing through a thick wall of clothes hanging at the back, we found another closet that exited into the next house. We descended some stairs, then down another hall and down more stairs into the basement, which did not appear to connect with the area we were in before. We were heading downhill, each basement lower than the previous. Then it was back up into another brownstone.

Mrs. Dunn moved through this labyrinth unthinkingly, automatically, without hesitation as if she had practiced the twists and turns a hundred, maybe a thousand times before in an emergency evacuation drill.

We were through our third building when we heard footsteps. Heavy ones. Coming up behind us and closing fast.

Suddenly, there was a sickly sweet scent in the air.

"What's that smell?" I could feel a burning sensation in my eyes, which caused me to blink repeatedly.

"This is where he makes his rum."

It was the heavy perfume of molasses.

As we rounded the corner, the odor intensified. There was a large stainless steel vat the size and shape of a king bed filled with black-strap molasses. It looked like a muddy hot tub.

A four-inch pipe jutted out the bottom and connected to another device with twisted tubes.

As I ran past, I stuck my finger in the dark brown viscous fluid. I dragged a string of syrup with me as I continued forward.

Into a living room.

Up a tight, two-hundred-year-old staircase hardly wide enough for a full grown man to pass through.

"How many flights?"

"Two," Mrs. Dunn said.

"And then?"

"It's too complicated to explain."

"Then wait for me at the top."

This was the place to make a stand. If I could bottle-neck them on these steps, I might be able to slow them long enough for us to escape.

But it meant leading them right to us.

I climbed down to the first floor. Into the living room. Now, the kitchen. Back into the basement. Then up into the second house. I started making noise. Slamming doors, walking on my heels. Exactly the opposite of the way Deganawa and the Mohawk had taught me when approaching prey.

Four men burst from the door at the end of the hall.

I had miscalculated. I had gone too far.

Gotten too close.

I turned and ran.

Two burly men and two smaller ones saw me and started for me. Down the hall. Into the kitchen.

One of the smaller ones was very fast. He was closing on me quickly. I opened a cabinet door into his face as he rounded the corner.

That slowed him down a bit. I heard a loud *whump* as he crashed to the floor.

Again into the basement. Up the stairs.

Past the vat of molasses.

I stopped.

I could hear them lumbering up the stairs.

I grabbed a heavy cast iron pot and smashed it into the four-inch pipe. It did nothing but shock me with how loud it was. My ears were ringing. I slammed the iron pot down on the pipe again.

Louder still.

Then again. Then again. Then again.

Finally, it gave way.

Hundreds of gallons of the thick, sticky fluid shot out from the busted tube, sending a smothering brown wave three feet high onto the floor and down the stairs. I heard a couple of thuds as the men slipped and fell.

I wish I could tell you they gave up, but they were determined.

I took off.

Back through the living room to the foot of the tight staircase.

My heart was racing.

I waited at the bottom of the steps.

I caught a glimpse of them. One of the big guys was now leading the way. He was glazed in brown, a basted turkey ready to be served.

Perfect.

I climbed to the first landing and stopped. When I heard them crossing the living room, I sprinted up the second flight of stairs, my shoulder skimming along the rounded plaster wall.

All four of them trudged up the staircase, their shoes sticking to the floor as if they were running in tar. The biggest guy was first. He squeezed his way through the narrow, twisting passage, the molasses made his shirt cling to the walls. The fast guy was behind him. Judging from the blood I saw, I may have broken his nose.

About three-quarters of the way up, the ceiling angled down, constricting the cramped space further.

When the big guy got to that point, he got stuck. He would have had trouble without the gooey mess, but the sticky sweetness teed him up for me very nicely. He tried to scream a curse at me, but couldn't. His throat was clogged with the suffocating syrup.

He was flailing, floundering, trying to get free.

I gripped the molding above the second floor landing and propelled myself, feet first, into his sternum. He flew back, taking one of my shoes with him. It got swallowed in the dark amber goo. My kick sent him tumbling and he landed on the next guy who fell on the guy behind him. The three of them, stuck together, slid down the treads until they blocked the path of the fourth man.

When I got to the third floor landing, Mrs. Dunn tried to see past me.

"Sounded like elephants."

"A herd of them," I said. "Let's go."

As Phoebe passed me, she said, "You smell like a gingerbread man."

After a hundred uneven paces, I ripped off my remaining shoe and left it behind.

Mrs. Dunn continued to lead us through the maze of buildings. A blur of rooms went by. In the sixth or seventh living room, Daniel barked his shin on a coffee table, hurling the IDs into the air. We had to stop and collect them.

Then it was down into another basement.

I was about done with all this and wanted out of the labyrinth. I was getting dizzy and could feel the beginnings of a headache.

But Mrs. Dunn wasn't done.

We went through a door that led to a long passage running under a street. At least, I assumed we were under a street. The ceiling above was arched and built to hold a great deal of weight, and we were moving perpendicular to the direction we had been going,

At the end of the tunnel, there were two choices. Mrs. Dunn turned right.

After about thirty feet, the rising passage turned left. We were under another home. Up a set of stairs again. It amazed me that Mrs. Dunn wasn't more out of breath. I couldn't say the same for Daniel. He was wheezing like an asthmatic in a smoking lounge.

"Fastest kid in a straight line, huh?" said Phoebe to me as she patted Daniel on the back.

"This is not a straight line," he said.

Emerging from the cellar, we found ourselves inside a beautiful mansion. It was exquisite, with an almost museum-like quality to the setting. The rooms I could see were enormous.

Mrs. Dunn pointed to the front door. "That is the way out. This place has numerous exits in the basement. Which hopefully will give you some time," she said. "He would laugh at me for saying this, but…good luck."

We stepped outside. I got my bearings. This was Mount Vernon Street.

Phoebe and Daniel were wound up like thoroughbreds in the gate. "Head east," I said. They didn't move. "That way!" I pointed. "I'll catch up with you."

They sprinted across the street but were tentative to put much more distance between us.

"I have to go back and get him," Mrs. Dunn said. "I have to make sure he's okay."

I nodded, but Engel had given one final instruction, even though Mrs. Dunn thought it was directed to her since what he said was so close to my Ancient name. Ἀλεξίμβροτος. *Protect the mortals.* I put out my hand to shake hers. When she took it, I gripped her palm tightly and pulled her out of the house. Once she was outside, I closed the door behind her, confirming it was locked.

"What are you doing?"

"He doesn't want you coming back for him."

"He needs my help."

"No." I pulled some cash from my pocket and handed it to her. "If you're as loyal as I believe you are, you'll honor his wishes. The way you moved through that maze, you've been preparing for this. You knew exactly what to do. I'm guessing you know exactly what you're supposed to do now."

She didn't have to answer. I could tell by the look on her face that she did.

I was sure Engel had some instrument in place—a trust or annuity—that would provide her with enough money for the rest of her life. Something she was aware of and would be able to access.

She surprised me by rushing past me, her hands grabbing the

door handle, pushing on the thumb press over and over as she desperately tried to open the door.

"Mrs. Dunn…" I said, calming her attempts to work the latch by gently placing my hand on hers.

She gave up, shaking her head despondently. She pulled one last time, and the door gave way as it was blown off its jamb, rocked by an explosion. We were knocked to the ground. The windows on the house shattered, sending glass into the street. A warm blast of air brushed over me.

As I lay on the ground, I stared at the fireball rising into the sky a block away. It lit up the street and the houses like a gigantic campfire.

"Mrs. Dunn? Are you all right?"

I helped her to her feet. She appeared uninjured.

"No, Master Grant, I'm not."

I rushed her away from the house, getting her around the corner and out of sight as neighbors began streaming into the street.

"Go," I said, backing away from her. "Get very far away from here."

As I was about to turn and race after my friends, I saw Mrs. Dunn's eyes well up with tears. Taking care of Engel had been her life. I came back and squeezed her hand, this time in genuine friendship. My grasp moved her watch, revealing what was hidden by the leather band. Two triangles. Smaller, darker, but the same symbol as the tattoo on Mrs. Avery's ankle. She noticed me notice.

"He called it a mark to protect me."

I stared at her, watching her for a long moment. "Thank you, Mrs. Dunn. From both of us." Then letting go, I slipped away into the night.

I caught up with Daniel and Phoebe about a block away as they were making their way along the edge of Louisburg Square.

Phoebe checked me over for lacerations and found only bits of broken glass in my hair and on my clothes.

Daniel stared at the flames shooting into the air. "Do you think…?" He didn't finish the question.

Sirens cut through the night. Not only the high-pitched wail of police cars and ambulances, but the low growling honks of fire trucks, the ones telling you something big is heading for you, and you better get out of its way.

"We have to go," I said.

Phoebe couldn't believe it. "We have to go and help him," she corrected.

I marched past her, up Mount Vernon. Looking back, I saw the flames and smoke coming from Acorn Street.

"If Engel wasn't ready with an escape, then it's already too late to help him."

Phoebe's eyes became slits. "How can you be so callous?"

Daniel said nothing, but I could see the disappointment on his face.

Without slowing, I said, "That explosion. That's Engel's work. Not the people chasing us. Those houses were rigged to explode. He set them off. Either he got out. Or he decided to die. Either way, it was his choice."

This may sound more heartless than my refusal to go back for Engel, but I felt a pang of loss in my stomach as much for that old street and its history as I did for the old man.

Well, maybe that's a lie.

The wind whipping up the narrow lane caused my eyes to tear up. I convinced myself that's all it was. Just the wind.

I wiped the tears away.

- THIRTEEN -
Sometimes Life Is A Walk In The Park—Where You Get Mugged

The mix of cobblestones and old pavers was difficult to run on, especially without shoes. Traveling over the lumpy, rutted path quickly tired my legs and made my calves burn and my feet cry out. Daniel twisted his ankle fairly badly when his half-burnt, zero traction soles caused him to slip on the uneven surface. Phoebe faired better in her cheerleading shoes.

I felt their displeasure with me, their disillusionment. It hung all around us, like the constant blaring of emergency vehicles. Rather than get quieter as we moved further from the blast, the sirens grew louder, more desperate.

We reached a brick sidewalk, an improvement. Still, it undulated and heaved. Jogging on this in the daytime was a challenge. At night, it was dangerous.

I have to say, streets like these are one of the things I admire about Boston. Just about any other city would look at this sidewalk and see a liability nightmare. There'd be a maintenance crew out here with orange cones and lime-green safety vests. The whole thing would be ripped up and resurfaced. That they haven't turned this city into a perfect Disneyland version of itself is one of the most admirable qualities of the people of Boston.

My feet felt like they'd been set on fire. It's strange how pain often gets worse right after removing the cause of the agony. The pavers had done their damage. My brain was just catching up to the suffering.

I could feel my pulse in my ears, at my temples. Every sound was amplified. Every image enhanced.

I was confident we had escaped the men following us. They'd been in the blast zone. I don't know why I was so optimistic there weren't others waiting for us around the corner. Every place we had gone so far, we'd been discovered. But I felt no imminent threat.

"I have to stop," Daniel said, sitting on the ground. He took off his shoes and massaged his feet. "Where are we going?"

I took in a deep breath and leaned against a tree that was heaving up part of the brick walk. Stopping made the pain feel worse.

My feet were never this soft when I played *tewaaraton*.

I missed my friend, Deganawa. So very much.

I looked at Daniel and knew, all too soon, I'd be missing him, too. I wanted to grab him and physically stop him from growing. I didn't want to be alone anymore.

"We're going to Logan Airport and then..." I shrugged my shoulders. "Out of the country."

"I can't leave the country," Daniel said. "My feet hurt."

I could see my comment had set off an internal battle in Phoebe. She didn't say anything for a long time, but her face betrayed her worry and indecision. She knew I was watching her, yet she never returned the gaze.

Finally, she spoke. "Every time I have a second to think during the brief moments we're not in immediate mortal danger, the thought occurs to me..." She glanced up with those eyes bearing into me. "You should have made us go home."

This time I averted my eyes, staring down at my feet. The base of the tree had scattered bricks knotted into its roots and rising into the trunk. How long does it take for a brick to get so intertwined with a tree that it's now a part of it? A hundred years? Two hundred?

"My parents think I'm at a homecoming dance. In about an hour or so my father is going to be out with a shotgun looking for Craig."

I have to admit I got a significant amount of pleasure envisioning Phoebe's father taking a shot at Craig. Not hitting him. Maybe winging him. Some birdshot in the tail.

I obviously have a little problem when it comes to Craig Coulter.

"I'm not trying to scare you or anything," I said. "But I think, right now, it's safer for you to come with me than go home."

"Safer with *you* than at home? With my family?"

"Yes."

I think she saw in my face just how serious I was. Her eyes blinked quickly. She was trying to process this.

"They've found us everywhere we've gone," I said. "I don't want them following you home. Because they will. I can't protect you or your family if you do that. Once we get some place secure where I can get help, then we can put together a plan to get you both home. At the moment, this is safer. For you and them."

"You're really shitty, do you know that?" She fought back the emotion. "At not scaring people."

Daniel slipped on his shoes. "You *are* shitty at it. I mean, just *horribly* shitty."

"I haven't had a lot of practice being honest with people."

"Let's hope you don't get any more practice for a while."

At the top of the hill, we turned down Walnut.

We walked the two blocks to Beacon Street in silence. Crossed the four lanes without waiting for the light and entered the Common.

Saturday night revelers were coming home from parties or being out. There were a few couples here and there, holding hands. In the shadows, homeless covered up for the night. A Freedom Trail tour guide still in his Colonial dress walked by. Had he been wearing that red sash around his waist in the 1770s, he might find himself tarred and feathered. Luckily, the only Patriots in the park were a group of four men and two women staggering toward us down the path, wearing player jerseys. They were singing. Badly. It appeared the partying for tomorrow's football game had started early.

Daniel limped a few steps behind Phoebe and me.

My mind wouldn't quiet down. *Had* Engel gotten out? My insides were a lot more conflicted than I'd shown earlier. And where were we flying to once we got to the airport?

We passed a police officer on horseback. He eyed us as we went by. I was suddenly conscious I wasn't wearing shoes, but I think it was more our age than my lack of footwear that drew his notice. Teenagers out late are always suspect.

That's when the crooning, intoxicated Patriots caught his attention, and he spurred his horse in their direction.

I steered us down another path. My plan was to head toward the subway entrance at the Southeast corner of the park.

We passed a playground off to the left.

Several teenagers were sitting on swings that were much too small for them. Others in the same group were standing on the brightly colored play structures. They watched us. It was a different kind of gaze than the cop on horseback, but it was just as unnerving. A moment later, three of them appeared up ahead, having crossed behind the playground to cut us off.

They were moving toward us with that slow, singsong sway that projected confidence—or tried to, anyway. That thuggish gait that says, *I'm not worried about you in the least.*

"D'you guys have any cigarettes?" one of them asked no one in particular, glancing everywhere but at us.

I didn't answer, just kept walking.

Before I could stop him, Daniel engaged with them. "No, we don't have anything."

Anything? He should have said anything other than anything. Now they were really curious.

"What's in the backpack?" the leader said to me, directly this time.

If they only knew I had almost thirty thousand dollars in cash in there, they might need a change of pants. They were hoping we had forty or fifty bucks on us. Maybe they might net a smartphone, a computer, or a tablet if they were lucky.

"Schoolbooks," I said.

"Kinda late to be studying," the one doing all the talking said. "On a Saturday." The others laughed.

They slid smoothly into a more threatening formation. With the talkative one moving directly in front of us. The other two on each flank. We were covered on three sides. The only thing we could do is turn and run back the way we came. But I had a suspicion we would've found ourselves meeting up with a few of their playground friends if we did that.

"Why don't you show us what's in there?"

I had the briefest urge to open up my backpack and use their momentary shock against them.

The two on the sides had both their hands in their pockets.

They were trying to make it look like they had guns. I could tell by the outline on their jeans they were just pointing their index fingers. The kid on the right was faking like he had a firearm in each pocket.

Gunslinger.

They could have weapons tucked in their waistbands, but I was confident they didn't. You don't hang around a playground in the middle of Boston Common with guns. That's a good way to get yourself arrested.

But the leader, he was more difficult to read. He had only one hand, his right, in his pocket. He was gesturing with his left whenever he spoke. Judging by the way he moved his arm, he was right-handed.

He stepped closer. "I said, what's in the backpack?" Left hand waving in front of me. Right hand coming out of his pocket, holding a knife that he flipped open with a flick of his thumb.

I didn't bother to look at the knife. That's the mistake most people make. They look at the weapon. All it does is let them know how afraid you are.

I fixed my eyes directly on his, piercing him with my stare.

This surprised him. But it didn't unnerve him.

It should have.

Daniel let out a loud groan behind me. "Are you kidding me? Do you know what we've been through? Do you have any idea who you are dealing with?"

"Shut up, fool," said the leader.

Phoebe looked back at Daniel. As if to say the same thing: Shut up, fool.

But Daniel was right.

I was angry. I was upset. Mostly at myself. That's probably why they picked us. Because I looked like I wasn't paying attention. And I hadn't been.

If I'd been more alert, they probably never would have bothered us.

I didn't plead with him. I didn't bother to negotiate. I didn't reach for the butterfly knife I'd used to cut the seatbelt that was still in my pocket.

When the kid shifted his weight to get into a fighting stance, I launched at him, seizing his knife hand. My left hand gripping the base of his thumb, my right over the top of my left. Even if he had been quick enough or strong enough to slash at me, the blade would've sliced harmlessly between my arms. I twisted my hands, rotating his wrist counterclockwise. I hadn't gone three-quarters of a turn before he dropped the weapon. The blade clanged on the asphalt.

It took less than a second from the start of my move to the knife hitting the pavement.

Still clutching his wrist with my left hand, I raised my right arm and thrust my elbow down, striking the middle of his forearm.

It snapped.

Cleanly.

Both bones.

They poked through the tattooed skull on his arm, making the eyes bleed red.

The kid screamed in pain. The sound echoed off the buildings a hundred yards away. I stepped over him, walking up to the closer of his two stunned comrades and simply said, "You should get your friend to a hospital. Quickly. There's a cop not far in that direction. I'd start yelling for help."

The cries of agony would probably draw the officer. But I stared at him. It was not a request.

He began calling out for assistance.

I turned to the other. "Give me your kicks."

He took off his shoes immediately and handed them to me. I reached back and grabbed Phoebe's arm, then pulled her down the path. Daniel followed, looking back every few steps, swearing under his breath.

There were a dozen ways I could've gotten out of that situation without hurting that kid. And under most circumstances, I would have attempted every one of them before resorting to brute force.

But I wasn't feeling very charitable at the moment.

I was alert again. Focused.

That had been my mistake. Not paying attention.

No one else in the park seemed threatening. In fact, late-night park goers we passed seem to fear our presence. They altered their path, changed directions or simply tensed up.

They must've seen it in my eyes.

It was the cold stare of a wolf.

I might have done something worse had anyone else messed with us.

We descended the covered staircase that led down into Park Street Station. I picked up the pace when I felt the rumble of an approaching train. At this hour, it could be some time before the next train arrived and I didn't want to be standing around, waiting for the police to comb the area.

I handed Phoebe and Daniel cash.

"We need to make that train."

I didn't bother to look at the transit map. We had to take the Green Line and transfer to the Blue Line to get to Logan Airport.

We used three ticket machines in unison to speed the process along, but it seemed to take forever anyway. While waiting for the tickets to print, I slipped the borrowed shoes onto my feet. The machines finally spit out the transit cards. I ripped mine from the dispenser and raced to the turnstile.

I slid the ticket in the slot and passed through the gates. I could hear the train now. We needed to get to the other side. I thought about crossing the tracks. They were only a few inches below the platform in this station, but we'd surely get the attention of Transit police. I sprinted down the stairs to the tunnel linking the two sides. Phoebe kept up with me. Daniel's turned ankle hampered his progress.

I wheeled around and yelled at him, "C'mon!"

He tried to move faster.

In the tunnel, I could feel the train pass overhead. The train was already in the station.

I was taking four steps at a time. The train was getting ready to leave. I raced across the smooth concrete. I was a dozen feet away when the doors started closing. Two big steps.

I leaped.

My face smashed into the doors, and I bounced off, getting spun a half turn by the train moving down the tracks before I crashed to the ground.

"Owwwwwwwwwww!"

My nose stung.

My head throbbed.

I hit my fist on the floor.

Now my hand hurt as much as my face.

Phoebe sprinted up to me, then rested her palms on her knees as she tried to catch her breath.

"You were gonna leave us here?" she said, breathing heavily.

"I was hoping to keep the door open."

"Okay," she said, not convinced. "He can't run. You know that, right?" She motioned toward Daniel with her head.

I sighed. "Yeah."

She watched me for a moment, then stuck out her hand, offering it to help me up.

"Thanks," I said.

"That's what people do. They help each other."

I nodded. She had made her point.

Once on my feet, I walked over to Daniel.

"Sit down."

I could tell he didn't want to comply, but after a moment, he sat on one of the benches. He averted his eyes, avoiding my gaze.

I squatted down and squeezed Daniel's ankle, running my fingertips over the ligaments. He yelped in pain.

"Can you not do that?" we said at the same time for very different reasons.

I lifted the bottom of his jacket and tore off a strip of its lining.

Now he was looking at me. Daggers.

"I'm going to wrap your ankle."

We had to keep moving. The police would be looking for the unknown assailant who brutally snapped the arm of one poor teenager and stole the shoes of another.

That incriminating knife the kid had was long gone by now.

I gently slipped off Daniel's shoe. The ankle was visibly swollen. It needed to be iced down, rested, elevated. We didn't have time for any of those things.

I wrapped the torn ribbon of lining around his foot, then his ankle, crisscrossing back and forth. I wound the fabric tight. His ankle needed support if he was going to keep up.

I asked a woman walking by when the next train was supposed to come.

"Maybe fifteen minutes," she said.

I looked around at the old station. Fifteen minutes was an eternity. When this place first opened, the entire subway trip took three and a half minutes.

Whenever people think subways, they usually think New York

City, but at six AM on September 1, 1897, a single car stuffed with a hundred passengers started down the tracks, disappearing into that tunnel right over there, and Boston officially opened the first subway in North America, beating New York by more than seven years.

I didn't want to be here that day, but I'd been forced into coming by one of my classmates. We ditched school. I think that was as much a lure for him as hoping to take a ride on the splashy new underground. We waited eight hours in the overcrowded, suffocating terminal before we were let onboard to roll from here to Boylston Station.

One end of Boston Common to the other. About five hundred yards.

It would've taken all of seven minutes—only twice as long as the train ride—to walk that distance, *and* we wouldn't have had to stand in a sardine-packed cave for half the day.

The experience was so bad, I didn't ride a subway for five years after that day.

I finished tucking the fabric strip up underneath itself, sliding Daniel's sock over the dressing to hold it in place.

"You might want to think about some new shoes and socks...and maybe feet." I waved the air under my nose.

"Thanks!" he said, grabbing his shoe and slipping it on for himself.

He got up and put weight on his foot.

I checked his ankle again. "Better?"

"Yeah," he said reluctantly.

"I'm sorry I lost my cool back there. I just don't like people taking advantage of the weak."

Phoebe came over and put her hand on my shoulder, patting me gently. I had earned back a small bit of her respect.

As I glanced up, I caught a glimpse of a face. One of the men from the woods. Standing on the platform. I got to my feet.

"We've gotta leave."

"What is it?"

I spun around looking for him, but he was gone. He couldn't have exited the station that quickly and the smattering of people wasn't dense enough for him to get lost in.

"What did you see?" Phoebe asked.

I realized I was seeing things. Like glimpsing Elam Khai on Commonwealth. Fear editing my vision.

"Nothing."

I walked over to the bench and leaned on it as I let the rush pass. I continued scanning the station for the man, even though I knew he was an illusion, my brain working overtime to find the next danger even if my mind had to make one up.

As I was navigating the most disagreeable parts of my brain, I stumbled over a thought.

"Braeden said something to me in the woods. *'The key is at the beginning of time.'*"

Thinking about him brought it all back. Phoebe gripped my upper arm, squeezing it, then slowly letting her hand slide down to my elbow. It calmed me. Calmed me and excited me at the same time. How did she do that?

Daniel scrunched up his face. "I don't remember him saying that."

"He said it just before we left." I didn't complete the sentence. *Before we left him, left him there to die.*

I'm sorry, my brother.

"When you two were talking in that strange language?" Phoebe said.

"That wasn't *a* language. It was a mix of three or four."

Maybe that had something to do with it. The Parthian jumbled with Ancient Greek and Vulgar Latin. It could have been part of the message, or it could have been to confuse anyone listening.

Phoebe looked like she was trying to figure it out. "What do you think he meant?"

"Again with the stupid riddles!"

"I'm not sure. He was passing along a message from my father. I know my father. It would be something he and I shared. Something that when I figured it out, I would just *know*."

Daniel was working over the phrase in his head. "It's obviously not the *beginning* of time. You people aren't that old."

Phoebe pushed up the sleeves of my sweatshirt that was way too big for her. "Maybe it's the beginning of humanity. Could your father be talking about Africa?"

"Maybe," I said, not really convinced. My father wasn't interested in the origins of humanity. Advanced civilizations, powerful empires, that was his amusement. "If it's anything like that, it'd be the beginning of recorded history. Mesopotamia. Indus Valley."

Daniel put more pressure on his ankle, testing it. "So we've got the choice of going to the Congo or the Sahara Desert or Mesowherever—"

"Mesopotamia. Iraq and Iran."

"Of course. *Or* the Indus Valley. I'm guessing that's in India?"

"Mostly Pakistan and Afghanistan."

"Even better. There isn't any Caribbean island possibilities? Maybe the Florida *Keys*. The Keys are at the beginning of time?"

I gave Daniel a hard look.

"I'm just saying. Blue water. White beaches. Girls in bikinis."

Phoebe glanced down at Daniel. "With your skin tone, we'd lose you in the sand. That is, until you burned."

I spent a couple of days last summer on Cape Cod with Daniel. The shade of red his skin turned after three hours in the sun was something I had never seen before. And frankly, hope never to see again.

"My father wouldn't be that vague. It would be something clever." My brain started to hurt. Where was that train?

Daniel shook his finger. "Maybe it's the beginning of *your* life. Where were you born?"

"Constantinople."

Phoebe jumped in before the confused look could appear on Daniel's face. "It's now called Istanbul. It's in Turkey."

"Istanbul," he muttered. "It couldn't have been Waikiki?"

"Could it be where your father was born," Phoebe asked.

I didn't answer. That's because—and this may sound strange—I didn't know where my father was born. Whenever I asked him, he deftly maneuvered the subject to something else. It's information that could be very useful at the moment. I know he was born somewhere around the Mediterranean.

"I don't think it's anyone's birthplace. He wouldn't have said *time*." I thought about this for a moment. *The key is at the beginning of time.* Could it be that simple? "Maybe it's the letter *T*."

"What?"

"The beginning of *time*."

"How does 'T' help us? Are we in some Scrabble Death Match?"

My mind suddenly registered something I'd been seeing the last few minutes. "This is the T. The subway here is called the T."

I motioned toward the signs in the station. A circle around a T.

That's when I spotted a policeman talking into the walkie-talkie mic clipped to his shirt. This was not a mirage.

Over the radio, I heard a female dispatcher giving the cop a description. White male, approximately sixteen. On foot. She got my eye color right, but my hair color wrong. Then she described my shoes. The color and brand.

I looked down. Celtics Green. Just as reported.

Just great.

They thought stealing the shoes was the motive for the attack. And for a moment, I gave up. I felt the muscles in my face fall. My shoulders slumped.

"You think they're looking for you?" Phoebe said, watching the officer.

I nodded. "We can't wait for the next train," I said, pointing at the brightly colored stolen sneakers on my feet.

Then again, leaving the station wasn't the ideal solution, either. That would put us back on the Common. But we didn't have much choice. I was about to head up to the street when I remembered there was a block long underground walkway that connected to Downtown Crossing.

"This way," I whispered. "Try not to look suspicious."

"We're teenagers out after midnight, how do we not look suspicious?" Daniel hissed.

"Shhhh!"

We followed the Orange Line signs on the walls that led to the Winter Street Concourse.

"Stop looking back," I said to Daniel.

"I can't help it."

"If someone was going to break your arm if you didn't stop, you think you could help it then?"

He got the message.

But it was already too late. I heard the muffled squawks of the walkie-talkie echo in the long corridor. The policeman was following us. From the sound of it, he wasn't far behind.

I fought the urge to turn and take a look.

Up ahead I saw one of those round parabolic safety mirrors mounted on the wall. As we passed under it, I could see the cop in the fish-eyed reflection.

He looked a little heavy, with a barrel chest. You could tell it was a struggle for him to keep up with our pace. He was winded.

I realized after a second glance that he wasn't overweight, he was wearing body armor.

The burden of his equipment—the ballistic vest, his nightstick, his gun, his walkie-talkie, the thick leather belt holding his handcuffs, extra ammunition clips, his flashlight, and mace—was weighing him down.

I didn't want to start running. That would force him to chase after us. The slower, the better. If we could maintain the distance between us, keep it constant, we might be able to stall until...

That's when I felt it.

The tremor. The rattle. Followed by the high-pitched squeal of a train coming around a corner. I tried to gauge how soon it would reach the station, and how far we were from the platform.

My nose tingled, reminding me of the earlier failed attempt. Me versus metal door. I didn't want a repeat of that.

"I think we should run," I said.

"Run?"

"As fast as we can."

Instead of sprinting ahead alone, I clasped my hand around Daniel's wrist and I dragged him. We got down to the platform just as the Orange Line was pulling into the station. I didn't really care which way it was going.

It happened to be heading in the right direction.

The train came to a stop. We still had to cross the platform.

There is a quiet that comes after the doors open. Especially at night when there aren't many passengers. It's this whoosh. And then it passes, and there is nothing left but background noise.

In that relative quiet, all I could hear were our heels on the concrete, the clock tick of time passing, counting down the seconds until the train doors closed.

Click click click. Tick tick tick.

The cop was closer than I thought. Sweat was streaming down his face, which was beet red, the perspiration rolling off his chin.

I could hear the hiss. The one that comes just before the doors begin to close.

"We've gotta sprint for it!"

We pushed ourselves and hurtled toward the train, jumping onboard at the last second. I felt a sense of deep satisfaction as the doors began to close. Daniel whooped in celebration, but the doors stopped halfway, jerked opened, and then hissed and closed again. The train operator must have seen the officer. The cop was able to get aboard.

The train lurched forward. No way off now.

The police officer had entered one set of doors behind us. He was no more than twenty feet away.

He was gasping for air. "Why you running?" he wheezed, his lungs barely able to push out enough breath to make an audible sound.

There wasn't a single response I could think of that would make our situation better.

I turned and yelled, "Go through the door!"

"What door?"

"To the other car." I pushed Daniel and Phoebe toward the end of the subway car. "Go!"

"But we're not supposed—" Daniel trailed off as he realized this would be the least of our crimes committed this evening.

We were plunged into complete darkness. The lights flickered, then returned as we entered the tunnel. Phoebe pulled open the door, and she and Daniel stepped into the breach between the two cars. Glancing down at the tracks speeding past, Phoebe suddenly lost her nerve. Her hands fumbled with the handle, and she couldn't get the door to the other car open. There wasn't enough room for me to fit. I had to wait until she stepped into the next car.

Anger fueled her effort, and she was finally able to unlatch it. She fell through the door.

I pressed myself into the breach. It was loud. The clickety-clack of the wheels on the rails were amplified by the smooth walls and curved ceiling of the tunnel. There was nothing but a small foot-hold on each end of the breach and grab rails on either side of the doors.

Daniel's foot slipped off the step, but he was holding on with both hands.

He wouldn't let go long enough to open the door.

Seeing this, Phoebe came back and pulled it open for him. He passed through into the other car. This left me alone in the breach.

The cop had recovered and was standing on the other side of the door. He was holding his flashlight, tapping the bottom end of it against the glass. It looked more like a nightstick. His movements were measured, cautious. This wasn't one of those tough-guy cops itching to break some heads. He seemed like the kind of cop they send to walk the neighborhoods and get friendly with the residents. The kind that takes a seat on a hot day and accepts a free cannoli from Mike's or a complimentary cold soda from a grateful merchant.

I held the handle so that the cop couldn't pull it open.

It was dark. I didn't think he could get a good look at my face. Then he flipped the flashlight around and shined the light at me. I quickly covered my face, pretending to shield my eyes from the brightness.

There were security cameras everywhere, on the platform, in the cars, and my image could be out to the world in a matter of moments if I didn't act swiftly.

I stepped away. And pressed my back against the door behind me, one hand clutching the grab rail, the other on the handle ready to push it open. These were tight quarters. If I could bring him closer, I would have the advantage.

A thought came to me.

Straddling the two cars, I let go of the handle and put up my hand in surrender.

The cop used the barrel of his flashlight to jack open the door, the other hand rested on the grip of his gun.

"We didn't mean anything by it, officer."

Both my hands were visible. The one out in front in a sign of submission, the other holding on to the grab rail.

"What didn't you mean?" The cop was thinking maybe he had a major collar on his hands.

"Not paying the fare. It's not that we can't. We have money." I slowly reached into my pocket. When I pulled it out, I waved three twenties in the air. "We just thought it'id be *brill* to be able to blow over, you know. Like we'ad seen in the movies." I was affecting a slight Africanized English accent. One that would be hard to place.

"Where are you from?" he said through the half-closed door.

I was ready and flipped open the passport from Ghana.

The train pitched and squealed as we cornered. The officer struggled to maintain his balance. After gauging I wasn't a threat, he felt comfortable enough to open the door all the way, leaning against it to keep it from closing. He beamed his light on my passport.

"Where the heck is that? You're not American?"

I shook my head.

"You speak English good."

"English is our official language. We used to be part of the British Empire."

The cop laughed. "So did we. I guess we both showed those SOB's, huh?"

"You a bit sooner, though."

"We don't take shit from anybody in this country, that's for sure."

He studied the ID. Slid his fingers over the type, making sure it was raised. Checked a couple of the other no-tech security features. He was thorough. I'm glad I used Engel.

"My friends and I are willing to pay for the tickets. It was just a daffy prank."

He aimed his light toward the heisted sneakers. But they were black, not the bright green he was expecting. As lethal as I appeared in Boston Common, that was how meek my demeanor was now.

"Here." I stuck out my hand with the money.

He looked at me. Looked at the bills. It wasn't so much cash that it seemed like an outright bribe, but it was definitely more than the amount of three tickets. It was a gamble. He hesitated. And I thought maybe I should've thrown out a couple of the hundreds instead.

"Where are you guys coming from?"

I nodded to the passport. "Ghana."

"No, I mean, right now."

"The Burying Grounds."

The Granary Burying Ground is an old cemetery across the street from Boston Common. Several people I knew are buried there, including John Hancock and Paul Revere. As well as a friend of mine named Christopher.

"We wanted to see the gravestones at night. We thought it might be brilliant."

"The gates close at five. You jump over those, too?"

"Ah, you know, bring a pretty girl to a scary place, they grab your arm tighter."

"You didn't see anything in the park?"

"We did. Yes."

He got excited. "What did you see?"

"The graves."

My awkward phrasing and faux misunderstanding were sufficiently annoying that he reached out and snatched the sixty dollars from my hands.

"Don't do it again," he said.

I shook my head like a three-year-old does when you tell him not to throw his toy truck in the toilet bowl. Wide-eyed with big side-to-side movements.

He stepped out of the way, and the door slammed shut.

I relaxed and let out a deep, slow breath, trying to cleanse my body of the stress.

I pushed on the handle and leaned back into the other car.

Before the door closed, I heard a dull crack.

I glanced up, The cop nodded at me through the doors. Only his head never came back up. His face fell forward into the window, flattening his features against the glass, then he slid out of view.

Behind him was the attacker from the woods. The man with the short cropped red hair I had seen for that instant in the station. The one who slashed my step-brother and cut him open.

The cop's unconscious body was in the way, blocking the man from opening the door.

The train was slowing. We were coming to the next station. State Street. We needed to transfer here to the upper tracks. Take the Blue Line out to the airport. Get rid of a maniacal attacker.

I called out, but Phoebe and Daniel weren't in the car. They had moved up further, thinking we were on the run from the cop. When I found them two cars later, Phoebe asked, "Where's the policeman?"

"The police are the least of our worries." I glanced back and saw the man had gotten past the obstacle and was now in the next car. "Remember the guy in the woods, the one who sliced open Braeden..."

Phoebe cupped her hand over her own mouth to stifle a scream as she saw him through the window.

I gripped the handle, hoping I could keep him out of the car, but he was much bigger than me and stronger.

"You beat him once," Phoebe said, her tone fearless.

Her unexpected confidence in me may have been misplaced, but it motivated me. I put one foot up on the door's glass and pressed my shoe against it for more leverage.

"Your shoes are covered in grease," she said, wrinkling her nose.

In the breach, I had rubbed the sneakers against the couplers, hoping the grime would camouflage the emerald footwear.

"They were looking for green shoes," I said.

I watched the man open the door on the other side of the breach with battle-scarred hands.

"What do we do?" Phoebe said.

"I think we stick with the plan. Get to the airport. Get out of the country."

"Seems like we need to get off the planet to get away from these people," said Daniel.

I looked forward, hoping to see the station in the window. I didn't. Just more tunnel. "We're running out of time."

Time. How could I be so stupid? The clue would have to be easy to find, and yet easy for others to misunderstand.

I grabbed at Daniel's watch, looked at the time and tapped the face repeatedly.

"It's not the beginning of time or my father's life or my life, or the beginning of the word time, it's the beginning of time on the clock. The zero hour."

"Midnight?"

Phoebe waved Daniel off. "The Prime Meridian? You think we need to go to England?"

My father hated England. It's the last place anyone would think he would go. But first, we had to get off this train.

"I don't want to alarm anyone," I said to the other people in the car. Of course, these words immediately alarmed everyone. "Does anyone have any mace?"

"Why do you ask?" said a woman in her twenties, curious and a little wary.

"There is a guy who's going to try to get in this car who just knocked out a police officer."

People sprang out of their seats and rushed the doors.

"We're almost at the station," said a man.

"He doesn't look like he's going to wait that long."

A woman in her thirties glanced around. "I've got something. But it's..."

She came over to me and opened her purse. In it was her wallet, some makeup, a large set of keys...and a stun gun. Electronic weapons were illegal in Massachusetts. Not that it had stopped Mrs. Avery. I raised my eyebrows.

She shrugged. "I have an ex-husband who threatened me once too often." She nodded toward the device. "You didn't get that from me."

"I don't even know who you are."

I took one of my hands off the handle and grabbed the stun gun, annoyed that I had left behind so useful an item on a Back Bay sidewalk.

Phoebe wrestled the fire extinguisher off the wall and got ready to use it as a weapon. Her stance was pretty good, and I wondered if she had taken self-defense classes. I motioned toward the red canister, shaking my head.

She shook her head back at me. "I'll put this down when we're off this train."

"Fine. Just don't hit me." I said. "When the doors open, you and Daniel run as fast as you can up to the Blue Line and take it to the airport. Don't book a flight. Don't even ask about flights. Just stay in the ticketing area of the international terminal. No matter what happens, you get there, and stay by the security checkpoint."

I slipped the backpack off my shoulder and tossed it to Daniel. He looked at it, his eyes as big as quarters. His hands trembled just thinking about how much money was in there.

"What are you going to do?" she said.

"I'm planning on running as fast as I can and coming with you. Now, get by the doors."

When I turned back, the redheaded man who had mortally wounded Braeden was no longer at the end door. In his place stood another attacker from the woods. His hair was longer, darker, and he looked much younger. He was holding the cop's nightstick. I hadn't anticipated there would be two of them.

Where was the other man, the redhead? The younger attacker was blocking my view. I tried to get a glimpse, but it was no use. I stayed put. I could at least take one of them out. I'd deal with the other man in the station if I had to.

One problem at a time.

The train was slowing. The younger attacker entered into the breach. The smart play would be to wait, converge on me in the station, but remembering the fight in the forest, they were more about brute strength than tactics. He would go for the door, try to force it open.

I pushed as hard as I could against the door with my foot. Rubber sole shoes. Good thing. I let go of the handle.

The younger attacker's hand disappeared from view as he reached for the door.

I flipped on the stun gun. And when I saw the handle turn, I zapped it, sending a crackling bolt of energy into the metal. I kept sparking the device for several seconds. Snap snap snap, like a squadron of wasps flying into a bug zapper only a million times more powerful. Through the glass, I could see the man on the other side convulsing.

He slid out of sight, unconscious.

The doors whooshed open. And everyone bolted into the station. The metal canister made a satisfying chime when Phoebe smashed the base of the fire extinguisher into the jaw of a third attacker lying in wait to the left of the train door. He dropped to the cement.

"Run!"

I saw the attacker with the short cropped reddish hair exit one car back. Our eyes met. He snarled. My muscles reacted before my brain even realized he was sprinting towards me.

I made for the stairs, taking three at a time, and sprinted down the passageway leading to the other platform. At the far end, I could see there was a Blue Line Wonderland train sitting in the station. Phoebe and Daniel were about to get on it. I headed for the train, but the short-haired man from the woods had beaten me upstairs.

I stopped.

If I got on that train, we'd be back where we started. The three of us and him. Normally, those odds would be in our favor, but I had a better chance of escaping him if I was alone.

When Phoebe saw me no longer moving toward them, she screamed, "Alexander!"

"Get on the train!" My tone was so firm, she and Daniel hesitated only an instant before stepping onboard just as the doors closed.

I wouldn't be joining my friends just yet.

- FOURTEEN -
It Would've Gone Better
If I Could Fly

I stood on the platform, watching the train begin to pull away. Phoebe and Daniel were safe. It was just me and him.

We were underneath Devonshire Street and the Old State House. They had redone the ceilings, made them more pleasing to the eye and probably less toxic, but it didn't look like the MBTA had made any structural changes to the tunnel.

That was good.

The train was rolling down the tracks.

I cut across the platform toward the tunnel the train was heading for. I tried to time it right. The man charged toward me, like I knew he would. His ruddy skin flushed red with rage.

Red, that was what he was. His hair. His face. His eyes.

He had the angle on me. But I had the speed. Just as I could feel his hand on the fabric of my shirt, I launched myself onto the back of the moving train, my hands clutching at the grab rails, my shoes dragging painfully along the railroad ties until I hauled myself up. My feet struggled to find purchase on the narrow landing below the end door. I got a toe on the step, and after a moment found my footing.

I reached for the handle, but it didn't budge. As hard as I tried, I couldn't open the door. It was locked. I slammed my hand against the glass in frustration.

The sound of the wheels on the curving track pierced my ears. I could hold on until the next station if I could just block out the ear-splitting squeal. I looped one arm through a grab hold so I could use my free hand to cover one ear. I pressed my shoulder against the other. It deadened the sound enough that I stopped involuntarily wincing.

When I opened my eyes again, I saw the redheaded man chasing the train. He had jumped into the pit and was running down the middle of the track into the rat-infested bowels of the hundred-something-year-old station. We were slowly picking up speed, but a person could sprint faster than we were currently moving.

He was going to catch us.

As the back of the train entered the tunnel, the resurfaced ceiling ended and the rough, exposed steelwork began. This section of tunnel was built using a method called "cut and cover." They would literally cut through the street, jack up buildings, dig a trench, lay down the tracks, build a support structure, then cover the whole thing and replace the road.

I remember sitting here after school and watching them work for hours. I'd never seen construction equipment like that before. At night, I would sneak under the fence and explore. This tunnel wasn't bored out of rock. It was built with steel beams, more like a building. There were all kinds of hidden passages down here.

The man was closing in on the train.

I used the door handle as a foothold and climbed higher until I was perched atop the grab bars on either side of the rear door, my fingers gripping a ridge on the roof. About twenty feet ahead, passing over the middle of the train, I saw what I was looking for: An access ladder in the ceiling leading up toward the surface. The lowest rung was an arm's length above the train.

Now the ladder was ten feet away.

The man reached for the grab bars, inches away from the soles of my shoes. It would be close.

Five feet.

The man's hand wrapped around the metal bar. He reached for my feet.

Now.

I threw my hands up and held on. Even moving as slow as we were, I realized it would be difficult to seize the small ladder. Instead, I latched onto one of the steel cross beams and hung by my fingers over the tracks as the train continued on to the next station without me.

The man cursed at me and let go of the grab hold, stumbling off the train and onto the tracks.

I reached out for the bottom rung of the ladder and seized it, first with one hand, then the other.

My feet were dangling no more than eight or nine feet above the tracks.

I put my hand on the next rung, but before I could pull myself up, the man jumped up and grabbed my right leg with both hands, tugging me, trying to drag me off the ladder.

I reached back for the stun gun in my pocket, but my grip was failing, and the device dropped to the tracks, smashing into pieces. The pain was excruciating. He kept jerking down with all of his weight while pulling himself toward my knee. I kicked at him with my free leg.

I let out a guttural scream as I continued to stomp on the man's head and hands. He pressed his face against my shin for some protection. Then he got inspired and sank his teeth into my kneecap.

My hands were slipping.

A voice in my head was screaming for the pain to stop.

I had a thought. Maybe I should let go. Maybe I should just drop. If I landed on him, he would break my fall.

That might end the fight right there.

The pain said, let go. I started to loosen my grip. But something in my head urged me to keep using my feet.

After delivering enough blows to KO a heavyweight champion, I was eventually able to knock him off with a final kick to the head.

He plummeted to the tracks, barely missing the third rail and the six hundred volts traveling through it. He stumbled to his feet, but I was already a few rungs up the ladder, too far for him to reach.

I rested for a moment and let the pain fade. When I looked down, the man was gone. My line of sight was constrained now that I was within the vertical access tube.

Less than a minute later, the man reappeared, lugging a fire hose that still seemed to be connected to the wall of the station.

The man flung the hose up toward the ladder. He missed the first time, and the metal nozzle landed on the third rail. Sparks flew, but the fabric grounded the electric charge. He tossed it again and missed again. A third attempt hit the mark. The nozzle caught the bottom rung. He jiggled the hose until gravity pulled the metal tip toward the ground.

I had missed my chance to descend and kicked it free.

I started climbing again and didn't bother to watch as the man fashioned a rope ladder for himself. At the top of the vertical passage, I let myself take a peek. He was climbing hand over hand. Not using his feet at all. Just his tremendous upper body strength. He had a narrow pack slung over his shoulder.

I was mesmerized. I had to force myself to look away. At the speed he was moving, he'd have me in seconds. I searched for a latch or a handle or something, but couldn't find any. It seemed the access door was locked from above.

I smashed it with my forearm. Nothing.

I glanced down afraid I'd see the man climbing the ladder.

I was relieved that the man couldn't maintain his grip using only his arms and had slipped to the ground. But he was climbing again and this time had shifted into a *break and squat,* using his arms to pull his knees toward his chest—the *squat*—then tangling his foot in the hose so he could stand back up, giving his arms the *break* before reaching up and repeating the move.

But...

Instead of coiling the hose around his leg like I'd seen soldiers do in rope drills, he kept the hose on the outside of his leg, locking the hose under his foot, while pinching it off with the opposite foot. It was twice as fast and half as taxing as trying to hold all your weight with your arms for the three or four seconds it took to wrap the hose around the leg.

I'd have to remember the technique next time they make us climb the rope in gym class.

That is, if I lived.

I was driving my forearm into the access door over and over and over and over. Stabbing pain shot through my arm. It wouldn't budge. The only damage I was inflicting was to myself.

The man was at the bottom of the ladder now. I could feel his motion transmitted through the metal rungs.

I hit the door one more time. It was no use.

I caught my breath.

He was now only fifteen feet below me and closing.

I maneuvered myself and braced for a fight. I had kicked him off once, I could do it again.

That gave me an idea. I quickly curled around, contorting my body until my feet were above my head. I kicked at the door, slamming my feet against the wood and steel, dust falling in chunks. I closed my eyes and gritted my teeth and struck it again and again until the access door burst open.

The man was only a few feet away. I didn't have the time or the separation to reposition myself to climb out, so I thrust my legs through the opening and used my feet to pull and my hands to push like a crab moving over the top of a rock.

I scrambled to my feet.

I was in the basement of the Old State House. To the right was an ugly cinderblock wall that didn't fit with the rest of the three-hundred-year-old structure. It was where the entrance to the subway station had been carved out of the building a hundred plus years ago. I tried to remember everything I knew about this building. They had restored it recently. But to what? Its original layout or the form it had during the Revolution or the one after it became the Massachusetts State House?

I slammed the access hatch closed. The lock was intact, but I had torn the hinges out of the floorboards. I looked around for something heavy. It was mostly boxes and papers and...

There was a filing cabinet in the middle of the room. I tipped it over, and it landed on top of the access hatch with a satisfying thud.

It wouldn't be enough to keep the man out, but it might slow him down.

I turned to look for a way out of the basement. There are thousands of times a day when you have to make a choice. Right or left. Up or down. Cash or credit card. Paper or plastic. Fries or a fruit cup. I should have hightailed it out of there. I should have run screaming into the street. But toppling the filing cabinet had revealed a desk. And on that desk sat a computer. Now, I'm not completely without mental faculties. I knew I had to escape, and quickly. I also needed information. The phone I had taken from the safe was a *dumb* phone. Messages and phone calls only. It didn't play games. It didn't give you directions. Or tell you the weather. No browsing, no touchscreen, no watching television while you drive down the street.

I chose this over the smartphones in the safe because I didn't want anything with GPS, nothing that could be used to track us down. Triangulating a cell phone using only the signal distance from cell towers was complicated and time-consuming.

Was I paranoid?

Absolutely.

But then someone had hacked into the grid and made the traffic lights turn green.

I glanced toward the exit. Sometimes you have to choose the more dangerous option.

I shoved the filing cabinet out of the way, then dragged the much heavier desk onto the access door.

I sat down behind the desk, and immediately, I let my fingers fly across the keyboard. The login screen came up, asking for a password. I knew how to get in without one, but it would take a few minutes to restart the computer into terminal mode and more time to hack in. I glanced around the desk. Moving some papers, I found—taped to the right-hand side—a Post-it note with "Something" written on it.

I understand. It's difficult to remember all the passwords we use. And as we force people to choose ever more complicated logins "*for their own protection*"—must have at least one Capital letter and one number, must not be a previously used password, can't contain repeating numbers, etcetera, etcetera—it has only exacerbated the situation.

So, people write them down. Where other people can find them and hack into their computers.

I typed it in.

> *The username and password you have entered do not match.*

I couldn't believe it. I thought that was it. I tried it again, just in case I had made a typo. The same. I could feel the man trying to force up the access door. I was going to have to abandon this. I looked around for something else, anything that might be a password, but nothing on the desk stood out. Just the Post-it, "Something."

I thought about it for a moment.

Then I started typing again.

BANG, BANG.

The floor reverberated with the man's considerable efforts.

I wanted to kick the access door.

"Shut up!"

I was answered with an even more powerful BANG!

Instead of an "O," I entered a zero. 5-0-mething.

I was in.

I'm embarrassed to tell you how excited that made me.

I started with a simple search of the web.

Elam Khai.

The screen popped up with a list of links, most of them for doctors with the last name *Khai* in the U.S., Pakistan, and India. There were several people with *Elam* or *Khai* in their name. Not both. It gave me suggested alternatives, which led nowhere. I hadn't expected to uncover anything, but you always start with the obvious and work your way out. If you get too clever, sometimes you miss something right in front of you.

I moved on to the more obscure search engines. There I found much the same thing. Nothing. I skimmed the first two pages of each search, giving up after realizing it was a waste of time.

Next, I logged into one of several high-end research databases I pay for. These are a great help when I'm writing term papers for school. I'll admit, it's an unfair advantage, but I figure it's better than what I used to do, just turn in the same papers over and over every four years. Of course, access to these databases cost thousands of dollars per month.

Good data is one of the few luxuries I always afford myself.

I finally got something on an anthropology database.

Elam means "forever, eternal," and, strangely, "tree." I had the feeling he wasn't named because of the meaning, but the meaning came to be somehow because of him.

Again, all that came up were the names of people, doctors, and scientists. I glanced at a few of the articles. There weren't any red flags that made me think: *I'm an Eternal, click here.*

I even tried searching anagrams of the letters.

Lama Hike. Make Hail. I Kale Ham. Alike Ham. I Leak Ham.

I was getting nothing but hungry.

My friendly assassin, Red, was starting to move the desk. The idea of abandoning the chase probably hadn't ever occurred to him.

I got out of the chair and sat on top of the desk. Adding my weight arrested his progress for a moment. I could hear him yelling at me, but I wasn't paying attention.

I combed through databases in Europe and Asia.

I flicked through history papers, war research.

I tried reversing the spelling of the first name and dropping the H of the second.

As Engel said, he gave us a name, one that would mean nothing to us.

The desk jumped, and I was nearly knocked to the floor. I was glad for the brief rest, but it was time to go. I felt a twinge in my knee as I stood. The bruise caused by the man biting my kneecap was a minor nuisance. But his hanging off me, tugging at me, torquing my leg, had tweaked my knee. Not moving had allowed it to stiffen up.

I erased the recent history, cleared out the cache and deleted the cookies, then closed the browser and logged out of the computer.

I had spent less than five minutes. It wasn't a total waste. I knew one thing I didn't know before. Whoever he was, Elam Khai was powerful enough to have scrubbed his ancient name from the pages of history.

Even more impressive given the meaning of his name.

I kicked open the door that led out to the center staircase and took it up to the lobby. The antique white paint looked fresh. Its warm tone made more welcoming by the dim incandescent lighting.

Standing on the top landing, I felt dizzy. At first, I chalked it up to fighting for my life, jumping from a train, having someone try to drag me off a ladder. But it wasn't that.

It was seeing this place again.

And not in that déjà vu way like before.

This was not feeling like I had been here before. Because although I have been in this building several hundreds of times, it never looked like this. This was a mishmash—a beautifully elegant mishmash—of different times. I had wondered which building I was going to walk into, the British royal governor's, the seat of the colonial legislature, the Massachusetts State capital, or the one that was used for businesses and shops in the late 1800s. The commercial period had been completely eradicated, but the place was a muddled mix of those earlier political eras.

If you hadn't been here back then, it wouldn't seem strange. But I had. And it did.

Every light was on. It was a waste of energy, I know, but I was glad for this concession and not simply because it helped me navigate. There's always been something comforting about passing by this building—whether it was called the Town House, the State House, or the *Old* State House—and seeing its lights burning through the dark night.

I've been in America most of the last four hundred years. There have been periods I've lived elsewhere, Europe mostly, Asia some, South America a little. And there have been stretches where I've traveled the world, staying only a few months in each city or town or village before moving on. But I'm never gone long. A few years at the most.

Boston has been a place I've returned to often. I've made it my home on numerous occasions, more than any other city in America.

I've always been attracted to places that are flashpoints of change. I like the action, sure, but it's during these upheavals, these cataclysmic reshaping of ideas that great men and women are forged.

These leaders, thinkers, creators, they draw me like a moth to a flame. It's why I've met so many notable people throughout my life. It isn't chance. It isn't me just happening to be in the right place at the right time. *It is because I seek them out.*

Or, at least, I seek out the caldrons that create them.

There have only been a few times in fifteen hundred years—I wouldn't need all the fingers on one hand to tick them off—that a single society changed a way of thinking, brought forth something so new, so bold, so quickly as America did in the hundred years after the Declaration of Independence. I'm sure my father might have others. Rome. Greece. Macedonia. Early China. Engel might add the Indus Valley. Mesopotamia. Egypt.

But the list is short.

I made my way along the blood-red carpet to the front doors and freedom.

I pushed on them, realizing only after I had done it, that they were chained shut. I could hear the man coming up the stairs. He had already broken through my shabby defenses.

My only option was to head to the roof. Up there, my agility would trump his brawn. Any strength advantage he had would be negated.

And so I went up.

My knee throbbed.

I attacked the stairs, using the handrails to take weight off my leg, moving with haste. The white rungs and the lacquered wooden balustrade twisted upward, giving me a sense of vertigo.

I climbed.

I reached the third floor landing and the end of the spiral staircase. I continued up a cramped set of stairs set off to the side. Now, I was above the roof, but I had another two flights to the tower that stuck out of the building as if a church steeple had been stabbed into the roof.

The man was relentless. I heard him pounding the floorboards in pursuit.

When I finally got to the lower deck of the tower, the view grabbed my attention. For two centuries, men stood here watching for approaching ships. To the east, there were still intermittent views of the water.

However, in all directions, newer buildings soared above the Old State House. All I could think about was how different things looked. The water's edge not so far away as it was now. A smaller, more organized layout. Not this hodgepodge of styles, this jumble of new, old, tall, taller, and taller still. Its confusion assaulted my sensibilities. Not because I didn't like the new or modern—I do— but that there seemed to be—there *was*—no master plan.

The man's footsteps pulled my focus back.

The last time I was up on the roof was over a hundred years ago when they were building the subway. I'd sneak in through the gaping hole in the basement.

I went to a window and was grateful to find they still opened. I unlocked the latch, lifted the sash, then slid out onto the tower's thin balcony. I scrambled over the balustrade, using the railing to lower myself. It was a good six feet to the roof, which wouldn't be a problem, except that it pitched at a steep angle.

At one time, wrought iron struts lined the edge of the roof, but they'd been removed.

Oh well, no safety net.

If I didn't land right, I would fall to my death.

I let go of the railing and dropped onto the roof, grabbing the peak, but my momentum ripped me free, and I slid down the steep slope much faster than I expected. The pitch was significantly higher than it appeared from above. I was scraping and clawing at the shingles with my hands and feet. It didn't help that some of the axle grease on my shoes had gotten onto the soles.

I could hear the man laughing.

"Where are you're going? Why don't you make this easier. I will throw you a line and you won't have to die."

I couldn't get enough traction to stop my descent. Desperate, I grasped at one of the dormer windows that protruded from the sloping roof and caught the underside of the eaves with my fingers.

I was breathing heavily. But I was defiant.

"Why don't you come down here and get me?" He didn't move. "No? Maybe you're too afraid?"

"I will if I must."

I wanted the man to come after me, wanted to get him out on the roof alone, so I could send him over the side, make him pay for what he did to my brother.

But for all his talk, the man wouldn't venture onto the roof, no matter how much I baited him.

"Not so tough, now, huh?" I said as I used the dormer to climb back to the peak.

There were no nearby buildings to jump to. No fire escapes. The dormer windows led to packed storage rooms with boxes and art blocking access to the door. There was only one way down. Well, only one way that was survivable.

I had to scale the brick façade at the east end.

The man smiled, his dark reddish close-cropped hair framing his face, making it look like his head was on fire.

"I don't need to come down. I can reach you from here," he said, pulling a small spear gun—twenty-four inches, maybe thirty—from the bag on his back. A thin line was attached to the end of the spear. The tip had a barb that would definitely hook into my skin if it hit me.

On the upside, I wouldn't plunge off the roof.

The instant I realized what it was, before he could aim, before he could get two hands on it, I was moving.

I stepped off the top of the dormer, vaulting onto the next dormer, then leaping again, reaching out to grab onto the façade. I fell short and landed hard on the roof, my momentum pushing me horizontally across the steep pitch, while gravity pulled me down. I braced myself for pain. I had one chance to take hold of the iron strut supporting the façade. If I missed it, I might be able to grab on to the gutter, maybe, but my hands would pay a terrible price.

Believe me, I had no intention of falling off the roof or losing any fingers.

I caught the strut. It was old and rusted and it sliced my left hand. In one fluid motion, I used the bar to swing myself upward. I was able to cat grab the top of the façade under the hind legs of a unicorn statue. I felt bile rising in my stomach as I stared at the unicorn. A gold lion up on his hind legs stood on the other side of the façade, the animals looking inward toward the clock. These emblems of the British Empire had been torn down from the roof and burned not long after the Declaration of Independence was read from the balcony below.

As I mentioned, I had fought for England, not by choice—I was forced into battle alongside other children in the late 1300s—and so I gladly lit the kindling for the bonfire that destroyed the original lion and unicorn.

These replicas were installed in the late 1800s. Had they tried it any sooner, the whole place might have been burned down.

As beautiful as these carvings were, they were symbols of oppression.

I'm a person who respects the past. I am part of it. But I didn't feel the least bit of remorse when I kicked off the unicorn's chains—shackles that represented England's stranglehold on Scotland—splintering the gold-painted wood before muscling up onto the crest.

It was satisfying to hear the pieces hit the pavement below.

Standing on top of the façade, I felt a gentle push from behind as I jumped for the flag pole sticking out of the side of the building. Hanging in midair in that second before gravity took hold, I looked down to see a spear sticking out the front of my jacket, just under my arm. I had been harpooned. Like some whale.

As I began falling, I didn't feel any pain and wondered if it was shock.

The line was pulled taught and I slammed hard into the clock face.

Dangling there, I realized that only my jacket had been caught. The spear had missed torso. I rested for a moment.

"Oy!" yelled the man. And the word struck a chord. Tickled something in my brain. *Oy.* It was a call to children, to nephews and nieces, grandsons. Old Scots. "Aye, I remember you," he said, his voice spilling over the façade and echoing off the surrounding buildings. "Ye dinnae remembur me, do ye?"

I pulled the butterfly knife from my pocket and flipped it open. If I cut myself free, I had to be sure I could catch the flag pole. I'd have to drop the knife immediately. And I'd still have the spear in my jacket. If I landed wrong, things could go badly.

I glanced down and prepared myself.

The clock on the façade ticked off another minute, the movement getting my attention. The hands looked like they could hold me. I grabbed the hour hand for support. I could safely sever the line now.

"Careful, oy." The Scotsman's face appeared off to my right in the gap where I had maimed the unicorn. "Else you're gon stairt a weir again." He patted the neck of the unicorn gently, then pulled off the last remnants of the chains and waved them at me. "You are gonna start a war again if you not be careful," he said, discarding most of his accent.

His face. I had seen him somewhere. And not in the woods. Before. Long before.

He disappeared, then after a few seconds reappeared directly above me.

"And this time, your side won't prevail!" he said as he grabbed at me.

Instinctively, I slashed at him, slicing his cheek. He let out a roar, then ran off the edge of the roof. I could feel the line tighten. I was lifted higher. He was attached to the other end of the line. He swung like a pendulum toward the balcony below me.

I cut the line mid-swing, felt it slacken and the Scotsman disappeared, crashing to the street.

I dropped down the face of the clock, noting the time as I used the hour and minute hands to get lower.

You're not supposed to look down, but I did. Took a deep breath. Tried to tell myself I had done things like this a thousand times before and survived every time. Another part of my brain told me that just means you're a little bit closer to it not working.

I could barely reach the flagpole with my toes.

I let go of the clock and dropped to the pole. Took a direct hit to my balls. Which hurt. Oh, man, did it hurt.

The spear came free and clanged on the asphalt.

I immediately swung off the flagpole, using the Stars and Stripes like a fireman's pole, slid down, and landed on the balcony. From the veranda, it was only about fifteen feet to the sidewalk. I climbed over the railing, hung down as far as I could and dropped to the ground.

The Scotsman had landed about a half a block away. He was getting to his feet.

I froze. Not out of fear, but waiting for him to make a move. So I could react without giving him any indication of my direction.

Blood was dripping down his face, but he didn't bother to wipe it away. He was smiling.

Pain just seemed to drive him.

He took a step and tottered. He was dazed.

I took the opening and sprinted past him, past the small, nondescript entrance to the transit line at the southeast corner of the Old State House. I didn't bother to go inside. I had missed the last train heading to the airport.

The man tried to follow, lumbering after me.

I was six blocks away before I stopped to catch my breath.

I examined my injured hand. It had a gash sliced across the palm.

People today don't realize how dangerous a cut like this used to be. For most of my life, a laceration gotten outdoors on rusted metal would cause a panic. The wound would be cleaned. Leeches might be employed to suck out the bad blood. If it wasn't properly taken care of—and sometimes even when it was—you could end up unable to move. Spasms in your arms and chest and stomach would twist your body unnaturally. In the worst cases, your back would arch off the ground and you'd be locked into that position, looking like you were suspended by some invisible force, lifting you by your belt.

I tried to remember my last tetanus shot. It was definitely less than a decade ago.

There weren't any taxis around. I wouldn't have hailed one anyway. They were too easily traceable. "Oh, yes, I remember the young man. He was bleeding all over the back seat of my cab."

Ridesharing apps were worse. Public transportation was more anonymous, even with cameras watching everything.

I gazed down at the red strip that lined the path of the Freedom Trail.

For the first time all night, I was beginning to feel the cold. The late November wind nipped at my face, and no matter how deep I buried my hands in my pockets, they wouldn't get warm.

As I continued past Cross Street, making my way north, I tried to put the Scotsman's words and the enraged way he gripped the fragment of the unicorn's chains out of my mind.

But I couldn't.

I was going to start a war *again*.

- FIFTEEN -
One If By Land, Two If By Sea, Three If By Air

I'm staring at the man's face. The Scotsman on the roof.

I have this memory of looking at him. But when was it? Where was it?

He obviously hadn't tried to kill me. *That* I would remember.

I was moving quickly, slipping in and out of the shadows, making sure I wasn't being followed by this redheaded giant I felt I had seen somewhere in my past.

For the moment, I had eluded him, but he was not the type to give up.

I was nimbler, faster, more adaptable without Daniel and Phoebe. I was also more isolated and alone.

Everyone says that family and friends are the most important things in life. But what if you don't have a family? And what if you have to start over, replace your friends every three or four years?

It's not easy to separate the thousands of people I've known. Events and individuals can bleed into each other. Even someone like the Scotsman can get lost in the blur.

Sometimes I wake up and don't know where I am or what century I'm in. I know there's no such thing as time travel—except perhaps on the quantum level, but in a way, I travel through time every night. So much of my life is in the distant past, my dreams are filled with it. I can visit a place and see it change before my eyes like watching a time-lapse of photos taken years apart. I can rewind through the last three centuries and glimpse the handful of people who stand out from the vague and indistinct.

Daniel had become someone I looked forward to seeing every day. A year and a half, a blink of an eye, but he had wormed his way into my affections.

And Phoebe...

I've spent that year and a half trying to convince myself she's just like all the rest. Even though I know that isn't true.

That face. That stunning, distinctive, uncommon face.

I was thinking of Phoebe's, not the Scotsman's, but the image too quickly morphed back to his.

I had to get off the street. I had to sit down. I had to think.

I turned off Hanover Street and cut down Richmond, then left onto North where it forks at Garden. I looked up at the house.

It's a place I bought with my own money, costing me $12,000 in 1902. It was a few years before I told my father about it, mostly because I knew he'd be upset with me, which he was.

"Flashy," was all he said. He didn't mean flashy in a glitzy or extravagant way. The house was dilapidated and in serious need of repair.

He meant *conspicuous*.

I explained that I'd been careful and had done everything through surrogates.

He surveyed the interior. "It's going to take a lot of work before you can move in."

"I'm not going to live here. I'm going to turn it into a museum."

My father glared at me. "What are you going to do, go around and buy up all the houses of anybody who has ever done anything? You're going to end up with a lot of homes that aren't going to make you a penny."

My father was big on real estate that produced profits. We owned a substantial amount of it.

"I couldn't let them tear the place down. I just couldn't."

He sighed heavily and shook his head. Then he offered to put up

$5,000 as seed money for the foundation that technically owns the house.

I pulled out a key from its hiding place around the corner and slipped it into the lock of the front door of the building—by far the oldest in Boston—and entered the house that had been home to Paul Revere for thirty years.

I turned off the alarm that was cleverly hidden behind a portrait.

Breathing in the house, my nose was tickled by the scent of old wood. The pine floorboards creaked under my feet.

The muscles in my thighs and calves were buzzing with fatigue. I sat on the floor not wanting to disturb the furniture and rested my legs. I unzipped my coat and pulled it off. I surveyed the damage. A clean shot. Just a tear under the arm. I slipped the jacket back on. It was still chilly inside.

I hadn't thought through giving the backpack to Daniel, it happened so fast. Although, I probably would have lost it during the chase. I had the phone, a driver's license, and the Ghanaian passport, but I only had twenty dollars in my pocket. The rest of the money was in the backpack.

It's amazing how quickly you get used to being able to get cash anytime you want or pay for something instantly with a credit card or phone. I've lived most of my life without the ability to easily access my wealth, let alone carry it in my pocket.

I'm not sure why I came here. But it comforted me. Maybe because it was the oldest part of this young city. Maybe because I was proud of saving it.

My father was right. I couldn't go around rescuing the home of everyone who did anything, but I could protect this one.

I would give anything to have saved my house in Constantinople.

The Revere House was eerily quiet. In the darkness, I could almost imagine Revere and his wife and children sleeping in their beds. Most people know Paul Revere because of the poem by Henry Wadsworth Longfellow:

Listen my children and you shall hear
Of the midnight ride of Paul Revere

It tells the story of the night before the first shots were fired in the Revolutionary War as British soldiers marched north hoping to apprehend the rebellion's leaders and capture a hidden cache of weapons, and how one man's heroic effort saved our nation from defeat.

Hang a lantern aloft in the belfry arch
Of the North Church tower as a signal light
One if by land, and two if by sea;
And I on the opposite shore will be,
Ready to ride and spread the alarm
Through every Middlesex village and farm,
For the country folk to be up and to arm

The poem, written eighty-five years after the events of April 18, 1775, gets the story completely wrong, of course. *And* it leaves out the other two major riders because, apparently, Longfellow couldn't find anything to rhyme with Dawes or Prescott.

Listen here and I'll tell you the cause
Of the ride of Revere & Prescott & Dawes

Or maybe...

I'll tell you, everyone, of the plot
Of the ride of Revere & Dawes & Prescott

Yeah, we gotta lose those two.

This is how history is remade. Because names don't rhyme.

I remember that night.

I was wolfing down some leftovers right over there. The table was larger than the one in here now. Revere was eating as well. He and his wife were quiet. The younger children were asleep. His son paced the room, sullenly. It wouldn't be safe for his father to return to Boston after tonight, which meant he had to stay behind to look after his stepmother, her infant, and his five sisters until they could leave Boston.

But it was that night that Paul Jr. wanted to be a part of.

I was one of the lads being used to keep track of the British soldiers. Paul Revere was part of a group of thirty men known as the "mechanics" that had been gathering intelligence on British movements. They were the tinkerers, the builders, the doers. The British were catching on, watching everyone, and it was getting more difficult for them to skulk about.

It was easier for me to look innocent.

I'd like to say that I was doing it for patriotism—well, patriotism alone—but there was another reason. Sarah Revere was thirteen, and like her father, she had a rebellious streak that ran deep. I guess I started to notice girls around the time I began living with the Mohawk. Deganawa was my best friend then, one of my best friends ever. He was always talking about girls. Out hunting. Shivering in the cold. Gathering firewood. Skinning deer. In the field during *tewaaraton*. I found girls interesting in much the same way that a cat finds the tail of a rattlesnake interesting. It's drawn to it, not exactly sure what to do with it, and things usually don't end very well.

Sarah watched me from the new kitchen Revere had recently put in. She was pretending to do chores, cleaning things that had already been cleaned before. I smiled at her. I didn't know it at the time. Otherwise, I might have spoken to her, kissed her, something, but tonight would be the last time I'd ever see her.

There was a knock at the door. It was about ten o'clock.

A stable boy had a message from Dr. Joseph Warren to come with all haste.

Revere whispered final instructions to his son. He kissed his wife. He kissed Sarah and then did the same to the heads of each of his sleeping children. A moment later, he led me from the house.

The last thing I remember was Sarah's worried look and the jealousy on Paul Jr.'s face.

We reached Dr. Warren's house a few moments later.

Dr. Warren answered the door himself. "Ah, yes, Mr. Revere. I understand you are not feeling well."

"Not as well as I should, sir."

"Come in."

Warren spoke quietly. He informed us that seven hundred British regulars were given secret orders to destroy the weapon supplies in Concord. The soldiers would cross Boston Harbor tonight in boats for Cambridge. From there they would take the road to Lexington and then on to Concord. Neither Warren or Revere seemed all that concerned about securing the weapons.

They were worried the target of these troops was more than the military supplies. They felt the objective was also to capture the leaders of the rebellion, specifically Samuel Adams and John Hancock, who were making war plans at a home in Lexington.

"Go to Lexington immediately and acquaint them of the troop movement. And tell Adams and Hancock that their lives may be in danger."

Dr. Warren informed us that he was sending another courier by land.

Revere would take the shorter, more direct route across the Charles River.

We were outside a moment later and ran into William Dawes who was already on his horse.

"Good luck, Mr. Revere."

"Same to you, sir."

Dawes nodded. "Either way it turns out, live or die, I will see you on the other side."

With that, he spurred his animal and rode off. Dawes would be taking the long way around, riding from Boston down through the narrow finger of land called Boston Neck that barely connected the city to the rest of the colony.

Revere turned to me. "We away to the church."

We walked briskly and reached the Christ Church in only a few moments. The caretaker responded after a few muted knocks.

"It is tonight," Revere said. "It is to be two lanterns."

The man nodded. He was old, and I wondered if he could survive a hurried climb to the top of the church tower.

"Should I stay and help him?"

Revere shook his head. "I need your arms in the boat."

The water seemed like a black abyss as we approached the wharf and I saw a rowboat with a man inside. His face was shaded by the night. I tried to look closer, to see him in this memory. The Scotsman was here, somewhere in my mind, in this time—his reaction to the unicorn told me that. I just had to find him.

Revere cursed. He had forgotten to bring rags to muffle the oars against the oarlock. Any sound might alert the British.

The man in the shadows smiled. It was not the Scotsman. Not his grin.

"Not to worry." The man pulled out a petticoat from under his seat. "From my girlfriend. She made a bit of noise over it, but when I said it was her modesty or my life, she relented."

As we made our way steadily across the wide mouth of the Charles, the HMS Somerset moored off Charlestown drew closer. The moon was beginning to rise, and its light was brightening the dark. My eyes spotted the duty watch on board the ship. If they were alert, we would be discovered. We quieted our oars, slipping them out of the river. I held my breath as we glided past the ship, its hull rising above us.

As soon as we landed, Revere leaped out of the boat. "Gentleman, this will be a night to remember. Thank you for your efforts."

I followed Revere away from the shore, keeping my distance so he wouldn't order me back to the boat. Several men were waiting for him. Revere was given a large mare named "Brown Beauty," borrowed from the deacon of the local church. He climbed onto the powerful horse and quickly made his way toward Lexington.

While the men watched him ride off, I jumped on another horse and was nearly shot.

"What are you doing, son?" asked a man, aiming the barrel of his gun at me.

"I mean to follow Revere and keep watch for him."

He lowered his pistol and shook his head, amused. "You'll never catch the man. He rides like the devil is chasing him."

"Then it won't be much harm in my trying." I threw him a pouch with ten pounds in it. "That will pay for the horse."

He glanced inside, surprised. "How is it someone your age has this many coins of such value?"

"If we fail tonight, those crowns will be worthless to me. And if we succeed, they will be worthless to us all!"

He laughed. "Away then, lad."

I spurred the horse, and it galloped off.

I am a fair horseman, and the steed I was riding was hearty, but no matter how fast I rode, I couldn't catch Revere.

Around midnight, Revere reached the home of Hancock's relatives to find nine men standing guard outside.

After Revere explained that he had a message for Adams and Hancock, one of the men said, "The family has gone to bed. They have requested we not make any noise."

"Noise? You'll have noise enough before long. The British are coming out!"

The family and their guests were roused from their sleep. Samuel Adams and John Hancock were told that the troops were targeting them for capture.

Dawes arrived half an hour later.

Other riders were dispatched to warn the surrounding towns. By the time I reached the home, Revere and Dawes were gone.

As they rode on toward Concord, the pair was overtaken by Samuel Prescott, a twenty-four-year-old doctor who was heading home in haste.

"Sir, what brings you out at this hour and so quickly?" asked Dawes suspiciously.

It was now past one AM.

"The same as you, I'm sure," the doctor said, smiling.

"Preparing for war?"

Prescott looked at them strangely for a moment. "No, then not the same."

Prescott had been visiting his fiancée and had slipped out the back window so as not to cause her any embarrassment that might arise from his departure at this late hour.

Once they determined Prescott was a friend of their cause, Dawes and Revere shared the details of their mission.

"I will race you there then, gentlemen, as that's my home I wish to defend."

They sped off to cross the five miles to Concord, rousing the inhabitants of each house they came to.

It was here, along a dark country road, that I finally caught up with Revere.

There was a checkpoint ahead manned by redcoats. The three men had been riding so fast they came upon it too quickly to turn away.

Given the urgency of their mission, they attempted to break through the roadblock, turning their horses off the road and charging them into the darkened countryside. They split up to frustrate the soldiers' efforts.

I followed through the fields far to the left of Revere.

Revere knew he couldn't escape. I could see it in the way he was changing directions, but perhaps, he could give his companions a chance if he did not give up until the last possible moment.

Prescott grew up nearby and traveled often between Concord and Lexington to see his fiancée. He used his knowledge of the land to his advantage.

The soldiers were closing on Dawes and Revere. Their horses were spent from the long ride.

Prescott's horse was the freshest, and aided by his familiarity with the area, he successfully eluded capture, jumping his horse over a stone wall.

Revere dragged out the chase as long as he could.

Dawes was thrown from his horse and somehow escaped on foot, hiding in a nearby farmhouse.

Only Prescott made it all the way to Concord, alerting his hometown that British troops were headed their way.

Finally, the soldiers caught Revere. I watched as he was asked to get down from his mount. I trotted softly into a stand of trees and tied my horse to one of the oaks. "Easy, boy," I whispered. "We've come to make a rescue. Don't give us away just yet."

I looked in the saddlebags and found several gunpowder cartridges. I untwisted the paper and pulled out the musket balls, then rewrapped the ends. I put the metal balls in a pouch on my belt.

I untied the reins from the bridle, then fixed nine cartridges to the leather, spaced so that when one exploded, it would light the next. After securing the charges, I attached the strap to the right stirrup.

"I'm sorry, boy. This is going to be loud."

Revere's engraving of the Boston Massacre made him known to the British. The interrogators thought he might have information about militia strength and preparations. They threatened his life unless he revealed what he knew. But Revere knew less than I did of the operational details, which was almost none at all. That didn't stop him from dragging things out. Finally "relenting," Revere gave the British greatly inflated estimates of how many militiamen were in the area.

I took out my flint and lit a small strip of fabric on fire. I bound the smoldering material to the reins, then slapped the horse on the hind quarter. My horse loped off slowly until the first cartridge exploded and the horse bolted into the woods. The cartridges popped every ten seconds or so, making it seem as if the area was surrounded by rebels. Bells started ringing and other shots were fired in response to mine. Fearing that Revere's exaggerated estimates were true and that they were in danger of being attacked, the soldiers released Revere, leaving him stranded in the middle of the road.

I found him walking back toward Lexington.

"You're safe," I said.

"Was that you in the woods?"

"More the horse than me, but yes."

"Well, we are a horseless pair now, aren't we?" He shook his head and looked up at the sky. "If they run off after the trickery of one boy, I don't know what they shall do when they see what they are facing at Concord."

Including those alerted along the way by Dawes and Revere and the men dispatched from Lexington and others who saw the signal from the church tower and still more that witnessed the troop movements with their own eyes, nearly fifty riders were racing through the night spreading the word.

Rather than the lonely ride of one man warning a sleepy countryside that Longfellow's poem portrayed, Middlesex County was bursting with activity that night.

At Lexington, we met up with Samuel Adams and John Hancock. Revere and I were given fresh horses. The entire command retreated on horseback through the woods. We hadn't gone more than a mile from Lexington when Hancock discovered he had left a trunk filled with important papers in the tavern there. The papers detailed war strategies, militia numbers and their leaders, as well as the locations of hidden weapons and ammunition. There was even information about spies inside the British army.

"I'll go back and get them," I volunteered.

It was nearly five o'clock in the morning, and the dark of night was turning into the purple of twilight.

"It's not a task for one man alone," said Hancock.

"Then I will join him," Revere said.

I didn't wait long enough to give them time to disagree. I grabbed the reins, turned my horse, and sped off toward Lexington. I knew we had to hurry. The British would arrive there very soon. As able a rider as Revere was, it took him a full minute to catch up with me.

"We would do our best to avoid the green at all cost. That's where they will mount a line of attack."

"Let's approach from the fields then," I said.

He turned his horse off the dirt path, and I followed soon after. We crossed the pastures that spread out from the center of Lexington, keeping the buildings between us and the green. I could hear the fifes and drums of the British, and my heart jumped into my throat.

They were already in town.

Our only hope was that it was too early for any of the regulars to break into the tavern for a drink. We reached the back door, and I quickly worked the lock free.

"I fear Master Alexander that you are an accomplished thief."

"Not accomplished enough to make a living at it."

We didn't need to search the premises. We found the trunk instantly. So would have any British soldier who had one half-able eye.

We slipped out the back and carried the trunk swiftly to the house of Reverend Clark.

It was heavy.

"I think he has a keg of ale secreted in here along with his papers," Revere said.

As Revere and the Reverend discussed hiding the documents, I went to the window after hearing shouts coming from the green.

The British were charging at the militiamen in a disorganized mass. The redcoats were screaming, telling the local men to disperse.

A single shot echoed across the green.

I heard it.

It was as if everything froze.

I don't know who fired the shot, which side, or even where it came from. But at the sound, the line of redcoats immediately opened fire. I saw an older colonist fall to the ground, struck by a musket ball. He was in his late sixties, perhaps older than that. As he lay there, writhing in pain, a British soldier approached the man. It is a moment that played out then and now in slow motion. As the old man reached up a hand in surrender, the British soldier ran him through with a bayonet thrust, killing him.

Almost immediately, several Americans returned fire.

Under a cloud of morning mist and smoke from gunpowder, it was difficult to make out what was going on.

This was the fog of war.

War.

It had come to that.

Revere came up behind me, and we watched the chaos for a moment. "We should leave this place and inform the others of what has happened."

I nodded.

We made our way toward the back of the house. Through an open window, I could see a lone British soldier creeping toward our horses. I pulled the musket balls from the pouch on my waist. I waited for a volley of gunfire, then hurled one of the metal balls against the wall behind the young man's head. He ducked, his legs quaking. At the next round of gunfire, I heaved the remaining musket balls at the wall. Thinking he was under attack, he scampered off.

Revere smiled and shook his head. We charged out the back and had our horses running before we had fully mounted them. We raced through the fields as musket fire crackled behind us. One ball went whizzing between me and the head of my horse. I slung myself low over the left side of my mount, using the horse to shield me from further fire. I didn't climb back into the saddle until we were deep in the woods. I later found a nick in the seat where my leg should have been.

The British marched on to Concord unprepared for the strength of the resistance swiftly put in place by the colonists. By the end of the day, the British attack would fail, and the redcoats would retreat all the way back to Boston under heavy fire the entire way.

∞

It's ironic to me that Paul Revere's most famous ride was arguably not his most important. The previous Sunday he had ridden out to Concord to warn that this attack was being planned, allowing time for the weapons and supplies to be moved and the surrounding militia to prepare. And four months earlier, Revere delivered information that led to the capture of hundreds of muskets, thousands of pounds of gunpowder, and sixteen cannons. Much of this haul was used to drive the British back to Boston and keep them there.

I had witnessed the beginning, been part of it. The Scotsman said I had started a war. But I had not started *anything*.

I got up from the bare floor and dusted myself off. Phoebe and Daniel would be wondering where I was.

I ran my hand across one of the wooden chairs on which Rachel Revere and her husband would sit and discuss the events of the day. Chairs where Sarah sat two centuries ago.

I took a last look around.

I went to turn on the alarm hidden behind the portrait. My hand froze as I grabbed the frame to swing it open.

Behind the glass was the face of the Scotsman. Darker skinned, eyes somewhat exaggerated, the reddish hair made black, but it was him.

The work was Revere's, a hand-painted print from an engraving. It was supposed to be the image of Metacomet, leader of the Wampanoag tribe in the mid-1600s.

Metacomet's father was the chief who welcomed the settlers at Plymouth in 1620. The food and assistance the Wampanoag gave the settlers ensured the Pilgrim's survival during those first few harsh winters. Metacomet mixed easily with the English. He attended Harvard College and took the name Philip. After becoming chief, he continued his father's treaty of friendship for many years.

Until finally, the constant stream of settlers threatened his tribe's existence.

Determined to survive, Philip formed an alliance of tribes hoping to force out the settlers. In a little over a year, Philip and his allies attacked more than half of the towns in New England, causing extensive damage and bringing the economy to a halt.

Philip was hunted down and finally killed. His head was mounted over the entrance to Fort Plymouth where it stayed for two decades. As a trophy and a warning.

I remember King Philip. I found him intelligent, wise and brave. A man of peace who waged war only when forced to. He looked nothing like this. Not when his head was on his shoulders. Not when it was stuck on the end of a pike.

Revere could have lifted the image from another work as he often did, but there was something that made me think he was in the same room as the Scotsman, using him as a model.

I reset the alarm and took a last look at the Scotsman dressed like an American Indian.

A rush went through me. Like someone had stabbed a needle into my stomach. I knew what the Scotsman was talking about! I knew how he and I and Revere were tied together. He was right. I had started the war. *We* had started the war.

Not in Concord or Lexington, but long before and right here in Boston.

I was running now, the cold air searing my lungs.

I knew who the man was.

Or rather, I knew *what* he was.

My babysitter.

After neglecting the colonies for most of the previous hundred and fifty years, the British attempted to reassert control over its New World territories. Governors and other high officials who had been paid by the colonists now received their compensation directly from the British to ensure their loyalties were to the Crown.

In 1773, Parliament passed the Tea Act, raising taxes and forcing the colonies to buy their tea from the East India Company and no one else.

The colonies responded by refusing to unload tea from British ships. Patriot leaders in Philadelphia and New York sent the ships back to England, their cargo holds full. In Charleston, the tea was left to rot on the wharf, its tax unpaid.

In Boston, well, you probably know what happened here.

It was late November 1773. I was standing watch in the tower of the Town House—that's what we called the Old State House then—when I saw the *Dartmouth* sail into port with the first shipment of tea.

Two more vessels arrived.

British law required the ships to pay import taxes within twenty days of arriving or customs officials could confiscate the cargo.

The governor wouldn't allow them to leave until they paid the tax. The captains couldn't pay the tax until they received payment for the tea. They wouldn't receive payment until the tea was unloaded. We wouldn't allow them to unload the tea.

On December sixteenth, the last day the *Dartmouth* could be unloaded before its contents were seized, seven thousand people showed up for a meeting called by Samuel Adams. Revere was in the audience. So was I. So was just about everyone else. The crush of people overwhelmed the meeting house and spilled into the street.

The show of force guaranteed the tea would not be brought ashore that night. That didn't mean it wouldn't be unloaded.

It was my idea to dress as Mohawk warriors, not only to conceal our identities but as a symbolic gesture.

They were the lion. We were the Eagle and the Brave.

Less a dozen of us were disguised as Mohawk, but it's enough to be remembered in the history books.

As the crowd watched, first in amazement, then in cheering support, we boarded the ships—one hundred and fifteen men and boys, including Revere and myself.

The others wearing warpaint, it was done haphazardly and without meaning. The patterns on my face were distinct and personal. They were the markings Deganawa wore.

It took us three hours to dump a hundred thousand pounds of tea into Boston Harbor.

It wasn't until fifty years later that the Destruction of the Tea became known as the *Boston Tea Party*.

I don't know who started calling it that.

It was *never* a party. It was a protest.

When England got word of what happened, the King and Parliament went mad. Instead of backing down, they passed the Coercive Acts, laws created to strangle the independence movement. It closed Boston Harbor to all commercial traffic. The people of Massachusetts could no longer hold town meetings without permission. The people's elected representatives would no longer have any say. Judges and juries were put under the control of the royally appointed governor. Life, liberty, and property were to be decided by those who had no allegiance to the people and received no authority from them.

The punishing effects did not stop at the Massachusetts border.

British officials would not be subject to local courts throughout the colonies for any criminal acts. George Washington called it the "Freedom To Murder Clause."

Military commanders could confiscate buildings and supplies to quarter their troops without permission.

In going so far, the British alienated moderate colonists and even a good many Loyalists whose businesses and fortunes suffered.

The first courts were to be held under the strict new provisions in Great Barrington—the sleepy little town that Daniel and Phoebe and I called home. When the British-appointed judges arrived at the courthouse, they were blocked from entering by fifteen hundred people.

A few weeks later, four thousand people shut down the court in Springfield. A few days after that, forty-eight thousand marched on Boston in protest, dwarfing the capital's population of fifteen thousand.

Not one British-controlled court was allowed to sit. The people had, without firing a single shot, taken back control of their colony.

This was the Revolution.

As I replayed that night on the deck of the *Dartmouth* in my mind, I could see the people on the dock, watching, the others around me working in unison, and something else: the Scotsman, pushing one of the four-hundred-pound crates across the deck.

I remember walking over to help, amazed that he had gotten the heavy wooden container as far as he had by himself. I stood shoulder to shoulder with him as we shoved the chest over the side and into the harbor. I can see now his conscious attempt to avoid eye contact with me. It was the practiced nonchalance of someone who does not want to appear to be watching, but *is* watching. Always watching.

Always watching *me*.

You may wonder why I kicked the shackles off the unicorn atop the Old State House. It was because of these words:

> *"For, as long as but a hundred of us remain alive, never will we on any conditions be brought under English rule. It is in truth not for glory, nor riches, nor honors that we are fighting, but for freedom—for that alone, which no honest man gives up but with life itself."*

These words could have been written by the colonists in the 1770s, but they were instead from a declaration of Scottish independence made four hundred and fifty years earlier. England's hold on Scotland—symbolized by the chains on the unicorn—remained to this day.

The Scotsman had been sent to Boston on a very specific mission, one that required him to remain inconspicuous, out of sight, but he couldn't help himself. The bitterness and hostility he had for the English ran too deep.

We were brothers that night on the ship.

We had ignited a war.

Now, we were foes.

- SIXTEEN -
We Came Here On Different Ships, But We're In The Same Boat Now

I needed a boat. I needed to get out of Boston. I needed to speak to my father.

I tried calling him. And just like the last ten times, I got this recording:

The person you are trying to reach is not accepting calls at this time. Please try again later.

My father believes in voicemail in the same way the rest of us believe the world is flat, which is to say, it's a stupid concept that, in practice, allows you to fall off the face of the earth.

He'd been against answering machines before that. I'd tell him I was trying to reach him.

He'd say, "I wasn't home."

I'd say, "If you got an answering machine I could leave a message."

He would just look at me. "Why in a donkey's ass would you want to talk to me when I'm not home. Seems like a waste of time to me."

And that would be it.

To be honest, he wasn't thrilled by the invention of the phone or the radio either, except that their military application would've made communicating with his troops a whole lot easier during his numerous campaigns.

As I approached the end of Hanover Street, I saw the Coast

Guard station. There was a cutter, two navigation aid vessels, and a response boat capable of over forty knots. I'd be at the airport in a minute with that. I decided stealing a Coast Guard ship was unwise. I didn't need the military and the federal government teaming up against me. I had enough trouble facing a band of four-thousand-year-old warriors.

My best option was a few blocks to the east. There was a condo complex built on the water that had boat slips.

It took me two minutes to reach the wharf. I gazed up at the buildings that rose eight stories from the pier, so close to the sea and yet so far from its way of life. I thought about the sailors of my past, their weathered faces making them look years older, and the women sorting the catch in the bitter cold of winter and the stifling heat of summer. All of them, the men and the women, their bodies permanently tainted by the smell of fish.

I followed the unmistakable sound of ship bells and found the slips quickly. The dock ran along the front of the southernmost building. There was a public promenade just above the dock that weaved its way around the complex. The walkway was well lit, and dozens of apartments had a clear view of the slips. I wouldn't have the luxury of jumping from boat to boat, trying them all. I'd have one shot to select and steal a vessel.

There was an eight-foot-tall security door at the head of the gangway leading down to the floating dock. I pulled out the driver's license Engel had made for me, jammed it hard between the latch and the strike plate and pushed the gate open in one fluid motion that made it appear as if I'd unlocked it using the keypad.

In the first slip, there was a small aluminum fishing boat. I know, not very flashy or very fast, but it would've been my first choice had there been an engine. Easy to steal, easy to handle, easy to come ashore just about anywhere without being noticed. Honestly, I would've made off with the thing if there'd been even a single oar.

The next few spaces were empty, as were two at the end of the dock. The other slips were filled by two bowriders, a small motor yacht, and several cabin cruisers. About halfway down the dock, I hopped on board the oldest of the cabin cruisers, landing on deck without a sound. The controls were topside and easily accessible. I kicked open a fuse panel under the helm with a single blow.

I chose this particular vessel because the older boat would be easier to hot-wire. Unfortunately, the cockpit controls had been updated. The newer, more sophisticated ignition system would slow things down. It wasn't impossible to steal. Just not *touch two wires together and we're off.*

I traced the wire back to a bundle, looking for the two that matched. I was searching for something conductive to span the gap when I heard a boat pulling up to the dock. Moving too quickly to see who it was, I cracked my head on the sharp edge of the control panel. I cursed and saw stars simultaneously for a good thirty seconds. Have I mentioned how much I hate banging my skull? I pulled my hand away and there was a speck of blood on my palm. It looked black in the darkness.

I peered over the gunwale and saw several people stepping off a water taxi. They were swaying in that lazy fashion people do after a late night of dancing and drinking. My choices were: spend another—I don't know how long—trying to hot-wire the cruiser *or* break the leave-no-trail-behind rule and have the water taxi give me a ride.

I climbed down from the helm with my head still throbbing and stumbled off the stern onto the gangway.

I hurried toward the far end of the dock, brushing past the three passengers that had just disembarked. The pilot of the boat was about to leave the dock when I placed my hand on the cleat at the back of his vessel.

"I need to get to the airport," I said.

The man glared at my hand gripping the cleat, then up at me. If he engaged the prop, he'd pull me into the freezing bay.

"Sorry. I can't. That was my last fare of the night. I have to get home. It's late. My wife worries about me."

He had a strong accent that I recognized even though my head was throbbing. It took me a couple of seconds to access the words—it had been at least a decade since I'd used them. Eventually, phrases bubbled to the surface from the dark recesses of my mind, and I began to speak Russian. The words came out slowly, simple sentences at first.

"I have need for to get out of here. I are have being followed," I said. It was awkward, jerky, uneven. Russian is not my best language. It's not even my tenth best. It ranks just above Esperanto—this engineered universal language meant to foster world peace that frustrates me so much every time I hear it that I want to beat up the person using it.

Hearing me, the man's eyebrows shot up so high in astonishment, they disappeared beneath his bangs. I wasn't sure if it was my speaking Russian or how poorly I was speaking it.

"You're not from Russia," he said, his eyes narrowing into slits, brows covering them like furry lids. He took his hand off the throttle and stepped away from the wheel. That was a promising sign.

"No. It were some language that I tried to have learning." I wondered if I was helping or hurting my cause by butchering his native tongue so meticulously.

I've spent time in Russia. Mostly while working for Benjamin Franklin when he was ambassador to France. The language spoken at the Russian Royal court was French, which I speak fluently. I had no need and absolutely no desire to learn Russian. None whatsoever. That was until it seemed like the United States and the Soviet Union might annihilate each other with nuclear weapons. I immediately got much more interested in the Russian language. I wanted to hear for myself what their leaders were yelling about at the United Nations while banging their shoes on the podium.

"I am having only twenty dollars and I did not receive the last train. From where of Russia are you coming?" I asked him.

"Saint Petersburg."

Saint Petersburg is one of the strangest places on earth. It is the world's northernmost city with a population of over a million people. The winters are long and cold and dark. Months go by without a sunny day, and even when the sun peeks through the clouds, it hangs low on the horizon, appearing only dimly between ten AM to two PM. But it is during the summer when Saint Petersburg shines. Literally. The sun sets for no more than a few hours only to come back up again. You can't even call it night. It's more like an extended dusk. Known as the White Nights, the city explodes with life. The people seem to celebrate a continuous two-month-long party.

"Are you having not been back?"

"Never! The Soviets were terrible. After them, the crooks were even worse."

Many cities in Russia went through a difficult transition after the fall of the Soviet Union. Perhaps none as dramatically as Saint Petersburg. Organized crime filled the vacuum left by the old communist regime.

I had heard the old city had come back to life.

"I'm having not been there since a long time," I said.

He looked at me and laughed. "A long time for you is a short time for me."

I didn't bother to correct him.

He stared at me for a moment, then in Russian said, "Jump in."

"Your wife, call her you should if she worry."

"What my wife worries about is that I am out with another woman. And I am. Every night!" He kissed his fingertips, then patted his boat. "She is a good girl," he said, more to the water taxi than to me.

I tried to give him the twenty dollars, but he wouldn't take it.

"You do something good for someone someday."

"I will," I said.

He powered up the engine, and as we moved away from the wharf, I gazed back at the city, toward the low, dark forms of the North End, then the explosion of height downtown.

The Charles River meanders in and around and through Boston, but it was almost a straight line from the wharf to the boat landing by the airport.

The water taxi jumped after hitting the wake of a cargo ship that passed sometime earlier. Rocked by the wave, I grabbed the railing to catch my balance. The Russian man didn't seem to notice. He lived on the water. More at home here than on land. I wondered, did his room sway back and forth as he lay in bed at night?

"Who was chasing you?" the man asked.

"Someone from my past."

He groaned a little and curled up the corner of his mouth on one side.

"I do not like those people from the past. They're always up to no good. So, you are going to the airport to get away from them?"

"Yes," I said.

He was quiet for a moment.

"Strange. I come here to get away from people in my past. And you have to leave here to do the same." I thought he might say something like, *you can't run away from your past.* But he didn't. "Make sure when you run, you go far enough away where they can't find you."

I was about to respond when I felt a buzz in my pocket. I pulled out my phone and flipped it open, hoping my father had seen my missed calls. I had one new message. It took several steps on this dumb phone to reveal the contents. There was nothing but a photo.

I stared at the picture for, I don't know, seconds, minutes, hours, as I tried to make sense of it: Daniel with his arms outstretched, his wrists fastened to an iron fence. Over his head was the word "Wonderland."

I felt my throat tighten. I couldn't breathe. I wanted to hurl the phone at the ground, crush it with my foot, make the truth go away. I could no longer hear the engine of the water taxi over the pounding in my ears.

"Stop," I yelled as much to the noise inside my head as the man.

His reaction was swift. He thrust back the throttle, slowing the boat to a dead stop.

"What is it?" He wore a look of genuine concern on his face.

I didn't know how to explain to this stranger that my friend was being held against his will. And it had nothing to do with my Russian being rusty. It was that I was racked with guilt for sending Daniel and Phoebe on ahead, alone, unprotected. How did this happen? And where was Phoebe? Why did I put them in danger in the first place? I was worried about their families. That's why. It was about protecting them.

But if I was honest with myself, part of it was that I didn't want to be alone. I spent much of my life on my own. I was used to it. Sometimes preferred it. But losing Braeden, not being able to reach my father, not knowing Engel's fate, made me feel more isolated than I'd felt in centuries. There was an emptiness in my stomach, and I struggled for air as if I'd been underwater holding my breath too long.

Friends and family. With all the gifts that living a long life gives, it exacts a high price.

I couldn't lose another person right now, especially not one of them.

I held out the phone and the man took it from my outstretched hand.

He moved it farther out, then closer in, then out, then in, then arms-length away as if he was trying to get the picture in focus. "My eyes aren't so good as they used to be. Who is this I'm looking at?"

I started to answer in my broken Russian, but the man waved me off.

"English, please. My head hurts from trying to understand you."

"He's my friend."

"The person after you, they did this?"

"Not the same person, but the same people."

My mind zoomed off in a hundred directions trying to come up with a plan. Wonderland Station was at the end of the Blue Line, a half dozen stops past the airport. Why go there?

I ran my fingers over the cut on my palm. The wound was raw, but the bleeding had stopped. Noticing the injury, the man retrieved the First Aid Kit from the storage compartment under his seat.

"Who sent this to you?" he said, as he handed me back the phone.

He worked quickly, ripping open a pack of gauze pads and some medical tape, then expertly wrapping the laceration.

I glanced at the number. It was from Phoebe's phone. I couldn't be sure if she had sent it or if someone else had. No text accompanied the message.

"It's from my friend's phone."

"The one in the picture?"

"No, another friend. A girl."

The man raised his eyebrows in concern. It was a look that told me he had daughters of his own.

Without a word, he finished dressing my wound—expertly done—then went back to the helm and thrust the throttle to full. The boat lurched forward.

"What are you doing?"

"I'm taking you to get your friends. Wonderland Station is by the water. I can land my boat on the beach. It's a few hundred meters from there to the station."

I thought of things in digits, cubits, paces, and miles. Although my idea of a mile (two thousand paces) was slightly shorter—about nine-tenths of a standard mile. I was comfortable with yards, which was just two cubits to me. Meters was an easy translation from there: multiply by one-point-one to get the number of yards.

My instinct was to tell the man that he shouldn't get involved in this, that it wasn't safe, that he should get home to his wife and daughters.

I said, "Thank you," in Russian instead.

"You are a good boy, no?"

"It's nothing I did. Nothing I did wrong, at least. My father is powerful, and these people think that he will pay a lot of money to get us back."

I was taking a risk telling him this.

"And will he?"

"Yes. He will also send people to destroy them."

"You sure your father is not Russian?" he asked with a sly smile. "I like him already."

We fell into a comfortable silence.

I tried to clear my mind and not think about Daniel or Phoebe or my father.

As we sped toward Wonderland Station, the lights of downtown receded and the darkness of the Atlantic Ocean spread out before us, the boat rhythmically bouncing as it skimmed the ripples on the surface. These ripples gave way to larger waves as we curled around the sharp point of Deer Island and into the choppy waters of Massachusetts Bay.

I let the undulating movement lull me into a focused state. I embraced the cadence and felt the anxiousness drain from my body. Meditating might seem like a strange thing to do before heading into a fight. It's more common to picture people getting psyched up for war, screaming and shouting, and there are times that letting loose a guttural war cry will prepare you to face the physical violence of battle, but I must find the calm. A straight forward fight is easy. Retreat or attack. Live or die.

This would not be that. I had to prepare for anything, for everything.

I don't recall anything about Wonderland Station. I knew the tracks ran alongside Revere Beach, which stretched three miles from top to bottom. Like so many other things in Boston, it was a first. The first public beach in the United States. I've walked along the sand many times, its texture not too coarse, not too fine, just right.

The beach used to be lined with arcades and amusements and roller coasters and rides of all kinds. It was known as the Coney

Island of New England, and at night the ballrooms would be filled with music and dancing. The lights and the atmosphere and the carousels and the twirling on the dance floors made you dizzy with excitement and the world felt magical.

They were all gone now, the towering wood roller coasters, the sparkling ballrooms. By the time this new century started, Revere Beach looked very much like it had at the beginning of the previous century.

Nothing but sand.

It was almost as if those hundred years in between had never occurred.

But they had. And I remember the simple, terrifying pleasure of dancing with a girl I just met. The guts it took to cross the floor to ask her. Sometimes I think facing a thousand men across a battle-field is less daunting.

I remembered swimming in the cool water and drying off in the sun. I let the thought of sunbaked sand warming my body bring me deeper into my calmness. I breathed in the unmistakable scent of the sea.

I was conscious of my breath.

In and out.

Breath is life.

I didn't know what I would be up against. But I knew who.

Elam Khai.

I had never heard the name before a few hours ago, and in that short time, he had become my enemy. The Scotsman and the others were simply his tools, extensions of Elam Khai's hands. What they did, they did for him. He was responsible for their actions. As if his own hands had held the sword that cut into Braeden or tied Daniel to the fence.

We had incapacitated several attackers in the woods, one or two more on the T, but I had the feeling Elam Khai could replace each man lost with a hundred more.

I felt my mind go deeper. Images flashed in my head. My brain was looking for something, sifting through the memories. I could see the beach and its surroundings, the fields of asphalt, a vague outline of the station, but nothing about the station itself. Almost everything I knew was gone, torn down, destroyed.

"What do you know about Wonderland Station?" I asked the Russian boat pilot.

He shrugged his shoulders. "Not much. I've been to it a few times. There's a beach that runs along the water."

"Revere Beach," I said. Revere. I smiled at the irony of it.

"And..." I could see the man was trying to make sense of something in his memory. "And there is a State Police barracks right on the other side of the parking lot, between the beach and the station."

Normally, having a dozen State Troopers around would be good news, but if Elam Khai felt comfortable enough to tie Daniel to a fence in public a hundred yards from a building full of cops, things were not exactly as they seemed.

I decided it would be foolish to seek the help of the Troopers until I knew what was going on and whom I could trust.

The breeze coming off the ocean was steady. The crescent moon reflected enough light that I could see the beach off to the left. The sand looked gray in the moonlight. Everything lacked color. The water. The sky. The water taxi. My skin. It was life through a black and white television.

One thing didn't make sense to me. If Phoebe had been grabbed along with Daniel—and using her phone to send the closeup photo meant that was a possibility—why didn't they send an image of both of them? I mean, if you're trying to lead me into a trap, using Phoebe as bait would evoke my natural urge to protect even more strongly. Sorry, Daniel.

Maybe she escaped. Or maybe she had taken the photo herself. But if Phoebe *had* sent the picture, why hadn't she conveyed more information, like where she was and what had happened?

There wasn't a single plea for help.

Just the photo of Daniel.

I wanted to answer the message, but if she didn't have her phone, it would let them know I was coming.

The logical assumption was that she had gotten away, but they had her phone. I couldn't contemplate the other possibility.

We were getting close to Revere Beach. I flipped open the phone and tried to glean something, anything from the photo.

Daniel was alone in the picture. There was something in the background.

"Are those—what are those?" I showed the screen to the man again.

"I don't know. They look like—"

"Stands?" I said.

A vision of sleek, gray dogs racing around a dirt track came to me. Then a spark of illumination. It wasn't Wonderland Station. It was the Wonderland Greyhound Park!

"It's the dog track," I said.

He shook his head. "That's closed. They made it illegal to race dogs in the state a few years ago."

"Of course!"

Suddenly, everything made sense. Proximity to the police barracks meant nothing. The track would be empty and protected from view. If you had to pick a location to lure me in, this offered complete privacy.

"How far is the race track from the beach?"

"Maybe six hundred meters. It's straight in from here," he said pointing toward land.

It was high tide, and the water taxi could get right up to the beach. I wouldn't have to wade in through the surf. I could see the shore. We were closing quickly and the man had no intention of cutting back the engine and taking it in slow. He meant to put me *on the beach*. I prepared myself for impact. When the boat hit the sand, scraping the bottom of the hull, both of us were thrown forward.

I scrambled out onto the front of the boat.

"I will stay here and wait for you," he said.

Standing on the bow, I glanced back at him and nodded. I didn't deserve this kind of loyalty from him. "My name is Alexander."

"A powerful name," he said. "You sure you're not Russian?"

I had to laugh. "I'm sure."

"I am Nikolay."

"Thank you, Nikolay."

"You want me to come with you?"

I shook my head. "We'll need an escape if I succeed."

I could tell he was relieved, although he tried to hide it in a mask of disappointment. "Then I will wait." He reached into a compartment and pulled out a gun. I raised my eyebrows. "Is flare gun," he said.

He rolled the gun over in his hands, then unexpectedly tossed it to me. I almost lost it in the surf, but I managed to grab it out of the air after it bounced off my hand.

"Hurts like the devil if you hit them in the chest. And, is very hard to see after. Very bright."

The gun had five extra flare cartridges hanging off the grip. One was preloaded. I tucked the gun into my jacket. Without a word or a look back at Nikolay, I launched myself off the bow, sprinting as soon as my feet hit the sand. My lacrosse coach forced us to run wind sprints the length of the field, up and back, three times, before and after practice. Five hundred meters was a little less than a third of a mile. I could run the 400 in just over fifty seconds. But this wasn't anything like running on a track. The sand under my feet absorbed most of the energy and I felt like I was struggling to gain any ground. Thankfully, the beach was narrow and I came to the end of it almost immediately.

The surfaces changed rapidly after that. Stairs. Pavers on the boardwalk. Asphalt street. Concrete sidewalks. Grass along the green space where the roller coasters used to be. More asphalt as I crossed Ocean Avenue.

I could see Wonderland Greyhound Park straight ahead, maybe four football fields away.

I was almost at the train tracks. Crossing them would mean climbing over two ten foot high fences topped with barbed wire, one on either side of the tracks. The closest through street was three blocks in the wrong direction. I veered off and raced toward Wonderland Station. I put on a burst of speed when I saw the walkway bridging the tracks.

I zigzagged up the ramp and over the span.

Exiting on the other side, I charged toward the street.

The dog track was less than two hundred yards away. There were patches of dead grass everywhere and the trees were skeletons. I hurdled over a guardrail and entered the desolate parking lot of Wonderland Greyhound Park.

SEVENTEEN

Malice In Wonderland

The park looked menacing in the darkness, a jumble of buildings thrown together over the years with no unifying theme or pattern. I was so close. I wanted to run faster. Wanted this to be over with.

The cold air seared my lungs and my muscles were tightening up. I had to ease up. If I used all my energy getting there, I'd have none left to fight.

And a minute or two or even ten wasn't going to make a difference. They were after me. They've waited this long. They could wait a little longer.

I stopped.

My chest heaved as I caught my breath.

I rested my hands on my knees and let my heart rate recover.

I was standing in the middle of a soulless wasteland, exposed, nothing but crumbling asphalt for a hundred yards in every direction.

If anyone was watching, they'd see me rising up like the creature from the blacktop lagoon. I didn't care.

I put my arms out and threw my head back.

There is a statue in Boston, in front of the public library, done by the same artist who sculpted the statue of Paul Revere near the Old North Church. Called *Appeal to the Great Spirit*, the statue is a Native American chief atop his horse, his arms outstretched, his head thrown back, much like I was standing now. When I opened myself up like this, like the Chief on his horse, I felt the power of the universe rushing into my body. It is in this prone state that the warrior gives himself up. There is nothing more pure, more graceful, and more vulnerable.

I breathed in. Then opened my eyes and saw the moon. The crescent that it was—waxing or waning, I don't know—and the faint shadow of the face mostly in darkness.

Goddess of the moon.

Phoebe.

I flipped open the phone and texted a message.

where r u

I waited in the cold. In the middle of the gray moonscape. I stared at the screen. Like watching water boil, it seemed to take forever.

The phone vibrated.

r u here

Frustrated, I almost let out a groan but strangled it in my throat. I still couldn't be sure Phoebe was the one on the other end. Calling her was out. The sound of the ringer or her voice might give away her location. Texting was dangerous enough.

Time to verify who I was talking with.

who wz ur d8 2nite

u

Clever. Pretty sure, but still not convinced.

4dance

cs

Cs. Phoebe's pet name for Craig Clifford Coulter. My fingers typed faster.

where r u need 2 c u

The answer came back:

flag

Light from the adjacent boulevard's street lamps spilled onto the parking lot and the grounds. Up ahead, just past where the stands ended, I could make out a white flagpole flying a tattered American flag, outside the curve at the southern end of the track.

The rest of the track wasn't visible. The stands blocked my view.

Perhaps there were other flags. I dismissed the idea. Phoebe was intelligent. She would've texted something more specific if there were others.

flag @ end

Or something like that.

The flag pole was close to the street. I didn't know how tall the fence running along the edge of the property was, but no matter the height, it would be safer to approach Phoebe from the sidewalk. Less chance of being seen.

Phoebe's texts didn't seem forced, like someone was prompting her. Still, I'd feel more confident if I could get a good look from above, assess the situation before going to her.

The roof at the rear of the building wasn't very high where it edged up against the parking lot. A wide wooden swing gate closed off access to an entry tunnel leading under the stands. There was a gap of at least three feet between the top of the gate and the roof.

As I ran toward the gate, I could see my breath and felt it against my cheeks. The cold reacted with the humidity exiting my lungs forming frost around my nose and mouth.

Directly in front of the gate stood a stanchion, about four feet tall with a padlock at the base.

I elongated my stride to correct my timing, stepped off the crown of the stanchion, launching myself onto the roof. When I landed, a layer of pebbles crunched loudly under my feet, and I rolled twice before I could stop my momentum. The din was replaced with silence. The wind. My breath.

Sound is magnified at night, especially when you're trying to be quiet. In the day, I could jump up here, stomp around, and no one would hear a thing. Could people spot me easier in daylight? Sure. But they'd have to be looking. At three in the morning, no one had to be watching. Sound carried farther, and there wasn't the noise of traffic and construction and machines to drown out the pebbles that resonated like a tub of ice dumped on a tile floor.

I scanned the roof to see if anyone had observed my ascent. Hard to tell. There were vents and other objects in the way. The roof pitched up toward the front. Wonderland was not a coherent, elegant design. Halfway across, the roof stepped up several feet. I couldn't see anyone, but I suspected I wasn't alone up here. I rose slowly and moved quietly toward the rise. As I got closer, I could see the difference in height was almost eight feet. I grabbed the edge, lifting myself as if I was doing a pull-up. I peeked my head above the roofline, allowing me a view of the rest of the roof. I was surprised to see a single figure in the darkness. He was standing on the leading edge of the building, his eyes focused toward the field. He seemed uninterested in defending his rear flank.

A bow rested comfortably in his hand. This wasn't an ancient weapon. From its silhouette, it was a split limb compound design with cams at the top and bottom and a counterweight jutting forward. It was a bow in name only.

I prefer a modern recurve, which has a more traditional look over a compound bow, but in the hands of someone skilled, either weapon was lethal at long range.

And silent.

You would be dead before you knew you'd been hit.

He had a carbon arrow nocked and ready to sling.

He wasn't scanning, his gaze was fixed at about eleven o'clock. I could easily catch him off guard. Run at him, shove him over the edge.

But that would announce my presence to the others.

I pulled myself up the rest of the way. Why wasn't he scanning his six o'clock? I don't trust anyone this oblivious to a weakness, especially with such easy access to the roof at the back.

I knew I was walking into a trap, that was obvious, but was this part of it? Or was I over thinking? Sometimes people really are this stupid. But only *sometimes*, I reminded myself.

As I inched forward, the crunching pebbles cut through me like fingernails on a chalkboard and made dashing quickly from one spot to the other impossible. The only way for me to advance was slowly padding toe-heel, toe-heel, as Deganawa had taught me.

I took cover behind one of the air conditioning units dotting the roof and peered around the corner to check the archer's position. The same. His attention focused forward and down.

I do not take pleasure in harming another human being. I've been trained to defend myself and will do so without thinking. But that does not mean I don't have a conscience.

Elam Khai was my enemy. And anyone who stood with him was my enemy as well.

In keeping with the code I'd been taught since I was a boy, I would make every effort not to kill another Eternal. But I would not hesitate to incapacitate them. And if there were no other way, I would kill without question.

The area around the man was clear of obstacles. I couldn't charge him without alerting him. If he had barely an instant of warning, he would turn and fire an arrow into my heart.

I decided on a new strategy. Make him come to me. I went to the left side of the structure, moving further away from his position.

I glanced over the edge.

About six feet below was a self-supported exterior stairway covered by a metal roof that was flat on the landings and angled like zigzagging playground slides over the stairs. I dropped onto the stairway, no longer worried about making noise. I wanted him to hear me, wanted him to investigate.

There was a glass transom between the top of the stairwell and the roofline. I was concerned I might be visible from inside, but the upper level was empty except for the remnants of the restaurant and bar—tables, chairs, and stools—that were strewn about the room.

Elam Khai had underestimated me before. I don't think he'd make the same mistake. So, why only one spotter on the roof?

The first lesson of war is that all battle plans fall apart the instant fighting begins. You can plan for contingencies, but you are never truly prepared for the unknowns that come. He had come at me with ten men in the woods. There were less than that here. If he had more people, he would've put more men on the roof. Preferably one at each corner. At the very least, he would have two. One at the front, and one covering the back. That was the *minimum*. Anything less meant that he did not have enough personnel.

He knew by now my goal was the airport. Daniel would've spilled that in the first few seconds. Perhaps he believed I would abandon my friends, and he had concentrated his numbers in and around Logan.

I waited. But the archer didn't show.

I tapped my foot lightly on the metal, continuing until, a moment later, I saw the tip of the arrow appear over the edge. I reached up and seized the dart, dragging it down, and pulling the man over the side. He landed on the roof of the stairway and slid down to the landing below me. He lay there, motionless. I still had the bow in my hand, the arrow, hanging precariously. I snatched the dart out of the air as it started to fall. The rest of the arrows were in their quiver under the man.

I pulled myself back onto the main roof. I stayed on my belly for a moment, checking for anyone else.

When I was convinced I was the only one left on the roof, I crept to the front. A line of lights ran along the edge of the roof aimed at the track and the stands below. I nocked the arrow and peered over. The roof was much higher on this side, perhaps the equivalent of three or four stories. Below, embedded in the infield along the final straightaway were six feet tall letters that spelled out: WONDERLAND.

I searched the shadows, desperately trying to find anyone. There was a sound behind me, and I spun around, raising the bow, ready to fire.

I saw nothing.

The arrowhead was my sight as I panned side to side looking— *hunting*—for a target.

I heard the sound again. One of the dormant AC units contracting in the cold air.

I went back to searching the track.

Human night vision is relatively poor. We have difficulty picking out objects in the dark, colors blend into shades of gray. One of the main reason we've survived as a species is the motion detection capabilities of our peripheral vision. It is embedded in us to be wary of things in the shadows, things just out of our view. It is sometimes more difficult to see slight movement directly in front of you than it is to sense it out of the corner of your eye.

There was a disturbance in the blackness off to my right.

I spotted him. One man in the far corner of the field. I examined the rest of the property for several minutes and couldn't locate anyone else. Two men. One on the roof. One on the field. If I had to guess, Elam Khai had only four to six men besides himself. It was better than ten or a dozen or whatever, but it didn't change things.

Elam Khai was formidable enough. He didn't need anyone else to defeat me.

But I had one big advantage. I didn't have to defeat him. This wasn't about victory for me, it was about escape. All I had to do was get Daniel and Phoebe safely away from here.

That I could do—maybe.

I walked the length of the roof, keeping enough distance between me and the edge, so I wasn't visible to the man in the field. I made one more visual sweep of the grounds. I was ready to join Phoebe.

I thought about going off the back of the roof, the way I'd come. There was a large fuel tank in my way, and I moved to see around it.

All clear.

I stared at the fuel tank. The skin was rusting at the seams, more so along the brackets attaching it to the roof. I found a warning label displaying a propane logo. The track probably used the gas in the kitchen and maybe for heating.

I tapped the side of the tank. It sent out a hollow sound. Empty. I turned one of the relief valves at the bottom of the tank an eighth of a turn. A quiet hiss came out. Almost no pressure inside. I opened the valve all the way, and I felt a coolness on my palm. I ran my hand through the invisible gas, and a pungent odor wafted into my nostrils. I moved my face away, but the sickening scent fell away quickly. The gas was heavier than air.

I heard laughing, and my body tensed, ready to react.

It was Daniel. *Laughing.*

It sounded as if it was coming from the trees on the other side of the track. But it was just a reflection. I moved to the front edge. He was somewhere underneath me, deeper, where I couldn't see.

It was time to get Phoebe.

I snuck back toward the left side of the roof as quickly and quietly as I could. I vaulted onto the head of the stairwell, holding the bow and my single arrow out to protect them. Then slid down the angled metal roof to the archer who was unconscious at the next landing. I slipped the quiver off his shoulder and examined the remaining arrows. The tips were bent or broken off. Useless. He began to stir, and I hit him in the face with the butt end of the quiver, knocking him out again.

I had one arrow.

I slid down to the next level, then leaped to the ground, absorbing the hard landing using my legs. Rolling would've been less painful, but I couldn't risk damaging my only weapon.

I peered through the chain-link fence that separated the track from a driveway. I could see the flagpole ten yards away. The fence was about six feet high with piping at the top, making it easy to scale. But this entrance was too close to the stands.

I headed out to the street.

Cars passed unaware of the life and death drama going on out of view.

I ran along the sidewalk for a hundred feet before I could see the flag again, peeking out from behind an ivy-covered building. A dilapidated wooden fence about nine feet high bordered the side-walk. The paint on the fence was nearly gone and the wood was weathered and gray. I jumped up, grabbing the top of the fence, pulled myself up, and rolled my body over the top.

I dropped to the ground. I was in some kind of maintenance

paddock. It was scattered with hoses, tools, a wheelbarrow, and rusted parts to equipment that had been long since scrapped or sold off. A large chunk of the fence that kept the dogs on the track was missing. It appeared there had once been a rolling gate, but all that was left were the wheels.

The flag fluttered twenty-five feet above my head. I crouched beside the wooden flag pole. Where are you, Phoebe?

I went to the rail. The stands looked smaller from here, and there were entire sections where the seats had been removed. The field was in terrible shape. The track hadn't been groomed in a couple of years. Grooves cut deep into the soil where runoff from rain and melting snow had eroded the dirt.

The building had power. Exit signs dotted the stands and restaurant. But everything else was in darkness.

Without warning, I felt a hand on my neck, gripping me tightly. Instinct commanded my body to strike. I tensed my arm, loading it. The elbow is the strongest bone. Straight into the sternum. I sucked in a lungful of cold air, getting ready to exhale through the attack.

Something tickled my nose.

It was the light scent I enjoyed for fifty minutes every day in History class.

Phoebe would not let go. Her arms squeezed me tighter. She was shivering.

Her mouth hovered near my ear. "Alexander." She said my name in a way I'd never heard it said before. It was as if no one had ever been this glad to see me. "Alexander, I didn't know what to do."

My pulse quickened. The presence of her had a way of making me feel stronger and weaker at the same time.

"It's okay," I said. "It's okay."

There was a moment where the emotion changed. Her breathing slowed, and I could feel the warmth of her body against mine. A warmth that suddenly grew more intense.

She pulled away, just far enough to look at me. She bit her lower lip. Her stare was fearless, bold, heated. Her fingers dug into my upper arms. Then the situation came back to her, and I could see the color leave her cheeks.

"It's okay," I said again, staring into her eyes.

She let go of me, held her arms at her side and looked away. "I'm sorry. I—"

I turned her face toward me again and brushed her hair over her ear. "I'm glad you're safe."

"But Daniel isn't." She glanced in the direction of the stands. "I started to call the police, but you were worried about our families, and I was afraid. I thought if there was a record of who we were, these people might be able to trace it back to our homes and put them in danger, too. I should've called the cops. I'm sorry."

She couldn't fight back the emotion any longer.

"There's nothing to be sorry about, Phoebe. We can still call the police if we need to. There's a state police barracks on the other side of the tracks. It's a minute away."

I could see tears on her cheeks reflecting in the moonlight. I put my hand to the side of her face and used my thumb to wipe away the streaks.

I pulled her deeper into the paddock. This was how she had kept herself out of sight.

"Tell me what happened," I said. "Everything."

It took her only a moment to regain control. She avoided my eyes. She seemed almost annoyed with herself for losing it. When she returned her gaze to me, it showed no fear.

She wiped away any lingering evidence of crying. "I'm not one of those girls who bursts into tears because some boy didn't ask me out."

"That's because they always ask you out."

"Not *always*," she said.

Guys ask out Phoebe all the time. I've seen it happen in stores, at the pool, at the gas station, there was even some guy who asked her out at her grandfather's funeral. I couldn't imagine any guy *not* asking her out—as long as it's not at a funeral. And then I realized: I hadn't asked her out. Was she talking about me?

This was not the time to find out.

"How did you end up here?"

She pulled in a deep breath and stared out over the track.

"We were on the T. I saw you chasing after the train. I was in the second to the last car, and it took me a moment to pass through to the last one."

"You should be a pro by now."

"Apparently not." She paused. I had interrupted, and it took her a moment before she found her place in the story. "I was just entering the last car when you suddenly started climbing. By the time I reached the door, you were gone."

"The door was locked," I said. "Our redheaded friend from the woods nearly had me."

Her eyes flashed. "He's here," she whispered as if the Scotsman were only a few feet away.

"Are you sure?"

She nodded.

"He wasn't at first. But he showed up a little while ago. That's when I really got frightened. I thought something happened to you."

A single tear pooled in her right eye and she smoothed it aside as it fell.

"I'm okay," I said. "See?"

She smashed her fist into my chest. Her breathing was heavy as she patted my chest more gently. Then finally, she nodded.

"How did they get Daniel and not you?"

"We were in different cars. At the next stop, some transit agents leaving work got on board. When I tried to get to Daniel, they told me I couldn't go between the cars. They said to change cars at the next station. Only we went through the next station without stopping. Maintenance work. When we got to the airport station, I saw him."

"Who?"

"The man from your house."

"Elam Khai."

"He was standing on the platform with a device. It was making a beeping sound that kept growing louder and closer together until he was right in front of the door Daniel was about to walk out of."

"Tracking device."

"Daniel must have recognized him," she said. "Because he froze. Elam Khai stepped into the car. I couldn't hear what they said, but I jumped back on the train. Elam Khai waved the device over the backpack and the tone was constant."

That's how they knew where we were. They had been tracking us—or at least the backpack—this whole time. But Elam Khai never touched the backpack at my house. How long had that homing device been in there?

"Was he alone?" I needed to know how many men Elam Khai had with him.

"He had two men with him. Two others were waiting at Wonderland Station. I should have called the police." She was angry with herself. After a moment, she continued. "They led Daniel out of the station. I was surprised Daniel wasn't screaming. He was acting strange. I mean, stranger than normal. He was laughing like someone was tickling him. It was weird. I think they drugged him." She glanced up at the moon. Did she know her name was tied to that silvery orb? "I was afraid they'd shove him in a car and drive off. I was just hoping I could get a license plate. But they dragged him across the parking lot to here."

"Is that when you sent me the photo of Daniel tied up?"

"I never sent a photo. I tried texting you and calling you like a hundred times. It kept getting cut off. And the texts wouldn't go through until I finally got all your texts at once ten minutes ago."

I opened the phone, struggled to remember how to open an old message, and showed her. "You didn't send me this picture?"

Her hand went to her mouth. "Is that Daniel?"

"You didn't send this?"

"No."

Instantly, everything around me crystallized. My attention zeroed in on the grandstands. The remaining seats. The deep shadows. The abandoned restaurant and bar that sat cantilevered above the stands behind glass.

I heard the flag whipping overhead and glanced up at it. The *flag!*

"We have to get out of here."

"What about Daniel?"

I pulled Phoebe toward the end of the paddock.

"That photo came from *your* phone number."

She still didn't understand.

"They spoofed a cell tower. That's why you couldn't get through to me. That's how they got my number and cloned your phone."

And that was why the archer on the roof wasn't worried I'd be coming up behind him. He knew—they knew—I was going to the flag pole. They had intercepted our texts.

This was the trap.

There was a crawlspace at the end of the paddock just big enough for us to squeeze through, one at a time. The chute had been built for the dogs to run through. But run to where?

They were coming for us. They knew we were here.

Escape. That was all that mattered now.

"Go, go!"

I frantically motioned for Phoebe to get into the chute. Using her hands and feet, she bear-crawled through the passage, disappearing through the wall of the paddock.

I saw movement out of the corner of my eye.

Someone was behind me.

I went to climb in after Phoebe but was grabbed by the waist and dragged back into the paddock. Fingers tightened around my throat. I squeezed the muscles in my arm, tightened my core, then thrust my elbow into my attacker's sternum. Immediately, the hands around my neck slackened. I heard a body slump to the ground. And the sound of wheezing. I looked back and was surprised to find a woman, slightly bigger and definitely stronger than me, gasping like a fish on land.

Diving into the chute, I scrambled away as quickly as I could. I didn't have enough room to crawl like a bear, I had to drop on my belly and army crawl, which wasn't as efficient as Phoebe's method. I was grateful Nikolay had bandaged the wound on my hand.

About ten feet in, I realized I had left the bow behind. I cursed loudly. Phoebe glanced at me.

"Are you okay?"

I waved her on. "Keep going!"

I quickly looked toward the paddock. The woman was on her back, coughing. It was too risky to go back for the bow.

Keep moving, I told myself.

Rocks dug into my elbows and knees as I crawled, sending sharp pains through my legs, reminding me of my twisted knee.

The chute dead-ended into a padlocked wooden door. Phoebe pushed on the wire roof, searching for a way out as she neared the door, but it was futile. Then…she disappeared. The chute made a ninety-degree turn to the left!

I was only a few yards behind. Suddenly, the enclosure rattled. I peeked over my shoulder and saw the woman aiming the bow down the length of the passage. I roared in anger. My own weapon! Before I could scramble to turn in the passage, she let the arrow fly. I pressed myself tight against the side of the chute as the carbon dart pierced the wood door, the feathered vanes an inch from my face fluttered with each breath I took. I stared at the shaft, my breathing shallow and quick. I yanked on the arrow, trying to pull it free. I didn't want to give her a second shot at me. The cage rattled again. The woman was crawling in after us. I really, really, *really* wanted to know what was so important that they were willing to expend this much energy to capture me and lure in my father.

Unable to free the arrow, I snapped it with my foot and grabbed the shaft, scrambling into the off-shoot that led away from the track. I passed through a fence that was a continuation of the wood barrier that edged the road. But this far down the street curved to the left and the fence and property line stayed straight.

Phoebe was twenty feet ahead of me. I could see holding pens along either side of the chute. A small building, its crimson color faded, sat between the fence and the road.

It was a Veterinary Hospital.

At least, that's what it said on the washed out sign hanging precariously over the back door.

When the dog track was operating, it was a savvy business decision to open a veterinary clinic here. A vet could supplement the business from the track with animals brought in by the public.

The woman's progress through the maze was slower than ours, due partly to her size and partly because she was still suffering from having the wind knocked out of her.

Phoebe exited the chute. Ten more feet and I'd be out as well. Above me were cage dividers, their purpose was to force the dogs into a particular pen. The first dog would go into the first pen. The divider would be pushed down, forcing the second dog into the next pen. And so on.

Free of the enclosure, I got to my feet.

Phoebe tugged at me. "C'mon, let's go."

I started to run, but seeing the woman reach the pens, I stopped and grabbed Phoebe's arm.

"What are we waiting for?" she said.

"Look."

As the woman made for the exit, Phoebe struggled to break free of my grip.

"Look!" I said again, this time more firmly.

It took a moment, but Phoebe finally saw what I was seeing. She whispered in my ear. I nodded. This was the place to make a stand. The woman was vulnerable and had limited movement.

The woman caught my eye and slowed her advance.

If she wanted me, the only way out was through the narrow

opening at the end of the chute with the two of us waiting for her, she would be defenseless.

She stopped.

The chute was not big enough for her to turn around. She would have to back her way out.

There was a moment where nothing happened.

I smiled.

The woman sneered back at me. It was a feeble threat.

Phoebe and I bolted for opposite ends of the holding pens. Before the woman understood what we were doing, I slid the first of the dividers down. The shriek of metal on metal pierced the night. One after the other, we slammed down the dividers until she was trapped. Four dividers in front. Three behind her. Latches locked the gates in place. As she cursed at us and kicked at the chute, we fastened them shut. They were good enough to keep a dog from getting out, but a human could work them free in a few seconds.

I noticed a tangle of roadside debris to the right of the veterinary hospital. Most of the litter had been blown into the brush. I grabbed the torn remnants of two plastic trash bags. I ripped out the ties incorporated into the mouth of each bag.

These would do just fine.

I walked over to the pens. The woman was barking obscenities as she fought to break free. I heard the squeal of metal as she got one divider open. Phoebe immediately slammed it shut with her foot.

I calmly used one tie to bind the divider in front of the woman. Then used the other to fasten the divider behind the woman. I found more bags and secured the remaining dividers.

"She's going to be able to tear through those. They're just plastic bags."

"The bags tear, but not the strips at the top. They're almost impossible to break or untie when they're cinched that tight."

We watched the woman vainly try to undo the ties.

"So where is this police station?"

"Why?"

"We need their help."

"The state police barracks is on the other side of Wonderland Station," I said.

She turned and made for the sidewalk. I held her hand, gripping firm, then more gently. She looked at it. My hand in hers. It should have been awkward. But it was comforting.

"Phoebe, if we go to the police, they're gonna ask a lot of questions we don't have the answers to. At least, not very good answers."

"As much as Daniel bugs...the...shit out of me, if something happens to him, I couldn't handle it. I don't care if I get in trouble."

"Do you think I'm worried about us getting sent to juvie?"

"Juvie?" She seemed surprised.

I raised an eyebrow. "Phoebe, c'mon. My house. The stolen car. The *exploding* cars. Acorn Street. The incident on the Common."

"We're going to jail," she said, gloomily. "I can't go to jail." She slapped her hands to her side like she does on the sidelines and I thought she might break into a cheer. *Ready? O-K! Gimme a J. Jayyy! Gimme an A. Aayyy! Gimme an I. Eyeeee.*

"No," she said, her voice strong and determined. "It doesn't matter. We have to help Daniel."

A chill ran through me, more than the wind finding its way through the openings in my jacket. I admired her bravery. I wondered why she got so angry with herself when she cried. I wanted to know all her secrets.

"We do have to help him. And the police might be able to protect us. For a while. But Elam Khai will not stop until he gets me, and nothing is going to get in his way. Not cops. Not a jail cell. And certainly not your life or Daniel's."

It was then I realized, the only option was for me to surrender.

- EIGHTEEN -
I Learn Who
My Father Really Is

My father has always said that the hardest thing for him is knowing when it's the right time to give up. Whether it's an argument or a battle or a life. For me, the last one, at least, is easy. Every three or four years. I get a new life. Almost like clockwork. Kids my age change so dramatically it would become noticeable if I didn't shed my name and put on a new one. For adults, it's a lot more complicated. Someone like my father can slip into a life for ten, twenty, even thirty years or more. That's enough time to build a life, have a family, be someone, do something important.

"But in every endeavor comes a point," he'd say. "Where a decision must be made. When do I yield?"

I reached into my pocket and pulled out the flare gun. The barrel was orange with a black handle. The extra cartridges dangled from the grip. I gently pressed the gun into Phoebe's palm. "I want you to use this if anybody comes near you. Aim at their chest. Close your eyes when you fire. Since it's dark, they'll be blinded for a few seconds. Then...you run."

I let my hand linger and felt the softness of her skin as I closed her fingers around the grip of the gun. I held on a moment longer, then I turned and headed toward the track.

"What are you doing?"

"I'm going to give myself up. And hope if I do, it will save Daniel's life."

As I walked away, I could feel Phoebe's stare burning the back of my head, but I knew it was just my mind playing tricks on me, my own doubt bubbling to the surface. She had to understand this was the only way. I glanced back to prove it and found her glaring at me, harder than my imagination could ever have envisioned.

It made me stop.

"How can you turn yourself in?" she said. "Why did we fight this whole time if you were going to just give up? Where's this honor you talk about? I almost got blown up in a car. Was that for nothing? And Braeden. He fought for you. If it wasn't for him..." She wanted to give in to the sorrow, but she resisted. "Did he die for no reason? Imagine what he would think of you right now." Her voice was steel.

She shook her head. I couldn't tell if the look she was giving me was dismay or disgust. Whichever it was, she was disappointed in me.

Her words had an effect. Perhaps not the one she expected.

"I'm going to the police," she said, marching toward the street.

Her strides were measured. It was almost as if she was daring me to come after her, then she disappeared behind the Veterinarian Hospital.

In a moment, I was blocking her path on the sidewalk.

"Phoebe."

From her, nothing but a piercing look.

"I need you to trust me."

Her face showed the kind of disdain reserved for only tax collectors and traveling salesmen. "I *have* trusted you. *Daniel* trusted you. Trusting you is what's gotten us here. That man, he wants you alive. Giving yourself up isn't brave. It's being a coward."

She meant these words. You'd think after fifteen hundred years I'd be immune to other people's opinions. That I'd have a strong enough sense of self that I could weather any criticism that came my way. For the most part, I can. But as much as I hated to admit it, some people's opinions mattered to me more than others.

"You said, think about Daniel. I am. If he's going to have a chance of surviving till morning, I'm going to need your help."

I took her silence as a sign she was willing to listen.

"He knows we're out here. But he doesn't have enough people. If he did, they'd be combing this place for us, not sending out one or two people. But he knows he doesn't have to. All he has to do is play defense. He's got Daniel. Sooner or later, we will come to him."

"Once he has you, they're going to kill Daniel," she said.

"Which is why I can't let him think he has me too quickly." I put my hand on the gun. "These flares go about a thousand feet into the air. When I leave, I want you to go to the edge of the track." I pointed to an area of bushes on the near side of the oval. "Hide there. Make sure you're outside the rail. No matter what, do not cross the infield or come toward the stands."

"Hide there? We need to alert the police."

"Give me ten minutes. Exactly...ten minutes. And then fire the flares in the air toward the building." I held her arm out at a forty-five-degree angle. "Fire all of them. Pop the spent cartridge out. Slide the next one in. Tilt between this angle and this angle until you're out of flares." I moved her arm up a few degrees and down a few degrees. "Just like that. Okay?"

She dropped her arm, shook out her limbs, then she lifted the gun, holding it firmly with both hands in a ready stance. She targeted the gun from just above to just below forty-five degrees. Phoebe was accustomed to learning routines quickly. She had a natural understanding of balance and her muscle memory was impressive.

"Perfect. I guarantee you the police will be here a few minutes after you fire these. Without you having to answer any questions. There's a man in a water taxi on the beach, straight out that way." I motioned with my hand like I was signaling a first down. "He's our escape." I didn't bother to add, *if we get to him.*

We checked our phones and compared the time on each.

"You're not really giving up, are you?" Her eyes pleaded with me.

"Yes, I am. I'm just not giving in."

She smiled at me, wanly. Bittersweet. "Ten minutes."

"*Exactly* ten minutes."

Phoebe was right. The moment Elam Khai had me, Daniel's usefulness would end and so too could his life. I hoped ten minutes would give me enough time to come up with a way to free Daniel while I dragged out negotiating my surrender to Elam Khai, but not so long that Daniel would already be dead.

∞

On the side of the track the patrons of the Wonderland Park never saw, there wasn't anything as elegant as a decaying wooden fence. A tetanus-riddled, run-down eight-foot high chain-link fence that was a danger to life and limb bordered the property. The edges were jagged and rusty and at least half the tie wires were missing, which made the fence sag in places.

I reached up and grabbed the links using the detached section as a spring to whip myself over the top and gently cushion my dismount as the fence bent in. I released and landed in a crouch.

I surveyed the grounds. The figure I'd seen earlier on the far end of the track was gone. Looking down from the roof, I had mistaken the shadow for a man. I'd taken out two. The archer on the roof and the woman locked up in the pens. That left Elam Khai, the Scotsman, and two others.

That I knew of.

I stood and walked to the perimeter of the track.

"I'm willing to listen!" I shouted as I crossed the infield. "Do you hear me?" My voice bounced around in the dense night air. "But you need to release my friend!"

There was no answer except my own words reflected back to me.

"You want *me*," I said. "I'm willing to negotiate. A simple trade. Me for him."

The lights that ran along the roofline suddenly came on. They blazed the night. I was momentarily blinded, which threw my equilibrium off, causing me to stumble on the uneven turf. I caught myself at the last second.

A familiar voice cried out, "Alexander! Alexander!" A chant of admiration, as if he had shouted "Caesar! Caesar!" in the Colosseum. The man's hearty laugh reverberated in the empty stands. After it faded away, he spoke again, his tone playfully stern. "I don't think you are in much of a position to bargain."

The lights illuminating the track made it impossible to see details in the stands. I shielded my eyes against the glare, hoping to catch a glimpse of Daniel. Once my eyes adjusted, I could make out several dark figures.

Daniel was smiling and singing to himself.

He was no longer simply tied to the iron gate. There were glints of light from two pairs of handcuffs, one set on each hand, locking him to a horizontal bar just above his head.

Two men stood near Daniel, stupid grins on their faces. I spotted the Scotsman unhurriedly moving across the stands, his head turned in my direction. He nodded to me, smiling. Everyone was so *happy.*

Stepping out of the shadows, closer than I expected, an imposing figure—

"Elam Khai," I said as I stopped at the inside edge of the track. He was less than twenty feet away. I could see his face, the scar, the dark stare. His posture was—I can't think of a better way to put it—regal.

He grinned. "Ah. The Old Man told you, didn't he?" He clicked his tongue and wagged his finger. Tsk. Tsk. Tsk.

My throat tightened. I hoped my expression didn't betray my concern for Engel.

Weakness. I cannot show him weakness.

"Don't worry, Alexander, he has nothing to fear from me. The Old Man gets special treatment."

He must know about the explosion. Does he know Engel's fate?

I didn't realize it until I exhaled that I had been holding my breath since the lights came on.

"How are you doing, Daniel?" I said, raising my voice.

Daniel glanced at his wrists, handcuffed to the iron fence. "I'm hanging in there." He laughed, his body swaying, head rolling from one side to the other, very amused at his own joke. He was shivering. "Just chillin." This time more of a giggle. "How are *you*? You look...you look *angry!*" He said it with an excited lilt in his voice, as if he'd actually said, "You look *great!*"

He kept swaying back and forth. I realized he was swinging the pendant Braeden had given him.

"Gives me strength. Gives me strength. Gives me streeeength."

"I'm worried about you."

"I *knoooow*. Me, *too*."

Phoebe thought they had given something to Daniel. I was sure of it.

Elam Khai hadn't used Engel's name. I played along. "The old man gave us a name. Nothing more. Which doesn't tell me who you are."

"I am nothing but a soldier. That is all I have ever been, and all I have ever wanted to be."

His arms rippled. It wasn't an attempt at intimidation. He did it instinctively. He said these words with such sincerity, without pretense, that I believed him. Though I knew he was much more than that.

"But who are you?" My tone was sharp and slightly defiant.

"Alexander," he said, scolding me, shaking his head in mock disappointment. After a few seconds, his face broke into an easy smile, his white teeth reflecting the lights. "I was once called that. Long ago."

There was something about the way Elam Khai held his head. Rotated noticeably to the left, chin slightly up. Not just regal. More than that. Then it came to me:

The *hero* pose.

Mimicked in the statues and portraits of leaders great and small that came after him. Forced upon him by a deformity in the vertebrae in his neck.

I could feel all the blood in my body drain to my feet.

"Alexander...The *Great*?" I said, my voice barely above a whisper.

My mind blinked out for a moment. Even when it came back, I felt fuzzy. Alexander the Great, considered the most successful commander in the history of the world.

My father would often scoff at historians' exaggerated praise of famous leaders, picking apart their weaknesses one by one. Alexander of Macedon was the exception. There were other generals my father admired and respected, but none more than Alexander III.

My father forced me to study his life, his style of leadership, and his tactics above all others. I would have to recite every battle plan, from the formations to the makeup of the troops to their positions, how they matched up against the enemy's forces and plans, how the tactics were altered once the fighting began. Every battle. Every innovation. The wedge. The sarissa. How he defeated great naval powers without raising a navy of his own, simply by cutting off their access to the water.

Fresh water.

The greatest Navy in the world was useless if they didn't have water to drink.

Less costly. More effective.

There were a hundred other touches of brilliance.

He was tutored by Aristotle. And seemed at times as interested in the arts and classical learning as he was in the art of war. And he loved war. In twelve years, he amassed one of the largest empires of the ancient world. Ruling lands that ran from the boot of Italy to the sands of Egypt to the snow-covered peaks of the Himalayas, and the plains of India, bringing with him a culture that he helped spread far beyond the boundaries of his empire. He was undefeated in battle. A genius of strategy. He was loved and respected and even deified. He inspired greatness in others and made warriors out of ordinary men. He demanded loyalty and punished cruelty.

He was arguably the greatest conqueror of all time.

And he was standing in front of me, holding my friend hostage.

"Alexander, son of Philip of Macedon, is only one part I played," Elam Khai said. "A fairly good part." His right eyebrow arched.

I remember my father telling me that as a young prince, Alexander III defeated the Sacred Band of Thebes—who had never been vanquished in four decades of war—at the Battle of Chaeronea. His skill and bravery were so inspiring that Philip's own men shouted, "Philip is our General, but Alexander is our *King*!"

"Why do you think you were named after me?" Elam Khai asked.

The next words to come from my mouth burned my tongue. "Because my father named me after someone he admired."

"Alexander," Elam Khai paused for dramatic effect. "I *am* your father," he said, drawing out the words in a way that seemed familiar.

I felt like I had been punched in the stomach, smacked in the head, and kicked in the balls. My father? No. *No.* My father was Marcus Grant. Not this man. The words cut through my skull and echoed in the void that used to be my brain. I've heard these words. I've heard them repeated. Many times. Seriously. Jokingly. As I glared at Elam Khai, gazed into his smiling, evil eyes, I realized: *Darth Vader. My father.*

"It's not true," I said, not meaning to parrot the dialogue of the movie, but it's what you say. It couldn't be true. Could it? Had everything in my life been a lie? The greatest betrayal. The most wretched scenario. My worst enemy is my own father. Any resolve I had melted away.

Elam Khai laughed. Again the sound echoed in the cavernous space behind him. "I'm not really your father. But it's such a great line, don't you think?"

My relief was flavored with rage.

"I find movies fascinating," he said, ignoring my fuming gaze. "Fascinating, and frustrating as well. Strange things, other people's visions in your head."

It's impossible for you, born after the birth of film, to understand having only your own images in your mind. You may think you can fathom it, but you can't. Having lived so long with nothing but my own visions, facing someone else's seemed like an invasion. When audiences saw the first publicly shown movie—nothing more than footage of a train heading toward the camera—people in the crowd were terrified, believing the train would burst from the screen and run them over. Some scattered in fear, others ducked out of the way.

Now, major cities of the world explode in movie after movie and we chomp on popcorn.

Moving pictures have expanded our vision. But they've also poisoned it. Things you could never imagine—and some you would never want to—are imprinted in the mind. And once an image is there, it can never be as it was before.

At times, I miss having nothing but my own imagination.

"I couldn't resist," said Elam Khai, sounding almost apologetic. He came closer and grabbed my hand. "We are blood, however, you and I." There was an incredible strength to his grip. I was powerless against it. "You are my brother's son. One he never revealed to me," he said, regretfully. "I had to discover you all on my own."

If yesterday you had told me that Alexander the Great was my uncle, I would've been overcome by a sense of awe and wonder. I would've stood taller. Felt gratitude for the extraordinary gifts I've been given. But today, the news filled me with dread.

My father did not dwell on the past, other than to force me to learn from it. He rarely talked about his family or his other children. Just once when I asked him about a memory I had as a young boy—from when I was not more than three hundred—of a gathering of people, did he tell me anything about his family. He revealed little, saying only that he had a brother and a sister. I've tried many times to recall that gathering. But I was so young, and like regular three-year-olds, memories from that age don't take hold as strongly. I remember flashes of laughter. A group seated around a table that seemed colossal to me. It was a glimpse of a normal life. A semblance of a family.

If Elam Khai had been Alexander The Great, who had my father been?

I tried to pull away from his grasp. He didn't release my forearm until I had struggled in vain long enough for me to understand he could have held on forever. One of the greatest weapons a warrior has at his disposal is getting the enemy to focus on matters other than the battle at hand.

I swallowed my embarrassment, and I pushed the question of who my father had been from my mind.

I had to stay in the present.

Tugging at his handcuffs, Daniel strained to see what Elam Khai's slightly turned head was looking at. "You keep looking off to the left. Is there some hot girl over there? Hi, hot girl! Wanna go to Homecoming with me?"

Elam Khai glared at Daniel. So did I.

And...

...something was missing.

"Whoa!" Daniel said, startled as he noticed our harsh gazes. "You *both* are very *angry*." He furrowed his brow and frowned. Then he burst out laughing and crooned like a child, "I just peed in my pants. It feels *warm*. I'm not chillin' anymore." He got very serious. "I think I *like* peeing in my pants."

I shook my head.

Focus.

"You still haven't explained what you want from me," I said, directing my gaze at Elam Khai.

"I want nothing from you. I want your father."

And that's when I heard the whoosh of a sarissa cutting through the air and aiming straight for the back of my head.

NINETEEN

I Am Completely Irrelevant—
And Absolutely Necessary—
To The Plan

It's not easy hearing that you're unimportant. Inconsequential. That the reason someone is interested in you is not because of you at all. That you are simply a tool, a pawn, a path to get to someone else.

It's even worse when that someone else is your own father. The blade goes in a little deeper.

The sarissa is not a terribly elegant weapon. It is nothing but a very long stick with a steel tip and a counterweight at the opposite end, but it enabled Alexander the Great to wreak havoc on the battlefield by allowing several rows of his soldiers—not just those in front—to project an overlapping wall of spears at the enemy. It's meant to be deployed in a phalanx. Used alone, it is an unwieldy, overly-long pain in the ass.

I ducked out of the way of the attack, felt the breeze tickle my ear as the shaft passed over me. At twenty feet long, even a swift swipe on the part of an attacker meant—due to geometry and physics— that the tip of the sarissa was moving in slow-motion. I was able to catch up with the rotating shaft and yank it toward me, dragging the long-haired man I'd seen standing beside Daniel to the ground.

After the *Titanic* went down, my father kept me close for several months, first in Paris, then in Rome. There was a woman in Rome that I had a brief crush on. She was probably twenty or so. I know what you're thinking, she was a little old for me, but I was nearly fourteen hundred at the time, and I'd had my share of dalliances. My father traveled often, and I was treated like the lord of the manor by his domestic staff when he was gone, which is one of the reasons I didn't run off. She was the other reason. She'd come over to the house several times a week and seemed genuinely interested in talking to me. I looked forward to her visits. I was an idiot, of course. What she really wanted was for me to introduce her to my father. I told her how I felt anyway. She said, "You're just a boy. I'm not interested in boys. I'm interested in men." I love my father, but I never hated him—no, not him—never hated being his son so much as I did at that moment.

Until now.

"Why do you want my father?"

"Because I really miss hanging out with my brother. He's such a great conversationalist. And I love it when he braids my hair." Elam Khai's wide grin slowly collapsed and turned dark. "Your father's been interfering with my plans."

"He's been stopping you, you mean."

"Delaying me."

"From doing what?"

Elam Khai seemed more interested in our fight than answering me. He prodded us to continue our sparring.

Long Hair got to his feet. I remembered him from the woods. He and I hadn't fought. Braeden had taken him on. I feinted a move to the right and instead jammed him, catching Long Hair in the midsection.

Elam Khai half-groaned, half laughed.

"From doing what?" I repeated.

I was interrupting his entertainment and Elam Khai let me know with a heavy sigh. "From doing the difficult thing. The thing that needs to be done."

How long had it been? Two minutes? Five? There wasn't much chance of me releasing Daniel with his hands cuffed to the iron, especially with my long-haired friend here monopolizing my attention.

Clutching opposite ends of the weapon, we briefly played tug of war until it was clear neither of us was going to let go. Then began moves and counter moves as we jockeyed for control.

Elam Khai and the Scotsman watched the dance in amusement.

"You look like banner carriers in a Fourth of July parade," roared Elam Khai.

When Long Hair saw how ridiculous we looked zigzagging across the field, he became self-conscious. Once he realized I was winning this "race," he doubled his effort. Which is why when I rammed the shaft into the timing pole at the finish line, the force of the collision snapped the sarissa in three pieces. The two ends and a short middle section that spun wildly into the stands.

I came away with the more useful end, a six-foot-long steel-tipped pike. Long Hair had the counterweight.

It was spear against war hammer.

"You are full of surprises, Alexander Grant."

"What is this *difficult thing* that needs to be done?" I asked, knowing I would be given no information from Elam Khai without effort. It reminded me of how my father made me work for answers. The similarity annoyed me.

"Let me ask you a question, Alexander. You seem to be a smart, capable boy."

I bristled at his patronizing tone. *Boy.* I let my anger simmer. I couldn't afford to lose my cool. So, I took it out on Long Hair instead with a flurry of aggressive attacks.

"Just how long do you think we can go on living undetected?" Elam Khai let the question linger in the air, the silence adding weight until it seemed everything around me was being dragged down.

The steel tip suddenly felt heavy.

"How long, Alexander? In the past, I could be anyone. I would move from one life to the next. The hardest part was knowing when to make the jump. How long to remain quiet. Marcus was always better at that than I was."

Long Hair came at me, swinging the counterweight. I was able to quickly parry the attack. I found it easier to use the splintered end of my spear to fend him off. Deflect, block, counter and spin the shaft under my shoulder and over my back to bring the steel tip to bear.

Elam Khai continued. "But now, fingerprints, surveillance cameras, facial recognition, DNA testing. If I become anything close to what I've been in the past, I'll never be able to be anyone else ever again." He followed me with his eyes as I clashed with his underling. "Do you understand?"

I did. Completely.

When I came in third at the 1948 chess championship, my father almost killed me. He cut the photo and headline from the front page of one hundred and sixty-three newspapers from around the country and around the world and had each individually mounted under glass. They crowded the walls of my room for three years. Hung not proudly, but shamefully as symbols of what *not* to do. He constantly warned me about being too good at anything. He barely tolerated my playing lacrosse. It drew too much attention. I knew scouts from Syracuse and Rutgers had requested video of my games. If my father ever found out, it would be the end of my playing *tewaaraton*.

"I do understand. I worry about those things, too." I saw Elam Khai wince a second before a blow caught me in the shin. I roared as the pain hit. "But what does that have to do with this?" I shouted in anger and agony.

"Everything. As long as technology continues to evolve and spread like a virus, we are in danger. Even without being famous, the time is coming when none of us will be able to hide anymore. A few decades maybe. Fifty years, if we're lucky. A blink of an eye. But I don't believe we'll be that fortunate. The day is coming much sooner."

ALEXANDER X | 319

I thought about Engel's operation. How much it had grown, how complex it had become in the last two decades.

Evade, sidestep, lunge.

I could see where Elam Khai's not unwarranted concern was leading.

"I will not let it come to that," Elam Khai said, his voice growing darker. "I will march us back a hundred years, a thousand if I have to." His hand formed a fist that looked like it could crush a diamond into dust. And I was drawn in by the gravity of his unshakable determination.

Perceiving my lapse in attention, Long Hair got in another good shot. This one to my hip.

I rolled the shaft around my neck, and grabbed it with the opposite hand, immediately going into a backhanded baseball swing. I caught Long Hair square in the jaw, sending him to the dirt. I narrowed my eyes to show my displeasure at him using my distraction to his advantage.

"Ragar, you're letting a boy beat you," Elam Khai said.

I decided I needed to finish this. I went on the offensive. Slash, stab, deflect. After crossing weapons, each of us trying to push the other back on their heels, I rolled the shaft under my arm and behind my back, letting Long Hair think the strike was coming from his right, but when I caught the shaft, I rolled my wrist and struck him on the left side of his head.

Reeling from the blow, Long Hair staggered and half-heartedly raised his weapon to parry. I did not let up. No more sparring. No more performing for our Master. I clubbed the shaft in his hand, sending it flying. Swinging around on my follow through, I caned him behind the knees. He collapsed onto his back.

I kept him from mounting a counterattack by using my weapon as a barrier. Like playing the 'knife game,' only instead of a knife rapidly stabbing the spaces between fingers, I was stabbing the ground between his legs, his arms, and his head as he tried to punch, bite, roll, reach for his weapon, or get leverage to stand.

Every move he made, I checked. His shins had to be in excruciating pain as many times as he went to kick me and found the wooden shaft instead.

Every time I put my weapon's tip to his chest, he knocked it away rather than submit to me. Finally, tired of the knife game, I let him get his arms close enough to his body to push himself off the ground. As he rose, I tossed my weapon and used my fists to pummel him. He hadn't been the one that killed Braeden, but he had been a part of that ambush. He was halfway to his feet when I side-kicked him in the chest and sent him careening into the rail on the inside of the track. As he tried to recover, I lunged at him and shoved him back on the rail a second time. When he took a feeble swing that I easily avoided, I smashed my clenched hand into his jaw just below the ear.

I don't know how many more punches I threw before I heard Elam Khai shout, "Enough!"

I was panting. My knuckles were bloody. I nudged Long Hair with my foot.

"Get up, Ragar! Get up!" urged Elam Khai, laughing as the Scotsman and the other man joined in.

Long Hair didn't respond.

"Feel better?" asked Elam Khai. "This is the life you were born for. Not that facsimile you've been living over and over. People think their need for stimulation can be satisfied by watching a screen or playing a game. Let them play with me. Let them attend a party of mine." He smiled wickedly. "I'll show them stimulations." He kicked at some fast food wrappers left behind by trespassing teenagers. "We have become soft. We have grown too dependent on technology. Have you seen what happens when the power goes out? People are lost without computers to think for them. The water doesn't flow. The food doesn't grow. Mankind has lived in a sustainable way for tens of thousands of years. This new way of living cannot survive for two hundred. I will lead us back to the way it should be."

"Who says the rest of us want to be led?" My tone was defiant.

"Almost everyone wants to be led. Change is uncomfortable. It's so much easier to be forced into it."

"You say you're Alexander the Great—"

"That is a *life* I lived."

"Semantics. For the most part, Alexander of Macedon was a good man."

He laughed. "Good. Evil. It's all a matter of perspective. It's not who wins. It's not even who writes the history. It's who rewrites it. Just because you are a hero today or tomorrow or even a hundred years from now, doesn't mean you'll be looked upon as a hero in a thousand years. History is fickle with whom it chooses to honor. I have been other names, not as beloved or worshiped as Alexander of Macedon, but I am the same. It is others who see me differently." He was quiet for a moment. "What do you think will happen when they figure out who...we...are?" He poked at the air to punctuate the last three words. "Do you think they will welcome us? Do you think they will honor us? The conqueror used to have legitimacy simply because he had won. The vanquished accepted the victor's will. Today you defeat an enemy, and he has no respect for you." Elam Khai met my gaze. "When they find out who we are, if they let us live at all, it's going to be to test us, to study us, take us apart bit by bit, gene by gene, until they discover why we are as we are. They will hunt us down and destroy every one of us because their inferiority will make them fear us. I think I'm being restrained in my response."

"What is that response? Exactly."

He seemed put out by the question, as if I was disappointing him, boring him. "I've already told you. I am going to erase the last hundred years."

He waved his hand, wiping away a century. Like the roller coasters and dance halls on Revere Beach. Gone. Like they'd never been there.

"You were a king, nearly a god, now you're just a terrorist."

"Terrorists poke you in the eye." He mimed this, closing his left eye and tapping it with his finger. "Which only makes it easier for their enemy to focus their revenge." His right eye glared at me. "The security measures that threaten to reveal us are a response to their random acts. Terrorists are weak because they hate their enemy. I do not hate my foe. I will not poke him in the eye. I will stab him in the heart." Elam Khai pounded his fist on his chest. The passion with which he spoke and the complete belief in his words was captivating. "I *love* my enemy. Anyone who hates his enemy fights forever. You understand what I'm saying? Can I not more quickly, more easily, and with less suffering completely destroy my enemy by loving him, by honoring him, by making him my friend?"

"You want to make friends?"

"I wish to eliminate enemies."

"You want to destroy the world."

Elam Khai shook his head. "Alexander. A third of the world lives in poverty. From the time we climbed down from the trees until a hundred years ago, humans barely made a mark on the planet. Since then, we have built a society on resources that will run out in a century. And it's not just oil and gas and coal. They are raping the planet, stripping her of every precious thing. Things that can never be replaced. Let's not even talk about unsustainable population growth. I don't want to destroy the world, Alexander, I want to *save* it."

"There are other ways to do that."

He brought out the jazz hands. "Oh, let's *recycle!*"

"I recycle!" gurgled Daniel.

"*Other* ways to fix the problems," I said. I tried to offer up some viable solutions. I couldn't. It reminded me of our limitations. "We're not the inventors. Or the discoverers. We're survivors. We learn and perfect and master, but it takes new minds to create new thinking. We could use our considerable resources to foster the change the world needs."

Elam Khai stared at me through a veil of sadness. "Don't you think I've tried."

He was being patient. Maybe it was because I was his brother's son. Maybe it was because he was in control. But I was acutely aware that Elam Khai's patience had a limit.

"Listen," I said, respectfully. "Maybe two thousand years ago you could change the course of history by yourself."

"You think it's been that long?"

"No, but it's different now. Different than even fifty years ago. There are no Einsteins or Galileos or Newtons or Marie Curies anymore. Not because there aren't any more geniuses, but because the average high school student's understanding of science surpasses those great minds. *He*," I pointed to Daniel, "knows more about the Universe than Isaac Newton."

Daniel wearily tugged at his hands. The cuffs clanged the iron. "I could go for a couple of Isaac Newtons."

"One person can't do it anymore," I continued. "But if we could marshal the others like us. Together. We could change the world."

"I'm afraid your father wrongly believes the same thing."

I felt my face flush with anger. "He will stop you. You know that."

"He will try. As he has tried in the past. Maybe he'll do better this time. He very nearly stopped me off the coast of Actium. If it weren't for his puppy love, he might have won."

Actium. The word slammed into my chest.

"That…was…" I couldn't finish the sentence.

The Battle of Actium wasn't fought by Alexander the Great. It was waged in the year 722 *ab urbe condita*—after the founding of Rome—which translates to 31 BC, three hundred years after Alexander.

The engagement pitted the forces of Octavian, the nephew of Julius Caesar, on one side, and Marcus Antonius and Cleopatra, Queen of Egypt, on the other.

Mark Antony had been Caesar's second-in-command, one of his closest friends, and his most loyal supporter. He rose to Consul, the highest elected office in the Roman Republic.

The traditional wing of the Senate feared Caesar's power had become too great. It was for this reason, Julius Caesar was assassinated. Knowing Mark Antony could thwart their attempt, he was delayed at the entrance by one of the conspirators as his friend was being stabbed inside. Antony's life was spared. The conspirators' plot was only to depose the man they believed had illegally commandeered the Republic.

The conspirators, however, hadn't understood the public's love for Caesar—the people worshiped him—and those who plotted his demise realized too late that they would never be hailed as heroes or liberators.

The conspirators had a more immediate problem. The fate of their own lives.

All they had to do was declare Caesar a tyrant, then their actions to remove him would be legitimate. However, if they did that, all of Caesar's actions would be illegal. Since it was Caesar who appointed his killers to their positions, they would be retroactively stripped of their political immunity and be tried for murder.

Mark Antony was instrumental in pointing this out to them. Two days after Caesar's assassination, the conspirators struck a deal with Antony for amnesty. In exchange, Caesar would be honored as a hero and held up as a God.

The murder of Caesar began a decade-long struggle for power between Mark Antony and Octavian, who Caesar adopted as his son posthumously in his will. Octavian, Mark Antony, and Marcus Aemilius Lepidus formed the uneasy Second Triumvirate. For a time, they brought peace to Rome.

When their alliance fell apart, Octavian persuaded the Senate to declare war on Cleopatra who had been Caesar's lover and was now married to Antony and mother to his three children, despite Antony still being married to Octavian's sister.

Declaring war on Cleopatra was Octavian's way of declaring war on Mark Antony. This would be the final war of the Roman Republic.

I studied the Battle of Actium with my father. From the way he spoke, I assumed he'd been a part of it, but he never gave any indication he was the leader of one of the factions.

After a brilliant military and political career, where he quelled uprisings in Gaul and cleverly used public opinion against Caesar's assassins to solidify his power, the Battle of Actium was a stunning and uncharacteristic defeat for Mark Antony. He would never recover from it, and his army—that had been equal to or greater than Octavian's—deserted him.

My father told me Antony lost because one of his top generals—upset by the influence Cleopatra had over Antony—defected prior to the decisive battle. Mark Antony had over four hundred ships. Octavian had two hundred and fifty. But with Antony's battle plan in hand, Octavian repositioned forces and altered tactics to counter Antony's numerical advantage.

In the middle of the engagement, Cleopatra, who had been at the rear, made a sudden break for the open sea, withdrawing her ships. Antony soon followed, leaving his flagship and fleeing with just forty ships. While the larger battle raged on, their escape went unnoticed. The conflict continued until Antony's fleet was set on fire. Three hundred ships and five thousand men lost.

The battle decided the war and ended the Roman Republic. Lepidus had been marginalized, Mark Antony defeated. Only Octavian remained. Although Octavian kept the institutions of the Republic, they were hollow and powerless. Gaining complete control over all of Rome, he renamed himself Augustus Caesar, the first Emperor of the Roman Empire.

There's been much debate over why Mark Antony gave up the battle and followed Cleopatra. On the subject, my father offered no insight. It was one of the reasons I didn't think he was close to the action. I should have suspected something. My father always had an opinion. And he was always in the middle of things.

If he really had been Mark Antony, then I didn't know my father at all.

Elam Khai gave me that same condescending look he had earlier. "So left in the dark. He didn't tell you who he's been, did he?" He shook his head. "What a waste. Your father was not much older than you when we conquered Persia. If I *was* your father, you would not be throwing away your life repeating high school like some remedial idiot. I've taken men and transformed them into warriors that conquered the world. Turned my generals into kings and emperors." He leaned in. "Just imagine what I could do with you."

We stared at each other. I could feel my eyelids flashing rapidly. He never blinked.

"My brother will come for you," he said. "And then, he will be mine. One way or the other."

This is how a great warrior defeats you. Before the battle begins. I had a million thoughts swirling in my head. Everything that I knew was being reprocessed, reexamined. One question kept bubbling up to the surface. And it was more my own curiosity than any attempt at gathering actionable intelligence.

"How?" I asked. "How will you do it?"

"Despite that high school education you keep limiting yourself to, I'm sure you're smart enough to come up with something."

The idea was so massive. Take us back to the way it was for most of my life. No light. No electricity.

He smiled. "Don't feel too stupid if it seems a bit too great a task. You've been reined in your entire life. And I..." His grin grew wider. "I have been planning this for nearly a century." He motioned to the Scotsman. I readied my body for another fight. "And now it's time."

The Scotsman stepped toward me, the heavy sword that mortally wounded Braeden in his right hand. I could smell his breath. It was foul, the scent of half-digested meat.

"It's the twenty-first century," I barked. "Haven't you heard of the toothbrush?"

He smiled and laughed, then took a deep breath and exhaled in my face. My eyes fluttered as my nostrils fought against the stench.

"I'll take that as a *no*."

Across the track, I saw a flare. Had it been ten minutes?

There was a succession of bright lights, one after another. Phoebe was firing flares, but not toward the stands. I could make out two figures illuminated by the harsh red light. Phoebe and the woman we had locked in the pens. The woman had her hands up in front of her eyes.

Even if I could escape the Scotsman and Elam Khai, I was too far away to help. The fight would be over by the time I arrived.

Run, Phoebe. Run!

She did run.

She ran straight at the woman and did a front flip off the grass, propelling her feet into the woman's jaw.

Then the lights went down on the little play.

The flares died out before we could witness its ending.

So much for my clever plan.

Had she used all the flares to defend herself?

The answer came a few seconds later as Phoebe fired three flares into the air. She arced them exactly as I'd hoped. The red glow flickered in the night sky. It would only take one for this to work.

In a few moments, the state police would certainly come.

I turned toward the Scotsman. "I remember you," I said as our eyes met.

Before I could say another word, the Scotsman grabbed me by the throat and hoisted me off the ground, my feet dangling at least half a yard above the cement. Gasping for breath, my Adam's apple jammed into my esophagus, I was unable to speak. I couldn't help but be impressed by his strength as he held me aloft with one hand while wielding his sword with the other.

"I would have preferred you come of your own accord," said Elam Khai. "We should not be enemies, you and I." I could see he believed this. "I have patiently explained my reasoning. Why I must do what must be done. I would be very displeased if that turned out to have been a waste of my time." He turned toward the Scotsman. "We have what we came for. Kill the other one," he said regarding Daniel, like someone asks a waiter to clear plates from the table after having had too much to eat.

It took Daniel a moment to realize they were speaking about casually ending his life.

"Oh, *c'mon*! Really? You're going to *kill me*? I thought we were getting *along*. What about all that crap about loving your enemy, making friends?" He stared at me, his gaze floating between the two or three of me he was seeing. He whispered to me...loudly. "He's not very nice." Then even louder at Elam Khai, "You're not very nice!"

The Scotsman lifted me higher. I would not give the Scotsman the pleasure of seeing me capitulate. I would not give in to him. I narrowed my eyes until they were daggers cutting into his pale skin and red eyes. It was as useless a gesture as the sneer the woman gave me in the pens. But it cannot be contained. It is the warrior.

In her. In the Scotsman. In me.

My options were limited. Daniel was shackled. Phoebe was fending for herself. I was suspended several feet in the air. I wasn't worried about my own safety. Elam Khai needed me alive. But there was no reason to keep Daniel alive now that I was in their hands. Literally, in their hands, dangling off the ground.

But then…there was no reason to kill him, either.

I wanted to point this out, but the Scotsman made sure I couldn't speak.

The way the Scotsman was squeezing my neck, I would lose consciousness in a minute or two. I learned in the woods and in the subway tunnel, hitting him had little effect. It was as if he didn't feel pain. I didn't waste my energy trying.

"Oy. What about d' gurl?" asked the Scotsman.

Elam Khai breathed in, considering the Scotsman's question. "Let the girl live." He turned to Long Hair who was staggering to his feet. "If you find her, bring her back alive."

I fought to squeak the words out. "Then…why…*kill him*?"

He glared at me. "Because you defied me."

I used the last bit of strength I had to kick at Elam Khai. He easily deflected my attack.

"Give me trouble, boy, and I will kill her, too."

With his head rotated to the left, his posture upright, his stance balanced, Elam Khai looked majestic, intimidating, and unbeatable. Forget saving Daniel, how could I ever stop this man?

"I came into your home alone and unarmed. Open-handed. I gave you a chance to make this easy. You turned this into what it is. Blame yourself. You're the reason he is going to die."

"Oh, God," moaned Daniel. "I just crapped in my pants."

The man standing guard next to Daniel laughed, and exaggeratedly pinched his nose at the smell.

"I don't love that as much as ur-urinating. I'm very uncomfortable."

"Dohna worry," said the Scotsman. "You wont be fer long."

Daniel made a high pitched whine.

Elam Khai glanced over his shoulder at Daniel, then back at me. "He is amusing. I can see why you kept him around." He smiled, darkly. "Whether you or my brother or any of the rest join me...I *will* change the world." Stepping away from me, he shouted, "Τώρα."

The Scotsman brought his face closer to mine. "I wont you to watch," he said as he lifted the broad sword to Daniel's throat.

"I'm going to kill you," I promised him, my voice a strangled whisper.

"I'm dead already," he said.

Not quite the reaction I was expecting. It briefly interrupted my strong desire to rip his head off. I saw his arm tense. Saw him slash at Daniel. Two quick whips of the sword. My heart broke as I heard the sound. Steel hitting the iron after passing through flesh. I closed my eyes, unable to take in the image of my friend's life bleeding from his body. I didn't open them until I heard another sound. My own breath returning. The Scotsman relaxed the fingers around my throat. I crumpled to the ground, my hand going to my throat to staunch the pain.

I struggled to open my eyes as I pulled in a breath that seemed to go on forever. I didn't know my lungs could hold that much air. When my vision came into focus, I saw the flares trickling down.

I could taste the sickening scent of the gas.

Too late.

Ten minutes had been too long.

As the first flare disappeared behind the edge of the roof, I closed my eyes again and whispered, "Boom."

A second later an explosion rocked the building and knocked anyone standing to the ground. The concussion shattered the windows of the dining room cantilevered over the stands. Glass shards rained down and I watched a large unbroken sheet slowly pivot as it fell. Catching the air, the pane gracefully glided horizontally, like a bird swooping down to land. My awe at the sight turned to gut-wrenching horror as the glass sliced through the man who'd been standing on Daniel's left, cutting him in two. It should have cut through Daniel's lifeless body as well, but Daniel wasn't hanging on the iron fence, which had been blown apart and twisted.

The scene surprised me. Not the level of destruction. I expected that. The flare ignited the propane pooling on the roof. The flames climbed up the valve I'd left open, sparking the fuel inside, detonating the tank.

Burning metal shrapnel, pieces of the tank, and parts of one of the air conditioners slammed into the track. A section of the roof at the rear of the stands collapsed onto the seats, emitting a wave of sound as deafening as the blast.

What surprised me was seeing Daniel, his hands held tight over his ears, an attempt to protect himself from the piercing noise as he tried unsuccessfully to crawl only using his legs. An inept inchworm.

He was alive.

In one piece.

The Scotsman hadn't slashed Daniel. He'd severed the cuffs with his blade, setting Daniel free.

But that wasn't the only surprise: Long Hair at the tip of the Scotsman's sword.

At the mercy of the redheaded menace. Without a word, Long Hair slipped his hand under his shirt and raised a small, silver version of the symbol. The Circle, X, Square. He touched the medallion to his lips. Lifting the chain over his head, he offered the piece to the Scotsman. It hung there in Long Hair's outstretched hands for an uncomfortably long time. The Scotsman slowly lowered his blade away from his throat.

Long Hair closed his eyes, bowed slightly to the Scotsman, then turned and ran.

In a moment, he was gone, enveloped by the night.

I advanced toward Daniel, keeping an eye out for Elam Khai. Daniel was deeper under the roof than I was. A roof that was failing quickly. The structure was engulfed in flames. It could collapse at any moment. There were pops and small booms as items were incinerated. The intense heat slowed my progress. My exposed flesh felt like it was being cooked over a barbecue pit. The building's skeleton became visible as its skin burned away, reminding me of the Hindenburg crashing in flames.

The extreme temperatures caused metal fatigue along the length of the grandstands, bending the beams. The building groaned and twisted and shrieked. With a crack that sounded like lightning, the roof broke free from its supports, slowing tilting down toward us, creaking loudly as it dropped. Flames shot forward. It felt as if a blowtorch were being directed at my face. I threw up an arm to shield myself from the searing heat.

I reached Daniel just as the roof gave way. The backpack was on the ground next to him. I grabbed it as we dove out of the way of the falling debris. The steel and wood and burning embers crashed to the ground barely missing us.

The force of the impact thrust the flames at us, briefly engulfing Daniel and me before it retreated, sucking the oxygen away as it withdrew.

I felt the vacuum drawing the air from my lungs.

I couldn't breathe. But the vacuum also extinguished the flames around us, dragging them back toward the conflagration engulfing the building.

If we had been indoors, we would have suffocated. Out in the open, there was enough air to fill the void. In a few seconds, air penetrated my lungs, the oxygen reaching my bloodstream.

Oxygen, that thing I didn't know existed for most of my life.

My ears were ringing. I couldn't hear. And I found it hard to balance.

I saw Phoebe out of the corner of my eye, and I wondered if it was a mirage from the heat.

Elam Khai was on the ground under some smoldering rubble. He moved slowly. Leveraging himself, he pushed at a heavy chunk of debris, first with his shoulders, then his arms. His face showed the strain of the effort. Then it cleared. His expression became placid. He threw the debris off him, making it look easy. His legs were black with soot and bloodied.

Regaining my balance, I ran at him, stopping just out of his reach. I screamed, "I will destroy youuuuuuuuuuu!" The veins in my neck bulged.

And then suddenly, I was dragged away as Elam Khai got to his feet, the fire in his eyes rivaling the flames all around him.

The Scotsman had Daniel under one arm, me under the other. He tossed us through an open gate that led to a tunnel running down under the seats. Phoebe was already in the passageway.

She rushed us, wrapping her arms around Daniel and me.

The Scotsman slammed the gate, locking it from the outside. We were trapped. The building above us was disintegrating. I turned to escape, but the Scotsman grabbed my forearm, stopping me, pulling me, ramming my face back into the gate.

"Alexander…" he said, his face pressed between the iron pickets, his breath hot and fetid. "Tell your father, I am sorry. Sorry for—"

He never finished the sentence as a flaming pipe was thrust into his back, the jagged tip piercing the front of his chest. He managed to get out a last hissing breath that sounded like "done."

Elam Khai came into view as the Scotsman's body slumped to the ground, flames spreading from the pipe to his clothes.

I wanted to feel joy over his death. But I didn't. I felt my sadness deepen instead of lift.

Sorry for…

For what?

I could feel Phoebe urgently tugging at me, yelling at me to come, but the sound was muffled and distant.

More pieces of the building fell, the gate was blocked by burning debris. I could see Elam Khai through the flames, his face golden in the flickering light. We stared at each other.

The flash of anger I'd seen in his eyes a moment ago was gone.

He didn't scream. He didn't say a word.

He didn't have to. It was clear.

He relished the challenge.

Behind his eyes, the next hundred moves were being plotted. We had not stopped him. Or deterred him. If anything, he was more determined to take me, hit back at my father, and move against the technology that threatened our secret and endangered our existence. The same technology that allowed billions of people to survive on this planet.

Millions, Braeden said. It would be many more than that.

I knew something else.

This wasn't the end. This was the beginning.

This wasn't a skirmish. It would be a war.

Somehow, some unconscious part of my brain took over, and I turned and disappeared into the darkness.

- TWENTY -
Even If We Get Away,
There Is No Escape

I ran toward the rear of the tunnel as cracks formed in the ceiling, sending fragments of concrete down on me. The world around me glowed red and was crumbling.

My head was foggy and I wondered if I'd been hit by a chunk of cement. Up ahead, Daniel and Phoebe frantically struggled to open the gate. They screamed at me. I don't know how long it was before my head cleared.

The first thing I remember was boosting Phoebe up to the space between the gate and the roof. She squeezed through, dropping to the other side. Then I lifted Daniel. He disappeared into a black void and was gone.

My head itched, and I scratched it. My fingers came away with blood. When did I get hurt?

The tunnel was collapsing. But there was no one left to hoist me. I clawed at the gate, its rusted edges digging into my hands. I pulled myself up. Smoke clung to the ceiling, spreading like an evil spirit in a horror movie. It got into my lungs, causing me to violently hack and cough. This is how most people die in a fire. From the smoke. A thick, black, billowing shadow danced on the ceiling. Reaching the top, my head entered the dark soup. My eyes burned as I straddled the gate. I couldn't see. I couldn't hold my breath. I was choking. I struggled to find the strength.

Then everything went black.

∞

When I came to, I was falling. My limbs were frozen. My mind flickered on and off, but my body was useless. I saw the pavement rising to meet me. Then something stopped me from slamming into the ground.

I called out, but my lungs convulsed, gagging me.

I heard my name.

"Alexander!"

A hand reached through the darkness and grabbed me, dragged me, my back scraping across the asphalt. As I looked up, I could see no stars. Only darkness and the blurred face of Daniel.

In a few steps, we were out of the dense, toxic air.

It was still dark, but it was the dark of night, not the void of suffocating smoke.

Daniel let go of me, and my head hit the blacktop. Still stoned, he marched off without me.

I don't know how we got out of the parking lot without being seen. I remember sirens, and red and blue flashing lights. The bellowing horn of a fire truck from the north, and the high whine of police cars from the south. The same disturbing cries we heard leaving Engel's.

The Scotsman apologized. To me. *Tell your father, I'm sorry. Sorry for—*

For Braeden?

The Scotsman said he was dead already. Did he set us free, knowing it would get him killed? Or was freeing Daniel and helping me escape an act of contrition, a desperate offering to my father who would surely hunt him down for what he did to Braeden?

We were a few blocks away on Kimball Street, behind one of those huge discount stores. I could see the black smoke rising into the air, but the shopping center blocked the view of the flames and destruction.

People were emerging from their homes, curious to see what was going on after having been awoken by the explosion. Everyone on the street was headed in the opposite direction, toward the fire, toward the excitement. The most suspicious thing about our behavior was that we were running away from such a spectacular event.

Even though we were exhausted, I chose the long way back to the beach, going south three blocks to the wide street that crossed over the tracks rather than use the walkway at the station.

No bottlenecks. No enclosed spaces.

When we reached the beach, we approached the water taxi from the south. Nikolay was watching the smoke and flames in the distance, and we startled him.

With surprising strength, he dragged us aboard. Then he slapped both my arms hard. "You are safe," he said, relieved to see me. He looked as if he wanted to kiss me on the cheeks, but thankfully he restrained himself. "I am glad. These are your friends?"

"Phoebe, Daniel, this is Nikolai. Nikolai, Phoebe and Daniel."

He took Phoebe's hand. "Niko*lay*.

"Isn't that what I said?"

"Nikolai. Nikolay. You see the difference?"

None of us could.

He stepped up to the helm.

"I saw a huge explosion and flames, and I thought something bad had happened."

"It did." I took the flare gun from Phoebe and tossed it back to Nikolay. "Is *very* bright," I said, mimicking his phrasing.

He looked at the gun with a great deal more respect than he had before. His hand was on the throttle. "Now we go?"

"To the airport."

"Away from the people from your past?"

"Far away," I said quietly, even though I knew I would soon be heading toward them.

Nikolay reversed the throttle and backed the boat away from the beach. The underside scraping on the sand sent shivers through my body.

I checked on Daniel. "Are you okay?"

The blast had partly awoken Daniel from his stupor. He nodded. "You know, back there, the middle one of you was quite unpleasant."

I shrugged. Then remembering his fearless act, I said with perhaps too much astonishment, "You rescued me back there."

"When did I do that?"

"At the gate. The smoke. I must have passed out."

"I have no idea what you're talking about. All I remember is a lot of angry people wanting to kill me. And you being not as adamantly against the idea as I would've liked."

I wanted to tell him that I was relieved he was alive, that I wanted to know him for as long as I could, wanted to see all of the phases of his life. That I wanted him to change his soiled pants as soon as humanly possible. In the end, all I said was: "You're my friend."

He glanced over the side at the black liquid shimmering in the moonlight. "I hate boats."

I made Daniel lay down on one of the benches. I found a blanket and draped it over him. I touched the black stone pendant Braeden had given him. "It gave you strength," I whispered.

"*He* did," Daniel said softly.

Daniel began shivering, the steel cuffs on his wrists clinking rapidly, as if the warmth of the blanket had reminded him how cold he was.

As the water taxi turned, Nikolay thrust the throttle forward. The engine churned the water behind the boat. In a moment, we were traveling at full speed, skimming across the choppy surf.

I stepped to the back of the boat. Phoebe was gazing out to sea, her hair fluttering in the wind. Her arms were tucked tightly against her body. She was shaking. Maybe it was from the cold. Maybe it was from what we had just endured.

"You saved us," I said quietly in her ear.

She turned and looked up at me. "I'm sorry about what I said. Calling you a coward."

"Don't be. That's part of what you did to save us."

I don't know if she could ever fully understand how her words had driven me. Kept me from giving up and giving in. How her fearlessness had rekindled my own courage.

"Why didn't you ever ask me out?" she asked, her tone bittersweet.

I took a step back, surprised. "You were seeing someone," I said.

She gave an exhausted laugh. "As long as you've been alive...you haven't figured out the best people are always 'seeing' someone."

I stared at her. "I'm not seeing anyone."

"Maybe you're not so good then."

I shook my head. "Looking..."

"Not seeing?" she said, playfully.

"*I* see," I said, nodding.

"I think you do."

She reached up and kissed me. It was soft and warm. And my lips tingled at the touch of hers. There was more than friendship in the kiss. Maybe there was even passion in it, at least, as much as she could muster under the circumstances. She was weary, drained. It had been a long day and night, and it was about to be day again.

And then, just at the end, she pressed harder into my mouth. Deeper.

As our lips parted, she went flat-footed, and I could feel her shiver again. I removed my jacket and draped it around her, overlapping the front to make it fit snugly.

"You're going to freeze."

My heart was pounding. I was anything but cold. "You should get some rest."

As soon as she sat down, her muscles went slack. Her body could finally give in to the exhaustion. She lifted her head. It seemed like a struggle. "This isn't over. Is it?"

I wanted to tell her it was, wanted to offer her a lie that would give her a moment of peace so she could let go of the last eighteen hours. For a person who's had to do it every day of his life, I'm not very good at being deceptive.

"Soon," I said.

I let my hand rest on her shoulder a moment longer than it needed to. Her chin dropped to her chest, and she closed her eyes.

I picked up the backpack by her feet. Then walked to the center of the craft. I asked Nikolay if he had a bag I could use. He pulled a canvas duffel from one of the storage compartments.

I dumped the contents of the backpack into the bag, checking twice to make sure I had everything, including that stupid baseball that I cherished so much.

I handed Nikolay a stack of bills. Fifty thousand dollars.

"That should cover it."

"Cover what?"

"*Spasiba*," I said. *Thank you.*

He stared at me. Then at the cash.

"I told you, my father would pay a lot of money to get me back. I'm just paying the debt myself."

"Too much," he said.

"Not nearly enough," I countered.

He understood pride and honor. He accepted the money with a nod.

"What is that smell?" he asked in Russian.

I shrugged, making sure not to glance at Daniel. "*Ja ne znayu*," I lied, telling him I didn't know.

I patted Nikolay on the shoulder, grateful for his help, then stepped out onto the bow and leaned my leg against the rail.

I stared down at the water rushing past.

I tossed the backpack overboard and watched it float away, receding into the distance as we sped forward.

I was free again. And for the moment, untraceable.

I didn't feel cold at all. My blood was hot. I wanted to strip off my clothing and paint my face like I had done on the deck of the *Dartmouth* as I dumped tea into the harbor.

I felt something deep within me growing stronger, felt the weight of the centuries falling away.

I pulled off my shirt and let the cold air hit my bare skin.

I am the warrior. The brave.

Once again.

I looked off the left side of the boat. There were the faintest hints of light peeking over the horizon. The sun's promise of a new day.

Toward the light. That's the direction we would travel in search of my father.

My father.

I am the son of Marcus Antonius, Consul of Rome. The nephew of Alexander the Great.

I stared into the distance, at the pale glow at the ocean's edge, my head turned to the left, my chin slightly raised, unintentionally striking the pose my uncle can't help but make.

They call me *Alexander the Pretty Good.*

If we are going to have any chance of preventing the destruction of the modern world, the deletion of a hundred years or more of advancements, I'm going to need to be much, much better than that.

Because Elam Khai has a plan.

And he has *never* been defeated.

THE BATTLE FOR FOREVER CONTINUES...

VOLUME II:
ΛNCIENT ΛMONG US

ENHANCE THE EXPERIENCE.
LISTEN TO THE AUDIOBOOKS READ BY WIL WHEATON.

About the Author

Edward Savio grew up in Connecticut. He has written numerous film projects for Walt Disney Studios, Sony Pictures Entertainment and others. He is creator of the political cartoon, "Ourmageddon." He makes his home in San Francisco with his family.

You can send comments to the author at:
writeme@edwardsavio.com

Visit edwardsavio.com
for more on his books and comic.

Other books by Edward Savio

Adult Contemporary Fiction:
Idiots in the Machine
Love on Haight
The Velvet Sledghammer (2019)

Sci-Fi/Action:
Ancient Among Us
Kids:
The Stupor Heroes vs. Dr. Earwax

Support Your Local Bookstore. Get Exclusive Content.

Reading a book however you can is great; on your phone, on a reading device, or in print. But a real book is special. And the places that sell real books, they're special, too. **So, if you're holding this book, do me a favor. If you can, take a photo of yourself with it in or in front of your local bookstore. The best pics get a free audiobook.** It's easy. It'll help this book and that bookstore more than you can imagine.

Post ANY photo of the book on social media through **edwardsavio.com/realbooks**

When you do, you'll get a link to exclusive content, backstories, lost chapters, audiobook mishaps, etc. that will take you deeper into the **Battle For Forever Universe**, future, present, and past.

www.ingramcontent.com/pod-product-compliance
Lightning Source LLC
Chambersburg PA
CBHW031059260626
47172CB00001B/124